"Kiernan Antares has truly entertained greatly and taught gently, cleverly woven into a fascinating story are a number of significant lessons in life for us humans living an emotional and physical experience in a crazy world. *Phoenix Star* is absolutely gripping and a wonderfully created story with characters I was disappointed to part with when the story ended!"

Andy Higgins,
Author of *Best Coaches Best Practices*

"Kiernan's debut novel puts her on the map as a masterful storyteller who develops very real characters that pull you into their adventure of enlightenment and transformation of the spirit. You can't help but finish it with a smile on your face."

Chris F. Allen,
Partner, Deloitte & Touche

"The first few pages of *Phoenix Star* drew me right into the book; it was hard to put down. I enjoyed the characters and all the twists and turns around a very interesting plot. *Phoenix Star* teaches us how to listen to our inner voice, follow synchronicity and grow to higher levels of consciousness."

Cherie Friendship,
Photographer

"Kiernan Antares is a purveyor of powerful words, a custodian of fantasies and a possessor of rich spiritual insights. As such, more than just a novel, *Phoenix Star*, is a journey for the mind, body and soul, consistently providing opportunities to live out its characters very real and life altering experiences. There is no time, need or chance for you to come up for air. You're hooked from the very first page."

Anita Erskine,
Radio Show Host, 93.5 FM

"*Phoenix Star* is a mesmerizing edge of your seat novel!"

Yasmin Virani,
Abundance Coordinator, Humanity's Team Canada

"As I read *Phoenix Star* it made me aware that my purpose in life is to be at a special place at a special time to help in putting the pieces of a puzzle together. The pieces might be insignificant and with no meaning to myself, but to another it might mean everything. It also revived my faith, my trust, and my hope in the Universe."

Louise Laroche, Toronto, Ontario

Phoenix Star

Phoenix Star

AN ADVENTURE OF THE SPIRIT

Kiernan Antares

For Janice,
Victory to Love!
Kiernan Antares

iUniverse, Inc.
New York Lincoln Shanghai

Phoenix Star
AN ADVENTURE OF THE SPIRIT

iUniverse, Inc.

iUniverse books may be ordered through booksellers or by contacting:

iUniverse
2021 Pine Lake Road, Suite 100
Lincoln, NE 68512
www.iuniverse.com
1-800-Authors (1-800-288-4677)

ISBN-13: 978-0-595-39883-6 (pbk)
ISBN-13: 978-0-595-84282-7 (ebk)
ISBN-10: 0-595-39883-9 (pbk)
ISBN-10: 0-595-84282-8 (ebk)

Printed in the United States of America

For Paul, whose smile reaches down and touches my soul, warms my heart, and makes me feel that we are made for one another.

For my son Kevin, who inspires me to be a better person and whose wisdom never ceases to amaze me.

For my parents Pauline and Harold, who teach me to believe in myself and never give up on my dreams.

For Robyn, Brittney & Ashley, who teach me compassion, understanding and joy.

Acknowledgements

I would like to express my eternal gratitude to my partner Paul, for his unwavering love and help in creating this book.

I would also like to give a special thanks to my son Kevin, my parents Harold and Pauline, my brother Gord and his wife Sandi, for always providing love and support, and Adalene for welcoming me into her family.

I am also grateful for my friends, colleagues and companions along the way who believed in my dream with a special thanks to Cherie Friendship and Anita Erskine. My thanks to Lynda Simmons for her extraordinary insights and recommendations in the evolution of this story.

Also, many thanks to the spiritual teachers whose works have inspired me to be the person I am today including James Redfield for following his vision and being a leader in changing the way humanity interacts. And Grace Cirocco whose coaching and book *Take the Step, the Bridge Will be There* provided me with some amazing insights to heal the past and connect more deeply with my creative voice.

I'd also like to acknowledge Damion for the element symbols used in this book, Dennis William Hauck and his book *The Emerald Tablet*, and the wonderful people at iUniverse including Rachel Krupicka who guided me through the process of publishing.

May the blessings of Love, Light and Joy be present in their lives each and every day.

Author's Note

While *Phoenix Star* is fiction, it was inspired by mythology that does indeed exist. The lost legends of the Emerald Tablet go back over 10,000 years and are resurfacing once again with unlimited transformational possibilities for anyone in search of a higher meaning in their lives.

It was my intention for this book to be a symbolic representation of what each person experiences on their journey of awakening to their own destiny. While the characters are fictitious, they reflect aspects many of us have that require healing in order to break through the barriers that hold us back from reaching our full potential.

Everyone has a unique and special purpose in uplifting humanity to higher levels of consciousness during this critical time in history.

Can you look deep within yourself and allow your inner beauty to be revealed? Do you have what it takes to face your own demons and act in spite of fear? As your own story unfolds you will discover the rewards are more than worth the challenges, not only for yourself but also for our planet and the unlimited universe.

I challenge you to be bold, be daring. Embrace the principles of transformation and become the Enlightened Beacon of Light you were meant to be.

With Love and Blessings,

Kiernan

Prologue

POCONO MOUNTAINS
3 December 1979

He hovered among the trees waiting. His shoulders shuddered from the cold December night air, and he pulled the zipper up on his black leather bomber jacket to keep warm.

Just over six feet tall, his broad, thick shoulders, narrowed hips and chiseled face led one to assume he was powerfully athletic. His short slicked back hair, piercing eyes, and set jaw added an ominous presence on the deserted country road.

Darkness swept over the winding hills just south of the Pocono Mountains in Pennsylvania as a patch of clouds drifted across the sky, concealing the illuminating full moon.

The stranger cocked his head slightly and his body stiffened at the sound of a vehicle coming towards him from the north. Knowing the time was approaching, his swift movement as the car rounded the corner was imperceptible in the isolated area.

The man driving the green, two-door Ford Escort glanced back to check on his three month-old-daughter, sleeping in the back. The smile of peace and contentment on his face swiftly disappeared when his wife screamed in shock.

"Grant! Watch out for the deer!" shouted the terrified woman. She grabbed the dashboard to brace herself for impact. Her face contorted in fear.

He slammed on the brakes and frantically turned the steering wheel to the left. But the car skidded across a patch of black ice and spun out of control. Plunging into a ditch it toppled, end over end, before smashing up against a tree, forcing it to come to an abrupt standstill.

The deer escaped death and disappeared into the night without a trace of its existence.

The mysterious stranger, appearing from the dust, walked slowly and purposefully towards the accident. Looking down into the ditch he saw the car, crunched and mangled with steam hissing from under the hood.

Loosing his balance as he sidestepped down the edge of the ditch, he grabbed onto the log of a dead tree to steady himself. He inched his way down the partially frozen and slippery brush filled bank. Reaching the bottom he stopped and brushed the dirt off his lambskin jacket. "Damn!" he muttered to himself noticing the rip on the right sleeve.

Shrugging off his annoyance, he straightened himself up and returned his attention to the car ahead and kept moving. His keen hearing detected the sound of the baby crying inside the car. He approached slowly, taking care not to trip over the busted branches and debris left behind from the collision.

A low tree branch had ripped through and shattered the windshield. The stranger peered inside and whistled at the devastation. The branch had pierced through the man's chest, pinning him to the seat. The woman's eyes were glazed, her hair soaked with blood, her right arm snapped in two from the impact.

Both husband and wife were dead.

Moving along the side the stranger inspected the vehicle's damage. He stopped to study the baby girl strapped into a child's seat in the back. Although she was still wailing she appeared to be unharmed. Satisfied, the man straightened, his expression as cold as ice. He adjusted his jacket, turned and walked away, into the darkness of the night.

Chapter One

HARRISBURG, PENNSYLVANIA
24 January 2012

A searing pain in her belly woke Maya Maxwell up from a deep slumber. She screamed and her legs jerked out uncontrollably kicking her sleeping husband.

What the hell! "Maya?" he called out in sudden apprehension.

"Brian! Something's wrong with the baby! Something's very wrong! Oh God!" she screamed. Another stab of pain shot through her and a warm flood of liquid escaped from between her legs. The thought of something happening to the baby filled her with panic. *Oh God, please don't let anything happen to my baby!*

Brian shot up in bed and grabbed her hand. The icy cold feeling of her skin fueled his anxiety. He reached over and turned on the bedside lamp. Looking at her escalated his fears. Her face was white. Her normally beautiful lush red hair was soaked and pasted to the sides of her head. He touched his hand to her forehead. "You're like ice!" he exclaimed, his voice cracking.

"I think I wet myself. Brian I'm scared."

"Shhh, it's okay, I'll help you. Let's get you into some dry clothes." Pulling back the comforter and sheets, he gasped in a shallow breath not wanting to frighten her any further but it was too late. The alarmed expression on his face was obvious.

Maya lifted herself up onto one elbow and looked down, following the direction of his eyes. She burst into sobs. "The baby! What's happening?" Her eyes were glassy. She was becoming delirious. *I can't lose this baby! Not now! It doesn't make sense. It took me so long to finally get pregnant. Please God, don't let anything happen to the baby!*

Her nightgown and sheets were soaked with blood. For a brief moment he wasn't sure what to do as panic claimed control over his normally calm nature. "I'm calling an ambulance, hold on!"

Dialing 911, Brian waited for someone to respond. One ring, two rings…*Come on, hurry up! Answer the phone!*

He slammed the phone down after finally getting through. "An ambulance is on the way," he reassured Maya. "I'm going to get you a clean nightgown." Walking quickly, his feet hit the hardwood floor heavily under the weight of their situation.

He grabbed his jeans and sweatshirt that he had tossed on the chair earlier and quickly dressed. Turning to her honey colored pine dresser; he pulled out a light blue flannel gown and rushed back to Maya.

She was shaking and her eyes started to roll back in her head. "Maya stay with me!" he commanded. Gently he moved her to lift the blood-soaked garment up over her head and replaced it with the dry one. Sitting himself beside her he pulled her away from the soiled sheets and wrapped a blanket around her. Holding her tight, he rubbed her arm to comfort her and warm her up, then waited.

I won't let her hear the fear in my voice. Stay in control. She needs you. He rocked her gently and kissed her forehead. "It's okay dear, everything's going to be all right." But his words felt empty.

Leaning up against the headboard he looked around the room feeling helpless. The full moon was shining so brightly through the window he noticed the light reflecting on the walls. He had never really spent much time in the bedroom but he appreciated the way she decorated it. He took comfort now in the warm earthy colors she selected. "Maya do you remember when we painted this room?" he asked in an effort to distract her from thoughts of losing the baby.

She was trembling but he could feel her nod her head.

"You kept following me, pointing out all the spots I left bare." *I know it frustrated her but she just kept joking with me.* "Sage, that's what I think you called it, right? I don't know, to me it's just green." He realized he was just babbling now but he thought the sound of his voice might help to keep her conscious.

He stopped talking when he heard the sirens turning onto their street. "Maya, the ambulance is here. I need to go downstairs to let the paramedics in. Will you be okay? Maya?" He realized she had lost consciousness. He got up, propped the pillows under her head and ran out of the room and down the stairs as fast as he could.

He reached the front door and opened it before the paramedics rang the bell.

"Thank God you're here," Brian said frantically to the two men approaching the door. "Hurry, my wife is upstairs in the bedroom. I think she's unconscious. I don't know what happened. She woke up screaming and she's lost a lot of blood."

"It's okay, calm down. Show us which room," demanded one of the men.

Following him they raced up the wooden staircase to the master bedroom facing the back of the house.

Brian held Maya's hand tightly and watched the paramedics at work. They said her pulse was growing weak and her blood pressure was dropping. They attached ECG leads, got the IV going, and put an oxygen mask on her.

They had to force him out of the way so they could load her on the stretcher and down to the ambulance. Brian jumped in the back with her and as soon as she was secure they raced through the streets of Harrisburg to the Pinnacle Health Hospital on Front Street.

* * * *

Half a block away Nicholas Rhodes sat in a black SUV, on standby orders. He'd been waiting for a couple of hours with the motor turned off not wanting to bring attention to his vehicle.

He glanced at the digital clock, one twenty-three A.M. and rubbed his hands together to warm up his cold fingertips. Having been assigned to monitor Maya on occasion in the past, he was familiar with the neighborhood. Colonial style two-story brick houses lined the quiet suburban street. They had some decent lot sizes, not crammed in like many subdivisions.

Fresh snow clung to the bare branches on the maple and evergreen trees. Garbage cans were lined up at the edge of the driveways beside the snow piles, waiting to be picked up the following morning.

He watched the lights go on in the living room of the house next door to Maya's. The neighbors pulled the drapes back and peered outside to see what the commotion was all about. Fortunately for Nicholas they didn't notice him.

A couple of minutes later the paramedics came out of the house carrying Maya on a stretcher. Brian locked the door behind them and climbed into the back of the ambulance. He looked frantic and disheveled. His brown hair was a mess.

The pant legs of his jeans stuck inside a pair of untied tan work boots. His navy and brown coat was hanging loosely, unzipped.

Watching the scene, Nicholas pressed the first speed dial number on his cell phone until it rang. "Hello. Yes it's Nicholas. Looks like your plan worked. She's in the ambulance now."

"Is he with her?"

"Yes."

"Good. Stay with them. Follow them to the hospital and see what you can find out. I want to know the minute you hear any news. Just make sure he doesn't notice you and don't leave the hospital until you've reported back. I'll be waiting."

"Got it." Nicholas snapped the phone shut and tossed it on the console. He watched the ambulance back out of the driveway, put the sirens on and pull away. Turning the key in the ignition and putting the gear into drive he concentrated on keeping up with them while maintaining a respectable distance. He thought about his boss and the recent events while he drove. *This is a pretty risky move. If she dies, he's screwed and he'll never get what he's after.* He had to admire the man's determination to succeed. No matter the cost.

* * * *

"I'm sorry Mr. Maxwell, you'll have to wait outside."

Brian tried to push through the door of the trauma room.

"Mr. Maxwell, you can't come in here. The doctor will come and see you as soon as he can." The nurse closed the door in his face.

The drive to the hospital had been a blur. He vaguely remembered hearing only a few words as the paramedics reported in over the radio. "Pregnant…Heart rate dropping…Hemorrhaging…In shock…" Now he stood feeling powerless outside the room where the doctors were trying to save the life of his wife and baby.

He was numb, staring into the distance waiting, oblivious to everything around him. He refused to allow his thoughts to wander to the possibility that anything bad would happen to Maya or the baby. She was his anchor. For the longest time he couldn't understand her obsession about getting pregnant, as much as he tried. Lately though, the idea of becoming a father started to grow on him. Seeing the ultrasound image of the baby a couple of days ago made it very real. He even gave in to Maya's pleading to get the nursery ready by painting it and putting the crib together.

He rolled his stiff shoulders and leaned back in the chair. *My life before her was so meaningless and self-serving.* He felt shame and guilt for the stupid activities he participated in during his youth. Chasing girls, doing drugs. *I still can't believe Maya ever agreed to go out with me. She always saw the good in me. It's because of her I've experienced more happiness than I deserve.*

The door to the trauma unit opened. A doctor, of average height, pulling his facemask off walked through. Looking around to the people waiting he narrowed his sights on Brian. "Mr. Maxwell?"

Brian's heart skipped a beat. He jumped up and moved to meet the doctor. "Yes that's me. How is she Doctor? How is the baby?"

"Unfortunately, there's no improvement. The bleeding hasn't stopped and she's in a lot of pain. She's suffering from what's called a placental abruption…"

"I'm sorry, a placental abruption?" His voice held a hint of annoyance at the doctor for speaking in medical terms. "I don't understand. What is that?"

"Normally the placenta separates itself from the wall of the uterus and delivers itself right after the birth of the baby."

Brian's eyebrows drew together in confusion and ran his hands through his hair. "But she's only twenty-seven weeks pregnant. Why is this happening? She just had an ultrasound last week and everything was fine. I don't understand."

"We don't know what is causing this yet," the doctor said and paused for a few seconds. "Has your wife had any other children?"

"No. This is our first. We tried to get pregnant for over three years," said Brian anxiously.

"Does she suffer from high blood pressure?"

Brian shook his head.

"What about diabetes? Is she on any medication?"

"No. Nothing." He was growing aggravated with the situation and felt like striking out at something. "Is she going to be okay?"

"I'm recommending we perform a cesarean section."

"A cesarean? But the baby is only twenty-seven weeks. What will happen?"

"The situation is critical Mr. Maxwell. We have no choice. We have to perform a cesarean before your wife loses any more blood. Many babies have survived and live without complications at this stage. There's no reason, at this point, to believe the baby is in any danger. But there is a chance the abruption has caused some serious damage to Maya's uterus and we may have to perform a hysterectomy. We need you to sign some forms." The doctor waited for Brian to comprehend his recommendation. "Can we go ahead?"

"Yes. Yes, of course I'll sign the forms. If you think this is the only way." He felt like his nerves were on the edge of losing control. "Do what you have to do. Just make sure to save my wife."

The doctor patted Brian on the back. "Don't worry. We'll take good care of her."

"When can I see her?"

"Once you've signed the forms I'll make sure the nurse takes you back to see Maya before we take her to the OR." The doctor rested his hand gently on Brian's shoulder. "Just go over to the nurses station, they should have the paperwork ready for you."

"Thank you doctor…" Brian's voice trailed off realizing he didn't even know the name of the doctor who was trying to save Maya's life.

"Henderson."

"Thank you Doctor Henderson."

Brian felt his heart pounding as he walked up to the nurse. She was talking to him but he struggled to hear what she was saying. He barely remembered signing the forms when the nurse opened the door to the prep room. He had to choke back the tears when he saw Maya hooked up to machines, tubes, and bags. She looked ghastly white. *O God, Why is this happening?*

Maya felt a pair of gentle hands wrap around hers and the warm sensation stirred her awake. Through the pain she struggled to open her eyes but it was too much of an effort. "Brian, is that you?" she croaked. Her throat felt parched and raspy.

"Yes it's me. I'm here." He noticed how limp her hands felt in his and he kissed the tips of her fingers. They felt so cold.

Her eyes flickered open and she saw Brian's face filled with anguish. "The pain…I can't…"

"I know. The doctor has to do a c-section. You've lost too much blood. Neither you nor the baby will survive unless they remove it now. But you're going to be just fine. They're coming to take you to the OR any minute."

Her eyes closed again and she felt like she was floating into darkness. She saw a White Light appearing. It came closer. She thought she could hear Brian still talking in the distance but she couldn't focus on his voice any longer. *The pain is fading away. The Light looks so peaceful and inviting.* She saw a woman in the distance. She had long wavy chestnut hair. Her skin glowed and she wore a gold colored flowing skirt and matching blouse. It looked like…*Momma, is that you?*

One of the machines started to make a loud piercing noise. Brian looked up as the pulse line went flat.

"Maya!" he yelled. Don't go! Maya I love you!" He cried in desperation. "I need you! Please don't leave me!"

He heard a rush of activity behind him and he was pushed out of the way.

"Sir, you have to leave now!"

"No! Do something!"

Two nurses grabbed him under the arm and pushed their weight up against him. "We're going to help her but you can't stay. Do as we say."

He resisted. "Maya!" He tried to get closer again.

"Sir! Get out now!"

Giving in, he backed out of the room. He watched for a few moments through the doors as the team worked fervently to resuscitate Maya, but then another nurse escorted him back to the waiting room.

Chapter Two

BEL AIR, MARYLAND
24 January 2012

Douglas Mercer leaned back in his luxuriant executive chair feeling on top of the world. A black leather briefcase sat opened on his desk in front of him filled with bundles of crisp one hundred-dollar bills stacked neatly in rows. One and a half million dollars in total.

Not a bad profit since the opening four months before of Charlie's Corner restaurant and nightclub in three locations. Each one was built virtually identical in appearance and layout. The decadently decorated restaurant with marble pillars and floors, lush plants and artwork was on the main floor. The nightclub was located on the top level and designed to be exclusive for members only.

It wasn't easy finding just the *right* corner spaces in all three cities, Manhattan, Los Angeles and Chicago, where they could gut the buildings and start from scratch. In fact, finding the investors was much easier than finding the locations since Douglas was quite the charmer and knew how to convince even the most skeptical person to invest in his business ideas.

Their efforts that took over two years to pull together were finally proving to be well worth it. It looked like they were going to be cash cows and profitable additions to their portfolios.

"Excellent. You're certain none of the investors or managers will be able to detect that we're skimming money out of the business?" questioned Douglas. He picked up one of the bundles of bills and fanned through them. Returning it to the case, he continued to run his fingers across the top of the money.

"Positive," said his business partner, John Damaskas who sat by the fireplace in Douglas' home office. "It's well hidden and even if one of them did discover a hiccup they'd never be able to trace it to the final destination. I've made sure there are loop holes at every turn that will trigger red flags in my system to notify me of any intruders."

"Well done John."

John forced a smile. He shrugged his aching shoulders hoping the heat from the smoldering fire in the fireplace would loosen the knots. It had been a long day and he came straight here from the office in order to give them the good news. He knew time was of no concern to Douglas who was usually up until four or five in the morning. He also knew that showing up at one A.M. would be appreciated, reflecting his loyalty and commitment. "You know I can't take the credit, it's a team effort. None of this would have even come together without your ideas and Vivienne's sharp mind."

"Well said," commented Vivienne, who was sitting quietly opposite John, absently looking over some paperwork. Vivienne was Douglas's wife and business partner. They had the controlling interest, which kept John in line as the third partner.

Douglas snapped the case shut. "You know the drill. Move the money to our banks in Dominica immediately."

"I've already got it covered. I have a flight early in the morning."

"You're looking tired John, why don't you go home and get some well earned rest," remarked Vivienne.

"I agree," said Douglas. "This next year is critical to continuing our success, that is assuming that everything goes according to plan in Egypt in December. Are you up for the challenge?" It was more of a test than a question. He liked to keep his people on their toes. It was his style of training and it weeded out the undesirables pretty quickly.

"You know I'll do whatever it takes." John's right eye twitched with a muscle spasm as it often did when he was over tired. Ignoring this minor annoyance he decided to plunge into his rehearsed speech. "Before I leave there is something I'd like to discuss with both you and Vivienne."

"Of course," Douglas said and paused, sensing whatever it was must be important to their partner. "Hold on, I'll come over there." Douglas rose from his chair, grabbing the briefcase in one hand and his whiskey in the other. He joined John and Vivienne by the fire. "What is it?" he asked.

"We've been partners now for what, five years? And friends for even longer. When we opened the accounts in Dominica and started transferring money there I didn't ask a lot questions."

Douglas raised his eyebrows and Vivienne put her papers down on her lap and smoothed them out.

"I mean why would I? Money looks good no matter what country it's in. But I think I have proven myself as a trustworthy partner and I think I deserve to know why Dominica? And why are we able to move our money around down there without any questions from the bank officials?" *There I did it.* You never knew how Douglas would respond to questions. His moods were often erratic. Sometimes he answered easily and others, well he'd react like he was being challenged and retaliate with stinging words or worse.

Douglas very deliberately picked up his drink and took a long sip. He crossed his legs and looked down at his house slippers. That was the advantage of working out of the house. Being able to work when he preferred and dress as casually as he wanted when they didn't have any business meetings scheduled.

He cleared his throat. "You're allegiance has been demonstrated, time and again, John. That is not in question. But we have not explained our decisions about Dominica for your own protection as well as ours. If I was to tell you the truth now, your safety could be jeopardized."

"I'd still like to know."

"I'd like to talk with Vivienne. Could you give us a few minutes? I believe Paige is still up. She could make you a snack if you'd like."

"Thank you. I'll be in the kitchen when you're ready for me." John left the room and closed the heavy sound proofed doors behind him. *My safety? That shouldn't come as a surprise.* Nothing should come as a surprise any more, he'd seen some pretty wild schemes during their partnership and he'd benefited on many levels because of them.

"What do you think?" Douglas asked Vivienne when they were alone. "Should we tell him?"

"It would certainly be the ultimate test of his commitment to us and our mission." She pondered this dilemma, lifting her hands and inspecting her manicure. "But still, it's a heavy burden to bear. There's a lot at stake if he cracks. Are you willing to take that chance?"

"We need someone we can rely on. Especially as things heat up over the next eleven months and beyond. If he's the one I'd rather know now so we can deal with the fallout if there is any and if not, well then it's perfect and I'll have a protégé."

She gazed into the fireplace. The logs she put in earlier were now broken pieces of charred wood, with a faint glow in areas where they hadn't fully burned down. Shadows flickered on the wall and the room was already feeling cooler. She studied Douglas. Despite the late hour he still appeared alert and full of vigor. She contemplated his argument in favor of telling John for several moments before making her decision. This was just the sort of thing he thrived on and knew it was going to be another late night. She didn't mind though, it was all for a good cause. "There's merit in your thinking. I agree. Let's find out what he's made of."

Douglas fixed his eyes on hers. He loved how closely they worked together and relied on her immensely to provide logical solutions. *Her eyes are such a magnificent green, just like a cat.* "You are so beautiful, my darling."

"Thank you." She recognized the seductive smile and where his thoughts had wandered. She also knew that meant there would be no rest for several hours yet.

He walked slowly and deliberately towards her. Stopping to stand in front of her, he kneeled down and met her gaze. "We belong together, you and I. You know that no matter what I must do to ensure the success of our destiny, we are inseparable."

"Yes darling, of course I know."

Delighted with her confirmation, knowing he was in complete control, he rose. "I'll go get John and we'll have that discussion now."

"Please join us John," said Douglas as he sat down with his refilled glass of whiskey and ice. "Vivienne and I have discussed your request at length, isn't that right darling?"

"Yes we have," she nodded in agreement. "John we need you to understand this is a very serious matter and we need your guarantee that what we discuss here tonight will not leave this room."

"Of course, you can count on me."

"We hope so," she responded gravely. "You have been very loyal and have always gone above and beyond what was asked of you. You have earned the right to be a part of the inner circle and what we are about to reveal to you is proof of that. Now I'll defer to Douglas and let him tell you about Dominica."

"Thank you darling." Douglas turned his eyes towards John. "You know of my connection with the government's remote viewing program. What you don't know is that the section of the agency I am involved with is a very covert organization and is not even known with most of the highest-ranking officials. What I am about to tell you is of national security. Are you certain you want me to continue?"

Wow, this sounds even bigger than I imagined. "Yes. I'm in." He wondered if the room was getting colder or if his nerves were on edge in anticipation as he felt a chill run through his body.

"All right then. During one of my missions in the program to locate an assassin, I stumbled across something that is known only by a very small, select group of world leaders. Something of such huge magnitude it has the potential to affect every person's way of life and topple the largest conglomerates in the world.

"Over the last number of years we have seen critical problems with the lack of available energy. Years ago more than half of the power supply came from nuclear power plants but many of them have been taken out of service as their safety deteriorated with overuse."

Where's he going with all this? John shifted in his chair and tugged on his suit jacket sleeves, determined to listen intently.

"While the technology in the operation of nuclear power has improved and it has other benefits of price stability and not contributing to air pollution or global warming, there is a downside. The costs of building or upgrading facilities involve high costs. Also, the development times are long and there are many complex waste disposal issues.

"There have been many attempts to build environmentally friendly alternatives like wind power and small-scale water power projects but for the most part we're relying more and more on natural gas and coal-fired plants.

"While natural gas plants can be built more quickly and for a lower cost than nuclear power or coal, the cost of gas, as we all well know has risen astronomically. But despite this dilemma and the escalating problems in the Middle East our government has chosen gas as our main power supply. I won't burden you with why they are doing this but I'm sure you have heard speculation in the news and in the business community."

Vivienne observed John. He lifted his chin and cocked his head to the side, his eye twitched continuously now, ever so slightly but even in the low light of the room she detected the spasms.

Douglas was in his glory. He felt a sense of power knowing he was about to reveal this well guarded secret to poor unsuspecting John. He couldn't possibly understand how this knowledge would affect him.

"This leads me to my discovery. While in the ether, scanning through the Caribbean islands, an energy field near the southern end of Dominica stopped me in my tracks. I had never seen anything like it before. It radiated a powerful electrical emission, which literally threw me against the wall. Do you remember when I dislocated my shoulder and broke a couple of ribs?"

A look of astonishment washed over John's captive face. "Yes, yes I do. I remember you were really banged up. But you said you were in an accident."

"Yes, well I obviously couldn't tell you or anyone else the truth. There are hazards to my job and it's not the first time I've sustained injuries as a result. In any case, my curiosity could not be contained and as soon as I was on my feet again I went back into the matrix and found the same location. This time I was prepared."

"What happened?" John asked, captivated by the story and eager to know more.

"I built up my own force field, which as you know I'm proficient at, and I was able to follow the signal line to the core of the energy at the bottom of Boiling Lake."

"Boiling Lake?" questioned John. "I've heard of it and always wondered what the hype was about but I've never taken the time to explore the island. I'm usually in and out pretty quickly."

"It's quite an unusual place. Mountains surround the lake and it's a good hike to find it but it's worth the trip. It looks like a cauldron of this bubbling grayish-blue water and it's shrouded in a cloud of steam."

"So what did you find at the bottom of the lake?" John asked, leaning forward with anticipation.

"One of the most remarkable sights I've ever seen. There is a crystalline energy covering the entire expanse of the bottom of the lake with the most magnificent array of colors you could ever imagine."

John's eyes widened in amazement. He decided to take a wild but estimated guess, "And you believe this could be a source of energy for the U.S.?"

"Not just the U.S. John, the entire planet." Douglas sat back basking in smug satisfaction.

"What? You're kidding right?"

"No I'm deadly serious."

"Jesus!" John stood and paced the room. His thoughts reeling in different directions. "Now I get it! If this energy was utilized it could take down the oil and gas companies!"

"Exactly."

John took some deep breaths to calm down his racing heart. "This is bloody huge!" He continued to pace trying to focus his train of thought.

Vivienne and Douglas watched in amusement as the meaning of the situation made its impact. They could sense his excitement rather than any forebodance, reassuring them that he would not spin out.

"Let me take another calculated guess," said John slowly. "You cut some sort of deal for unquestioned access to bank accounts in Dominica for your silence?"

"Impressive. You are correct. To guarantee my safety I have agreed to be at their beck and call to locate anyone or thing in the ether. I am after all the best damn viewer they have with an almost one-hundred percent accuracy rate."

"Sweet!" exclaimed John.

"There are some disadvantages. Unfortunately I can't escape from their grasp and I've had to participate in some very disturbing missions. But it serves us well for the time being."

"Douglas, I'm sorry. What an awful position to be caught in."

"Don't feel sorry for me. It's only temporary. I'm working on a plan to release me from this agreement and once our destiny is assured in Egypt I will be able to execute it flawlessly."

"Speaking of our destiny," injected Vivienne, "John, now that you are fully in the loop we expect you to take on higher responsibility. This will allow us to concentrate more on making sure all the other players are on schedule to deliver in December."

"I understand. As I said before, I'll do whatever it takes."

"Good," said Douglas. The phone rang. He looked at his watch. "That should be Nicholas." He answered the phone while Vivienne and John continued their conversation.

"Why don't you take an extra day or two in Dominica this time. See some sights and check out the Boiling Lake. It'll have more of an interest now," suggested Vivienne with compassion.

"I might just do that," John smiled absently, still lost in thought from the implications of this meeting.

John and Vivienne overheard the end of Douglas' phone conversation.

"Just make sure he doesn't notice you and don't leave the hospital until you've reported back. I'll be waiting," said Douglas into the phone. He placed the handset back on the desk and returned to the others.

"Was it Nicholas?" asked Vivienne.

"Yes. Everything's working according to plan. Maya's awakening is about to begin." Careful with his words, he looked into Vivienne's eyes to convey his real meaning. John didn't need to know everything. "It looks like I'm going to be up for quite a while. Both of you might as well retire for the evening." He had work to do in the ether to ensure the proper sequence of events took place over the next few hours.

John stood and picked up the briefcase sitting by Douglas' chair.

"John, good work. I feel better knowing you're on our side and I can count on you." Douglas reached out to offer his hand in respect.

The two men shook hands. "Thank you for confiding in me. You won't regret it," said John.

"We'll talk more about this and some other things we'll need you to get up to speed on when you return from your trip. Let us know when you're back," said Douglas.

"Absolutely, I'll let myself out. Good night."

"Have a safe trip," said Vivienne. When she heard the front door close she prepared to retire for the evening as well.

"Will you wait up for me my love?"

"Yes darling, I will. Please be careful tonight." She kissed him tenderly on the cheek and walked up to their bedroom already lost in thought. She had her own things to watch over that night.

Chapter Three

HARRISBURG, PENNSYLVANIA
24 January 2012

Brian sat looking desperate at the door to the waiting room. He checked his watch, five thirty-seven A.M. His nerves were frayed not knowing whether his wife was alive or dead.

Looking around the waiting room he noticed it was three quarters full. *Maybe I'll grab a coffee. No, forget it, I'm tense enough. That might send me over the edge.*

The room was so dreary looking. The walls were scuffed up. The chairs looked like they'd never been replaced.

He noticed a woman and child huddled up together. Her face tear stained. The child, a boy of about six years old, looked rumpled. Her arm was around him, holding him tightly while he slept. *Something must have happened to his father. Poor kid.*

A man, holding an ice pack to his head looked like he'd been in a bar fight. *He must have been having fun. Too much to drink and someone says something stupid. I remember those days.*

Others waited, for their loved ones, he supposed, just like him. Restless, frightened and tired.

The door opened and he jumped up when he saw Dr. Henderson. His heart was pounding loudly in his ears. "Is she…?"

"She's going to be fine," the doctor said.

Oh, thank God. Brian took a deep breath. It felt like he had been holding it for ages.

The doctor continued, "She's going to need blood transfusions though and we'll have to monitor her progress so she will have to stay in intensive care for a few days."

"What about the baby?"

"I'm sorry Mr. Maxwell..." He paused to clear his throat. "Brian. We did everything we could but we were not able to save the baby. She survived for only a few minutes. The trauma was too much for her to bear. If she had survived it's likely she would have suffered severe damage."

His shoulders slumped. The feeling of loss filled his heart. "She? It was a girl?" *A daughter. I would have had a daughter. Maya will be devastated.* "Does Maya know?"

"She's not awake yet. She's lucky to be alive. She's been through one hell of an ordeal."

"Doctor, will she..." pausing, afraid to ask, "will she be able to have children in the future?"

"Fortunately we were able to avoid doing a hysterectomy and she will require some ultrasound therapy to remove scar tissue. Right now, there's no way to know for sure because we have not identified the cause of the abruption..."

Brian felt anger and frustration rising to the surface. "Doc, just answer my question."

"All right. Yes, I believe it is possible."

Brian nodded his head, feeling some measure of relief then asked numbly, "When can I see her?"

"She's in recovery right now. We need to run a few tests to determine if there is damage to her organs. Assuming there are no further complications, I anticipate she will be moved into her room in a few of hours. You can see her then. Why don't you go home and get some rest."

"Thank you Doc." Brian turned and sat down in the nearest available chair. He leaned forward, placed his elbows on his knees and dropped his head. His mind felt too muddled to think clearly. Running his hands through his hair he attempted to focus. *Home. Yes, I'll go home and clean up.* He stood up and followed the corridor to the exit. He patted his coat pockets. *Damn I forgot my cell phone.* Finding a pay phone, he called a taxi and waited for it to arrive.

In his turmoil and haze, Brian did not notice the man by the vending machine across the lobby, watching him.

* * * *

Resting his head back against the back seat of the taxi, Brian closed his eyes. He could feel anger stirring in the pit of his stomach. He couldn't let his feelings rise to the surface. At least not yet.

"Did you hear they reported another outbreak of the Avian flu? Yup, this time in Chicago. They say one of these days it could turn into a pandemic and we won't be ready. I don't know what the world is coming to." The driver looked at Brian through his glasses in his rear view mirror and waited for a reply but none was forthcoming.

"That's not the only thing in the news this morning. Yes sir, there was an earthquake along the coast of West Africa. They say thousands are feared dead. Yup, don't know what the world is coming to. One disaster after another these days."

Damn it, why did I have to get a chatterbox this morning? The heat was rising in his body. *Keep your cool.* "You know what…" he said pausing to look at the name tag on the back of the seat, "Samuel? I've had a really bad night. If you don't mind, I don't feel like talking."

"Oh yeah sure, no problem. Sorry to bother you man."

Once in the house he headed up the stairs. Avoiding the master bedroom for the moment, he went into the baby's room instead.

They decided on the room facing the backyard for the nursery. It received the morning sun, filling the room with light and warmth.

Brian had just finished painting the bottom half in a butter yellow, as Maya called it. She selected a charming animated Noah's Ark wallpaper pattern for the top half with a handrail separating it from the painted bottom half.

The furniture was delivered just this past weekend. He leaned up against the doorway reminiscing about his exasperating experience assembling the crib. *I can't believe the stupid fight we had over the furniture. Why did I have to give her such a hard time over the cost? It was no big deal. She was right, it would have taken me months to build, even with all my tools. What a ridiculous waste of energy fighting over something so meaningless.*

His breathing deepened. His hands began to shake. He couldn't bear to continue brooding here so he turned and walked towards their bedroom.

Remaining stoic, he stripped the blood-soaked sheets and replaced them with clean ones. When he was done he sat on the bed and picked up the phone to call the office. "Rudy, hi it's me, Brian."

"Hey what's up?"

"I won't be able to work today or for the next couple of days."

"What's wrong? Are you okay?"

"It's Maya," his voice wavered and his bottom lip quivered. "She lost the baby."

"Oh God. I'm so sorry. Of course, take a few days. Is she okay?"

"She's lost a lot of blood and they said they have to keep her for a few days to run some tests. Probably do some blood transfusions. But the doctor says she'll be fine."

"Oh man, I am so sorry to hear that."

Brian could hear his boss flipping through some papers. *Probably the schedule.* "I'm supposed to be working on the installation of the kitchen cabinets at the Jacobson site this week. Can you get someone to fill in for me?"

"Yeah, I can probably get Jerry. I think he's just doing odd jobs on the side right now. Don't worry about it. Do you need anything? Is there anything I can do?" asked Rudy.

"Thanks but no. I'm going to head back to the hospital in a bit. I'll give you a call in a day or two."

"Righto. Give Maya my best. Tell her I'm sorry."

"Yeah. I gotta go. I'll talk to you later." Putting the phone down he looked around the room. Not able to contain himself any longer he picked up the lamp on the bedside table and smashed it against the wall. It fell to the floor in pieces, leaving a dent in the wall. *Damn! Things were finally going well. Maya was happy for the first time in so long. Having a baby meant everything to her. Why? Why did this have to happen?*

* * * *

Maya became conscious of pain radiating throughout her entire body. Her eyelids fluttered. They opened slightly but they were too heavy on the first try. Her eyes rolled and then they closed. She tried again, and again. Finally she was able to keep them open but everything was a blur.

The light in the room proved to be painful. *Where am I?* It was obviously daytime—perhaps mid-morning. She saw her husband slouched in the chair beside the bed. He was asleep. He looked rough with dark stubble growing on his face. His thick sandy brown hair with just a few strands of gray was in disarray from leaning against the coat he had folded up and used as a pillow.

Hospital. I'm in the hospital. What happened? She tried to remember but everything was hazy. She wanted to stretch but the IV drip she was hooked up to prevented her from moving around freely. She looked down to her legs. Panic filled her. Her hands jerked to her stomach and she gasped. "The baby!" She released a heartbreaking wail.

Her scream startled Brian awake. Seeing the look on her face he jumped up quickly and joined her on the bed.

"Brian, the baby?" She sobbed in his arms as the memory of the night came back to haunt her.

He held her tightly and let her cry until her body finally stopped heaving. When she settled down he tilted her face upwards. "I almost lost you. They did a c-section but the baby couldn't survive. It was too much for her." He let the words sink in.

"Her?" she asked weakly.

"Yes." It was all he could say. No other words would come.

"My baby. Our baby girl." She didn't think she had any tears left but she was wrong. The pain was too great to bear and she wept even more. She couldn't imagine how she was going to cope with the loss. Her whole world had become wrapped around having this child.

Brian knew how much she longed to have a baby and he ached at the emptiness he knew she now felt.

"I don't understand. What happened?" she asked.

He smoothed her hair away from her face and explained to her what the doctor told him. "They've run some tests but I don't know yet if they discovered the reason. The doctor seemed pretty confused about it. You didn't have any of the conditions that may cause an abruption."

Abruption. Conditions. "I don't get it. Everything was fine during the ultrasound. That was just…just a couple of days ago."

"I know hon. I told the doctor the same thing."

She felt panic and anger blending together, leaving her very confused. She looked up at him with desolate eyes. "It took so long for us to conceive. I thought this was *it.* I thought I was finally going to have the family I've always wanted."

"I know. But at least they didn't have to do a hysterectomy so there's still hope…" his voice trailed with the suggestion.

She rested her head against his chest. Loneliness filled her heart. She thought it would break. He stroked her hair but she felt nothing except the pain.

"Brian?" she called to him timidly.

"Yes Maya?"

"I saw my mother."

His body tensed. "What do you mean?"

"I know I almost died. I saw a White Light. It was so beautiful and comforting. It was like I was drawn to it so I walked towards it and I saw her there."

"But you've never seen your mother. You were only three months old when your parents died. How could you know it was her?" He wasn't sure how to digest what she was saying.

"I recognized her by the pictures I found before putting Nanny in the nursing home. She looked just as pretty and young as she was when I was a baby. I never realized how much I look like her."

"Hon…It was probably just your imagination trying to help you deal with the pain."

She didn't want to accept Brian's explanation. She felt a connection and she wanted to believe it was her mother. "Maybe…She took my hand," she added wistfully. "I felt like I was floating in the air. Then she told me it wasn't my time to pass over yet. That was how she said it, pass over. She said I haven't done what I came here to do yet and I have to go back. Then both the Light and my mother disappeared and my body vibrated violently. Now here I am."

"I know you've felt lost all your life without knowing your parents but I think your mind is playing tricks on you."

Maya felt a pang of anger but she was too exhausted to argue with him. She lay in his arms and eventually drifted back to sleep feeling numb and confused.

Chapter Four

HARRISBURG, PENNSYLVANIA
May 2012

"Don't forget you have a doctor's appointment at two fifteen this afternoon. I'll be back in time to go with you," said Brian, tossing the newspaper aside.

"You don't need to baby-sit me. I can get myself to the doctor," Maya said angrily.

"I don't want to fight with you Maya. I'm concerned about you. You've been depressed for four months now. Most days you don't leave the house or even bother to get dressed." He stopped himself from saying anything about her appearance. She had given up taking any pride in how she looked. Her normally beautiful, shiny, bouncy red hair was flat and lifeless most of the time now because she couldn't be bothered drying or curling it or whatever it was she did to make it look so lovely.

"I just want to make sure everything is okay," he added. It was obvious to him how much agony she was in and he was getting really worried about her inability to sleep too. The dark circles under her eyes were haunting and she'd lost so much weight all her clothes just hung on her now.

How dare he! He's not the one who lost all his hopes and dreams when Chloe died.

A formal death certificate had to be signed and they needed to name the baby as well as give her a funeral. Everyone says it helps in the healing process to have closure but Maya was unsure about whether that was really true. It didn't seem to help ease her pain.

"Well excuse me for mourning the loss of our child," she retaliated. "It's better than pretending nothing happened. Did you even want the baby? You certainly don't act like it meant anything to you."

"You know perfectly well it hurts but I'm not going to worry myself sick over what happened. It's done and there's nothing I can do to change it."

"I don't know how you can be so flippant about this."

"Maya, please. Let's not do this. Nothing I do or say seems to help these days. In fact, everything just ticks you off. I don't have time to argue I need to get to work. I'll be back here around one forty-five. See you later." *I hope that Doctor Walkerton might be able to do something to help her. She can't keep going on like this. She's getting worse not better.* Standing up from the round pine kitchen table, he gave her a quick kiss on her head, grabbed his thermos of coffee from the counter and left.

She held her breath, hoping it would stop her from spewing out all the obscene remarks she wanted to fling at him. Once she heard the door close behind him she put her head down in her arms on the table and sobbed. She didn't know how to deal with the anger, which had been brewing inside all these months and crying was her only release. It only helped for short periods of time though, then the tension would build up again and she'd take it out on Brian.

She stared absently through the kitchen window into the backyard. They were having an early summer again this year. It was only the middle of May and already all the trees and bushes were lush. Normally she would have been excited with anticipation to get out into the garden and decide what flowers to plant for the summer but like everything else these days; it did not have any impact. Besides, with the extreme heat they were experiencing it was already too late to plant anything new.

It had been months since anything had given her pleasure, including the kitchen, which she had decorated to be an extension of the garden she loved. It was painted green, softened with a ragging technique. Not gifted with the paint-brush she hired an artist to create a design of flowers and ivy leaves around and above the doors and windows. It produced a quaint English cottage feeling that was accentuated by the white cupboards and trim.

Part of her knew he was right about doing something to help herself but she couldn't work past the anger and betrayal she felt. It just wasn't fair. She missed the feeling of Chloe growing in her belly. She ached to feel her child in her arms and experience all the thrills of a new parent.

The morning seemed to disappear just like all the other days. If anyone asked, she wouldn't be able to say what she did all day. She hadn't been able to go back to work yet. Although her sick leave was going to run out soon and she'd have to deal with returning but she couldn't bring herself to think about it yet.

I better get myself cleaned up and dressed for my appointment. Absently she went upstairs, stripped off her nightgown and turned on the shower in their ensuite bathroom.

When Brian returned to take her to the doctor he found her sitting in the rocking chair in the baby's room. She looked up when he poked his head in but her eyes were vacant. *At least she's dressed and it looks like she even had a shower and made an attempt to fix her hair nice for a change.* "You ready to go?" he asked softly.

"Hmmm? Oh yes. Yes I'm ready." *How long have I been here?* She couldn't remember if she had anything to eat since this morning. She had trouble remembering a lot of things these days.

Brian held her hand in the waiting room at the doctor's office wanting to show his support but he found it lacked any warmth. In fact, it just lay there limply and it saddened him greatly.

Maya had trouble feeling any kind of emotion other than pain, anger, disappointment, and loneliness since the death of Chloe. It consumed her and overrided any feelings of love she had for Brian.

"I don't know why you insisted on coming. I could have just as easily told you about it later," she said to him bitterly.

The door to the doctor's area opened. "Maya?" The office nurse waited for Maya to rise. "You're next."

"I'll wait here. The nurse will come get me when the doctor is finished her exam," said Brian.

"Whatever," she said and disappeared through the doors.

Upon completing her exam, Doctor Walkerton, a woman in her early forties with chin length, dark brown hair slipped off the plastic gloves. She was a slim, plain looking woman who didn't wear any makeup or jewelry. With her hectic family practice and long hours she couldn't afford the time to worry about such things. "Everything looks like it's healing fine. I understand Brian wants to come in to hear the results with you. I'll let you get dressed and you can meet us in my office at the end of the hall." The doctor noticed the tension in Maya's body increase at the mention of Brian's name but she refrained from making any comment.

Several minutes later after putting her clothes back on, Maya entered the doctor's office. She was writing some notes in her file. Brian was already seated at the desk waiting.

The room felt small with all the books and files scattered everywhere. In odd contrast her desk was free from clutter, adorned only with one tray of files, a couple pictures of her husband and two children, a phone and a ceramic dish, colorfully painted with flowers. Maya assumed one of her children must have made it for her. She felt a pang of envy hit her hard in her chest and she couldn't breathe. The atmosphere in the room left Maya with an uneasy feeling.

Doctor Walkerton smiled at Maya and put her pen down. Glancing first at Maya then Brian she said, "As I was telling Maya, everything appears to be healing well. I received the follow up test results from the hospital and there doesn't seem to be any signs of damage to your heart or any other organs."

Maya gave Brian a smug look as if to say *see I told you I'm fine.*

"However, there is still some scar tissue in the uterus so I recommend you continue with the ultra sound therapy on a weekly basis. Your blood count is still on the low side." She eyed Maya carefully. "Are you eating properly? Sleeping?"

Maya's head dropped ever so slightly. Brian cleared his throat and spoke up. "She barely eats. She just picks at her food and she walks the floors most nights."

Maya glared at him. "I sleep," she said defiantly.

"Right, sure you do. Do you think I don't notice when you disappear from the bed at night? I hear you creeping around the house and I've seen you rocking in the chair in the baby's room." He turned to look at the doctor. "I'm really worried about her Doc. She's become so reclusive. She doesn't even keep in touch with any of her friends anymore."

"Why do you have to keep harping on me? Why can't you just leave me alone?" demanded Maya angrily.

"See what I mean Doc?" He looked to the doctor, pleading for help.

"Maya, Brian has a right to be worried. He loves you and just wants to help you."

Maya took a deep breath and counted to ten. "I know," she said sullenly.

"You are a good ten pounds under a healthy weight. Your eyes are sunken and your skin is pale. For starters I want you in here every week for a vitamin B-twelve shot. I'm going to give you a diet to follow to help put some weight back on and we're going to weigh you each week to keep track of your progress."

Brian was so glad he insisted on coming to this appointment. *I'll bet she wouldn't have told me any of this.*

Maya kept silent, biting her lip. She felt as though they were both ganging up on her and she resented their efforts.

Doctor Walkerton weighed her next words carefully. "Maya I'd like to make a suggestion," she paused to gauge her patient's attitude, "I know a really good therapist who specializes in dealing with death and I'd like you to consider meeting with him."

Maya stood up quickly in defiance. "Is this really necessary?"

"I have to agree with Doctor Walkerton. I think it's a good idea," pleaded Brian.

"Of course you do. You probably talked to her about it before we came and convinced her I needed help."

"That's ridiculous. Doc, talk to her please."

"If you won't go see a therapist then what about talking to a Priest or Minister," suggested Doctor Walkerton.

"A Priest or Minister?" Maya paced the room enraged. "You've got to be kidding me! Why on earth would I want to do that? God took my baby away from me! What God would do that? No! Absolutely not. I won't do it."

"Maya please sit down and listen to reason," said Doctor Walkerton. "If you don't get help to work through your emotions I'm very concerned your health will suffer severely. Right now there's every reason to believe that you will be able to have other children but if you continue in this way you may lose that opportunity."

The doctor's words hit her square in the heart. She stood peering out the window overlooking the Walnut Street Bridge. It is the oldest surviving bridge over the Susquehanna River and its nickname was *Old Shakey.*

Many of the buildings on Front Street were the original low-rise structures built in the 1800s, typically two or three stories. Some were still homes or apartments, others had been converted into offices. The State Capital building and office towers were added in over the years behind the older part of the city, giving it a mixture of a quaint town and city complex. Not a very large city with a population of only seventy-five thousand, Harrisburg managed to retain its old town feeling.

The vintage buildings were constructed with combinations of red, beige or brown bricks with white trim around the doors and windows.

Maya watched a mother pushing a stroller along the sidewalk just above the river's shoreline and had to fight back the tears.

She finally sat back down in the chair. "Okay, I'll do it. No church though. But I'll go see the therapist."

Brian felt a huge relief. He reached out to hold her hand and was happy to discover she didn't resist. "Hon, I'm so glad. I'll help you. Everything is going to be all right, you'll see."

* * * *

"Maya, can I get you anything?" asked Brian opening the door quietly. The bedroom was dark, all the blinds were drawn and the drapes were closed to block all the light.

The hall light felt like a beam blinding her and she rolled onto her side to protect her eyes. "No thanks. Please just leave me alone."

He entered the room and closed the door behind him. "Do you want any ice?"

"I said no thanks," she replied, annoyed that he ignored her request.

"You haven't called to make an appointment yet with the therapist have you?" he dared to ask. He tripped over something. Straining his eyes to adjust to the darkness he was finally able to see the garbage can. Bending lower he recognized the smell of vomit. He sat beside her on the bed and reached out to touch her forehead.

She pushed his hand away. "I don't have a fever. Please just leave me alone."

Why does she always push me away? He longed to feel connected to her again. To hold her in his arms and feel like she loved him. "Maya, you need help. You're getting worse and now you're getting these migraines all the time," his voice changed from caring to stern. "You can't go on like this. Your office called me and said you're not returning their calls. They said your sick leave is running out next week and they want a decision about whether you are going back to work or not."

She rolled onto her back again and rubbed her tender eyes with a groan. *Why can't everyone just leave me alone?* "What do you want me to say?"

"If you don't call the therapist and book an appointment on Monday then I will. I expect you to stop brooding and pull yourself together and that means getting ready to go back to work."

"Brian!"

"No. I mean it. Call or I will." He walked out of the room and closed the door. *Maybe that will get her attention.* He was growing tired of living a hermit's life with her and wanted to join the land of the living again. *We never have any of our friends over for dinner anymore and everyone has given up trying to invite us over because she keeps making excuses not to accept.*

He went down to the basement to finish sizing and cutting the shelves he wanted to add to his workroom. He loved the smell of sawdust from freshly cut wood and building things helped to take his mind off his troubles with Maya.

She knew she was sinking lower and lower. *How do I dig down deep and find the strength to go on?* She felt so lost and alone and she knew she was pushing everyone away. Drifting off to sleep she thought she heard a voice whispering to her in the dark. "Maya, don't give up. You're not alone."

* * * *

He transported himself in the ether with ease to her coordinates. Having tracked her throughout her life it was a snap to locate her and he had trained his perception to sense when something was wrong.

Douglas knew his visitations, which had become more frequent since the night Maya lost the baby, were causing her pain but that couldn't be helped. *She'll adapt.*

He found her in total darkness in the bedroom. *She must be having another migraine.* He stood by the foot of her bed watching her. Wanting to reach out but of course he couldn't. She didn't even know he existed. He moved closer and breathed her in.

Her hand passed through the air above her head and he smiled. *She senses my presence. Yes, she'll make an excellent student.* "Maya, he said softly."

She rolled onto her back.

He studied her face. Her skin looked pale and green. The circles under her eyes were even darker than his last visit. *She's getting closer to breaking.* He heard Brian coming up the stairs and moved away from the bed and stood by the closet entrance.

He listened to the exchange between them, what little there was. He shook his head when Brian changed tactics with Maya and forced the issue of visiting a therapist. *He's such a fool.* Stepping further back into the closet he fondled her clothes. He sniffed her scent. *Oh Maya, I so look forward to taking you in my arms.*

When Brian left he wandered back into the bedroom. He gave her a few moments to calm herself and waved a hand across her face, a few inches away. He leaned close to her ear and whispered, "Maya, don't give up. You're not alone."

Chapter Five

Knowing that Brian's threat to call the therapist was no joke, Maya gave in and called on Monday making an appointment for the following afternoon.

She sat on the brown leather couch with her arms and legs crossed. Her foot was swinging in nervous anxiety and she refused to make eye contact with the therapist.

Looking around the room she saw that the walls were adorned with various diplomas and scenic pictures of mountains and waterfalls.

Doctor Rupert took note of Maya's apprehension and closed posture. "They're beautiful aren't they? I grew up in North Carolina. Some of the mountains reach over six thousand feet and offer the most spectacular views on earth." *I imagine she's quite pretty without those dark circles under her eyes.* He could see she took care in dressing for the appointment wearing a soft green pantsuit and beige blouse. Unfortunately, it hung so loosely on her body that it only made her look frail and vulnerable.

"They are beautiful." She eyed him distrustfully. She guessed he was in his mid-fifties, balding and thought he was probably quite attractive in his younger days. "Why did you move to Harrisburg. It must be kind of boring here in comparison."

"My wife was offered an opportunity here to become a partner with a law firm." He shrugged his shoulders. "She didn't want to pass it up. So we compromised. We sold our house and bought a cabin in the mountains where we spend our vacations."

"I see." She uncrossed her legs, shifted her position and crossed her other leg over. She fidgeted with her suit, trying to smooth out the loose fabric. The suit felt ridiculously big and it made her feel even more self-conscious.

"Would you like to tell me why you are here?"

"I guess you could say I'm here under duress." She glared at him then fussed with her suit again.

"If you don't think you need to be here there's nothing stopping you from leaving, if you want."

She watched him suspiciously. "You're playing head games with me. I can see that. I'm not stupid."

He waited for her to make the next move.

She felt a pang of guilt for being rude. "My husband and doctor are worried about me. They think I'm not coping with the death of our baby very well," she said defiantly, pushing her hair behind her ears.

"What do you think?"

"I think they are over reacting."

"I see. Does you husband love you?"

His question caught her off guard. "Yes." She shifted again. Her foot started to twitch faster.

"Do you believe he cares about you and is just looking out for your well being?"

Silence. That's a rotten thing to do. How else am I supposed to answer?

"Maya?"

"Yes."

He noticed her back softened slightly. Gently he cleared his throat and asked, "Would you like to tell me what happened?"

The pain in her heart erupted with force and her carefully guarded wall came crumbling down. She lowered her head in her hands and sobbed.

"Let it out Maya. Don't hold it in." He offered her the box of Kleenex from the side table and let her cry.

After several minutes Maya looked up at the doctor with her tear stained face streaked with mascara and recounted the events from the night she lost the baby.

"And the doctors still can't explain why it happened," she continued. "They've run so many tests and everything keeps coming back normal. Except my blood count hasn't picked up because I've lost my appetite and it's such a struggle for me to eat anything."

"Are you able to sleep?" he asked jotting some notes down on his pad of paper.

"No. I usually end up sitting in the rocking chair we bought in the nursery. Sometimes I doze off for a while when I'm there. I just…I feel so alone and disconnected from everything and being in Chloe's room helps to keep her alive in my thoughts even though I never had the chance to know her, or hold her."

"What about your family. Mother? Father? Brothers or sisters? Are you close with them?" The minute the words came out of his mouth Doctor Rupert knew he hit a nerve.

She shook her head. "I don't have any family except my grandmother who raised me but she's in a nursing home now. She has Alzheimer's and doesn't remember me anymore."

"What happened to your parents?"

"They died in a freak car accident when I was three months old. Nobody knows what happened. The newspapers said my dad must have lost control of the car on the slippery roads. It flipped and crashed into a ditch. There were no witnesses so everything is just speculation. Strangely enough, I was in the car too and the papers said it was nothing short of a miracle that I survived without injury."

Now he understood why she clung to the pain. "Do you feel as though Chloe was your chance to feel connected to something bigger than yourself? To have the family you never had?"

Unable to speak at first, she nodded, staring absently at the bookcase behind the doctor. "I've spent my whole life trying to figure out who I am and where I belong." She started to cry again, softly this time. "I never got to know my parents. My nanny, well she would never tell me much about my mother or father. She led a hard life and losing her daughter just about killed her. I think I reminded her so much of my mother it was too painful for her to talk about."

"What was it like growing up? Did you have friends?"

"It was lonely. I never got to have friends over or join any school teams because Nanny was always tired," she said wistfully. "And I was always envious of the other kids, having parents, and brothers and sisters to play or fight with."

"Did all these things make you feel like you didn't fit in?"

"Yes."

Pleased that she was opening up he wanted to keep her talking. She needed to vocalize her feelings in order to understand her pain more fully. "What about when you met your husband? Does he make you feel like you belong somewhere?"

"Brian? In some ways, yes. But it doesn't take away from the questions I have about myself. I keep thinking that if I knew more about my parents then I'd understand myself better."

Doctor Rupert stopped taking notes and leaned forward in his chair. "Maybe that's part of the process of understanding yourself. The more you question things the deeper you dig. You learn about yourself just by the types of questions you ask. What do you think?"

"I suppose."

He paused trying to determine where to steer her next. "Do you love Brian?"

"Yes."

"How are things between you now?"

Maya played with a loose thread on a seam of her jacket. "We ah, we haven't made love since I lost the baby."

"Why is that?"

"My heart hurts too much. I…I can't let him in."

"Do you blame him for what happened?"

"Blame Brian? That's crazy! Why would I blame him?" She flicked her hair behind her ears again.

"Then who do you blame?" He waited. "What keeps you up at night?" He pushed her harder still. "Who do you blame Maya?"

"Blame? You want to know who I blame?" Anger rising, she stood and headed to the window. She stared out into the distance, not really seeing the view. "I'll tell you who I blame! I blame God! God took my parents away from me and now he's taken my baby! What am I supposed to do now?"

"It's your responsibility to take care of yourself. No one else can do that for you. Sure I could prescribe drugs to help you sleep and numb your feelings but they won't help you heal from your losses. Only time and facing each day one day at a time will help you do that. And of course, turning to the people who love you."

"I don't know if I can do that."

"Well Maya, you are the only one who can determine that."

* * * *

Nicholas put the file back where he found it and escaped from the doctor's office as quickly and quietly as he entered.

Back in his car, parked a block away from the office building he made the call to report what he discovered. "Hello? Yes, it's Nicholas here."

"Do you have an update on Maya?"

"Yes, I do. She met with a Doctor Rupert today, a therapist. I just reviewed the file."

"And?"

"She resisted at first but then opened up about how important having the child was to her. Apparently she suffers from a feeling of disconnection resulting from growing up without knowing her parents."

"What else?"

"It seems things are not going very well between her and Brian. They haven't made love since the baby died, she won't let herself open up to him. She's not able to let go of what happened and blames God for taking away her family and her child."

"Excellent. Everything is progressing as I hoped. Well done Nicholas."

"Thank you. What's next?"

"It's time to start working on Brian. His patience has got to be running thin by now and we need to step our plans up to another level. I'll contact him in the ether and plant a seed to take her to the Atlantis Resort in Nassau."

"I don't understand. Why the Atlantis Resort?"

"The resort has an area they built called 'The Dig' which has stone walls with symbols written on them. They also have artifacts claimed to be from Atlantis. It's kind of hokey but the psychometry of Atlantean times will resonate with her on a subconscious level and assist in preparing the restoration of her memories. When the time is right, of course."

"Will he be open to receiving the message?" He regretted the words the instant they were out of his mouth.

Silence. Douglas fumed with Nicholas' unforgivable error.

"That was a stupid question, sir. I apologize."

"I understand why you asked, but thank you for acknowledging the error of your skepticism. While Brian is not open to the concept of other worlds, he will be easy to manipulate for our purposes because of his love for her."

"I see," said Nicholas. The tension between Nicholas and Douglas was heavy. He'd been progressing well in his training over the past year after a rocky start. He'd butted heads with Douglas in the beginning, which resulted in humiliation among his peers, including verbal lashings and surrendering to Douglas' overpowering attacks in the tactical portion of their military like training.

He had moments of doubt and almost walked away from the vision on a couple of occasions. But he also quickly learned the rewards of performing well outweighed his need to assert his independence. There was no room for autonomy in this organization. You were either a team player or you were out and a team player meant doing exactly as instructed. He was on his way to being welcomed into the inner circle and his mission of watching Maya would be his ticket.

"Nicholas, may I remind you who is commanding this mission. It would behoove you to not question my actions or motives again." Douglas continued in a deadly serious voice, "I don't want to see you lose your position after putting so much effort into training you. Am I clear?"

"Yes sir."

"Good. Now let's move on. I want you to keep me informed and let me know when he books the trip."

"Of course."

"When that's done I want you to make plans to stay at the Atlantis resort at the same time. We'll orchestrate a meeting with both of them."

"A meeting?"

"Yes. I'll prep you for the message you will be delivering. Plan on taking Julia with you, it'll look better if you have a female companion. Again, well done Nicholas. You are a valuable team player and you will be rewarded handsomely for all your efforts when our time has come."

The phone line went dead. Nicholas removed his earpiece, started the engine and drove off into the night. This was the most important mission he had worked on so far and he felt privileged to be part of something that would change the course of history. *She's got a long way to go though, and she's such a frail looking thing. I'd never guess in a million years our survival depended on her. I hope she's got what it takes.*

* * * *

HARRISBURG, PENNSYLVANIA
June 2012

"Do you have the base salary review list ready for Mark yet?" Kristen asked, poking her head in the door of Maya's office.

"I'm working on it now," Maya said annoyed with the interruption.

"Mark's been asking for it for the past two days. I'm running out of excuses. Are you sure you don't need my help?'

"I got it." She looked up from her computer to glare at her over eager and perky assistant. *Geez, she's getting on my nerves.* "Tell him I'll send it to him before the end of the day."

"We're already past the deadline to get the lists to the managers. You know how Mark gets when he has to report delays in his department. If we screw up the timelines for the salary adjustments he'll be on the rampage."

"I said I got it, don't worry." She waved her assistant off with a wave of her hand. *Doesn't she realize I'm her boss? I could fire her little butt.* Maya, beating herself up for such an awful thought, dismissed it as quickly as it came. She propped her elbows on her desk and leaned forward to rub her eyes with the palms of her hand. *She's saved me from embarrassment on a couple of occasions because of my mistakes. I should be nicer to that poor girl instead of chewing her out.*

Maya had only been back to work three weeks but it felt so much longer than that. She stared at her computer screen. The numbers were starting to look blurry on the spreadsheet and she could feel a tension headache building again. She grabbed the bottle of painkillers from the top drawer of her desk and swallowed three of them with some water. *I can't afford to get another migraine right now, especially in the middle of the performance review process. I'm already in the doghouse with Mark.*

She leaned back in her chair and let out a long sigh. Looking around the office she thought about how boring and small it was. The glass tabletop desk, two chairs and a bleached wood credenza took up most of the room, leaving it feeling very cramped. Files were scattered everywhere, it was so unlike her. She was normally neat and organized but she just couldn't seem to get into a routine that worked for her yet.

She was the Human Resource Manager at Harper and Conner Architects. They gave her old position back to her when she returned to work but her boss had been replaced while she was away. Now she reported to Mark Harbinger, the Vice President of Operations. This was not a good thing. She didn't have an established working relationship with Mark and he wasn't showing a lot of patience for the time that she needed to get back up to speed.

She knew she had to deliver the salary review list today or she'd have to face a very annoyed Mark. She just hoped the migraine would hold off.

Pushing the hands free button on her phone she dialed Brian's cell phone number.

"Hi Maya. What's up?"

Hating speakerphones she picked up the handset as soon as he answered. "Hi. Sorry to bother you on site but I wanted to let you know it looks like I'm going to be late tonight. I'm swamped with some reports I need to finish today."

"No problem. How late do you think you'll be?"

"I should be home around eight."

"Okay. I'll make dinner. Just give me a call when you're leaving," he said. "Are you all right? You sound tense."

"I'm having a rough day. Mark's on my case and I'm fighting off another migraine."

"Did you have lunch today? You know you need to eat," he chastised.

"Of course I know, and yes I did eat. Kristen ordered in today because we're all in a crunch. I had a chicken salad. It actually tasted good with nuts, seeds and raisins."

"Good, good. Hey Jeff, watch out! Maya, sorry…I have to go. Call me later." Click.

She stared at the phone then hung up. *Okay, back to work.*

It was still light out when she arrived home just after eight o'clock that evening. As she pulled into the driveway she felt a pang of guilt for neglecting the gardening. The grass was looking spotty this year from the intense heat wave they'd been experiencing this summer. There wasn't much she could do about that anyway with the water restrictions imposed by the city.

She noticed the Dogwood bushes along the driveway needed trimming and the Juniper's by the front windows needed thinning to remove the dead undergrowth. *Oh well that will have to wait until the weekend.* Her life had become a habit of putting things off and now that she was back to work even less got done. She just didn't have the energy or the desire anymore.

Dropping her briefcase on the hardwood floor near the front door she entered the large vaulted foyer. She walked past the living and dining room on the right and the den on the left. Brian was just coming in the kitchen from the back patio when she entered. He carried a dish with a freshly barbecued steak and a couple of foil wrapped potatoes.

The table was already set with a salad waiting and he greeted her with a smile. "Hi hon. Dinner's ready."

She walked towards Brian. "I can see that." She gave him a quick kiss on the lips. "Thank you." She sat down in her usual spot, leaned back and sighed.

"You look tired. How's your head?" He put the tray on the table and moved behind her to rub her shoulders. They were still pretty boney but he could tell she had put on a few pounds recently.

"Mmm, that feels good. It's still just a headache but my eyes are really sore."

He nodded in understanding and picked up one of the steaks and placed it on Maya's dish. "Did you get your reports done?"

"Yeah. But it starts all over again tomorrow. I couldn't have gone back to work at a worse time." She resented Brian for forcing her to go back and she didn't hide her feelings in her tone of voice.

Guilt washed over him as he studied her sunken eyes. They used to be such a lively green. Now they're dark and reflect the sadness she held inside. *No, I can't let her do that to me.* "Maya, I'm not going to feel guilty. You need to get back to the real world and deal with life just like everybody else. If you think I'm being harsh, I'm sorry but even your doctor agrees."

"I don't have the energy to argue. I'm tired. I just want to eat and go to bed."

"Maya…"

"Brian please. Let's just eat and change the subject." She dabbed at the corners of her eyes to stop the tears from escaping.

"Okay. Why don't we go to dinner and a movie this weekend? We haven't been out in a long time."

"Sure. Sounds fine," she said in a mellow voice.

When they finished eating and putting the dishes in the dishwasher Maya headed upstairs to bed.

He watched her go. He thought about following her but it was only nine o'clock. *Besides, it's obvious she still doesn't want me around.*

She changed into a nightshirt, washed her face and climbed into bed. She thought about what her life had become. Get up, go to work. Come home, eat dinner, go to bed. This was the new bane of her existence. *Maybe Brian was right. Maybe it's for the best to have a routine to keep me busy to get through the days.*

* * * *

"Did you enjoy our night out together last night?" Brian asked Maya hopefully. It was a Sunday morning and he seized the opportunity to laze around beside her in bed for a change.

"Yeah. It's always nice when someone else cooks."

It was unusual for him to stay in bed so long. Normally, he was an early riser and started work on some project or other he had on the go. Now that she was starting to get some sleep again she'd often sleep until noon on the weekends and this was the first time he hung around. When he pulled her into his arms she started to feel a bit anxious.

He caressed her hair that hung loose from a ponytail, as she lay curled up beside him with her head on his chest. "I miss spending time with you. Why don't we spend the day together? It's a nice sunny day, we could go for a long walk."

"I'm still kind of tired."

"Oh come on hon. The fresh air will do you some good."

"Okay," she succumbed to his plea.

He rubbed his hand along her arm and shoulder tenderly. When her body stiffened slightly he continued anyway, hoping she would soften. He rested his cheek against her head. "Your hair smells wonderful." Lifting her face up towards his, he leaned closer to kiss her, gently at first then with increasing desire and urgency. "Oh God, it's been so long Maya."

He pulled the band from her hair to free it so he could feel its silkiness against his body.

She tried to push her discomfort from her mind and let herself feel something, anything other than pain, anger, and disillusionment.

His hand slid down her arm and moved across to reach for her breast. Gently he squeezed and a groan escaped from his throat.

It was too much. She couldn't cope with the flood of raw emotions. She pushed him away and gasped for air. "Brian, stop. I can't. I'm not ready yet."

He was confused and disoriented and he didn't want to stop, "Maya, hon I love you." He tried to pull her closer again but it was no use and he fell against his pillow trying to reign back his yearning to touch her, to make love with her.

She moved away from him, turning onto her side and wept quietly while he collected himself.

"I don't understand. What's wrong Maya? What's happening to us?"

"I just…I'm just not ready," she sniffled and reached for a Kleenex on the nightstand to blow her nose.

"Don't keep shutting me out, please talk to me."

"I don't know. I tried. Really I did. But the awful feelings of loss came over me and I couldn't control it. I'm sorry. I don't know what's wrong with me, why I can't let go."

"It's an awful thing that happened to us. But it happened *to* us Maya, not *between* us. If you don't talk to me about what you are going through I don't know how we are going to make it through this period."

When she didn't respond he sat up on the edge of the bed and ran his hands through his hair frustrated. Rising he said, "Well I hope you figure it out soon. I'm still going for a walk after lunch. Join me if you want to."

Chapter Six

HARRISBURG, PENNSYLVANIA
August 2012

"Mark was looking for you. He wants to see you in his office," Kristen said to Maya as she walked by her desk.

"Did he say what he wanted?"

"No, he didn't."

"Hmmm. Okay thanks," Maya frowned. *Great! I wonder what he wants. I couldn't have done anything wrong, it's only Monday.* She grabbed a notepad from her desk, smoothed her suit jacket and headed up to the fourth floor.

"Is he in Connie?" Maya asked when she reached Mark's assistant who was busy typing on her laptop.

"Yes, go ahead. He's waiting for you," replied Connie quickly glancing up.

She knocked on her boss's partially open door. "You wanted to see me?"

Mark had a corner office with windows on both sides of the building. The blinds were angled upwards to soften the blinding sunlight.

The office was bare of any personal items. No family pictures, no plants, and no inspirational art on the walls. He had a huge wooden desk, two chairs and a matching credenza at one end. At the other end were a sofa, a large round wooden table, and a couple more chairs. A large white board hung on the wall filled with flow diagrams of the new structure of the contact management system he was preparing to propose to the senior executive team the following week.

His office left people with a cold feeling and added to the brisk and impersonal reputation he acquired during the six months he had been working for the firm.

"Yes, come in Maya."

She didn't see Sheryl-Ann MacKenzie, Vice President of Design and Production at first. "Oh, I'm sorry. I'm disturbing your meeting. I can come back later."

"That's okay. Please come in. I asked Sheryl-Ann to join us." He got up to close the door behind her and ushered Maya in to sit in the chair beside Sheryl-Ann.

"Are you looking to hire some more people for your team?" she asked Sheryl-Ann politely. "I don't recall requiring additional staff as part of this year's operational plan."

"Actually Maya, she's here for another reason," Mark said pausing to look at the woman sitting across his desk. *Although she's looking somewhat healthier than when she came back, she still has those creepy haunted eyes.* He didn't have patience for people wallowing in self-pity. Her confused look indicated she didn't even realize why he called her to this meeting.

She stared at Mark blankly. He had a cold and calculating look about him with shifty eyes. He was only five feet nine inches tall with meticulously kept short dark brown hair. There was a quiet joke around the office that he had the short-man syndrome, tough talk to make up for the lack of height. Never seen without a full suit and freshly polished shoes, he was always meticulously dressed.

"I understand that you have been through a very difficult experience but things are not working out and I'm afraid we're going to have to let you go."

She blinked. "Excuse me?"

"Maya, your work has been very sloppy and you've missed every deadline I've given you. You've been back to work, what, about three months now? The amount of days you've called in sick is unacceptable. I realize you are not feeling well but perhaps it's best if you take the time you need to recover from your loss."

"That's hardly fair Mark! Doesn't my previous record account for anything?" Her head began to pound. She felt dizzy with confusion. "Sheryl-Ann, you've known me for a long time. You know I am dedicated and efficient. How can you agree with him?" She felt like she was being side swiped and it caught her off guard.

Mark jumped in, "Maya, we have too many important initiatives going on right now and you are not working up to speed. I'm sorry, my decision is final."

He picked up the receiver and punched in some numbers on the dial pad. "Connie, please send in Jonathan now."

The door opened and the office security manager entered.

"Jonathan will escort you to the building entrance and if you could let him know where he can find your purse and personal belongings, if you have any, he will get them for you."

"I can't believe how callous you are being! This is crazy!" She began to have trouble breathing and tapped her chest unconsciously. The room was closing in on her.

Sheryl-Ann noticed Maya's growing discomfort. "Are you going to be all right?" she asked with concern.

"I…I can't breathe." She rose from her chair hoping it would help but she lost her balance. She reached out to grab the back of the chair for support but her knees gave out from under her and everything went suddenly black.

Jonathan was quick on his feet. He rushed to her side and was able to catch her before her head hit the floor. He eased her down carefully on the ground.

"Great. Just what I need," said Mark in disgust as he opened his office door. "Connie can you please come in here for a minute."

When Connie entered the office she saw Maya unconscious on the floor. "Oh my gosh! What happened?"

"She fainted. Try to get a hold of her husband and see if he can come and get her," said Mark.

"Shouldn't we call a doctor or an ambulance or something?" Connie asked.

"No. I want to keep it a low profile. She didn't take the news very well and fainted, that's all." He looked at his assistant impatiently and raised his thick eyebrows. When she didn't move right away he barked, "Now Connie."

* * * *

Fed up with lying around in bed feeling sorry for herself all week, Maya walked into the kitchen, freshly showered and dressed wearing yellow Capri pants with a crisp white shirt buttoned loosely over her Capris. She carefully selected cheerful colors this morning in hopes of lifting her spirits from the consuming agony that filled her days. "Morning," she said.

Brian, who was reading the Sunday edition of Harrisburg's Patriot-News, gulped down his mouthful of toast in surprise. "Well good morning. I didn't expect to see you down here."

Doctor Walkerton had ordered some blood tests following the episode at the office. She discovered Maya's red blood count was still quite low, which the doctor explained, was the reason for the migraines. She also said the additional stress from being fired resulted in her anxiety attack and subsequent fainting spell.

"I think I was starting to get bed sores," she replied. "Besides, even I couldn't resist a beautiful August Sunday outside." Having been confined to bed rest all week, she found herself sleeping most of the time from complete physical and emotional exhaustion. She dropped a couple pieces of bread in the toaster and poured herself a cup of coffee.

It was plain for Brian to see she was feeling better. "That's great. What are you planning to do?" he asked.

"I'm going to Harrisburg Gardens to buy a few flowers for my garden. I know it's too late in the year but I've really neglected it this year and I thought it would be nice to spend some time puttering in the yard. Don't worry I won't spend too much."

"I think that's a wonderful idea. I'm planning on building that shed today so you'll be able to store all your gardening tools there. Do you want my help at the store?"

She spread some peanut butter on her toast then loosely smeared some jam on top. "That's okay thanks, I can manage." She joined him at the table for breakfast. "Besides I want to take my time and you would just get impatient waiting around for me."

"So how *are* you feeling today?" he asked tentatively. He asked her the same question a couple of days ago but she tore a strip into him so he was almost afraid to ask again.

Maya picked up on his tone of voice and understood why he asked it the way he did. She swallowed a piece of her toast. "Sorry about the other day. I was just so angry that my previous work record meant absolutely nothing to them and I took it out on you."

"That's okay. It's pretty scuzzy they couldn't cut you some slack until you were back on your feet again. You have every right to be angry. I didn't think they were like that. It seemed like they were always really good to their employees."

"I could understand if I was brand new to the company. I mean I know I wasn't pulling my weight but…"

"Don't dwell on it Red, it's done now."

He hadn't called her Red since before that dreadful night in January. She used to think it was sweet but for some reason now it seemed almost irritating. "I know. It's just…well it doesn't feel very good knowing I was doing such a poor job. I've always prided myself on my work ethics."

"That's because you're such a perfectionist and you expect too much from yourself. You need to stop beating yourself up. Let's forget about all that and enjoy the day."

They cleaned up the dishes and went on their separate ways.

Maya spent the next couple of hours forcing herself to concentrate on her plant shopping excursion while Brian worked on putting up the framework for the shed.

He whistled while he worked, hopeful that she would agree to his idea. He waited until she returned and had some time to get pleasure from her hobby before he brought it up. *Now's as good a time as any.* He put down his hammer and approached her from behind.

"Maya, I was thinking that we should get away. You know take a trip together. What do you think?"

"Brian, I really don't think now is a good time to be taking a trip. We don't know how long it will take for me to find another job." Despite the fact that Brian was bringing up this crazy suggestion right now, she was enjoying the warmth from the hot sun on her shoulders while stooped over a flowerbed in her garden. Now that she was finally free from the latest migraine, she didn't want to take a chance with the sun beating down on her head so she wore her favorite big floppy pink hat.

"That's true, but I think it would be good for us to get away and forget about everything for a while." Brian decided to take a break from building the shed. Wiping the sweat from his forehead he sat down under the green canvas umbrella at the patio table with a beer. He was so happy to see Maya up and about after being cooped up all week in bed. He decided to take it as a very good sign that things were about to improve.

She stopped digging. *Hmmm, I wonder if that's enough Lavender for this spot?*

Gardening was her joy and she desperately wanted to reconnect to something that gave her pleasure. It allowed her to forget about herself and her thoughts while enjoying the feel of the earth, the sounds of the leaves swaying in the breeze, and the birds chirping around her. She especially enjoyed it when butterflies, hummingbirds or goldfinches fluttered around her flowers. Watching them always made her smile.

"I don't know. You're the one who pushed me to go back to work," she said with resentment. Brushing a strand of hair away from her chin with the top of her gloved hand she realized she should have put her hair up in a ponytail.

Feeling the sting of her words riddled him with guilt. "Maybe I was too harsh, I feel terrible about forcing you to go back to your old job."

She joined him at the table. She wanted to resist saying the proper thing because she still felt angry, but she did it anyway. "You were probably right, I'll just make myself crazy if I don't keep busy."

"I do think it would be better for you but that job was too much of a high stress position. I should have suggested you look for something less demanding."

She leaned over, picked up another Lavender plant, shook it out of its container and went back to work. "Well to your point earlier, it's done now. I'll get my resume updated this week and start looking for something else."

"I know you're thinking it's the practical thing to do but I really think we need to get away and focus on us. Come on, just think, sun, sand…"

"Isn't it kind of silly to go to an island in the summer?"

He could feel her start to hedge and his hope grew stronger. "We can't go for walks on the beach or swim in the ocean here, right? Besides the weather has been so unpredictable here this month and we can probably get a really good deal now. Come on, say yes."

She stretched her legs out in front of her and noticed how pale they looked. "Oh all right." There really wasn't much point in fighting it. After all, looking for a new job wasn't exactly on the top of her things she wanted to do. But then again, that was part of the problem, she felt lost, no desires or ambitions. Everything felt right when she was pregnant. For the first time in her life she felt she had a purpose. But it was all gone now and she was faced once again with the uncertainty of where she belonged.

She pushed her thoughts aside. *For the moment I feel a small measure of hope that I might survive and I want to savor it, even if it's just for this one day.*

"All right then. Great. I'll go online when I'm done here and start looking for some deals."

"What about your work though? Summer is such a busy time of year for you. You're one of their best carpenters and you'd be putting Rudy in a tough spot."

"Got it covered already. I spoke to him about it a couple of days ago when I got the idea. He understood and sent me an Email this morning to let me know he was able to arrange for someone to fill in for me. I just have to let him know when we're going." He rose from the chair and took one last long swig of his beer to finish it off. "Ahhh…that was good."

Maybe there's a chance for us yet. He pulled off his shirt and scratched his chest. He didn't notice Maya stiffen when he leaned to give her a kiss on the cheek.

"Well, I better get back to work. This is great Maya. You'll see it's going to be good for us," he said cheerfully.

She watched him with indifference as he walked towards the shed he was building and she wondered how long it was going to take for her to feel love for him again, or anyone else in her life for that matter.

Chapter Seven

NASSAU, BAHAMAS ISLAND
August 2012

Brian found a great last minute deal for the famous Atlantis Resort and Casino in the Bahamas. The timing worked out great, leaving on Thursday. He scooped it up quickly before Maya could change her mind.

A week later they were cruising through the scenic Nassau Harbor on a large sailboat, returning from an exotic private island where Atlantic Bottlenose dolphins are known for gathering. A day filled with sun, sand, snorkeling and swimming with the dolphins left Maya pleasantly tired and relaxed.

Her long legs were stretched out in front of her while she leaned back on her elbows, enjoying the breeze in her hair and the heat from the sun on her body.

Sailboats and cruisers of different sizes drifted in and out of the harbor, leaving ripples spreading across the turquoise water. People waved as they passed each other like an unspoken law.

She found herself at ease being out on the water, far away from everything. Even though she struggled her whole life wanting to feel connected to a family, to other people, being alone was oddly comfortable and familiar to her. She wondered sometimes if she was crazy or had a split personality.

She looked over at Brian, drinking and laughing with a group who had also signed up for the Dolphin Encounter excursion. It looked like he had put on some weight over the last few months and his streaks of gray hair were growing more noticeable.

While she continued to observe him she thought about his need to be around people. It made him feel alive. They were very different in this way and she often wondered if she was holding him back, because while she enjoyed other people's company on occasion, she was more of an introverted person.

Feeling her gaze, he excused himself from the group of people he was talking with and rejoined Maya. "You look beautiful. It's nice to see you having some fun again. I hope you're glad we came."

She lifted her hand up to block the glare from her eyes. "It has been a nice break. Don't think I haven't noticed how busy you are trying to keep me so I don't start dwelling on things again," she smiled slyly in his direction.

"I don't know what you are talking about," he said bringing his eyebrows together in an inquisitive way but he couldn't contain his crooked grin.

"Well let's see, we've been here what? Five days? So far we've been snorkeling twice, played golf, oh let's not forget the helicopter tour." She paused trying to recollect what else they had done. "Um, we've driven around the island and of course swimming with the dolphins today."

"You forgot to mention the massages we had together," he laughed.

"Oh yes. That was very relaxing."

"It's working isn't it? Your skin is glowing from the sun and I think you've even put on a couple of pounds since we've been here. I almost wish I booked two weeks instead of just one."

"It wouldn't make much difference. We'd still have to go back home eventually. That's the problem with vacations, they always end."

"Maya, I've been thinking maybe it's time we thought about conceiving again. What do you think?" In his happiness he blurted the words before he knew what he was saying.

The gorgeous turquoise blue waters turned black in Maya's eyes. She held her breath without realizing it. Her heart began to race. Heat rose in her face so it felt like it was on fire. Her skin felt like it was being pricked by a thousand needles.

When she didn't respond he knew that he had made a fatal mistake. "Maya, I'm sorry. I shouldn't have sprung it on you like that. You're not ready yet. Forget I said anything."

The anger filled her so intensely she couldn't bring herself to speak for several minutes. Was she angry with Brian, the world, or with life? It was impossible to tell in the heat of the moment.

When she finally did speak, her words were carefully measured. "My heart would break if something happened again."

"Do you mean just now or ever?"

"I don't know how to answer that question. All I know is that it is too painful right now." *How does he put up with my moods? I don't deserve to be with someone so thoughtful and loving. I know he just wants to make things right.*

He was confused and disappointed. *I thought trying to have a baby again would make her happy.* "There's plenty of time, we don't have to rush." Despite his soothing words he felt a growing sense of restlessness.

* * * *

Brian chose Amici's Italian restaurant for dinner to celebrate their last night in Nassau. He hoped the romantic setting would help to rekindle some loving feelings between them after the disastrous conversation yesterday on the boat.

Stealing a glance at herself in the mirror by the restaurant entrance, Maya adjusted the strap on her shoulder. She felt pretty in her new, simple yet stunning black dress. It flattered her skin, now golden from the sun, and long wavy red hair.

The dress's clinging, low cut style accentuated her cleavage, which had filled back out some with the help of the few extra pounds she put on lately. It was the first time in a long while that she was able to feel like a woman, all feminine and pretty.

She kept her jewelry simple tonight, wearing only her wedding band and small diamond stud earrings.

"This a beautiful restaurant Brian."

He smiled and nodded in agreement, "Yeah. I thought you might like it."

Maya admired the rich mahogany columns and the marble floors while they waited to be seated.

"Do you have a reservation?" asked the hostess as they approached the dining room entrance.

"Yes we do, the name is Maxwell," said Brian.

"Ah yes, please follow me." The waitress seated them at a table overlooking Cable Beach. The large windows were open and a faint scent of bougainvillea drifted in the air. The flowering bushes in vibrant shades of fuchsia and red surrounded the restaurant in abundance, adding rich color to the atmosphere.

The hostess placed the wine and dinner menus on the table. "Your waiter will be right with you."

"Thank you," Brian and Maya spoke at the same time and for the first time since yesterday, they smiled at each other.

She recognized that he was going all out on this trip to help ease her pain and improve their relationship. It made her feel even more horrible for reacting so harshly yesterday.

"Look at the hand-painted ceiling, Brian, it's stunning." Gazing upwards at the garden setting alive with gazebos, an array of colorful flowers with lush green bushes and palm trees caught her attention.

"Yeah, it is pretty nice." He was encouraged by her comments and it helped to ease the anxiety he had been experiencing.

He was thirty-nine now, six years older than Maya and he had to admit the age difference was starting to bother him. He recognized last night, after Maya had dozed off and he lay in bed unable to sleep, that his comment about having lots of time to conceive again may not be his true feelings. He'd be forty next year and he didn't know how much longer he wanted to wait to have children.

"You look beautiful tonight," he said pushing aside his thoughts and reaching out to touch her hand.

"Thank you. You look pretty nice yourself." He was wearing dark blue dress pants with a patterned blue silk short-sleeved shirt, which brought out the blue in his grayish-blue eyes.

A waiter approached their table. "Good evening. How are you tonight?" he asked.

"Good thank you," said Brian.

"My name is Tom and I will be your waiter this evening. Would you like to order something from the bar?"

They ordered a bottle of Shiraz with their dinner then relaxed to enjoy the ambiance. The restaurant was partially open to the outdoors and their table was close to the terrace overlooking a bay. A small motor boat glided across the bay and the light from the moon danced on the rippling water.

Maya admired the view of the masses of fuschia bougainvillea surrounding the terrace, cascading over every wall their beauty filled her with appreciation for island life.

"So what did you think of the tour of the Lost City of Atlantis?" Brian asked taking a bite of his steak when dinner arrived.

"I don't know. It's hard to take any of it seriously but it would be nice to think a place like Atlantis really existed once. It made me think of Egypt with all the hieroglyphics carved on the walls."

"I can't imagine how long it must have taken them to build all the tunnels and the artifacts in the rooms. It's amazing how they created the whole thing like an underground aquarium."

"I know what you mean. It must have taken years. I thought the Treasury Room was pretty neat with all the carvings and records but the Submarine Room kind of freaked me out with the metal sentinels standing guard. They were creepy."

"Did something else upset you in the Navigation Room? You were staring at that round ball hanging from the ceiling for a really long time. It's like you were in a trance."

The look on her face turned sober and she toyed with the pasta on her plate. "I don't know. It was really weird." She cut her veal scalloppini into pieces. "There was something about it that seemed so familiar and I couldn't walk away."

"Have you seen one like it somewhere else or maybe in a movie?"

"That's just it, no. At least, not that I can recall. But you know, I haven't been able to shake the image from my mind all day." As she spoke the words she felt the hair stand up on her arms and she rubbed them to get rid of the goose bumps.

* * * *

The drive back between the restaurant and the resort was breathtaking. Maya felt like they were in an enchanted forest in a fairy tale. The trees arched over both sides of the roadway, almost totally enclosing it. In all the places she'd traveled, not that there had been many, this had instantly become her favorite stretch of roadway.

"Brian slow down. This is so beautiful, I want this road to last forever," she said wistfully.

The air was warm and humid as they drove in the rented open jeep. She breathed deeply, taking in the trees swaying in the breeze and the moonlight flickering through the tiny gaps in the overhanging branches.

Even though she knew there were no other cars on the roadway Maya thought she saw a shadow behind them in the rear-view mirror. She turned to look but nothing was there. She gave her body a shake to fend off the uncomfortable feelings created by the illusion.

"Are you cold?" Brian asked.

"Hmmm? No. I thought I saw something behind us but I must have imagined it." An image of a stone carved with symbols and the hanging metal ball flashed unexpectedly in her mind. *Why do I keep thinking about it? It's driving me crazy.*

She was surprised at how vividly she was able to remember the details of the structure she had seen earlier at the Dig.

The hexagon shaped stone was about three and a half feet high with hieroglyphs carved all around it. There were two pillars on top, which supported three metal rods extending upwards in a semi-circular fashion. They were bolted to the ceiling and surrounded the hanging metal ball. The ceiling was recessed in approximately an eight-foot circular area.

She felt hypnotized by the image and suddenly the metal ball changed to some type of clear crystal that somehow emitted a vibrant green color.

The pathway of trees came to an end on the road and the image disappeared from her mind as quickly as it arrived. *What on earth just happened?* She could hear her heart beating loudly in her ears.

There it is again! Seeing the shadow in the rear-view mirror she glanced quickly behind them but whatever it was had disappeared. Then she felt an ominous presence swoop across the back of her neck making her feel dizzy. She swung her head quickly back and forth looking for something to explain this sensation yet she couldn't see anything there.

Wow the wine must have affected me more than I thought. I didn't have that much though. Maybe it was bad. Yes, that must be it.

Chapter Eight

"It's been a wonderful trip Brian. I feel better than I have in a long time and I haven't had any migraines either." Wearing her pink satin pajamas, she pulled back the covers of the bed and climbed in beside him. She's always heard that women with red hair shouldn't wear pink but she didn't care, she loved the color.

"I'm so glad to see you in better spirits. It's so good to see you smiling and laughing again." He was sitting up watching television but when she got in he clicked it off.

She snuggled up beside him. "I know this has been really hard on you."

"It's been hard on *us*," he corrected.

"Okay us." She lifted herself up onto one elbow and leaned up against him to kiss him. It felt strange to reach out but she wanted to try to make things up to him.

He was hesitant at first, concerned about whether she would back away again. As she lingered with her kiss his body began to respond. *Would she finally…?*

She suppressed the feelings of uncertainty and anxiety that came to the surface again and went through the motions of making love to please him.

He groped her hungrily and the months of celibacy ended quickly. Too quickly. He lost himself in the feeling of her warmth around him and wasn't able to control himself.

When she lay in his arms afterwards she felt an emptiness inside. She wasn't able to persuade her body to rise to even the slightest of heights. She had wanted to show him how much she appreciated everything he was doing to help her but she realized she did it for the wrong reasons and it made her feel alone.

Even though he was able to release his pent up tension he experienced a sense of loss. Their lovemaking lacked any kind of emotional connection and he recognized afterwards that her heart wasn't in it.

She pretended to fall asleep and when she thought he was too, she turned over onto her side, facing away from him.

He lay still, believing she was asleep, not wanting to wake her. Disappointed, he tried to convince himself that their lovemaking was another step to fixing the rift between them, but deep down he recognized his efforts to alter the truth were pointless.

What am I doing wrong? Where is our life together heading? I don't know anymore how to fix things. His mood sunk even lower.

When he was still unable to sleep after a while he looked over at the clock radio to see the time and was frustrated to see it was only one-thirteen. Believing his attempt to get any sleep at this point was futile he rose from bed, quietly got dressed and slipped out of the room.

Maya remained still while he dressed and left. *What have things come to? What is wrong with me that I can't be intimate with my own husband?* She watched the stars flickering in the moonlight, from the bed where she lay. Wondering how and when she would ever feel happy again.

* * * *

Brian was lost in thought as he walked along the winding paths heading towards the Beach Tower Bar. *I don't know what she wants or needs anymore. The anger inside of her is destroying the woman I married.*

"Hey man, how are you tonight?" Joseph, the bartender, offered a wide toothy grin to Brian as he approached the bar. He spoke in the typical Bahamian English, a mixture of Queen's diction with some African influences. Joseph, a native from the island, was wearing a colorful red flowered shirt with khaki knee length shorts.

"Hi Joseph, I'm okay. How about you?" answered Brian as cheerfully as he could muster and leaned over to shake Joseph's hand. Brian met him yesterday, passing time at the bar while Maya had a nap after the dolphin excursion. He brooded over a drink, assuming she didn't want to be around him after his stupid comment about trying to have another baby.

"Good, good. What can I get for you tonight?"

"I'll have a beer, thanks." Brian looked around to see if there was anyone else he recognized as a new band was preparing to entertain the crowd for the next couple of hours.

Joseph came back with his beer. "Here you go, should I start a tab for you?"

"That would be great, thanks." Brian turned around and took a sip from the bottle. That's when he saw her. Their eyes connected and he smiled. He looked away quickly. *What am I doing?* He met Holly briefly yesterday during Happy Hour. She flirted with him and it felt dangerously good to be appreciated.

He found himself glancing in her direction again and watched her meander through the crowd to approach him. He admired her long straight blonde hair, which was pulled back on one side with a white orchid. She looked breathtaking tonight in a white sleeveless lace top and a matching long flowing lace skirt. She walked towards him and leaned forward and offered her cheek for a kiss.

He couldn't help but gaze down and appreciate her voluptuous body. "You look beautiful," he said.

"Thanks, you're looking pretty good yourself. The mood is very lively tonight. Are you planning on staying for a while?"

He was surprised by her interest, thinking she could land any guy here and wasn't sure why she was bothering with him. Not that he didn't consider himself attractive but he was married and not exactly a young stud. "Sure, I'll keep you company." *Why not? There's no harm in hanging out for a while.* He was suddenly in the mood for some fun conversation. "Can I get you a drink?"

"I'd love one, how about a strawberry daiquiri?"

Brian leaned over to Joseph and ordered her drink. At that moment a steel drum band named the Hillside Boys shook the floor with the rhythms of some dance music.

When Joseph delivered Holly's drink, Brian lifted his bottle of beer and clinked it to the rim of her glass, "Here's to the Bahamas."

"To the Bahamas," she laughed with Brian, "Come on let's dance." She grabbed his hand and pulled him out to the dance floor.

A few drinks and a couple of hours later Holly reached for Brian's hand again, "Come on let's get out of here."

"Whoa. Hold on a minute." He pulled away. "I'm a married man, didn't you know that?" He waived his hand in the air, showing off his wedding band as proof.

"Sure, I noticed the ring but you look like you could use some fun." She leaned up close against him and nibbled on his ear. "I know you want it, let's go to my room."

God she's beautiful. Her perfume filled his mind and he swayed on his feet. Her allure was becoming almost too great to turn down. "Holly you are absolutely beautiful, and as tempting as your offer is, I just can't. I'm sorry." He escaped before she could say anything to change his mind.

That was too close. I won't do that to Maya. As tough as things have been she doesn't deserve to be cheated on. But something has got to change soon. I don't know how long I can live like this.

* * * *

Holly watched Brian leave and lifted her shoulders. *Oh well, his loss.* She turned to leave and caught the man's eye sitting at the end of the bar. Walking towards him, she stopped just long enough to let him know what happened. "He was really tempted but he wouldn't go for it. I did what you asked, where's the rest of the money?"

Chapter Nine

Maya slept restlessly that night near the edge of the bed, curled in a fetal position. The sound of rain beating down on the balcony in the morning caused her to stir. She stretched out her long legs and felt comforted by the warmth of Brian's body and the sound of his slow steady breath, until memories of the night before slipped in to renew her anxiety and discomfort.

Confusion lurked in every corner of her mind. She shifted onto her back and lay quietly, weeping silent tears.

She looked around the room trying to distract her mind from traveling a lonely road. The walls, barren of pictures, with the exception of a large mirror, were painted a sand color, and seemed rather plain in comparison to the vivid fabrics on the furniture. A lime green chair stood near the balcony doors on one side while matching coral armchairs sat beside a small round bamboo table on the other. She studied the fresh bountiful arrangement of flowers on the table while listening to the rain pelting down even harder now.

Even though she liked to sleep with the drapes open she felt disoriented. The dark menacing clouds disguised the daylight hiding behind them. *What time is it?* She felt sure it had to be morning.

Gently pushing aside the turquoise bedding she lifted herself up onto her elbows so she could see the clock across the king size bed, on Brian's side.

He rolled onto his back, opened his eyes and was met with a surprised Maya. "Morning," he mumbled.

She smelled the alcohol on his breath and forced a smile. "Morning yourself," she responded.

"What are you doing?" he asked watching her squint across the bed.

"I'm trying to see what time it is." Her eyes finally focused. "Wow, I can't believe it's ten o'clock. It's so dark outside."

"Ten o'clock? I can't remember the last time I slept so late." He yawned and stretched out his arms. Impulsively he reached out and pulled her towards him. "Come here."

Her head was against his chest and his arms held her tightly before she could respond. He debated about whether to talk to her about what happened but he was afraid they would end up in another fight.

She sighed and rested there, listening to the beat of his heart. "This week has gone by so quickly," she said wistfully.

He decided to leave it alone and put it behind them. "It certainly has." They lay together quietly for several minutes, each lost in their own thoughts.

"We should probably get up and start packing," she said.

"You're right." He reluctantly released her from his embrace, swung his legs over the side of the bed and sat up.

"Wow it's really coming down out there," he said as he walked towards the balcony. He stood watching the storm raging outside. "It looks like it might rain all day."

"Oh you never know. It could disappear quickly. I've heard it's common in the islands to have flash storms that end as quickly as they come." Maya began opening dresser drawers to take stock of how she wanted to pack her things.

"Oh well, I guess we're not going to have time to do anything much anyway. Our flight is at five so we'll have to leave here around two thirty."

"That gives us time to shower, pack, and have a leisurely lunch," she said.

"Sounds good. I'm pretty hungry already."

They prepared for the day and carried on as though nothing was wrong. Believing that sweeping it under the rug for now was the best thing to do, they kept their conversations light.

*   *   *   *

"See I told you the storm might pass," yelled Maya from the balcony.

"You were right. I can't believe the sky is clear already." Brian was zipping up the last suitcase. They made arrangements for their bags to be held by the concierge until their bus was scheduled to leave so they wouldn't have to fuss with them while they had lunch.

Leaning against the white wrought iron railing on the balcony, she smiled and watched the seagulls as they circled around the beach area looking for food. *It's a new day…no tears today.*

People were already beginning to grab their lounge chairs, claiming their spots for another day in the sun. Children were scouring the beach looking for shells and colorful rocks to add to their collection. She found herself feeling envious of their carefree joy for living. Their only concern in the moment was waiting for their parents to let them run and play in the water.

A shadow of sadness clouded her heart, threatening to take over but somehow she managed to bury the feeling.

"Come on we might as well walk around and enjoy the sunshine," he said.

The Atlantis resort was stunning and luxurious. All the buildings were painted in various themes of coral, turquoise and green, spread over several acres of land and water.

"Where do you want to eat?" Brian asked.

"I can't decide. The Lagoon Bar is so beautiful, overlooking the water but we never made it to Fathoms. I wanted to see that restaurant. It looked really neat in the pictures."

"Is that the one that's surrounded by the giant fish tank?"

"Yes, that's the one," she said.

"Well we have some time. Why don't we go check it out and we can always stop for one last drink at the Lagoon Bar before we leave for the airport."

"Sure, why not."

They strolled through the resort enjoying their last moments of island sun and finally found themselves standing in the dimly lit Fathom's restaurant.

"It's really dark in here," she said disappointed after walking outside in the bright sunshine.

"Would you rather go to the Lagoon Bar for lunch instead?" Brian asked.

She looked around noticing a few groups of people laughing and enjoying the atmosphere. The massive room size fish tank surrounding the restaurant was very impressive. "No, let's eat here. It could be interesting."

They were seated at a table near the tank-providing full, up close viewing of all the sea creatures swimming around.

The walls were painted a muted shade of coral, consistent with the pastel theme throughout most of the resort. Soft lights from the ceiling provided a warm glow on the walls that were etched with markings.

"Those look like some of the symbols that were on the walls in the Atlantean Dig rooms," said Maya pointing above the doorways and tank.

Brian nodded in agreement, "Yes they do."

Once they ordered their lunch, an uncomfortable silence descended between them for a few minutes. To fill the time they took turns pointing out the different types of odd-looking tropical fish until their food arrived.

About to put a fork full of food into her mouth a shark swam by, startling Maya. She screamed and jumped in her seat, almost knocking her glass of iced tea over. "Oh my God! That scared me." It was a little too close for comfort even if there was a glass wall between them but they laughed it off together.

When she collected herself their attention became distracted by a group of people gathering around a table near the entrance.

"I wonder what's going on over there?" questioned Maya. She popped one of the shrimp from the pasta dish into her mouth and plucked the tail off.

Brian leaned back to try to get a better view. "I don't know. It's hard to see. There are too many people."

A large woman in shorts and a tee shirt moved, providing Maya with a brief glimpse inside the circle. "I see a couple in the middle. Everyone seems to be listening to the man talking."

Brian strained to see something but his view was still blocked.

The large woman shifted again, preventing Maya from seeing anything else and their waiter approached the table before Maya could speak.

"How's your meal?" he asked.

"Good thanks," said Maya. "Do you know who that couple is over there?" she pointed discreetly.

He glanced over his shoulder and turned back to Maya. "Oh, he's some big shot psychic from Detroit. He works with the police to help solve crimes. I believe his name is Nicholas Rhodes and that's his partner, Julia."

"Interesting, I've heard that is becoming more common for police to work with people like that," said Maya.

"Why is everyone gathered around them?" asked Brian.

"It's pretty freaky actually. He can tell you all about yourself. That's why everybody's around him. They are asking him questions because he can predict things too. You know, like looking into the future and stuff like that. Anyway, is there anything else I can get for you?"

Brian glanced towards Maya while she shook her head. "No thank you. That should do it. Can you bring us the bill please? Thanks."

"Everyone certainly looks mesmerized by this guy," said Maya. "Do you want to go over and check it out when we're done?"

"It doesn't matter to me. I don't believe in all that crap. You don't, do you?"

She shrugged her shoulders. "I don't know. It's probably nonsense but I'm kind of curious. Aren't you?"

Brian shook his head and sighed. "I'll go with you if you really want to. Ah, who knows, it could be good for a laugh."

Once their lunch was paid for they joined the crowd of people, standing quietly in the background, observing and listening.

Maya could understand why everyone was entranced, especially the women. She studied Nicholas and found herself becoming more intrigued, noting that he seemed to be full of contrasting traits. His voice was soft yet strong at the same time. His mannerisms were gentle but with a commanding quality.

His boyish good looks were enhanced with his loose golden locks, moussed back in a perfect unruliness, a slightly darker beard and deep brown eyes.

He's obviously very meticulous in his style. His soft yellow golf shirt and beige pants look freshly pressed, and his brown loafers looked recently buffed. His appearance seems oddly out of place for someone who works in such a tough environment.

Brian tried to focus his attention on what Nicholas was saying but he was having trouble concentrating, it was over his head and he couldn't understand what all the fuss was about.

"Life is a journey," Nicholas said, "I'm sure you've all heard that before. Everyday is an opportunity to learn something new. We have to walk the path, do the work, and listen, really listen to your heart's calling. Ego can make us believe we are ready to take on our life's work before we are actually ready, or on the other hand, it can convince us the time is not right. But the infinite divine wisdom knows the truth and will guide you if are open to new possibilities."

Brian shifted, feeling uncomfortable. *I've heard enough. This guy is full of himself.* He glanced sideways to look at Maya and wondered about the odd look on her face. "Come on, let's go," he said quietly.

"Shhh, not yet. I want to listen." The stranger's voice was having a peculiar effect on her, creating a feeling of resistance yet curiosity in what he had to say.

"Take a look at what your outer world looks like. This will guide you to see your progress. Is your life filled with turmoil and strife? Or does everything you do fall into place smoothly? If things are not going your way you need to stop and take time to contemplate what is motivating you to manifest your struggles. Ask yourself, what is holding you back from reaching your full potential? Listen to the voice within and allow your higher consciousness to reveal the areas of your life that need special attention."

As Maya listened, the feeling of resistance went up a notch or two to anxiety. She shifted her weight from one foot to the other and pushed her hair behind her ears.

"I think it would helpful if you explained to them how they can do this in a tangible way," said his partner Julia.

Maya wondered about the woman beside Nicholas. She had some similar qualities. Perfectly dressed and groomed, smiling when appropriate with a very formal air about her. It was obvious she took a back seat to him because she remained quiet most of the time but her tone of voice indicated she was also a person in authority.

Maya glanced around at the group of people who were listening to his every word and wondered what it was about him that seemed to be capturing their attention so completely.

"Yes, of course. Excellent suggestion. Thank you darling," Nicholas said acknowledging Julia's input. "Many people find it extremely helpful to explore their feelings by writing in a journal. Explore what angers you, what makes you feel sad, lonely, betrayed, and jealous. Ask yourself what your relationship is like with your spouse, children, family, friends and even money. Especially money. Something I have discovered is your relationship towards money is a telling sign of how you deal with all aspects of your life. Many people feel they are not worthy of having money. This feeling is likely to spill over into the other areas of your life. If you subconsciously believe you are not worthy you will sabotage yourself from experiencing true happiness. This is not an easy exercise and unfortunately, most people cannot face their inner beliefs."

Maya's anxiety continued to build to even higher levels. "Is he actually saying that people sabotage themselves?" she asked Brian quietly. "I mean, come on, why would anyone want to do that?"

"I've never heard of anything so ridiculous. Have you heard enough yet?" Brian asked impatiently.

"Yes, let's go." Maya touched his arm and they turned to leave.

"Excuse me," Nicholas said in a louder voice. He stood and moved gracefully towards the couple leaving. "Your name is Maya isn't it?"

They stopped to look at the man walking towards them. He was taller than Brian by several inches. Maya estimated he was probably six feet four. As he approached closer she could see his eyes twinkling and a mischievous smirk formed at the corners of his mouth. She noticed that he was older than she originally thought, his beard showed signs of graying and the depth of the lines on his forehead meant he must be in his late forties. There was something very mysterious yet earthy about him.

"How did you know that?" Maya questioned.

"I know many things." He extended his hand to Brian. "And you are Brian. Hello, my name is Nicholas Rhodes."

Brian, unsure how to respond, shook Nicholas' hand.

"I apologize if I made you uncomfortable. Sometimes I have that effect on people. Why don't you stay and have a drink with Julia and I."

Maya spoke up, "Thank you but we really should be going. Our plane is leaving in a few hours."

He focused his eyes intently on Maya's and she squirmed under his gaze.

Brian held a sudden flash of jealousy in check. "She's right. It was nice to meet you," he said with a tightened jaw line.

"Yes of course. I don't want to keep you. I just wanted to tell you I know that you have had a very difficult year with the loss of your child…"

Maya gasped for air and grabbed Brian's arm for support. *How could he know that?*

"Is this some kind of sick joke?" demanded Brian.

"No, no of course not. I assumed you knew of my psychic gift. Sometimes it's more like a curse. Please I apologize. I felt compelled to somehow reassure you that everything will be fine. You must believe that everything happens for a reason."

Losing any shred of sanity by his comment Maya burst out, "Reason? How can there be a reason for what happened? Brian please, let's go," she pulled on Brian's shirtsleeve.

"Maya," Nicholas said in a powerful voice.

She didn't know why but she felt drawn to stop and turn around. As he looked into her eyes she felt spellbound by their depth. She motioned for Brian to wait.

"That speech I gave about exploring feelings to understand what is happening around us, it was meant for you."

She stood still, unable to move.

"You have to resolve your issues about abandonment and self worth before you will be able to have a family of your own. God is not punishing you Maya. Quite the contrary, you have a special purpose to fulfill and the universe is helping you to prepare for your mission."

She blinked back tears. Her thoughts were jumbled and confused.

"That's enough," said Brian. "Thank you for your concern but we have to be going."

"I understand." Nicholas's hand swiftly fanned out across Brian's body then extended out to touch Maya's arm. He looked deeply into her eyes and spoke with intensity, "I strongly suggest you do not dismiss what I am about to say."

Brian tried to speak but no words would come. He wanted to reach out to Maya, but his body would not move. Everything seemed to stand still around him while he watched Nicholas' mouth move, but couldn't hear any words. He felt sealed in a vacuum chamber and lost all sense of time and space.

"Our meeting here was no accident. The universe conspired to bring both of us here at the precise moment in time that is most perfect. Any sooner and you would not be able to integrate the energy. Any later and it would be too late. The universe, as most usual, has waited until the last possible juncture to bring the necessary forces together."

Maya felt a surge of electricity pulse through her body. "I don't understand."

"Why don't I help you along. What you are experiencing is a life crisis. Everything that you thought you knew has turned upside down. Like a snow globe that has been shaken and now the snowflakes float down in all different directions. Is that a good analogy?"

"Yes…I'm confused and nothing makes sense anymore." She wondered why she was talking to this man but felt compelled to continue their conversation.

"What you are experiencing usually occurs when women and men reach their early to mid forties. You are going through it earlier than most because time is of essence," said Nicholas.

Brian was right about this guy.

"Brian is not capable of understanding, but you are. You just don't remember yet. You will have to figure out how to manage the situation with him or make some tough decisions. That is totally up to you and no one can interfere with that process."

What is he saying? A spark of anger flared through her body. *How dare he comment on my marriage.*

"Please there is no time to waste and I have no desire to upset you. I only wish to help you to awaken to your destiny."

Why is Brian just standing there and not stopping this insane discussion?

Nicholas nodded in understanding without her speaking. "I have placed a force field around us so that no one can hear our conversation and no one can interrupt."

"A force field? That's ludicrous!" She glanced nervously around. The world was moving around them, yet it seemed as though only they existed. She looked squarely at Nicholas with anger and resistance. "And what exactly is my destiny?" she asked trying to control her emotions.

"There is much you will have to discover on your own but I *can* tell you that as part of your journey you must awaken to your brightness and clarity. It is your destiny to shine a light for both yourself and others but your biggest weakness is your inability to follow through to completion. This lifetime is your ultimate test and the world's enlightenment rests on your success."

"Whoa, hold on a minute. That's a heck of an expectation. How can the world's enlightenment rest on my success? I haven't even been to church in years. I'm hardly in a position to provide any kind of enlightenment to myself, much less others."

"This is not about church or religion. It's about each person's ability to connect to divine wisdom through their heart and soul."

"I still don't understand what all this means," Maya said angrily.

"Our great planet is also experiencing a crisis of epic proportions. If humanity is going to avoid another disaster like that of Atlantis there must be a massive shift in consciousness and you are part of the solution whether you like it or not. You have much to do, and much to discover in a short period of time. Your first task is to uncover the secrets of the Emerald Stone. When you do this your destiny will be revealed to you and doors will open to show your next steps in your mission."

She felt like she was watching a sci-fi movie, except this was real life and she was the leading actress. "This is very overwhelming. I don't know what to think."

"Do your research and it will become clear."

"What if I don't?"

"That, of course, is your choice. We are all guaranteed free will but one thing you must understand is that the universe will never give you more to do than you are capable of handling." When she didn't respond he continued, "That being said, let's look at your choices. You can sit in the baby's room and mourn her death for the rest of your life or you can live to reach your fullest potential and help save our existence and create a whole new way of living."

She felt pain piercing her heart. How could she make these kinds of decisions? "You've said time is of essence. What do you mean by that?"

"Do you know about the end of the Mayan Calendar?"

"No."

"Then that is something else you will need to research. You must beware however, there are forces out there that once they recognize you are awakening, will work to dissuade or discourage you in any number of ways. Including making you feel crazy for believing in your unique situation. Now it is up to you to decide on your course of action, but please do not waste time."

"How much time do I have to decide?"

"Very little. There is only four months left to complete your mission."

"Four months! How can I possibly be ready in four months?"

"I know it's difficult to comprehend how, but you must trust that you were born with the necessary knowledge. I am taking a chance by telling you any more but drastic times call for drastic measures..."

"Yes?" she asked defiantly. *What more could there be?*

"It is not your destiny to have a child right now. The universe needs you. It must be enough to know that there will be time to have children upon successful completion of your mission. Now you must go. Don't worry, Brian will not realize how much time has passed while we spoke. Be well Maya. Perhaps we'll meet again someday."

In that instant she became aware of the noise in the restaurant and Nicholas was no longer standing beside her talking. Her breathing was shallow. Her heart beat rapidly. She rubbed her eyes and temples. *How on earth am I supposed to deal with this? It's ludicrous. Me saving humanity? I must be insane to even think there's any truth to this.*

Brian put his arm around Maya and gently nudged her to move. *Where did he go?* He shook his head, confused about why he felt so angry and how Nicholas could have moved back into the crowd so quickly. He couldn't remember what their last words were or if they even said goodbye. "Come on, let's get out of here." He escorted her outside, noticing a slight headache developing.

She walked silently beside him, lost in thought.

"Are you okay? You look a little green," said Brian when they were back outside.

"Oh yeah. Yeah, I'm fine." The world around her seemed hazy even though the sun was shining brilliantly.

The doctors had never been able to determine why I lost the baby. She wondered if there was any truth to what Nicholas said. Just to be safe she tried to focus on his message and burn it into her mind but she felt it slipping away. *Emerald Stone and the Mayan Calendar. That's what I have to remember. Concentrate.*

* * * *

"You were phenomenal Nicholas," said Julia later in the hotel room they shared for appearance sake. It was important to keep up the illusion they were romantically involved throughout the trip. "I had no idea you were so well versed. There were times I thought you sounded exactly like Douglas himself."

"He's an excellent teacher and I learn quickly, guess it makes for a good combination." He shrugged off the compliment but inside he knew he nailed his performance perfectly and was very pleased with himself.

"Do you think she'll act now?"

"I felt a spark there—I think I got through and I'm pretty sure she'll do something about it but it all depends on how much control she gives to Brian. If not, Douglas will put the pressure on her to move," Nicholas said with confidence in their leader. "I believe wholeheartedly that Douglas will succeed and save the world from destruction. I feel so fortunate to be a part of this and I'm looking forward to working beside him in the New World." Nicholas felt blessed to have been given such an important task as the one he just completed. To have been taught the gift of cloaking was all the proof he needed that Douglas believed in him and was holding a place for Nicholas in the inner circle.

Julia contemplated his comment while they packed their things. She agreed with Nicholas but the days were slipping away too quickly and December twenty-first was just around the corner. *Stay in the NOW.* She reminded herself about the techniques Douglas taught her to release fears. She concentrated, drawing in a deep breath to let go and she felt her worries slip away effortlessly. *I wish I were in Maya's shoes. I'd give anything to be that important to Douglas. He's the most remarkable man I've ever known. So loving and compassionate.* She deliberately avoided thinking about his other qualities that sometimes frightened her.

* * * *

"Do you think there's any truth to what he said?"

"Who?" Brian looked at Maya sitting next to him on the plane. "Oh, you mean that quack? No I don't." He studied her before continuing. "Are you still thinking about that? Don't bother. Come on, snap out of it."

"How can you dismiss it so quickly. There has to be some truth to what he says. He's obviously well respected and how could he have known about losing the baby? That's pretty specific."

"What are you saying? That you think you have some special mission? That's nonsense."

"I'm not saying that I believe that part but it really hit home when he talked about issues of abandonment." She kept the rest of the conversation to herself. Brian was irritated enough as it was, she couldn't imagine how he would respond if she told him everything Nicholas had said.

Brian sighed. "Only you can determine that. But I just can't buy into the universe causing you to lose the baby because you have abandonment issues. How does that make sense?"

"I'm not sure. I do know that this was a really nice trip and it helped me to let go of some anger. Enough to know I need to do something to help myself because I don't want to keep living the way I was."

"Maybe you should think about going back to the therapist. You only went once."

"Maybe." Maya didn't know what the answer was to her problems but she didn't think that was it.

Chapter Ten

"Join me in Egypt and I will show you a New World."

"Who are you? How will I know you?"

"Have no fear. You will recognize me by the dragon."

Maya woke up startled. She felt dazed and her heart beat rapidly. *That dream felt so real! It's like he was really in my head talking to me. Who was he?* The sharp pain at the base of her skull forced her to lie back down after trying to get up.

The clock on the night table read 11:11 A.M. *Damn! I can't believe I slept so late. Why didn't Brian wake me up before he left?* Waiting for the pain to subside she tried to remember the dream but all that came back to her were the words from an unknown man. *It's just a dumb dream and it doesn't mean anything.*

But it felt so real.

They had been home for a few days and Brian was back to work. She wanted to get up early and work on getting her resume up to date so she could start her job search today. *Oh well so much for an early start.*

She rose slowly from the bed, testing her head. Satisfied the pain was gone she got up and stretched her arms up to the ceiling. Lazily she wandered to the window where she stood, staring out at the deserted street, still dazed from the strange dream.

She was feeling better physically from the daily exercise on their trip and decided to keep her resolution to keep it up, before she started her job search for the day. *What are another few hours?*

She did a few more minutes of gentle stretching. Then dressed in a baby blue matching terry short set, brushed her teeth, slipped her hair into a ponytail and headed out for a long walk.

Whew, it's hot out here. I must have walked a couple of miles by now. She felt energized but decided she better start heading back. Allowing herself to go into an automatic pilot mode provided her mind the opportunity to wander in different directions and she found herself thinking about her meeting with Nicholas. It frustrated her that she could only remember bits and pieces of the conversation.

Whenever she thought of him she felt hypnotized and she had to keep herself busy to stop from dwelling on it. But here she was, a couple miles away from home with nothing to distract herself.

She was torn about whether to investigate the things he told her. They seemed too far out and unbelievable but what if they were true? *Ugh! It's crazy to think about it. Forget it Maya.*

Content with her decision, she started to jog lightly, enjoying the quiet neighborhood streets. After a few minutes she picked up her pace. It had been years since she ran and she had forgotten how much she enjoyed the feeling of her body working so efficiently. The doctors thought it best that she not tax her body any more than necessary while she tried to get pregnant so they recommended that she limit her physical activity.

Her breathing became heavier as she pumped her arms harder, pulling her forward. Suddenly a vibrant vision of a silver dragon with gold tipped wings blinded her sight. It disappeared as quickly as it came. But the image was so vivid and real, it startled her and she almost tripped.

When she gained her stride back she experienced a slight dizziness. *I must be overdoing it.* She slowed down to an easy jog, which seemed to alleviate the dizziness but then she was hit by a feeling of nauseousness and a tingling sensation up her spine.

She stopped and bent over. Resting her hands on her thighs, waiting for the feeling to pass. But the tingling grew stronger. It felt more like needles digging into her skin now. She straightened and took some deep breaths. The dizziness came back and it felt like there was a fire building upwards in her body. Her cheeks turned a bright red. *Oh God, I'm going to be sick.* She instinctively raised her hand to cover her mouth and looked for a place to sit. Reaching a big maple tree a few feet away she dropped to the ground and braced her back up against it for support.

The cool grass beneath her felt refreshing and thankfully the episode faded away after a few moments. She looked around in embarrassment to see if anyone was nearby. Realizing she was alone she waited several more minutes before standing. *Wow…that was pretty wild. I must be dehydrated or something.*

She walked the rest of the way and when she arrived home she immediately drank a couple glasses of water.

* * * *

Night after night Maya tossed and turned. "Who *are* you?" she pleaded.

"Maya wake up," Brian said groggily and tugged on her shoulders several nights later.

"Huh? What?"

"You were shouting in your dreams again." He sat up and turned on the light. "This has been going on every night for the past week. Are you all right?"

"I don't know. I've been feeling really weird." When she turned to face Brian she noticed everything felt wet.

"What do you mean weird?"

"Geez Brian, the bed is soaked I must have been sweating. Can you help me change the sheets?"

"Yeah, sure. Do you have a fever? Here let me feel your forehead." He reached across to touch her. "No, no fever. What do you mean you've been feeling weird?"

They got up from the bed and Maya walked to her dresser. "I keep getting these dizzy spells and then…" She pulled out a fresh nightshirt and changed her clothes.

"And then what?" he said getting slightly irritated. He tossed the blanket on the floor and yanked the sheets off the bed. It was three o'clock in the morning and he needed to get up for work in two and a half-hours. The thought of losing another night's sleep made him grumpier.

Pulling out a clean sheet from the linen closet she walked back to the bed. "It's like I can feel my blood getting hotter and hotter and it shoots up my spine. It's so strong sometimes I feel like I'm going to throw up."

He grabbed one side of the sheet as she aired it out and pulled the corners under the bed, tucking in his side. "Why didn't you tell me about this? How many times has this happened?"

"A few times."

"A few times? What do you mean by a few?"

She hesitated. "Actually it's happened everyday this week and today it happened twice."

"For Pete's sake. Have you called the doctor?"

Wincing by his reaction she debated about telling him about the visions of the dragon that appear along with these episodes. "Not yet."

"What do you mean not yet?" He was furious. The distance between them was growing even wider since they returned from Nassau and he didn't seem to know what was going on with her anymore.

"Because I was waiting to see if my dreams would help me to understand what's going on."

"Your dreams? How can your dreams help you?"

"I don't know," she said with resignation.

"Why haven't you talked to me about these things?"

"I guess I thought you wouldn't understand and you'd get mad at me."

He took a deep breath to calm himself. "I'm not mad, but I can't understand if you don't talk to me," he said. "Maya, why do you think your dreams would be able to help you understand why you're getting dizzy and sick?"

"Because they seem connected." Her stomach knotted up while she contemplated how much she was going to tell him.

"Connected how?" He picked up his pillow from the floor, tossed it on the bed and plopped down, pulling the sheets across his body. This conversation was agitating him. He wondered why and assumed it was because she seemed to be keeping things from him.

"Well…it was the same dream for the first few nights. I can never remember much of it except this voice telling me I need to go to Egypt and that I'll understand when I see the dragon."

Brian laughed. "Egypt? Dragon?" He laughed again. "I'm sorry I don't understand. What does this have to do with your dizzy spells?"

"I keep seeing a dragon when it happens."

"Maya, your imagination is just playing tricks with you. You are probably thinking so much about the dream that you are creating this image in your head."

"If that's true then what about getting dizzy and this unexplained heat in my body?

"I don't know," he said in frustration. "Maybe it's because you're not getting enough sleep. I want you to call the doctor, end of story. No arguments. Okay?"

"All right, I'll call the doctor."

Brian turned out the light and they relaxed under the blankets. "Wait a minute," he said, "if this has been going on everyday for the past week, have the dreams changed?"

"Pardon?"

"You said the dream was the same for the first few nights. What about the rest of the time?"

"After the first few times it changed a bit." She pulled the sheet and blanket up around her shoulder. "In the dream I am driving somewhere, I don't know where, then I stop for a break and go for a walk in the woods. There are really tall trees everywhere and then a large stone rises up from the ground with some kind of a crystal sitting on top. It's really strange, it's like the crystal speaks to me somehow, calling me to touch it."

"Then what happens?"

"That's all I remember. The next thing I know I'm hearing about Egypt and the dragon again."

"And you've been having these dreams every night?"

"Yup."

"Promise me you'll call the doctor?"

"I promise."

He turned onto his side, away from her. He felt his patience being tested. *Just when I thought things were going to get better between us. She looked so much healthier in Nassau. I don't get it though. She's still looking good. Christ she's even been running again. Maybe her hormones are out of whack.*

* * * *

"All the blood tests are normal and everything was clear on the MRI. I can't find anything physically wrong with you Maya. If anything, the tests seem to indicate you are healthier now than before your pregnancy."

"But what about the dizzy spells?"

"I can't explain it." Dr. Walkerton flipped through the results of the various tests. "Your iron levels are within normal ranges and so are your hormone levels. Your ears and ear canals are in perfect shape so it's not vertigo." She let the papers drop and looked at Maya. "I think there is a good possibility it's the stress from losing your job and having to start over again."

"Makes sense. Thanks for taking the time to check things out for me. Brian might not believe me when I tell him though. Is it okay if he calls you?"

"Of course. Let me know if it continues. In the meantime if I think of any other tests to run I'll contact you. Have you thought about going back to consult with Dr. Rupert?"

"Brian suggested it when we were in Nassau. I'll think it over." She stood up to leave the doctor's office. "Thanks again."

Maya drove through the busy city streets oblivious of the bumper-to-bumper traffic. She was relieved to know that Dr. Walkerton couldn't find anything wrong but it didn't explain what was happening to her. Frustrated with the medical community she decided to do some research. *Maybe I won't find anything but I have to at least try to get some answers.*

It was five-thirty in the afternoon when she arrived home. She made herself a cup of tea and went into the den. Her desk was littered with copies of her resume and letters she had sent on her job search. She pushed them aside and turned on her computer and waited for an active signal from her wireless connection.

She pulled up the Google page and typed the words: Emerald Stone, then she hit the enter key.

"What are you doing?" asked Brian casually entering the den.

Maya jumped and let out a yelp. "You startled me! I didn't hear you come in. How come you are home so early?"

"I was worried about you and wanted to find out what the doctor said. So what happened?"

"Dr. Walkerton couldn't find anything wrong. In fact, she said I'm healthier now than I've been in a long time."

"Right."

"Honest. I knew you wouldn't believe me. You can call her if you want."

"So how did she explain what is happening?"

"She said it might be stress from losing my job and having to start over again."

"That's it?" he demanded.

"Yes, that's it. She just said to let her know if I continue to have these experiences."

"Well that's crazy! Last night your body was jerking around like you were being shocked or something. It's been getting worse. There must be something we can do," he said desperately. "We should try another doctor and get a second opinion."

He started to pace but the Google listings on the computer screen caught his attention. "What are you looking up?"

"Something called the Emerald Stone."

"What's that?"

"I'm not sure exactly. That's why I'm trying to find out. It's supposed to be connected to the end of the Mayan Calendar and the world experiencing a massive crisis."

"What? Honestly Maya, I don't know what's gotten into you." He paced behind her, running his hands through his hair. "Where did you hear about this Emerald Stone?"

She took a deep breath. "Nicholas Rhodes."

"Nicholas who? Do you mean that quack from Nassau? For Pete's sake Maya, when did you talk to him?"

"That day in the restaurant."

"What? I don't understand. Did you see him again after we left?"

"No, of course not."

"Well then, when exactly did you talk about this Emerald Stone?"

Against her better judgment she decided to tell him about the force field Nicholas put around them and his message.

He bellowed out an overbearing laugh, "Force field! Oh now I've heard everything! I think you're really losing it. What's Dr. Rupert's phone number. I think it's time you booked another appointment."

"I am not crazy," she said in quiet determination, Nicholas' words about forces working against the quest echoing in her mind. His attitude was infuriating. "Look I know this sounds far fetched but you said yourself what's happening to me is bizarre. I need to figure it out and the doctors can't help."

"You're going to listen to that kook after only one doctor's opinion?"

Her hands started to shake. Her body temperature began to rise. "You don't know he's a kook. He seemed pretty well respected to me. As I said, I have to do something." She turned to face the computer to see what came up on her search.

"Then call another doctor. Maya, I'm against this. You don't know what you're getting yourself into." He was infuriated that she was totally dismissing his opinion.

She couldn't explain it but she felt driven and Brian's reaction was fueling her determination. Her right hand tremored and she shook it out. His reaction was unnerving but she felt pushed up against a wall and didn't like it.

"Maya! Come on, listen to reason." When she ignored him, he reached out to grab her chair and pull it away to get her attention and show her how serious he was. "For Pete's sake Maya!"

She pushed herself away from the desk. Anger consumed her. "How dare…" She looked down at her right hand as she rose from the chair.

They stood in shocked silence as they watched a crackle of flame escape from her fingertips. Shooting out it knocked over the garbage can beside the desk. They listened to the sizzle and watched the steam rising upwards.

Brian took a step backwards. He stared with a glazed look at the semi-melted can. "How?" he stammered, "What…What just happened?"

She was just as confused. "I…I don't know…"

He took a couple more steps back. Turned and walked away. When he reached the doorway of the den he turned around to face her. "Do what you want. I can't deal with this."

Speechless she watched him walk away.

Chapter Eleven

"Who are you?"

"Come with me to Egypt and you will discover the answers for your existence," whispered the dragon into Maya's ear.

She watched with apprehension as the brilliant red serpent with a golden underbelly and wings circled around her. "What do you want?" She squirmed backwards as its head suddenly swooped in close bringing them eye-to-eye.

"It's not about what *I* want," it said teasingly. "Don't you want to know *who you are* and why you are here?"

The fever she fought for two days continued to escalate and she thrashed about in bed. "Why Egypt?" she shouted. "Why Egypt?" The sound of her own voice startled her awake. Drops of sweat trickled down her neck. She reached up to rub her eyes and felt her soaked hair.

"Brian? Brian are you there?"

Her whole body ached and her teeth chattered. *What day is it?* She tried to clear her thoughts. *Oh yes, it's Sunday.* "Where is he? Damn! I forgot he went away for the weekend."

She gathered the comforter up and wrapped it around her as she stumbled to the bathroom. She grabbed a cloth and soaked it with cool water. Dabbing her face trying to bring her temperature down she screamed in discomfort. She clumsily opened the cabinet door and reached for some Tylenol.

"Damn these stupid child proof caps!" Fumbling with the bottle she finally managed to shake a few pills into the palm of her hand. She popped them into her mouth and swallowed with a gulp of water. Chills ran up and down her body and she grabbed the bottle again taking another one.

Stumbling back into the bedroom she stopped at the linen closet to get another blanket. Dropping into bed she wrapped herself up under all the covers and fell back into an uneasy sleep.

Her dreams became more vivid and bizarre. The same dragon haunted her, calling to her. A shadow descended upon a pyramid. The dragon swooped down and scooped her into its arms. It let out a loud roar of fire to destroy the shadowy presence.

She tossed and turned. Her eyes rolling in their sockets, delirious from the rising temperature in her body. Then she was vaguely aware that something was holding her down, pinned on her stomach, she couldn't move her arms. Somewhere in the background she heard a hissing sound. *I must still be dreaming…*

Sometime near noon, several hours later, her fever finally broke.

Her body ached. "Ouch! Geez why is my back so sore? It feels like it's stinging." Feeling stronger she threw aside all the blankets. Everything was soaked and she felt disgusting with her nightshirt sticking to her body.

She got out of bed and drank some water. Her legs felt unsteady, but the flu or whatever it was, had definitely passed. She stripped the bed and then took her nightshirt and panties off, letting them drop to the floor. She headed for the shower.

When she finished washing up and shampooing her hair she turned off the water opened the curtain and reached for one of towels hanging on the rack. Stepping carefully out of the tub she dried herself and wondered again why her back felt like it was still stinging. She wiped off the mirror and when she turned sideways to wrap her hair up in the towel something caught her eye in the mirror. *What's that?* She stopped abruptly and stared at the fiery red mark on her lower back in shock.

"What on earth is that?" It was difficult to get a clear look. She pulled herself up on the vanity and moved as close to the mirror as she could. *It looks...it looks like a flame of fire!* "How the hell!" She tentatively touched it to see if she could feel anything but there was no sensation. No blood, no trace of an outline. *It looks like it's under the skin!*

Her heart pounded hard in her chest. Maya continued to gaze into the mirror at the mark. "What is going on?" Her mind raced in different directions. *Am I possessed? The dragon! Did the dragon do this? That's crazy, how could it? It was just a dream. Wasn't it?*

She tried to remember what happened. No, the dragon protected me. But how did this happen?

She jumped down off the counter, ran into her closet and pulled on her thick white terrycloth robe. She scouted all the rooms upstairs, then ran down the stairs and checked the living room, the dining room, and the kitchen. But there weren't any signs of anyone having been in the house.

She wandered into the den, sat down in front of her computer and tried another search for the Emerald Stone, but once again, nothing came up that matched the criteria.

* * * *

She spent the rest of the day wandering around the house, not knowing what to do. Brian returned home long after she had fallen asleep and she was just as happy not to have to make conversation.

"Have you had any calls for interviews yet?" Brian asked casually the next morning over a cup of coffee at the kitchen table.

"Nothing yet. I've sent my resume out to all the online job search companies and several agencies. I've also applied to close to a dozen job advertisements," Maya replied. "I thought I'd get an early start today to see what else I could find." She hated lying to him but she had no desire to fight with him just now.

"I wondered why you were up so early. Well, don't get discouraged. Something will come up soon."

"You got in pretty late last night. Did you have a good weekend?"

"Yeah, the boys and I just hung out at Shane's cottage most of the time. We had some drinks and played cards. Nothing spectacular but it was fun. We haven't got together as a group in a long time so it was nice to catch up and just hang out. What did *you* do?" He wasn't all that interested but asked anyway out of politeness. Things were getting too weird and it made him uncomfortable. He tried to block out the bizarre incident the day they had the fight by avoiding having any conversations around it. But it hung in the air increasing the distance growing between them.

"Not too much. I puttered in the garden. You know, the usual." *He's going to see the mark sooner or later. You can't avoid it forever. God, how am I going to explain it?*

"That's nice. Well I better get to work." He stood up and kissed her on the top of her head. "Have a nice day," he said absently putting his mug in the dishwasher and left.

"You too." She went upstairs to their bedroom and watched Brian drive away through the window. She'd given a lot of thought about what to do next since her search on the Internet came up empty. She decided that she owed it to herself to see if there indeed was anything called the Emerald Stone. For some reason her old friend, Emma Jackson, kept popping into her head all night so she'd decided to get in touch with her.

They had been friends for several years but they lost touch when Maya lost the baby.

It's too early to call her. Maybe I'll go for a run, by the time I get back it'll be eight o'clock. Then I can shower and have some breakfast. That should bring me to just after nine. That should work.

Emma had retired a couple of years ago, having sold her award winning, preservative-free jam and jelly business to a large corporation for a lucrative profit and had since spent many hours of her time on the golf course during the summer months and studying that so-called New Spirituality.

Maya hoped she wasn't golfing today. She needed to talk to someone.

*　　*　　*　　*

"Should I make us some tea?" Emma asked Maya a few hours later.

They met during a cooking class Emma taught a couple of years ago and developed an easy friendship, filled with laughter, understanding, and acceptance of each other.

Emma was forty-nine years old and on her second marriage, which seemed to be as rocky as Maya's had become.

"Sure, that would be nice." Maya relaxed into the chair, taking in the view of Emma's rural backyard, covering an acre of land, through the wall-to-wall windows.

Emma lived in an area neighboring onto Amish country, where there were miles and miles of rolling hills and trees.

Maya watched a hawk circling gracefully over the area, soaring high above the trees. She admired her friend's knack for making her home so peaceful and inviting.

Emma came back with a fresh pot of her favorite strawberry kiwi flavored tea and a plate of shortbread cookies. "I know you have a sweet tooth. Besides you look like you could use a few extra calories. How are you doing Maya?"

"Thanks. I'm doing better now. It was pretty rough going for a long time." Maya picked up a cookie from the plate and took a bite. She savored the taste of the buttery shortbread melting in her mouth. Sighing she said, "Emma, I'm so sorry I didn't return your phone calls or keep in touch with you. It was just so hard to deal with the loss of our baby and I guess I became a hermit."

"I'm sorry you had to go through that. I know how much you wanted to start a family of your own. I can't imagine how difficult it must be for you."

Maya fought back the tears and cleared her throat. "Anyway, I'm here for something quite different and," she cleared her throat, "unusual.

Piquing Emma's interest she said, "Oh? What is it?"

"Have you ever heard of the Emerald Stone?" Maya asked.

"As in jewelry?"

"No. At least I don't think so. It sounded like it was a specific stone."

"Oh, well than no, can't say that I have. You don't know what it is?"

"Not yet but apparently it has the answers to the questions I need to be asking and I thought you might be able to help me figure out what to do."

"How so? What do you mean questions you need to be asking?" asked Emma biting into a cookie.

"I feel kind of silly telling you this but I know you're into all that new age spirituality stuff and I thought this Emerald Stone might fall into that category."

"You're kidding me right? After all the times I tried to get you to read some of the classic inspirational novels?"

"I know, I know. I told you I feel silly," Maya said sheepishly.

"Well this is quite an interesting turn. So tell me about why you need to find out about this so-called Emerald Stone," responded Emma.

She explained about the meeting with Nicholas in Nassau to Emma. Then she described all the strange things occurring in her body saving the appearance of the mark on her back until the end.

"No way! I don't believe you. Are you playing some kind of practical joke on me?" asked Emma.

"Unfortunately, no." She gripped the teacup tightly, tracing her thumb along the rim. God how she wished this was all some crazy dream and she would wake up soon.

"Does Brian know all of this?"

"Yes. Well, not entirely. He knows almost everything up until this weekend and the appearance of the mark and my back."

"Why haven't you told him about it?"

Maya took a deep breath and looked out the window before continuing. "First of all he believes Nicholas is a kook and he was pretty freaked out when I set the garbage can on fire. We haven't talked much since then. Plus, I guess I was afraid if I talked about it, then it would have to mean something. If it means something then I have to figure it out and do something about it. That scares me. It's like something you see in the movies. It's all so mysterious. I don't know if I'm up for this."

"I'm sure there's nothing to worry about. I think it's exciting. Can I see it?" asked Emma.

"You're going to be pretty amazed." Maya rose up, turned around and lifted her T-shirt high enough for Emma to see.

Emma's face lit up in obvious surprise. "Oh my gosh, it is an actual symbol! You really don't know how it got there?"

"None. Well, not really. I mean I remember something happening but I thought it was all a dream." Maya tucked her shirt into her jeans and sat back down in the chair. She picked up another cookie and broke it in two, nibbling on it. "So what do you think? Can you help me?"

"Well it's beyond my experience but sure I'll help you try to figure this out."

"You don't think I'm crazy?"

"I have to admit that I've never actually seen anything quite so extraordinary but I've heard stories. So no, I don't think you're crazy."

"Got any ideas on what to do next? How do we find out about this Emerald Stone?"

"Well I was thinking of starting at the Heartsong New Age Bookstore to see if anyone there has heard of them."

Maya cringed.

"Listen girl, you don't have any right to think the people who go to new age stores are weird."

She chuckled. "Sorry, you're right."

"Come on Maya, it's exciting don't you think?"

"Well, part of me is excited."

"But..."

"But I'm thinking of Brian."

"Maya, you're going to have to stop worrying about Brian and let things fall where they may! You have to do this for yourself."

"That's not so easy but I know you're right. You're such a good friend. You're always there for me." Maya looked at Emma filled with guilt. "I'm sorry I didn't turn to you."

"Don't worry about it. You're here now. Besides, it goes both ways you know," said Emma trying to reassure her friend.

"How has everything been here?"

"The usual, nothing different. Now, if time is running out, whatever that means, we'd better hurry up and start investigating."

"Right. By the way, don't think I didn't notice you changed the subject." Maya could respect the fact that Emma didn't want to talk about things with Jeffrey. He could be a real jerk, especially when he was in a losing streak during one of his gambling phases, so she didn't push her to talk.

Emma smiled sheepishly. "I'm free anytime, when do you want to go?"

"What about tomorrow?" *Do I really want to do this? Quit worrying, it'll probably turn out to be nothing anyway.*

"Sounds good. Why don't we just meet there around two o'clock? Do you know where it is?"

"Yes I can find it. Two is okay with me. Well I guess I should get going." Maya got up to leave. "Here let me help you with the dishes."

They gathered up the dishes and Emma gave her a warm embrace as they stood by the front door of solid oak underneath a rounded archway saying goodbye. She squeezed Maya's shoulders. "This is exciting. I'm so glad you came to me about it."

Maya squirmed. "Well I'm glad you think so."

"Oh come on. Don't worry, everything's going to be just fine. Think of it as an adventure."

Maya rolled her eyes. She tried to feel reassured but inside she was shaking.

Chapter Twelve

SALT LAKE CITY, UTAH
August 2012

Douglas concealed himself behind the pyramid in Maya's dreams. He took on the form of the silver dragon, one of his preferred shapes to contact his disciples.

The time for the branding of her sign had arrived. He'd known of this date for almost a year now and had waited patiently for its time to come.

He'd watched over her since the day she was born and he deserved to be there to witness this grand moment in her life. She would not be able to deny her heritage any longer and he would be right by her side to guide her to fulfill her destiny.

Oh yes, she will come to love me and trust me as others have before her. She will soon see that I am the Ultimate One, the next leader of humankind and she will do everything I ask. In return I may let her live and she will have the honor of working along side Kanïka and I. We will be the supreme triad. Yes, I might let her live if she proves herself worthy of my love.

He cocked his head around the side of the pyramid and watched his opponent take a swift dive bringing itself in close to Maya. They were now eye to eye.

"It's not about what *I* want," it said teasingly, "don't you want to know *who you are* and why you are here?"

Wanting to be fully present in her awakening the silver serpent climbed up the side of the pyramid and perched himself on the apex. He raised his glorious wings, reveling in his power.

Oh yes, he was enjoying this dance immensely. We're not so different you and I, we both want her to succeed and open the portal to other worlds.

"Be gone! You are not welcome here!" roared the mighty red dragon as it protected Maya in its arms and blasted its fire.

The unexpected impact knocked the silver dragon off balance, sending it tumbling down to the ground.

He vaporized into the air on impact.

* * * *

He berated himself for being so careless. It reminded him of his amateur days when he took uncalculated risks all the time. This was too costly and he couldn't afford to jeopardize himself again.

Douglas considered himself to be in better shape than most men twenty years younger but at fifty-six he was becoming more susceptible to injuries.

He suppressed a groan from the shooting pain while climbing out of the car. But his grimace did not escape Vivienne's attention as he held the door open for her.

"Darling you should have stayed at the hotel. You're in too much pain and you shouldn't be driving around looking at houses. I could have done this by myself."

"Nonsense. I'm not going to let a couple of cracked ribs hold me back. I've sustained much worse injuries than this and kept going." He had pulled out of the dream before the fall but unfortunately not soon enough to avoid banging up against the side of the pyramid.

She knew his pride was injured far more than his body and she also knew that he did not accept defeat very well. There would be repercussions over this incident and it worried her. She had to find a way to keep him occupied and distracted long enough for him to recognize any attempts to retaliate could put all their efforts at risk.

The real estate agent joined them and was disappointed to discover that his clients had been too preoccupied to notice the house or the magnificent backdrop yet. "Well? What do you think?" He spread out his arms waiting.

Douglas was annoyed with the interruption at first but then they couldn't help but stare in awe at the beauty before them. The custom built house was constructed of light and dark shades of gray brick with lots of windows and a dark gray marley tile roof. The house itself was perfect but the mountains behind made it a prize home.

Vivienne was delighted. "Ken, this is spectacular! It's everything you said."

Douglas remained silent. He raised his hands in front of himself and spun his gold signet ring around his fingers. He nodded in agreement. He knew without even going inside that he wanted it.

An estate home, in a secluded area of Salt Lake City with mountains in the backyard. It offered all the prestige and privacy he desired plus it would be a nice addition to his growing collection of property. "We'll take it. How much did you say the builder was asking?"

"Douglas!" Vivienne exclaimed. She was the voice of reason to his impulsive and sometimes reckless ways. "We haven't even been inside yet."

"I don't need to see it. I want to buy it."

"We'll talk about this later." She gave him a scornful look. "Let's look around first."

Once inside she had to admit she wanted to buy it as much as Douglas but she didn't want to appear too eager in front of Ken, their agent.

There were vaulted ceilings and skylights, stainless steel appliances, seven bedrooms and five bathrooms. Most of the rooms had a view of the mountains surrounding the landscape.

As they toured the house Douglas ruminated on his plans. The Charlie's Corner chains were turning out to be everything he hoped and along with the several other business schemes they had set up over the past few years, money was coming in fast and steady. *Yes, everything was falling into place.*

In his mind the ends justified the means. *We will be victorious and people will see our way is the enlightened way. They will flock to me to lead them into the New World.*

"Do you have the paperwork with you?" asked Douglas feeling confident in his decision. "I'd like to put in an offer today."

"I'll have to take you back to the office to get the proper documents, but sure we could do it today."

"Not so fast Douglas. We need to discuss this with our business advisor to determine the best way to purchase it." She looked at Ken and shrugged her shoulders. "Legalities, you understand?"

"Of course. Take whatever time you need. This is a prime piece of property but houses in this price range don't disappear overnight," said Ken.

Douglas interrupted them, “No. I don’t want to wait. I want to put the offer in my name and be done with it.” This was one purchase he didn’t want to hide. He wanted to see his name on paper for a change.

She raised her eyebrows. “That’s not a good idea,” *What are you doing?* “An extra day or two won’t make any difference.”

“I made my decision.” Douglas said stubbornly. He turned to look at Ken. “Let’s do it.”

Vivienne shook her head. *He’s making a mistake. I can feel it.* But she decided to let him have his way, after all it might just work to her advantage.

Chapter Thirteen

The day after her meeting with Emma Maya walked nervously through the door of Heartsong New Age Bookstore. She glanced around the store to see if Emma had arrived yet but it appeared that Maya got there first.

She nodded and smiled politely at the woman behind the counter, noticing her eyes held a sparkling and joyful quality, which complimented her warm smile.

Maya continued on to wander through the aisles. She took in the shelves that were neatly arranged with books on topics such as self-help, channeling, meditation, healing therapies, Buddhism, and Taoism. Crystals, candles, fountains and Angel carvings could also be found throughout the store.

Mmmm... That incense smells wonderful. There was soothing flute music playing in the CD player which helped to relax her jittery nerves.

She meandered back to the counter near the front of the store and studied the crystals while she waited. Some were cut in shapes of pyramids and animals, while others were, in what she assumed was their rough natural state. She really liked the dark amethyst and rose quartz clusters; she found them quite beautiful.

There were larger crystals and meteorites, which were kept in a locked glass case. She thought it was really odd to see meteorites. But it was the smaller clear crystals in one corner that really caught her attention. *I wonder why these ones are locked away? They're not very big.*

"Would you like me to get something out of the case for you?" asked the sales woman.

"Oh hi," Maya said a little embarrassed. "I was just wondering what kind of crystals these ones are?" she pointed them out to the woman.

"They are called Herkimer Diamonds."

"Diamonds? Really?"

The woman laughed. "They're not like the diamonds you are thinking about, although they are one of the most expensive crystals. Herkimer's are known to stimulate clairvoyance and help remember past lives. Many people often sleep with them under their pillow because they encourage vivid dreams."

"Sounds interesting."

"Would you like to hold one?"

"Oh no, that's all right."

"Come on, show me which one you are drawn to. Crystals have that effect on people. It's like they know who should buy them, who needs their energy, and they call out to be held. You'll understand once you try it. Trust me."

"Okay, how about that one, I can't seem to take my eyes off it."

"Oh, you have good taste. We just got that one in a couple of days ago. It's one of the largest ones we've ever had in the store." The woman opened the case, removed the golf ball size crystal and handed it to Maya.

"Really? It's not very big in comparison to the other ones in the store." She turned it around between her fingers, studying its shape. "Wow, it's almost two hundred dollars!"

"I told you they were expensive. They are becoming very hard to find especially ones that size. Try holding it in the palm of your hand and close your other hand over it. Yes, like that." The woman watched as Maya's expression began to change and her eyes grew wide.

"Oh my gosh. It's like I can feel a pulse. It feels alive."

"I had a feeling it would speak to you. Why don't you hold on to it while you're here and see how it makes you feel. I suspect this one wants to go home with you."

"Thanks, but I can't imagine what my husband would say if I bought it."

"Don't make up your mind yet, give it some time."

"What are you trying to decide?" asked Emma as she strolled into the store and over to the crystal case.

"Emma! I didn't see you come in. Come here, look at this Herkimer crystal! Isn't it beautiful?" Maya said with delight in her newfound discovery.

"Wow, I've never seen one this large before." Emma turned to Helena and smiled warmly, "Hi Helena. How are you?"

"Hi Emma! So nice to see you," exclaimed the sales woman. She came around from behind the counter and gave Emma a big hug. "You look amazing."

Emma turned to Maya, "I see you've met Helena."

The two women hugged. "Sort of. She was explaining a bit about this crystal and let me hold it."

"Helena and I have known each other for years. She's an amazing woman whose reputation reading tea leaves with remarkable accuracy is attracting some very prominent people in the city," she said with pride.

"Tea leaves?" asked Maya.

"Yes, that's just one of the things I do. Oh excuse me, I have to help the woman at the cash."

"Of course, it was nice to meet you Helena," said Maya.

"Likewise. I'm sure I'll be seeing you around."

Emma smiled, "She's a wonderful person. Everything is an adventure to her and people seek her out because she makes them feel special. Did you ask Helena yet if she has heard of the Emerald Stone?"

"Oh my gosh no. I was waiting until you got here."

"Well let's go and ask, she's free now."

They walked towards the cash counter. "Helena, have you ever heard of the Emerald Stone?" asked Emma.

"I'm not sure. It sounds vaguely familiar. Let me check the store's database to see if it comes up with anything."

Maya and Emma went back to looking at the selection of crystals while Helena checked the computer.

"No. There's nothing here. Let me think about it for a while."

"Thanks for checking. Maya and I will wander around the books to see if we can find anything."

Helena shouted behind them, "Something tells me it might be Egyptian. Check that section."

"Thanks!" responded Maya and Emma together. They looked at each other and laughed.

There were many books on Gods, Goddesses and pyramids. Maya was getting frustrated after half an hour with no luck. "Maybe it's all just a hoax. There's nothing here. We should just go." She felt relieved and disappointed at the same time.

"Hold on. Don't give up so easily," said Emma. "Let's take some of these and go sit by the fireplace." The store had an electric fireplace with four chairs in front of it, offering a nice cozy spot to relax and read or chat with some friends.

"That sounds good," said Maya as she picked up a few books and joined Emma.

Maya was looking through a book on the Great Pyramids. She sat up, in anxious anticipation. "Emma here's something about an Atlantean Priest-King named Thoth who built the Great Pyramid of Giza. It says he brought the knowledge of ancient Atlantean wisdom to Egypt. Apparently he carved this knowledge on a stone tablet." Her heart started to speed up. "Listen to this:

> "Thoth the Atlantean was the wisest of all the Egyptian Gods. It was said he understood the great mysteries of the heavens and reincarnation. He was considered immortal, conquering death and passing through this dimension at will. His wisdom made him ruler of many Atlantean colonies. He engraved these cosmic mysteries using sacred symbols onto a stone tablet, which he hid here on Earth. According to legends these mysteries held information on how to achieve immortality.
>
> "The myths also indicates that this tablet is meant to be searched for, but only the highest of initiates, selected by Thoth himself will be able to utilize their energy."

"What else does it say?" asked Emma.

"Just a sec." Maya continued to read. "Okay…It says Thoth was the God of Wisdom and known as the Recorder. It talks about the Great Pyramid being a temple of initiation into the mysteries and that Jesus was one of the people initiated there. Did you know that?" The Herkimer that Maya was still holding began to vibrate stronger, in sync with her own heartbeat, and she could swear that the symbol seared into her back was beginning to pulsate too.

"I knew that Giza was connected to sacred mysteries, but I didn't know about Jesus. That's fascinating."

"Wait! Wait! Oh my God, listen to this," exclaimed Maya. "Apparently in Thoth's last life he was known as Hermes-Trismegistus and he carved the teachings onto an emerald tablet!" She read faster. "It was made through some process called alchemical transmutation. Whatever that means. This stone is supposed to be indestructible and the writings are engraved in the Atlantean language. It says that anyone who looks at the stone will be altered by the wisdom it contains."

Maya, feeling breathless stopped reading. She and Emma sat there, staring into each other's eyes speechless. Breaking the silence she asked uncertainly, "Do you think this is the Emerald Stone that Nicholas was referring to?"

"It would be a pretty big coincidence if it wasn't," commented Emma.

"But how is this connected with me?" Maya's heart was now pounding. Something told her this did indeed have everything to do with her. *I'm being silly...It's just my imagination getting away from me.*

"I think that book mentioned the stone was carved with Atlantean symbols. Maybe they hold a clue to the sign on your back. Wait a second! Didn't you say the name of the resort you stayed at in Nassau was Atlantis?"

"Oh my gosh, I didn't even realize that!" Maya's mind was spinning. "Do you think there really could be a connection to all this?"

"The signs certainly seem to point in that direction. Keep reading," said Emma.

"I...I can't read anymore. This is...it's too much to absorb." Maya shoved the book over to Emma, "Here you continue."

"Okay, let's see, where did you leave off?" Emma skimmed through and decided where to pick up the story.

> "The myths reveal that in every century there exists four individuals who bear the key Egyptian symbols for Earth, Air, Fire and Water on their backs."

"Did you hear that?" Emma exclaimed. "Symbols on their backs!"

> "These four Chosen Ones have been marked by the great wisdom of Thoth, containing within them the potential to unlock and integrate the ancient mysteries of transcendence and transmutation.
>
> "For thousands of years the ascended beings have predicted a phenomenon to occur at a specific moment in time, which is known as the Shift of the Ages.
>
> "If the Chosen Ones are successful in releasing this ancient wisdom, it will raise Earth's vibration and all humans will have the potential of achieving higher levels of consciousness."

Emma turned the page. "Oh my God! Maya, look at these symbols! The one for Fire...It's...It's the one on your back!" Emma quickly pulled her chair closer to Maya so they could look at them together.

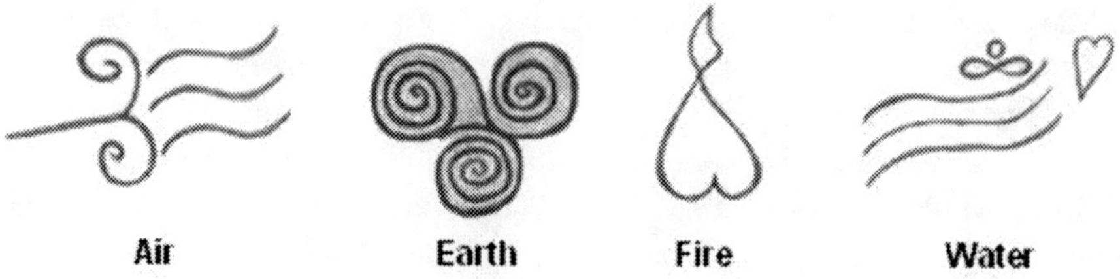

"Maya, this is unbelievable! You…You must be one of the Chosen Ones!"

"That's impossible! This can't be real…It's fantasy Emma! These authors keep talking about legends and mythology—that's all it is—fantasy."

"Really!" Emma sounded annoyed. "Then how do you explain the symbol on your back that just happens to look identical to this one? It's not just a few freckles that look like something if you use your imagination. It's real Maya. You were branded with it to signify who you are."

Maya felt like her world was spiraling out of control. She couldn't think or see straight. The damn symbol felt like it was literally on fire, burning her back. "Okay, okay…This legend mentions four people. That means there are three others out there somewhere who have the other markings. What else does it say?"

Emma flipped the pages back and forth. "I can't believe this! That's it, there isn't any more."

"Are you serious?"

"Unfortunately, yes."

"It didn't mention anything about timelines or dates," Maya mumbled, partially to herself.

"What do you mean?"

"Huh? Oh, well Nicholas also told me to find out about the end of the Mayan calendar. Somehow it is connected to the Emerald Stone."

Helena joined the ladies. "How are you guys making out? Did you find anything helpful?"

"I guess that's a matter of opinion but yes we found something," responded Maya.

Emma looked around and was surprised to discover how late it was. The store had emptied out except for them. "Helena, what do you know about the Mayan Calendar?"

"There's lots of information written on that theory. Basically the prophecies say that the numbers 11:11 are directly connected to the end of the Mayan Calendar and that at 11:11 in the morning on December twenty-first, 2012 there will be a rare astronomical and celestial alignment called the 'Dark-Rift.'"

Emma interrupted, "Yes, I started noticing the numbers a few years ago and discovered the books written by different authors on this phenomena. They wrote about triggering and unlocking the DNA memories too. I found it really interesting but I wasn't sure how much of it I believed. It's pretty far-fetched."

"So is The Arconion Prophecy, but millions of people have benefited from the insights. It was a best-seller for a long time," said Helena.

Maya had a look of realization on her face. "You know, come to think of it, I've just happened to look at the clock a few times in the last while when it read 11:11. What does all this mean?" she asked feeling more confused.

"The earth's axis has been shifting for many years and the final switch will cause an opening, a portal if you will. The Mayan's were considered geniuses, and believed this re-alignment to be so important that it will cause a transition in human consciousness. They call it the New World Age. There's a catch though."

"Which is?" questioned Emma.

"Well the forces of Light must overcome the forces of Darkness in one last battle for it to be successful."

"And if the Light doesn't win?" asked Maya tentatively.

"There are two theories. The most common prediction by the doomsday sayers is that it will be the end of the world. The second is that it could mean it's the last opportunity for humanity to make the transition into a New World. People who are more inclined to believe in new spirituality have been working diligently over the last twenty or thirty years to make the second theory the new reality."

Maya was feeling overwhelmed. "But December twenty-first is less than four months away! That's what Nicholas must have been talking about. God, my head is hurting." She pinched the bridge of her nose hoping the pain would stop.

"Would you like an aspirin or something?" asked Helena.

"No thanks. I'll be fine." Maya looked at Emma. "We'd better go so Helena can close up. It's getting late. Oh wait! I just realized I'm still holding the Herkimer. Helena, I think I'm going to buy it. It almost feels like it's embedded into my hand." She stared at the crystal in a daze.

Emma noticed that Maya's face had lost all its color. "Helena, we'll be right up after we grab our things."

"Sure, no problem," replied Helena.

Maya felt paralyzed. She stared in turmoil at her friend. "How am I supposed to get my head around this? It's not making any sense and I still don't understand how or what I'm supposed to do."

"Not to put any pressure on you, but it sounds like you are supposed to save the world from Darkness."

Chapter Fourteen

"I can't believe I didn't even buy the book," Maya said to Emma over the phone.

"You were in shock, it probably didn't even cross your mind. We can go back and get it if you want."

"That's a good idea. It's better than moping around here again all day."

"Have you made any decisions over the past two days about what you're going to do yet?"

"Not really. Well I don't know, maybe. I haven't been able to concentrate on anything since Monday. I feel like I've been walking around in another world."

"What do you mean maybe?" Emma asked.

"Everything seems so surreal and part of me just wants to forget it all and carry on with life like nothing happened. Yet…I can feel this energy or whatever it is moving around in my body and I look at the symbol…It forces me to question how I could possibly turn my back and walk away."

"What about the dreams? Anything new?"

"I felt a bit silly but I put the crystal I bought under my pillow because Helena mentioned that people do that with the Herkimer Diamonds to enhance dreams. I didn't have the dream about the dragon but last night something different came up. Remember I told you about finding the crystal in the middle of a forest?"

"Yes, I remember."

"I could never figure out where this forest was but this time as I was driving I saw a road sign."

"What did it say?" asked Emma curiously.

"Herkimer, New York. Ten Miles."

"Holy cow! And you're still wondering what to do?"

"I know. I know."

"Have you talked to Brian about any of this yet?"

"No. I've managed to avoid having any serious conversations with him. It hasn't been too difficult, he's really keeping his distance from me. I'm getting worried about us. Things have never been like this between us before."

"I know you guys have always had a really good relationship and if it's meant to be you guys will work things out. That might not be very reassuring right now but try to have faith."

"I guess you're right. Anyway, I might as well go to the store today to get that book. I'll call you tomorrow."

"Okay. I'll talk to you tomorrow. Maya?"

"Yeah?"

"Keep the faith. Everything will work out."

"That's easier said than done but I'll try. Bye." *Have faith? Those are pretty glib words people throw around so casually.*

*　*　*　*

"Hello Maya! It's nice to see you again so soon," said Helena.

"Hi Helena. I came back to get one of the books Emma and I were reading yesterday."

"Oh that's wonderful. I love it when new people come back. It gives me such joy to see them open up to new experiences for the first time."

"To be honest, it's a little scary."

"There's nothing to be scared about honey. We're all here to help each other awaken on our journey." Helena came around from behind the counter. "Come here and let me give you a hug, you look like you could use one."

Maya felt awkward and shy but welcomed the comforting embrace.

"You might as well get used to it. We're all huggers here," Helena chuckled. "You came on a good day hon. We're having an open house. A few of our healers and channelers are available for mini appointments. Fifteen minutes for fifteen dollars."

"Channelers? What do *they* do?" Maya asked.

"They bring in messages from the spirit world, like ascended masters, angels or other guides." Helena observed the skeptical expression on Maya's face and added, "We all have guides that help us, most people just can't see them. People who channel can see them and are able to deliver messages that often provide very valuable direction when we're confused about something that's going on in our lives."

"Uh huh, I see." Maya felt uneasy in this unknown world.

"The open house is a great way for newcomers to try out something new without making a major commitment. Why don't you think about it. Check out the board and see if there is anyone's name that captures your attention."

"Well I suppose it couldn't hurt to look. Thanks Helena."

"My pleasure. I'm here if you need me."

Maya strolled slowly to the board beside the office and read the names and descriptions of the services they offered. Roger Thurston—Reiki Master and Healer. *That one sounds intimidating, I don't even know what Reiki means.* She continued to look at the names. Kathy Jamieson—Massage Therapist, Celeste Withers—Angelic and Spirit Guide.

She stopped and studied Celeste's name. It has a nice feeling about it. *What the heck, maybe I'll give it a try.*

She put her name down on the list. There was one other person ahead of her so she went back to buy the book and look at the crystals while she waited for her turn. Instinctively she put her hand in her pocket to make sure the crystal she bought was still there. For some strange reason she was getting in the habit of carrying it with her all the time.

"Are you Maya?" asked an unknown woman.

"Yes I am," she jumped, feeling jittery and apprehensive.

"Hello, nice to meet you. I'm Celeste. Come on back in the room."

Maya followed the robust woman into a darkly lit room, complete with candles on a small round bamboo table accompanied by two bamboo chairs.

"I've never seen you here before. How did you find us?" asked Celeste.

"My friend Emma Jackson comes here often."

"Oh Emma! She's such a fabulous woman. I saw her just last week. Yes, she's definitely a regular here." Celeste noticed that Maya seemed jittery. "Are you nervous?" she asked.

Maya cleared her throat. "Yes, a bit I guess. I've never had a reading before. All this," she gestured with her hands, "it's all new to me."

"Well don't you worry about a thing. Now, let me get centered for a minute and we'll see what comes up for you today."

Celeste, like Helena, also appeared to have a warm and compassionate nature, which helped Maya feel a little calmer. She watched as Celeste took a few deep breaths with her eyes closed.

"What would you like to know, my dear?" asked Celeste.

"As I said, this is all pretty new to me but I am experiencing some things I don't understand and I was wondering what was ahead for me?"

Celeste paused to see what would be revealed to her. She took a deep breath and released it. "Well it's shadowed, indicating that we're not to know everything just yet, because we're not always to know. I *am* being told that all is not well in your relationship though. Does that makes sense to you?"

"I'm not sure..." Maya hesitated, taken off guard by the way things were starting. "Um, ever since I lost my baby I've been going through a lot of changes. Lately I've been trying not to view life in black and white terms anymore because nothing is making any sense, but Brian, that's my husband, he's not willing to see things differently and it's causing a lot of friction between us."

"He has to make his own choices, dear one. You can't do it for him."

"You're right Celeste, I know. But we've always had a good marriage and I just can't give up. Besides, it hasn't been easy for him. I've been a real bitch sometimes," she said and paused to wipe a tear from the corner of her eye. "I've been so angry and bitter. But I've been experiencing some really strange things that are forcing me to see things differently. Brian, he's been so patient and loving, until recently, and well, I think he's giving up on us."

"Some people are not capable of growing Maya, but if the love you share is real then it will sustain these tests."

Maya could not face the possibility that her marriage was in danger. She needed him. He's always been her rock.

"Everything happens for a reason and each challenge we face provides an opportunity for growth," said Celeste.

"So I hear," said Maya melancholically.

"Yes, and the more difficult the challenge, the deeper the reward. So what are you afraid of Maya?"

Ouch, did she have to go right to the punch? "I don't know."

"Yes you do. You're afraid to be alone," replied Celeste gently.

Tears filled Maya's eyes and slid quietly down her cheeks. She choked back a sob and reached for a Kleenex from the box Celeste offered.

"Are you all right?"

"Yes, thank you. I'll be fine." She dabbed her eyes and sniffled. "I'm okay, let's continue," said Maya.

Celeste watched for a few seconds with a compassionate heart as her client suffered silently. "They're showing me a gold diamond ring. Oh, now it's vanished, and it's become a gold rose. They're showing it blossoming and blossoming."

Maya watched Celeste in fascination. Her eyes were closed during the reading and Maya wondered who "they" were that she kept talking about?

Celeste's voice rose in anticipation of what Spirit was about to show her. "They're taking it up into the universe and flashing a series of symbols over the planet. This is Metatron!"

"Pardon?" *This is who? What is she talking about?*

"This is Metatron! He's an angel! He represents divine knowledge and wisdom. Oh my goodness, this is the first time he has presented himself to me! He's one of your guides and he's getting stronger with you each day. He's showing me some symbols and he's telling me that one of your lessons in this life is to learn discernment."

"Can you describe what the symbols look like?" asked Maya, ignoring the mention of learning discernment.

"Well let's see. One of them looks like a flame, one has wavy lines with a heart, another one has these three swirls that are connected." She tried to draw it into the air with her eyes closed. "The last one, sorry, it's gone now and I can't quite remember."

Fascinating. Sounds like the symbols in the book. "What else?"

"Your guides are materializing this energy for you as quickly as they can but it's very important for you to learn to meditate. It is especially important when you have a new guide working with you. You want to keep the combination of body, mind and spirit together. It helps them to adjust to your frequency, and you to theirs."

"I see," said Maya. *Do I?*

"This is really a major energy. Well done Maya! Metatron is one of the top fellows with the Galactic Council. He helps to ground the energies of the multi-dimensional reality into an inter-dimensional system."

"Uh huh. What does that mean?" *Do I really want to know?*

"You have a very powerful gift developing and that's the energy you are tapping into—you're bringing that line in, which makes complete sense that you'd be working with Metatron," Celeste said more to herself than to Maya.

"Can you tell me about this gift?"

"You have the Force with you and it will provide you with many abilities if you use it wisely," she paused. "Sorry that's all he is willing to share right now."

"Will he be staying as a guide for me?" asked Maya.

"Yes. You also have Archangel Michael's energy with you. He's much more fixed, meaning he's been by your side for a long time. Michael is an angel of protection—he keeps you safe from harms way. Of course, he also works with the Christ consciousness and Metatron works with the other dimensions, which is also obviously with the Christ consciousness. So I mean you've got a wonderful..."

"What do you mean by other dimensions?" Maya jumped in before Celeste could finish.

"Well the fourth, fifth, and sixth dimensions. He's bringing that inter-dimensional energy in for you." There was a tapping on the door.

"It's time for your next appointment," said Helena on the other side of the door.

"Thank you! Well that's all the time we have today. "Oh, I have one last message from Metatron. He's showing me this is all part of your spiritual awakening. You're A-okay. That's what he's saying, you're A-okay. Don't worry." Celeste said with laughter, holding her thumb upwards.

Apparently Metatron has a sense of humor but Maya didn't find it so amusing.

* * * *

Multidimensional reality. Galactic Council. What the hell does it all mean? I don't know who I am anymore. These thoughts plagued Maya on the way home and all through the evening.

"How's the job hunt going?" asked Brian while they were going upstairs to bed for the night.

The sound of his voice brought her out of her haze. "I haven't had any bites yet. I've been making some calls to put some feelers out there. I've had a couple of leads but that's about it so far." She had to work hard not to let her irritation with him come through in her voice. All he seemed to care about was her getting a job. What she didn't understand was that it was the only topic Brian felt safe to discuss now.

She went into the ensuite closet to undress and change into a nightshirt.

"What the hell is that?" demanded Brian.

"What?"

"Is that a tattoo? When the hell did you get a tattoo? And why didn't you tell me?"

Damn! She'd avoided it for as long as she could but in her daze she didn't even think about it while she changed.

"It's not a tattoo," she said in defense.

"It's not? Then what the hell is it? Maya, what's going on with you these days. I don't know you anymore! You go out and get this…This thing and you don't even talk to me about it. So what is it?"

Overwhelmed by Brian's animosity and the weight of everything else she was facing, Maya burst into wrenching sobs. Confusion tore into her heart and it was too much to bear in that moment.

"Maya! I'm sorry! Maya talk to me, what's going on?" He grabbed her robe from a hanger and wrapped it around her shoulders. "Come on, let's sit down." He guided her to the bed and sat her down with his arms around her.

She sniffed and put her arms through the sleeves, wrapping her robe around her tightly she heaved a few breaths. When she was able to finally speak she said, "You won't understand."

"Try me." He waited.

Slowly she told him what happened on the weekend while he was away. When he didn't say anything she felt her anxiety building again. "Brian?"

"Go on, something tells me you're not finished."

"Yes."

"And?"

"What's the point, this isn't getting us anywhere. Look at you. You've pulled away and you're shutting me out."

"Am I upset that all this stuff is going on around me and you're leaving me in the dark? Yes, of course I am. But go on, tell me the rest…*please*."

Maya gave him the details on her discoveries about the Emerald Stone. When she finished she waited for his reaction.

"So let me get this straight. You're telling me that this mark showed up mysteriously on your back while you were sick. You think you have a special mission to save the world from destruction and you believe what Nicholas said that it was fate that you lost the baby. That's what you're telling me?"

"Yes. I know it sounds crazy but…"

He laughed. "Crazy? That's an understatement. Maya, what do you take me for, an idiot? Why are you making all this up?"

"I'm not making it up!" Now she was getting angry. *Stay calm. I don't know how to control it yet, remember what Nicholas said.* "Look at this!" She stood up and pulled the robe away. "Look at it, I said. It's deep under the skin and I didn't put this there. This is real Brian."

He reached out and touched the symbol on her back. His shoulders slumped and he sighed. "Maya, I'm sorry. I don't know what to think."

"You don't know what to think? How do you think I feel? I'm scared. Nothing is as it appears anymore and I don't know what the future holds." She sat down heavily on the bed beside him.

"Come here." He pulled her close to him and held her tight in his arms.

They continued to hold each other, without any more words passing between them, until they fell asleep and Maya slipped out of his arms and into a deep slumber.

"Come to Egypt. You know your destiny awaits you. You can't escape it."

Maya stirred awake and lay there for what seemed like hours while she contemplated what she should do. Should she take a chance and risk pushing Brian further away or should she forget everything and go on about her life to keep the peace? Finally she gently slipped out of bed and quietly left the room.

Carefully avoiding the noisy stairs she maneuvered her way down to the den and turned on the computer.

She hoped that Brian would support her decision. *He came around tonight, he'll be okay.*

She kept her email simple and straightforward. *Emma, please meet me at the Heartsong Bookstore tomorrow*...she erased the word tomorrow and typed in *at 10 A.M. I need to figure out what to do. Thanks! Maya.*

Chapter Fifteen

"What are you going to do today?" asked Brian.

"I'm going to meet Emma at the Heartsong Bookstore to see if I can find out any more information." She refilled their mugs with more coffee.

"It's only seven o'clock, when have you had time to talk to Emma?"

"I haven't. I woke up after having another dream so I came down and sent her an email." She stopped him before he had a chance to say anything, "Why don't you come with me? Maybe it'll put you more at ease if you find out about some of this stuff for yourself? I'd feel better if you came with me…"

"You know I can't take any time off work right now. Things are too busy," said Brian. "Besides, I don't understand why you have to do this." He was discouraged to discover that she had contacted Emma after their talk. He desperately hoped that it would all go away and things would go back to the way they used to be.

"I can't just walk away, at least not yet. I need to understand what it all means in more depth and what I would be expected to do."

Brian watched her eat her toast smothered with jam. "Why can't you wait until the weekend, then I could go with you?"

"Because time is running out and if this is all true I need to act quickly."

He was relieved she wouldn't wait. He had no desire to get more involved in all this nonsense.

She finished eating and took a quick sip from her mug. "I thought you were okay with all this?" she asked looking at him thoughtfully.

"Would it matter if I wasn't?" he asked sullenly.

"Brian…"

"Well, would it?"

She sighed. "I don't know. I have to find out more. I hoped you would understand."

"I just don't want you to get caught up in all this and not be able to see what's real and what isn't."

"I can understand why you're worried but this is something I have to do."

He grunted. "I better get to work." As he approached the doorway he hesitated, turning to watch her, he questioned whether he would be able to cope if she decided to pursue this even further. The knot in his stomach gripped him and left him feeling like he was losing her.

* * * *

Maya and Emma chatted together by the fireplace at the Bookstore for an hour getting caught up on the events of the past two days, when a woman walked into the store, headed straight towards them and sat down beside Maya.

She was rakishly thin accentuated by the hippie style clothing. She had long, rather unkempt, brown hair and wore beaded dangly earrings in shades of blue. Her ankle length dress of navy blue with various geometric white designs was broken with a green sash around the waist.

Maya and Emma exchanged glances with a questioning look trying to determine if either one of them recognized this odd woman. They both shrugged their shoulders and shook their heads in denial.

They continued to chat with each other but felt uncomfortable with the stranger, who was obviously listening to their conversation. They refrained from discussing the Emerald Stone for the moment.

The woman pulled out a deck of tarot cards from her purse. "My grandmother has been teaching me how to read tarot cards," she said to Maya and Emma. "She gave this set to me. They're antique. You can't buy ones like these anywhere. She inherited them from her mother." Looking at Maya she asked, "Would you like a reading?"

"Sure, why not? What's your name?" asked Maya.

"Angelina," said the woman.

"Nice to meet you. I'm Maya, and this is my friend Emma."

"I've never seen you here before. Are you new to the neighborhood?" asked Emma.

"Oh, I've been around," responded Angelina vaguely and then began to spread the cards on the table in front of them.

Maya imagined generations of women handling the cards, causing the edges to wear away and the once rich colors to fade.

Angelina spread the cards across the table. "Please select three cards," she said to Maya.

Maya glanced towards Emma, raising her eyebrows and giving her a quirky nervous smile. She leaned over the table in front of them, pulled out three cards randomly and passed them to Angelina.

"Good. Very good." She turned the cards over and placed them on the table. "These cards are all connected. This first one indicates you are in great turmoil and are facing a major life altering decision. This one," pointing to the middle card, "shows you also thinking of taking a trip to a far away land. Correct?"

Maya glanced quickly in Emma's direction with surprise. Maya and Emma sat up straighter. *Okay she's got our attention.* "No. Well I don't know, maybe. I haven't really given any thought to going anywhere. What else do they tell you?"

"There is no need to hesitate about taking this excursion. You will find many answers to the questions you seek. You will discover your strengths. You will also learn of a relationship to another life where you were very powerful. This last card indicates that the flame burns strong within you. It represents your soul and the passion of your journey. You will meet others on the same journey—three people, and they are looking for similar answers. The four of you are ready to meet. The time is now. The world is waiting," Angelina said with conviction.

"Can you tell me more about this journey?" asked Maya, contemplating the odd synchronicity of meeting this woman, now.

"Let me feel the vibrations and connect to their message." Angelina slowly passed her hand across the top of the cards. "The Stone engraved with the ancient Atlantean wisdom you seek is in a hidden chamber under the Great Pyramid of Giza. That is where you must go. You will find the chamber and a pyramid priest, who stands guard in wait for this time. He will recognize you and the others and let you in."

Maya took a sip of water from the bottle she brought with her and noticed her heart rate rising. She felt it flutter causing a shortness of breath.

Angelina continued, "This stone is cut from emerald and above this great Stone hangs the largest Herkimer crystal known to man."

It was Emma's turn to gasp in surprise. "You love that Herkimer! Maya this is fantastic!"

"Uh-huh." Maya couldn't speak. Her heart fluttered again. "Emma, I don't know if I want to find out more. This is so bizarre."

Angelina leaned towards them and said in a grave voice, "There is more you must hear. There is a reason you carry that crystal with you now. It is helping you to raise your energy to the right frequencies so you can do what needs to be done."

Maya looked to Emma and back to Angelina, unable to speak she nodded her head. Taking another uneasy breath, she pulled out the Herkimer Diamond she bought last week from the front pocket of her jeans and shifted about restlessly in the chair. Holding it in the palm of both hands she felt it begin to pulse in rhythm to the beat of her heart.

"Are you ready to hear more?" Angelina asked.

"No, but let's hear the rest of this crazy story anyway, since I can't seem to escape from it."

"Once the four Chosen Ones are inside this chamber you must take your places in your respective spots that are marked with your signs; Fire, Earth, Air, and Water. If the four of you have attained the required level of spiritual awareness, the Herkimer Diamond will activate the engraved Atlantean characters on the Emerald Stone. When this happens the esoteric energy of the symbols will be released to the initiates, transforming your consciousness and connecting your human souls to the Divine."

"Oh my God!" Emma exclaimed.

"You got that right. How am I supposed to do this? I'm not ready!" Her palms were sweating. She tucked her hair behind her ears in nervous habit.

"I don't know but it looks like you're going to Egypt whether or not you think you're ready," said Emma.

"You're getting all this from these three cards?" asked Maya unbelievingly.

"I have learned not to question the ways of the messengers," Angelina said sharply. "Now are you finished ladies? May I continue?"

Emma looked startled by Angelina's abruptness. "Yes, of course."

"Thank you. This transference of wisdom is also known as the Zero Point Merge. It represents the coming together of the physical and spiritual aspects of the being or also known as, As Above, so Below."

Emma tried to lighten the tenseness of the situation with what she thought was a joke. "Not that we're going to put any pressure on you to succeed." She reached out to tap Maya's knee. "Sorry, I guess I'm getting giddy, or delirious."

"Very funny." Maya gulped for air. *God it's hot in here.* She reached for her bottle of water and took a long swig. "I assume there's more?"

"Yes," said Angelina. "Human DNA or genetic memory has been encoded to be triggered by specific digits to awaken the mind to this change. The most well known code for awakening the unconscious mind is the number 11:11, which represents the twin strands of DNA. When people see this number it means that their DNA is being activated to remember this time of mass awakening and it is their responsibility to take action."

"This is fascinating. You've talked about the 11:11 theory before," Maya said to Emma. "So how exactly does this fit in with the Emerald Stone?"

"In precise terms, the Chosen Ones must come together to activate the stone at exactly 11:11 on December twenty-first for the transition to be successful."

Reminded that this date was looming only a few months away added enormously to her anxiety. "And if we aren't successful? What will happen?"

"Then Earth will continue to experience natural disasters and wars with epic proportions will destroy nations everywhere. There is no guarantee the planet will survive." Angelina leaned closer once again towards Maya and spoke solemnly, "It is vital that Earth achieve mass enlightenment during this timeline. You must be strong. You must have faith in yourself and in the supreme consciousness." With that final message, she began to pack her tarot cards into a faded honey colored leather case and put them back into her bag. "I must go now."

"Wait!" Maya panicked. "How will I recognize them? The others?"

"The Chosen Ones are being organized to carry out the divine plan for Earth. Just be aware. Keep your eyes and heart open and you will know who they are."

"Well that's reassuring," Maya mumbled to herself. "Can I offer you something? Some money?"

Angelina glared at Maya, insulted by the offer. "No. There's no need. I came here to give you this message. My job is done."

"How can I reach you? What if I have other questions?"

Angelina looked back as she walked away. "There will be others to help you," she replied and then she was gone.

Reeling once again from another message she said to Emma, "I don't know about all this. It's sounding crazier every day."

"Maya, there's truth to the prophecies if you stop and think about it."

"What do you mean?"

"It seems like there's some sort of disaster on the news almost every day. Whether it's terrorist attacks, flash floods, hurricanes, tornadoes, earthquakes or fires. Wait a minute...Doesn't that represent the four elements? Water, Earth,

Air and Fire—yes, it does!" Emma's voice picked up speed. "We're destroying ourselves day by day. Our farms and rain forests are disappearing and in their places we're building malls and high-rise towers. We're becoming more and more dependent on large corporations to fuel our nations and keep us alive and they are forcing us to pay higher and higher prices," she sighed. "Whatever happened to living simple lives? People said technology would uncomplicate things but all it really did was help us do more things and do them faster."

"What are you getting at?" Maya had never seen Emma this passionate about anything before.

"Think about it…There are more people inhabiting Earth than ever before. What if the reason is because NOW is the time for mass awakening. That would make sense…All the souls who ever existed on Earth have incarnated during this lifetime to help Earth reach a new level of enlightenment!"

Terror was overwhelming Maya's ability to stay calm. She stood up and paced around her chair. "Okay but why does this have to involve me?"

"Why not you? It doesn't matter who it is really. It could be any one of us. But somebody has to step up and lead. Maya, you are one of the keys to this. You can't ignore it! It's your responsibility to act in spite of fear and find the answers. Will you please sit down."

When Maya did as she was instructed Emma reached out to hold both of her hands. "Take a deep breath. That's it, breathe. Again."

"You're right Emma. I have to do what I can to find the answers."

"That's my girl. Just stay focused and take it one day at a time. You can do this. It is your destiny. You just need to learn to harness your power and I believe that this is your opportunity to find out all that you can be."

Even though Emma's speech was very convincing, Maya was torn with indecision. "How can I believe this is real?"

"Only you can decide. But you're running out of time and you're going to have to make a choice soon."

* * * *

"So…I'm just supposed to hop on a plane and go to Egypt? Then what? Ask everyone I meet if they have a symbol seared on their back?" Maya asked Emma over the phone later that evening.

Her world felt like it had totally turned upside down and Maya didn't know which end was up anymore. She didn't understand what was happening to her but something drove her forward. How could she not? This was a chance to learn what she was made of. Who she really was and maybe, just maybe she would discover her purpose in life.

"The universe has guided you up till now. Maybe you just need to have faith that it will continue and show you what to do next," Emma said reassuringly.

"What would I do without you Emma? You are the most amazing friend I've ever had." Maya considered what Emma said. She had to acknowledge that her faith was indeed being greatly tested.

"It's been a long day and you've been through so much lately. I think you should take a nice bath and get some rest," Emma said.

"That sounds like a perfect idea. I can't thank you enough for being here to support me. I'll call you in a couple of days. I need some time to digest everything that's happened and figure a way to make things work with Brian. Maybe if I get him to listen I'll be able to convince him to take me to Egypt."

"Sure, I understand. Call me when you're ready, I'll be here."

They said goodnight and Maya put the phone back in its cradle on the kitchen wall. She stared out the window, oblivious to streaks of orange across the sky as dusk approached, the squirrels running across the backyard fence and the cardinal singing to her high atop the evergreen tree. Nor did she notice the raven watching her, perched on a hydro wire.

A shiver ran up her spine and she closed the wood blinds to give her some privacy from inquisitive neighbors.

She turned on the kettle to make some chamomile tea. *I'm not very hungry tonight but I better eat something to keep my strength up.* She opened up the fridge door and decided on some cheese with crackers and turkey slices because the thought of cooking drained her already depleted energy.

She took her tea and plate of food into the living room and relaxed on the sofa. She flicked on the television to keep her company and distract her from thinking any further. She desperately wanted to quiet her mind and forget everything, at least for tonight.

When she was ready to retire for the evening, Maya went upstairs and filled the tub. She lit a few candles for ambiance and some incense she bought during her last visit to Heartsong, NAG CHAMPA. The box claimed its properties promoted spiritual awareness during meditation but all she knew was that she found it relaxing.

Climbing into the tub she let the hot water enfold her, soothing her like the arms of a mother holding her child.

Climbing into bed after the bath, she let the fluffy expanse of the duvet pull her into a deep sleep. She refused to let her mind wander to think about the events of the day or about Brian. There was enough time for that tomorrow. Right now she needed rest.

For the first time in a very long time she slept peacefully and didn't hear Brian stumble in at two-thirty in the morning, drunk from his own attempts to forget.

Chapter Sixteen

It was mid-morning and the Saturday Patriot News lay spread across the table. Maya cooked breakfast for her and Brian, hoping a hearty meal would pave the way for a positive outcome for the discussion. She knew it was a silly attempt to get what she wanted but she tried it anyway. The smell of bacon and eggs was still in the air and the empty dishes were pushed aside when she finally told him what she was thinking of doing.

"You can't be serious!" Brian stood up pushing the kitchen chair back with such force it fell to the floor. "Ouch!" The sound of wood hitting the ceramic tile echoed piercingly in his head, reminding him he had too much to drink again last night. "Damn it! My head is killing me."

"Take it easy Brian," she said. She sat at the table, holding her coffee mug tightly while her body trembled, waiting for his tirade to pass. The sky was eerily dark. Thick with clouds pelting rain against the windows and ground, contorting her flowers in the garden and testing their will to survive. She jumped skittishly at the sound of the thunderous crack overhead.

"This fantasy of yours has gotten out of control now and I think you've really lost all sense of reality." He paced behind her, fuming inside.

"Bri…"

"Come on! Listen to yourself. You're really considering going to Egypt?"

"Yes. I know it sounds…"

"Sounds what? Crazy? Ludicrous? Dangerous? Yes! Maya how can you even consider it with all the problems in the Middle East?"

"Come with me," she pleaded. "It'll be an adventure." She waited for a response but nothing came. *Maybe I should have waited a few more days to think this through. Who am I kidding? I couldn't have spent another day like yesterday, waiting and wondering about his reaction.* She hadn't seen him in the last two days. He called to let her know he was going out with Shane again last night so she had all day and night to herself.

She spent the day in silence, working in the garden clearing her mind and sitting quietly in her rocking chair in the baby's room staring into nothingness. The dreams and visions had left her alone. Haunting only her memories for the past couple of days and even though it allowed her to sleep restfully, it made her feel oddly abandoned. If it wasn't for the symbol on her back to remind her she might have dropped the whole thing.

He stopped pacing and stood staring into the distance through one of the windows.

Maya gently pushed the chair back to rise. She walked up behind Brian and put her arms around him, resting her cheek against his shoulder. Still wearing her nightshirt, it rode up revealing her bare thighs that were starting to show signs of shape forming from running several times a week. "You keep complaining we're growing further apart. This could be our chance to change that."

He stiffened. Not even the sensation of her body pressed against him distracted his brooding. Resentment smoldered inside and clouded his thinking.

"Brian, please, I need you."

"Do you love me?" he asked.

His question caught her off guard.

He loosened her arms enough to turn around and face her. "Do you love me?"

She looked into his eyes earnestly, hoping that this was a sign he would come around. "Of course I do."

"Then don't do this."

She felt wounded and torn. Her head dropped and she took a step backwards, pulling herself out of his arms. "I'm not sure if I can walk away from it."

"Maya," he said and then stopped. Grief was overwhelming his ability to speak. His bottom lip quivered. His eyes reddened and filled with tears. He cleared his throat determined to finish. "I'm sorry but I can't be a part of this." His hands shook and he bit his lip to help stop him from totally succumbing to his despair. "If you insist on continuing, I…I can't stay with you."

She looked at him stunned by the meaning of his words. Pain seared into her heart paralyzing her with fear. "You can't mean that?" she said desperately.

"I'm sorry Maya but I do." He turned away from her and started to walk out of the kitchen.

"Where are you going? You can't just walk out on this conversation!"

"I'm going to crash at Shane's for the rest of the weekend. Maybe it'll give you some time to think about things. The decision is up to you. I just hope you come to your senses and save our marriage."

"Brian!" But her plea fell on deaf ears. He was already on his way out the door. She heard it slam behind him. The sound echoing in her ears.

* * * *

The down pour of rain continued all day and into the evening. The storm, violent at times with lightning touching down periodically and thunder booming near and far, released the intense heat wave that had plagued them throughout the past several months.

Fire engines, enroute to putting out blazes caused by damage from lightning strikes, could be heard every now and then in the distance.

Maya's hair was ruffled and her face stained with traces of mascara and tears from hours of sobbing into her pillow after Brian left.

She wandered from room to room throughout the house with a fleece blanket wrapped around her to ward off the damp chill now in the air.

Sorrow and remorse from causing so much damage to her marriage filled her to the depths of her being. She spent hours upon hours thinking of their years together. They both had their faults but they had saved each other.

When they met she was drowning with her insecurities. Always searching, often in the wrong places and in the arms of undesirable men, trying to figure out who she was and what defined her. Brian had changed all that. He gave her someplace to call home. He stood by her side all the years she tried to get pregnant and failed.

She thought about the months he tried to care for and comfort her when she lost the baby but she shut him out and turned away from him when she believed her reason for living had been taken away. For the first time she was able to really understand how hurtful that must have been for him.

Having tired of the party scene, Brian cleaned himself up pretty quickly when they met and devoted himself to winning her over. He wined and dined her, treating her with respect and adoration to the best of his abilities. He believed it was because of her that he turned things around and was saved from falling into a life of trouble and strife.

They'd been through a lot together over the years. *Could* she give it all up? *Would* she give it all up? These questions tormented her throughout the dark hours while she stared at the ceiling. Listening to the raindrops on the roof, reduced to just a spattering now. She wished for sleep to spare her from her own thoughts.

But sleep would not come that night and just when she thought the storm was over it came back with a vengeance forcing her to stay indoors for another day.

Having a cup of coffee the next morning she stared out the kitchen windows watching her flowers die. Beaten to the ground they lay limply, battered and bruised. The dark circles under her eyes were a reflection of the death around her garden.

Unable to eat she walked listlessly to the living room where she curled up with a blanket in the green plaid LazBoy chair.

She sighed, a long wistful sigh. *How can I let him walk away? He's a wonderful man and a loving husband. I can't do this. I can't bear to be without him. No I can't do it.* Her eyes closed and she finally drifted off to sleep believing her decision was just and final.

"Maya, my sweet child, wake up."

"Who's there?"

"Baby, open your eyes and look at me."

She did as she was told. The world around her looked different. Everything seemed so big. Except her body, it was a young girl's body. Her hands looked so small, her hair was long, longer than it had been since she was twelve when she cut it because it was becoming so unruly to tame.

"What's happening? Who are you?" she asked eyeing the woman who sat on the table in front of her. "Momma?" She reached out to touch the woman's long hair. "Is that you Momma?"

"Yes baby, it's me."

Maya lunged into her mother's arms and cried.

"It's okay sweetheart."

"I miss you. You hardly ever visit anymore."

"I know, I know. That's too difficult to explain right now. When you're older you'll remember and understand. But I'm here now and that's what's important. Baby, listen to me." She took her child's face into her hands and smoothed away the tears with her thumbs.

"What is it Momma? Why are you here *now*?"

"There's something very important I have to tell you. Can you listen? Listen real good?"

"Yes Momma, I'll try."

"That's my girl. Oh you are so pretty and I'm so proud of you." She held the young girl's hands tightly in her own. "There's something very important you will have to do when you are older. A great many people will be counting on you. You will have to be stronger than you've ever been before to do this very special thing. You are going to need a great deal of courage. Do you understand?"

Maya's eyes grew large and she nodded innocently.

"You will be given a very unusual gift to help you and you will have to learn how to use it wisely but don't worry, you will meet other people who have their own special gifts, and together you will help each other. Understand sweetheart?"

Maya nodded again, sucking in her lower lip and squeezing her mother's hands tight.

"There's one more thing honey. You can't let anyone make you feel bad about this gift and you can't let anyone stop you from doing this very special thing because you are one of the Chosen Ones. You have to promise me Maya, that you won't let anyone convince you it's not true. No one. Do you understand?"

"Yes Momma."

"Do you promise me you won't let anyone stop you? This is important, very important Maya."

"Yes Momma. I promise. Really I do."

"That's my girl. I knew we could count on you. I have to go now."

"No! Please don't go Momma!" she screamed.

"Bye sweetheart. Remember your promise."

"Momma wait!" But it was too late. Her Momma had left already. She sat in the big chair and cried.

"Huh? What?" Maya stirred. She lifted her hands to rub her eyes and discovered her cheeks were wet. Abruptly she sat up and the dream came flooding back. *Oh my God. I remember now! I had that same dream when I was only eight.* It came back to her now because it happened on her eighth birthday. She was feeling so lonely but the dream lifted her spirits for weeks as she tried to keep it fresh in her mind but after awhile it began to fade until it all but disappeared.

She leaped out of the chair. "I remember Momma! I remember!" Her heart raced and her body was shaking. She dropped to her knees and looked upwards. "I'll keep my promise!" She shouted and feelings of relief from making a painful decision washed through her body and soul.

Chapter Seventeen

Maya rose from her knees with a new clarity and determination. The storm ended sometime during her sleep and now sunshine broke through the clouds, filling her house with brightness. It made her feel alive. More alive than she could ever remember feeling.

Overcome with pangs of hunger she made herself a quick bite to eat. She chopped up an apple and made a tuna wrap to tide herself over for the next few hours.

When she was done eating she cleaned up the kitchen and wondered what she was going to do for the rest of the day. She didn't know when or even if Brian would return today but she was determined to put thoughts of him out of her mind while he was away.

Turning on the radio she laughed, filled with delight by an old uplifting song about surviving that now radiated throughout the kitchen. She turned it up loud and sang along. She hadn't heard the song in years and the coincidence of the timing was amazing.

Deciding to freshen the house up she grabbed a cloth with some polish and went into the den, singing and dancing while she dusted the bookcases and furniture. When the song ended she stood in front of her desk, looking at copies of her resume and letters she sent to companies in search of a job.

Well I won't be needing these for a while. She gathered them up and put them into a file in her desk. *There, that's better.*

Maya spent the next couple of hours straightening up and cleaning the house allowing her mind to wander. Memories long forgotten from her childhood began to resurface.

She remembered dreams of her mother visiting her, teaching her how to use energy to heal. One day she practiced her gift on a real potted plant of flowers that had died. She sat cross-legged on her Nanny's front porch with the plant in front of her. She put her hands around the yellow gardenias focused her thoughts, sending them energy, and watched them come back to life.

When her grandmother, who had fallen asleep in the porch swing, woke up and witnessed the miracle Maya performed, she became hysterical and grabbed the child. Dragging her into the house kicking and screaming. Calling her a witch.

Maya was so traumatized by the event she must have blocked it from her mind. She thought about it now and realized that must have been when she also stopped having the dreams with her mother.

Contented with her cleaning efforts, she still had lots of energy so she went for a five mile run.

When she returned she took a nice long shower, enjoying the feeling of the hot water spraying on her body and the ache in her muscles from her vigorous activities.

Ravenous, she cooked up a shrimp and vegetable stir-fry for dinner. Sitting down to eat she pulled out the travel section from the newspaper.

Hello, what's this? She found an advertisement from Mystic Tours & Travel Agency for a spiritual journey through Egypt. It offered a tour promising the *potential for personal spiritual growth not likely to be matched elsewhere.* It was to be led by Pamela Griffin, a world-renowned psychic who had received a guarantee from the Egyptian government for the safety of this spiritual tour, in recognition for her efforts to protect the sacred mysteries of the pyramids.

She picked up the phone and excitedly dialed Emma's number.

Emma picked up on the third ring, "Hello?"

"Emma, hi it's me. How are you?"

"Hi! Happy Birthday!

"What? Oh my gosh, I forgot."

"How could you forget it's your birthday?"

"I guess with everything that's been going on it never entered my mind." Then she remembered the dream with her mother on her eighth birthday, twenty-five years ago today, was the last time she saw her mother until the night she lost Chloe. It made her smile in understanding.

Maya jumped into the reason for her call. "I just came across this advertisement in the travel section for a spiritual tour of Egypt."

"Of course you did. Didn't I tell you to have faith the universe would guide you on your next move? Does this mean you've made a decision?"

"I guess it does."

"What about Brian, have you talked with him yet?"

Maya winced. "Yes. We talked yesterday. Basically he gave me an ultimatum, it's either this quest or him."

"I'm so sorry it's come to this."

Maya told Emma about the dream with her mother including her promise and the scarring event with her grandmother. Then she returned to talking about the trip. "It's a twelve-day tour of Egypt led by this famous psychic, Pamela Griffin…."

"Oh Pamela! I've read some of her books. She can see and talk to spirits on the other side. Her personality is a little on the gruff side but she means well. What else?"

"Well, the first week is in Cairo and surrounding areas. Get this; the second week is a cruise on the Nile River! Can you imagine that, the Nile River!"

"Wow, that sounds fantastic. When is it?"

"November thirtieth to December eleventh."

"The timing is a bit off, you'd be coming home before the twenty-first."

"I was thinking about that too. I'll probably look into extending my return flight or keeping it open. I won't really know when I'll be coming back depending on what happens of course."

"So you're really going to do it?"

"I still have to talk to Brian again. Maybe I can convince him to change his mind."

"And what if you can't?"

Maya considered this very carefully. "I made a promise and I have to keep it."

"Good for you!"

Maya hesitated, "I'm excited and terrified at the same time. I'd certainly feel safer knowing I'll be with a group of people. It's still three months away though. I don't know what I'm supposed to do with myself until then," she added pensively.

Emma laughed, "Aren't you learning anything? The universe will guide you along. You just have to stay open."

Maya laughed nervously. *Of course, how could I be so foolish?* She heard a noise. "Emma, I have to go. I think I just heard Brian come home."

"Good luck," said Emma.

* * * *

"Happy Birthday Maya," said Brian as he entered the kitchen. He carried a bouquet of daisies, which he thought were safer than roses with everything they were going through. He handed them to his wife.

She choked up in surprise. "Thank you." Wondering if the gesture meant anything more, she felt at a loss for anything else to say. "Would you like something to eat? I made enough stir-fry in case you came back."

"No thanks. I don't think I can eat anything." He felt a twinge of resentment that she was able to eat after their argument.

She got up to get a vase for the flowers, feeling very awkward, not knowing whether to give him a kiss or not. He seemed pretty stiff and unapproachable so she decided to keep her distance.

Brian spotted the newspaper open to the travel section. He looked closer and noticed something circled in a red marker. "What's this?" He picked up the paper.

"Pardon?" She turned her head sideways as she opened up a cupboard door and saw him looking at the paper. *O boy, here goes. Well we might as well get it over with.*

He felt outraged. His breath became shallow and quick. "I take it you've made your decision?" he asked defiantly.

"Brian please. Why can't you understand?"

"Oh I understand all right. Our marriage apparently means nothing to you!"

"That's not true! If you would just listen…Come with me…"

"I already told you how I feel about this and I haven't changed my mind. If you want to throw everything away and follow some stupid whim then I guess I can't stop you," he said with resignation. "But I sure as hell can't stick around and watch you do it either."

He held up the paper and waved it in her face. "Is this your decision?"

"Brian!"

"Just answer me! Is this your decision? Are you going to Egypt?"

"Yes."

"Well then. I guess that's that." He turned to leave the kitchen.

"What are you going to do?" Maya asked.

"I'm gonna pack a few things and go stay at Shane's until I figure out where I'm going to move."

"You're serious?"

"I am and I'd appreciate it if you could make yourself scarce while I pack. This is difficult enough as it is."

His words felt like a slap in the face but she stood tall and didn't falter. She heard his footsteps stomping up the stairs to their bedroom. *I guess this is it. Great Spirit, if you really exist, I'm going to need all the support, guidance and protection you can provide.*

* * * *

Later that night, all alone, Maya was still in shock over the events of the past few days. Needing some company, she drank a cup of chamomile tea and polished away the last of the chocolate chip cookies she kept stashed in the cupboard while watching television.

She flipped through the stations and paused when a constellation being shown on the Discovery Channel caught her attention.

They were discussing Pleiades and Maya was shocked to discover that this cluster of stars was also known as the Seven Sisters and the eldest sister's name was Maia.

Her heart beat faster and she wondered if she would discover some sort of clue about her identity as the dragon in her dreams indicated.

Maya leaned forward in her chair and rubbed her face in anticipation. According to mythology Maia was also the most beautiful of the sisters. She was shy and lived alone in a cave. Zeus met her and fell in love, visiting her often in her cave to keep his very jealous wife, Hera from discovering his secret.

This story was most intriguing but Maya wasn't sure what to make of it until she heard that Maia and Zeus produced a son, Hermes. The same Hermes-Trismegistus who wrote the carvings on the Emerald Stone.

Clicking the television off when the show ended moments later she sat dazed. Staring into the blank screen.

She became overwhelmed with the feeling that there was so much she needed to learn and do. She felt unprepared for what lay ahead.

Doubts about her abilities and fear slowly seeped into her thoughts. Thinking about the state of the world, filled with bombings and talks of war every day. Each passing year since 9/11 continued to worsen and Americans were hardly welcome in many countries overseas. Since 2001 there had been two other major terrorist attacks, one in Canada and another in Britain, killing thousands.

The thought of going to the Middle East alone, even though she would be joining a group, scared her immensely. The strength and exhilaration she felt earlier in the day was quickly disappearing.

Chapter Eighteen

HARRISBURG, PENNSYLVANIA
22 November 2012

"I can't do it!" Maya yelled out.

"Yes you can. Just stay focused," Emma said calmly.

"It's not working." Maya stomped around the fire pit in Emma's backyard as she looked at her miserable attempts to start a blaze using her powers. So far she was only able to ignite a few tiny bursts. She watched them fizzle into the ground and die away in disappointment. "I still can't control it. What am I going to do? I leave for Egypt a week from tomorrow and I'm no further ahead than I was three months ago."

"That's not true and you know it. Now you're just being dramatic. You've come a long way since then. You know how to call to your Fire."

"Sure I can call it up but it's so erratic." Maya rubbed her hands together to warm them up. The temperature had dropped to forty degrees Fahrenheit in the last hour as the sun started going down and the light jacket she wore wasn't keeping her warm enough. She reached into her pockets to pull out her gloves but realized it was an idiotic thing to do unless they didn't have any tips and were fireproof, which of course hers were neither. The cold damp air added to her tenseness. "I never know what will happen."

"You just have to have patience. You're learning how to meditate and use your healing powers and that will help you focus. I think that's fantastic. If you just keep practicing you'll learn to master it. Stop worrying so much. It'll all come together." The cooler air was beginning to affect Emma as well so she rubbed her arms and tapped her feet together.

"When? Time is running out fast! I can't believe it's November twenty-second already. There's only twenty-nine days left and I haven't discovered any more information about the prophecy." Maya felt a hint of hysteria slipping into her voice but couldn't stop it. "Every lead turned out to be a dead end and every time I tried to consult with Celeste our meeting would get cancelled, either she was sick or there was some emergency. I mean, come on! What's that about?"

"Maybe you're pushing too hard. If you keep knocking on doors that won't open you have to have faith that there's a reason. The universe will never give you anything to bear that you can't handle."

"That's what Celeste said," Maya sighed. She looked up and watched the intermittent clouds move slowly across the sky.

Three maple trees, hovering near the gardens were bare, the summer and fall flowers were long gone but the spruce trees lined up across the yard, creating a barrier to the roadway behind them, stood tall and proud.

"She's right," said Emma confidently.

"But even the dreams don't come as often and there hasn't been anything new in them either. I just don't understand what I'm supposed to do."

"Maya, listen to me. I think that the dreams and energy you experienced were all part of your awakening. It had to be forceful in order to get you to take action and make some decisions but maybe the rest is meant to come once you are actually in Egypt."

"Maybe." But Maya was reluctant to believe this.

"This has been a year of major life changes for you but the past few months have been really good for you, I can see that clearly. You've had a lot of time on your own. I know it's been tough but you've grown as a person. You've done some work on yourself and in many ways I think you are finally getting comfortable with yourself. Don't you agree?"

"I suppose," said Maya looking down at her feet.

"Okay then. So stop putting so much pressure on yourself and let go. Can you do that?"

"I don't know."

"I just had a thought. Let's try something different. Let's sit on the bench."

They sat down together on the black wrought iron bench just a few feet away.

"What are you feeling right *now*?" asked Emma.

"Angry and frustrated."

"That's good you were able to identify your feelings so quickly. Now I want you to really let yourself go into those feelings. Can you do that?"

"What do you mean?"

"Let yourself feel the anger and frustration. Build up the feelings. What is making you angry?"

"I'm angry that I've gone through all these changes that were asked of me and the universe hasn't given me any more direction."

"Okay, what else?"

"It makes me angry that this caused my marriage to end."

"Good, now do you think you can let these feelings go? Can you release them?"

Maya looked at Emma confused.

"Just answer, yes or no. What is your first reaction."

"I'd have to say no."

"What if I told you that if you release these feelings it will help you to get unstuck and maybe even allow your natural gifts to improve? Could you release them then?"

"I don't know."

"Let's go deeper then. What else are you feeling?"

Maya hesitated growing more uncomfortable, until she recognized what lay beneath the surface. "I'm afraid. Terrified actually."

"Of what?"

"That I'm not good enough. That I don't have what it takes to go through with this crazy quest." Maya's inner feelings came tumbling out into sobs. "I've never been able to stick with anything. Everyone thinks I'm strong, but I'm not."

Emma put her arms around Maya and held her tight for several minutes. When the crying slowed she pulled Maya away and looked into her eyes. "Now if I told you again that if you let go of these feelings it might allow your gifts to flow more easily, *could* you release them?"

Maya thought about Emma's words, "I think so."

"Then *would* you release them?"

"Yes, okay."

"When? Could you release them *now*?"

"Yes. I think so."

"Then do it. Just simply let them go."

Maya's shoulders shook slightly as she attempted to take a deep breath. As she exhaled she felt her body relax. "Wow, that was pretty amazing." She took a few more deep breaths and felt more of the tension melt away. "I feel so much better. I feel lighter."

"That's wonderful. I'm so happy for you. Can you understand that all those feelings stemmed from the limitations you placed on yourself?"

Maya nodded, "Yes, I can see that now and it wasn't nearly so difficult as I thought it would be."

"You are an amazing person and you have been chosen to lead the way into a New World. You might not understand what that means just yet but God, the Great Supreme Creator, or whatever term you want to use believes in you. Who are we to question that?"

Emma watched Maya shrug her shoulders. "Exactly, so just shine your Inner Light and everything will come together. Now, let's get back to work."

They stood side by side in front of the pit. The last bit of daylight slipped away as darkness from the early winter evening settled in.

"Concentrate and breathe," said Emma quietly.

Maya closed her eyes and focused on her breath, letting all expectations drop away. A soft breeze picked up a few remaining dead leaves on the ground, blowing them around the women's legs in a puff.

She thought about the book she read recently about a mystical force called Kundalini. It explained how energy moves in a spiraling motion within the body and it is the feminine psychic energy that lays dormant in most people, until one experiences a trauma or some event in their lives that is timed to awaken them to their spiritual journey and gifts.

It also said that Kundalini can be a dangerous force if pushed too quickly. It is a warm magnetic energy that swirls around the spine moving upwards to the base of the neck.

Maya was fascinated to learn that the awakening of Kundalini often creates symptoms of unexplained headaches or migraines, leaving most doctors confused as to their cause.

She pushed these thoughts aside to concentrate on the task at hand and was pleasantly surprised to find she was getting better at clearing her mind. She focused on relaxing every part of her body, one area at a time. Then she visualized a White Light entering the top of her head and moving down through her body. She couldn't remember what the different energy vortexes known as chakras were called, so she decided not to worry about it and do the best she could.

When the White Light reached her genital area she visualized the light passing through and spiraling up the spine like a snake, which represents the opening and activation of DNA into higher levels of consciousness.

She could feel her body getting warmer and warmer as the energy moved upwards. Her breathing became slower and deeper. She repeated the process again. This time the energy felt stronger and more powerful. She felt an electric energy building within her. Connecting her to a force far greater than herself.

Emma watched Maya in fascination. Something was going to happen, she could sense the energy building around them. She twitched involuntarily at the sound of a crackle of electricity in the air.

Bringing the energy around for a third time, Maya's confidence grew. She opened her eyes. She concentrated on the logs in the centre of the pit. She raised her hands, one, two, three…Blue and orange sparks sprung from her fingertips. Shattering the silence. A flare barely perceptible by the human eye broke free. Bursting the logs into flames.

Maya quickly looked at Emma who shrieked in astonishment. "I did it! I can't believe I did it!" She grabbed Emma and together they jumped up and down.

"You certainly did! Oh my God, that was the most incredible thing I've ever seen."

"It worked, it really worked! Emma, thank you so much. I couldn't have done it without your help."

"Sure you could. Don't give me the credit. It's time you started believing in yourself and your abilities."

"Okay, okay. I get it." Maya looked up to the sky and shouted with new confidence, "I'm here universe! It's Maya Maxwell, and I'm ready to stand up and be counted!"

*   *   *   *

When the colder weather approached the month before, Maya had joined Star-Fit. She found she was able to run harder on the treadmills and she liked the variety of weight machines to strengthen and tone her muscles.

The fitness club was bright and cheery with lots of windows and colorful walls, painted in shades of purple and yellow. It was not a very large club but it suited Maya's needs. She liked the fact that it was a women's only center, it made her feel more at ease.

This was the last day she was going to be able to run before she left for New York and then Egypt, and she didn't know when she'd be able to run again once she got there, so she wanted to make sure she pushed herself hard today.

She tried one of the aerobic classes but found it really boring and she preferred the solitude of running. She loved the rhythmic motion of her feet hitting the treadmill.

Running as hard as she could, her lungs felt like they were going to explode. After reaching her goal of five miles she cooled down and then moved to the weight machines, where she forced out every ounce of remaining energy and strength left in her body.

She left the gym feeling exhausted yet exhilarated, ready for her adventure.

A stranger stopped her as she walked up the front walkway of her house with her mail.

"Excuse me? Are you Maya Maxwell?"

Eyeing the short bald man warily she said, "Yes. What do you want?"

"I have this package for you. Could you please sign here?" He withdrew a pen from the case he was holding and waited for her to sign. When she was done he handed her the large manila envelope.

"What is this?" she asked.

"Goodbye," he said quickly and walked to the car parked on the side of the road.

Maya took her keys and opened the door. She dropped her gym bag in the hallway and hung the keys on the rack by the closet.

Ripping open the package she was unprepared for its contents.

Superior Court of Justice Family Court Divorce Order.
Applicant: Brian John Maxwell,
Respondent: Maya Caroline Maxwell.

There was a red tag with an arrow sticking out on the pages waiting for her signature.

Brian contacted her within a week of his leaving to begin the negotiations but she hadn't seen or heard from him since they came to an agreement. He wanted very little in the end and they had decided that since the down payment for the house came from the trust fund she received when she turned twenty-one that she would keep the house.

She walked numbly to the kitchen and sat down, staring at the documents. Even though she knew it was only a matter of time for the divorce papers to arrive she hadn't anticipated the feeling of being punched in the chest.

All this time she felt responsible for the breakup of their marriage but now, suddenly she felt anger towards Brian. *He's the one that gave up on us in the end…gave up on me. He couldn't accept who I am or what was happening to me.* She was filled with disgust for his cowardice.

Maya stared at the documents in front of her for a long time before she finally picked up a pen and signed her name. *Well I guess that's that.*

Chapter Nineteen

BEL AIR, MARYLAND
29 November 2012

Douglas meticulously stroked his brush on the canvas, put the finishing touches on the Atlantean temple that belonged to Diãntha. Blending shades of violet and royal purple with shimmering hues of turquoise on her beloved crystal.

He had labored over this piece of art for years, a little bit at a time as inspiration moved him to reconnect with their destiny together.

While he worked he envisioned the moment he would reveal this painting to her. She would fall into his arms with love and adoration for capturing her heart and soul so completely as no one else possibly could.

She would belong to him and no one else. He'd have to find a way to make sure she didn't merge souls with him, the other one. His name, he didn't know yet but they would all reunite in Egypt in only a few days. He would just have to stay close and look for opportunities to keep them apart. The thought of her being with anyone else, especially the one who stole her from him infuriated Douglas. No, he was not going to let her spurn him again.

Knowing that if he didn't take his mind off that thought he would destroy the painting. He relaxed his body and let the anger dissolve.

In only a few weeks our destiny will be secure. With the new consciousness the world will be ripe to expose the leaders holding the secret of the Boiling Lake and its source of energy. Once they are disposed of I will look like a hero. Especially when they see how my methods will reduce pollution and global warming for a fraction of the cost, changing the way we live and operate. Oh yes, my position will be secure.

He put the paintbrush down and stood back to admire his work. Someday he would organize an art show and display his work. *Everyone will see what a genius I am.*

There was a knock at his studio door.

"Yes," he said in annoyance.

"Douglas darling?" Vivienne opened the door and stepped gingerly inside.

"What is it?" he demanded not even looking in her direction. "You know I don't like to be disturbed while I'm painting."

"I know darling but John is here and he needs to speak to us together." She waited for a response but didn't receive one. "He says it's critical and can't wait."

"All right. I'll be right there." He would not allow business discussions in his studio. It was his sacred space and he didn't want it contaminated.

He took one final look at Diãntha and her temple before leaving. *Soon we'll be together.*

Joining Vivienne and John in the office, he closed the door behind him. "Well what is it that couldn't wait?" He glared disapprovingly at John, refusing to acknowledge him with a proper hello in retaliation for spoiling his mood.

"Perhaps we should sit down. I have some disturbing news." John waited to be directed where he should sit. He knew that Douglas would calculate the atmosphere and where he'd feel most in control to deal with the impending message. His attention to details and nuances was the most profound John had ever known and it never ceased to amaze him.

Douglas looked at Vivienne with raised eyebrows. He sat down at his desk and Vivienne, taking her cue, sat down at hers, which was kiddy corner to his.

"Why don't you bring one of those chairs over here," said Vivienne.

They watched John gather himself and sit down.

"Tell us what this is about," Douglas ordered.

John cleared his throat and hesitated before delivering his news.

"Come on, out with it. What could be so serious?" barked Douglas, losing his patience.

"I received a tip this morning that the Securities and Exchange Commission is filing a complaint against us and one of our holding companies."

"The *SEC*?" questioned Vivienne in disbelief.

"Yes they are filing a total of twelve fraud charges," responded John. "The claim is going to say we benefited from the sale of shares at inflated prices through an offshore account. That's the gist of the charges in a nutshell."

"That's ludicrous!" Douglas shouted. "Those damn idiots! Who do they think they're dealing with?"

John winced.

"I thought you said we had safeguards against this sort of thing?" demanded Douglas. His eyes were growing dark.

"Douglas please," said Vivienne calmly. "Nothing is ever one-hundred percent guaranteed. John has been very diligent in keeping the trails in order." She watched Douglas raise his clasped hands to his chin. His breathing was shallow and his mouth pursed together. Turning to look at John, she was the picture of unruffled elegance except for the steel edge in her voice, which gave away her inner state. "You said it was a tip. Does that mean it hasn't happened yet?"

"Yes, that's correct."

"How long will it take before we hear officially?" she asked.

"My guess is a few days." His foot tapped slowly on the floor.

"Well that's good then. We leave for Egypt tomorrow and nothing is going to stop us from taking this trip." Douglas leaned forward and narrowed his eyes. "John I want to know how this happened. We must have a leak somewhere and I want to know who it is. I want daily reports sent to us while we're away," ordered Douglas.

"Got it. I'll take care of it." He kept calm on the outside, knowing his performance under duress was being evaluated. He couldn't give away the apprehension he was feeling. He tried to remember all the nuances in human behavior he'd learned from Douglas over the years but the slow tap of his foot escaped his attention.

"What are the chances the charges will stick?" asked Vivienne.

"I may be able to dispose of some of the evidence in the next couple of days before this hits the fan but we could be in for a real tough battle," said John.

"What could be the possible repercussions?" asked Vivienne remaining stoic.

"For something of this magnitude, prison." Tap tap.

"You just keep me informed and I'll get in touch with my contacts. I'll make this go away, one way or another," Douglas said suppressing his anger. "You have work to do, I suggest you get on with it right now."

"On my way. I'll be in touch with you tomorrow before you leave. Would you like me to take you to the airport?"

"Yes John, that would be appreciated," Vivienne said with a sigh.

Once John left the room and closed the door Douglas picked up the phone.

"What are you doing?" asked Vivienne.

"I'm calling Harrison Gardiner. I want to know who is responsible for this."

"Are you thinking John had something to do with it?"

"For his sake I hope not. I will not tolerate that kind of betrayal. Whoever it is, just signed his own death warrant."

Chapter Twenty

JOHN F. KENNEDY INTERNATIONAL AIRPORT
30 November 2012

EgyptAir Flight 984A filled up slowly with people from all across the United States and some even from Canada. It was after midnight and the flight to Egypt was an hour delayed as a result of protests and uprisings occurring in the city of Cairo. There were rumors in the lounge area that their flight was at risk of being cancelled. But security at J. F. Kennedy airport finally gave clearance to depart.

Maya's nerves were on edge. This was not a good start to the trip. *What if there are terrorists on the plane? What if something happens when they arrived in Egypt?* She thought she must be crazy for getting on this plane. *What was I thinking?* As she approached the entrance to the plane a man behind her bumped into her and she had to stop from snapping out a sarcastic comment. *Where does he think I can go for Pete's sake? Can't he see the line is backed up?*

Archangel Michael, if you can hear me, I hope you are watching over me. She still had trouble getting used to the concept of angels and spirit guides being around her and felt ridiculous calling out to them. But desperate times call for desperate measures.

She tried to calm herself and drill into her head that the uprisings would be contained and would not affect her journey. After all, how could it? The universe had held her hand to get her there and it would not be in vain. Right?

She plodded down the aisles along with everyone else looking for their seats. She'd never been on a 747 before. Taking a quick scan of the plane she noticed there were three seats on both sides of the plane with a row in the center holding another four seats. *Here it is…33B. Figures…how was I lucky enough to get the middle seat? Well at least I'm not stuck in the middle section.*

She was hesitant to get settled in because the window seat was still empty and she knew she'd have to get up again but she closed her eyes anyway for a few moments to collect herself.

It had already been a long day getting to New York and they hadn't even left for Cairo yet. She'd never been on a flight as long as this and she wasn't looking forward to a ten-hour flight. She was never able to sleep much on a plane but she hoped that since they were flying overnight she'd be tired enough to catch a few hours of rest this time.

She overheard someone saying that there were over one hundred and fifty people going to Egypt on this tour. She noticed that most of them were traveling with friends and this made her feel even more alone and anxious.

She watched as people took their seats. Excitement was filling the air because they would soon be on their way. People joked and laughed with each other. She was surprised to see that there were several men on the tour. Over the past couple of months on her trips to Heartsong she noticed there were very few men that went into the store. She assumed they were not as open to paranormal or metaphysical experiences as women seemed to be.

"Hi! I guess I'm sitting beside you. I have the window seat," announced a bubbly voice.

Maya smiled up at the wisp of a woman grinning down on her. "Oh hello, sure, here just a sec. Let me move out of the way." Maya clumsily maneuvered herself into the aisle. Her foot caught on the edge of the seat but she was able to steady herself before tumbling. She laughed nervously.

Finally they relaxed into their seats after much noise and jostling.

"Are you part of the tour group?" the stranger asked.

"Yes. I am. Are you?"

"You bet." Extending her hand she cheerfully said, "My name is Arielle by the way."

"Nice to meet you Arielle. I'm Maya." Her back suddenly felt tingly and she twitched in discomfort. *That's odd…*

"Maya, oh that's such a pretty name." She studied her for a moment and said, "It suits you with your red hair and intense eyes. Exotic and mystical. Yes…It's you." Arielle admired the woman's beauty and simplicity and studied her classic style, jeans, crisp white shirt and black pumps.

"I'd hardly call myself exotic," Maya said shyly.

"Are you kidding me? Take a look at yourself girl! You're beautiful. Oh I get it. What jerk did a number on your self image?"

"What?" She shook her head in disbelief at the comment. "No, it's not like that." Looking at Arielle she took in her long blonde hair with soft highlights that must shimmer in the sun like gold.

Arielle's perky little nose and full lips emphasized her whitest of white and slightly crooked teeth when she smiled. And her eyes, well they were almond-shaped in a soft brown shade with tiny golden flecks that held the light. It made you feel like there were surprises waiting under the surface and suited her upbeat personality.

The red and orange swirl velveteen top was low cut with a scoop neck and certainly punched up the color of her faded blue jeans. A collage of silver bangles in various designs on both her arms announced her presence with flamboyance and the oversized silver hoop earrings only added to one's impression of confidence and vivaciousness.

Arielle took a swift look at Maya's ring finger. "I recognize a ring finger that's missing a wedding band. The indent is still there." She pointed to Maya's left hand.

Feeling taken back, Maya wasn't sure how to respond to this woman's outrageous personality. "I…Well…I mean…Yes my divorce was just finalized but if I have self-esteem issues it's entirely my own doing. Brian was an amazing guy."

Maya was disappointed to see the seat beside her on the aisle was being claimed and by a rather large man. She was hoping it would remain empty. She had to squeeze close to Arielle until he lodged himself into his seat.

"Hey listen, I'm sorry. I didn't mean to upset you. But if he was such a great guy why the divorce?" *Geez Louise, what the hell has gotten into you? You've practically reduced this poor woman to tears and it's only been a few minutes.*

Wow! Talk about jumping right into things. The plane's not even ready to take off yet. Part of Maya felt like she wanted to escape but here she was alone on this journey and she could really use a friend. "Oh that's a really long story but the end result is we found ourselves going down different paths and there was just no way to see eye to eye."

"I am sorry, really. Are you okay?"

"Some days are better than others, but yeah I'm okay. What about you? Husband, boyfriend?"

"Nope. I was engaged twice but I guess I'm holding out for the big bang. You know totally love struck with the stars, tingles and the whole bit." Her bangles clanged as she moved her hands around while she talked with animation. "Maybe that's only in fantasy books but I want it all and I just didn't feel it with David or Nick so I called it quits both times. Some would say I'm afraid to make a commitment but I don't think that's it at all." She stopped to take a breath and looked at Maya. "So do you think you'll ever get married again?"

"I'm not sure yet. Perhaps someday. I'd like to believe there is someone out there who knows me better than I know myself. Someone who will love me, not in spite of my quirks and oddities, but *because* of them. When I met Brian I thought he was the one but I guess I was wrong. I'm beginning to see now that it was my insecurities that wanted me to see something that maybe was never there. I wanted him to be something he wasn't but I guess you can't change people."

"If you can't love them the way they are then it's not love—at least not the kind of love that will last," responded Arielle sympathetically.

Maya stopped to look at Arielle with wonder. "Wow, how did you do that? I never open up like that to people I just met."

"I'm not sure. In a way I feel like I already know you. It feels like we haven't seen each other in a while and we're just catching up where we left off. Do you know what I mean?"

"That's exactly what it feels like." Maya wriggled in her seat and rubbed her back. She wondered why the mark on her back felt like it was heating up.

"Maybe it's fate at work," said Arielle sneaking a peak at Maya out of the corner of her eye.

"Humph..." Maya contemplated the remark with curiosity. The connection was too instantaneous to ignore. *She couldn't be one of them, could she? Nooo... That would be too remarkable.*

They had an opportunity to sit back and reflect on the peculiar bond they felt as the flight attendants began to walk through the usual emergency procedures.

* * * *

The plane began to move away from the terminal and head towards the tarmac. Looking out the window, all Arielle could see was darkness with a path of lights guiding them. The words, "Just follow the Light and the path will reveal itself," popped into her head and she smiled.

I can't believe I'm on a plane. You never could have convinced me that I'd ever fly again. Tension filled her body and she glimpsed at Maya who was turning to look at her.

"Are you okay?" Maya asked.

Panic was beginning to well up in Arielle, "Um, I'm not a real good flyer. Actually it terrifies me. I had a bad experience when I was a child and I've never been able to overcome it."

"Oh my gosh, what happened?"

Clearing her throat as if it might ease her discomfort, "My parents took my brother Tommy and I on a trip to New York. They never really traveled and this was the trip of their lifetime. They'd been saving up for it for years. We were going to go to Ellis Island, the Empire State Building, see the Statue of Liberty, you know the usual tourist stuff." She squeezed her hands together, her voice barely a whisper now. "But we never made it there. Something went horribly wrong in the engine shortly after we were in the air."

Arielle paused, trying to collect herself, the memories were flooding back. Unwanted tears filled her eyes and as much as she tried to fight them back, she couldn't. They began to drop onto her cheeks.

"Oh my God, what happened? Oh Arielle, this is too painful for you, you don't have to…"

"No, it's okay. I've got to work through this. It's been haunting me my whole life. Apparently negligence in the routine maintenance checks failed to discover a faulty component. The pilots lost control of the plane and we crashed. I don't remember much. It was such a blur of madness and chaos. I was sitting in between my mom and dad. Tommy had the aisle seat in the next row because he was older and wanted to feel like a grown up."

Taking a deep breath and closing her eyes, images flashed into Arielle's mind. "It happened so fast yet it seemed to go on forever in slow motion. I was too young to really comprehend what was going on around me. I must have lost consciousness during the impact. When I came to there was screaming and moaning towards the back of the plane. But I was the only one left alive at the front. A lot of the seats were missing. Mom, dad, and Tommy were gone. It was as though they were just plucked out." Her shoulders shuddered and she gasped for air as she tried to stay calm.

Maya reached over to take her hands. Their fingers clasped around each other tightly. Arielle felt a warm energy flowing from Maya's hand into hers. It seemed to surge into her body giving her the strength to continue. Looking into Maya's eyes she blurted, "My family died that day. Lots of people died that day. I was one of the very few who survived."

"Oh Arielle, I'm so sorry. That's so tragic. I can't even begin to imagine what you must have gone through. How old were you?" She felt her hands getting warmer and realized her healing energy was to flowing without effort or thought.

"I was only eight at the time. My mom's sister came for me. I was in shock and didn't speak for days. Aunt Grace was wonderful though. She held me and loved me and became my best friend over the years. I can remember her holding me close and rocking me. Telling me everything was going to be okay. She would take care of me. I can remember the smell of her perfume, she always wore Charlie by Revlon."

Arielle realized the tension in her body had momentarily lifted while she described her experience to Maya. It began to fill her again though as the engines came to full life and panic set in. Heart pounding, her breath quickening. Just as it felt as though terror was about to completely overtake her, she was overcome with feelings of love and compassion. They flowed into her body and seemed to completely surround her. She welcomed the warmth flooding through her. When she felt it begin to dissipate she realized that she had become oblivious to the fact that the plane had lifted off the ground and they were airborne.

"Wow! I feel so much calmer now. How did you learn to do that?" exclaimed Arielle looking at Maya with appreciative amazement.

"I'm just as surprised as you. Apparently I have a gift for healing. I can't really explain it and actually I only rediscovered it a few months ago but I've never used it on people before."

"I can't believe how peaceful I feel. This is the first time I've been in a plane since the crash. I've tried a couple of times but I seize up and can't go through with it. I even took the bus to get to New York."

"Where are you from," asked Maya.

"Coos Bay, Oregon."

Looking stunned, "Oregon! That's on the pacific coast! You took the bus from Oregon?"

"Yes. It's a wonder I'm here now. I almost turned and ran from the ticket check-in counter but something wouldn't let me back out. I knew it was either now or never."

"You should be very proud of yourself. You're conquering a lifelong fear. I just met you and *I* feel proud of you. There must be a very important reason you are going to Egypt?"

An announcement from the pilot that the flight attendants would be coming around to take drink orders distracted their conversation temporarily.

"Are you still close with your Aunt?" asked Maya when the announcement ended.

"Yes, we're very close. She's the only family I have left. Both my grandparents passed away before I was twenty. There are no other aunts, uncles or cousins in the States. I love the fact that Coos Bay is a very small community and we live only a couple of streets apart. It's quite cozy there and I wouldn't dream of living anywhere else."

"What do you like so much about it?"

"We have lots of beaches by the ocean and swimming holes hidden deep in the woods with lots of parkland. Everything you need is right there. Small boutique shops and the larger retail stores. The weather is mild and humid which is nice but we do get a fair bit of rain and the winds can get pretty wild at times. What makes it so special though are the little things the town does to get people involved in the community."

"What kind of things?" inquired Maya with envy.

"Well let's see, for example, recently there was a Lunch and Learn held at a nearby community center. The speaker was a member of the Coquille Indian Tribe. He taught people about the tribal perspective of the history of the Coos County Region. Things like what happened to their people when their culture was permanently disrupted by the changes. Other things like Shakespearean plays by the waterfront. Oh and Christmas is really beautiful. It's just so…so cozy."

"It sounds charming. I've never experienced anything like that. Harrisburg sounds dull in comparison. There's a lot of history in our area. Gettysburg, stuff like that. I've never felt attached to it and I think that someday I'd like to pick up and move somewhere else. Somewhere I can feel like you feel about Coos Bay." Listening to Arielle made her feel even more disconnected than usual and she wondered if she would ever feel like she belonged somewhere.

"I guess I'm pretty sentimental. It wasn't just my aunt who took me in, it was the whole town. I think in a way what happened brought people closer together. You know, taking care of each other and it always seemed like someone would be extra nice to me, doing nice things. Like our neighbor Miss Allison would bake cookies and invite me in after school for cookies and milk. Or dear old Mr. Parker across the street who surprised me with handlebar streamers for my bike." She sighed with the memory. "Listen to me going on and on. What was your childhood like Maya?"

"Well oddly enough I lost my family too. My parents were killed in a car accident when I was only three months old." A strange expression crossed her face.

"Maya? Is something wrong?"

She thought about Arielle inexplicably escaping death in the airplane and was dumbstruck by the coincidence of her own life. "I…I was in the car when it overturned into a ditch. Everyone said it was nothing short of miraculous that I survived…" Her voice trailed off, her heart beating loudly in her chest.

"Oh," Arielle didn't know what else to say.

"Yeah, oh. Don't you think that's strange?"

"Uh huh…What are you getting at?"

Maya, assuming Arielle would respond with some major insights to confirm her suspicions, felt a little disappointed by her reaction. "Nothing I guess."

"What happened after the accident? Who raised you?" Arielle asked politely, distracting Maya.

"My Nanny…I mean my grandmother. My childhood wasn't as pleasant as yours though. Sorry that didn't come out right. I didn't mean to imply…"

"That's okay. I think I know what you mean. What was it like living with your grandmother?"

What a stupid thing to say. She sighed, "It turns out I'm almost the spitting image of my mother, except my hair is red and hers was more brownish. Anyway, I guess seeing me all the time was very painful for my grandmother. She was pretty bitter and took it out on me a lot. Maybe she was angry that I survived and her daughter didn't. Her health also deteriorated quickly and she wasn't able to do very much so that meant I had to stay close to home all the time and help her."

"You must have missed out on a lot of things."

"Yeah. I wasn't able to establish any real childhood friends so I spent a lot of time alone. I only had one picture of my parents and I used to look at it all the time wondering what they were like. My Nanny…She wouldn't talk about them…So I grew up never really feeling connected to anyone. I guess I've always felt lost." She paused and sighed. "So here I am."

"Would you ladies care for a beverage?" interrupted a flight attendant.

Chapter Twenty-one

Sometime later, over the Atlantic Ocean, Maya continued to dwell on the special link she felt with Arielle and mentally deliberated about how she could investigate it further. "So why did you sign up for this tour of Egypt?" she finally asked.

Arielle shared the same curiosity to explore this unusual camaraderie that existed between them. "Do you want the long version or the short version?"

"Well we've still got at least another eight plus hours so you decide," laughed Maya.

"I'll go for a semi-short version because we should try to get some sleep soon." Arielle paused momentarily collecting her thoughts before proceeding. "When I was engaged to Nick I started feeling restless. It's hard to describe but he just couldn't fill the void I was feeling. On the surface there was no reason for it not to work. He was a great guy, handsome, gentle, and compassionate. He understood when I'd disappear in my art studio for hours on end to paint."

"But there was no magic," Maya stated.

"Exactly. I started to read spiritual books and go to New Age type workshops and did that for a few years. I discovered that what I was missing was inside myself all along. I'd touch upon it at times when I painted but it was only when I started listening, really listening to what my heart was trying to tell me that was I able to connect at a deeper level with myself and ultimately with God."

"Wow, that's very inspiring," commented Maya.

"Thank you. It's like that expression *to know oneself is to know God.* It's a tough lesson to learn isn't it?" Arielle exclaimed.

"Probably one of the toughest. I guess that's what I've been struggling with this year." She was reminded of the speech Nicholas gave in Nassau. "I think most people are afraid to really look at themselves. It's not easy to accept and love all aspects of ourselves including our dark sides. I guess we all have them."

Arielle nodded in agreement. "Eventually everything I was reading and hearing started sounding repetitive. So I took a break from it for a while."

"And something happened?"

Emotional turmoil erupted internally and she debated about whether to trust Maya or not. This was very personal indeed and they only just met…Still, their connection was strangely strong. "This is not something I'm comfortable talking about. People have been ostracized and crucified for such things. In my case I've lost a couple of friends because they think I'm crazy."

Maya straightened in her seat. "I don't know what to say to reassure you except that I know what it's like to risk speaking your truth. I lost my marriage because I needed to discover who I really am."

"I want to believe you Maya." Arielle still struggled with trusting her; after all she had a very strange story to tell.

"I'll stand out on a limb first. I'm going ask you something and if I'm right you have to spill the beans. Okay?" She couldn't believe what she was about to do. It was only a hunch and if she was wrong she was the one who would look like a total idiot. But December twenty-first was only three weeks away and she was getting fed up with playing it safe. It was the story of her life and she decided it was time for a change. She had to start trusting her intuition sooner or later. It might as well be now.

Arielle took a deep breath and thought about what Maya said. "All right. What's the worst that can happen? I hardly know you so if you decide to walk away thinking I'm crazy what have I lost?"

"Exactly! And if *I'm* the one who's wrong, believe me you're going to think *I'm* the crazy one."

They looked at each other, both afraid to put themselves on the line.

Arielle gave in. "Fire away."

Maya blurted out the question before she had any time to change her mind. "Do you have a symbol seared into your back?"

Gasping with shock Arielle's voice was barely a whisper. "Yes. Wait a minute lots of people have tattoos on their back. That's hardly a deal breaker."

"I'm not talking about a tattoo—I said a symbol. There's a difference. Did it mysteriously show up one day out of the blue?"

"How did you know that? Are you psychic?" she exclaimed in surprise.

Maya laughed at the question. "I wish I was but no. Maybe it would make things a whole lot easier." She reached for Arielle's hand, looked directly into her eyes and whispered. "I have one too."

Arielle's eyes grew wide. "You do?"

"Yes. When did it happen to you?"

"The day after the plane crash. I was only eight years old." Her hands came up to her face and she burst into heart wrenching sobs.

Maya grabbed Arielle and put her arms around her as best as she could, given the constraints of the seats. "It's okay, cry. Let it out. I'm here for you." Stroking her long golden hair she felt love pouring out for her newfound friend.

Straightening up and catching her breath Arielle wiped away the tears streaking down her face. Lifting her eyes to meet Maya's they found the tether that bound them together. "I've spent most of my life thinking I was some freak. Even studying spiritual anomalies didn't explain what it meant."

"It happened to me just this past August," began Maya. "I…I experienced something awful this year, a life crisis I guess you could call it. I lost my baby in January."

"Oh Maya, I'm so sorry."

"Thanks. It happened when I was twenty-seven weeks pregnant and what made it even worse was that the doctors did a c-section and she was born alive but she was too weak…" Maya dabbed the tears forming at the corners of her eyes.

"Maya, you don't have to go on, it's okay."

"No, I'm all right. Anyway, I really went downhill after that. I sunk into a deep depression and became reclusive for months. Pain became the only emotion I could feel. I couldn't even love Brian. That was really the beginning of the end of our marriage. I kept turning away from him because I couldn't or wouldn't feel anything but the agony that became my friend. I even lost my job because I couldn't function properly. Then after experiencing some very bizarre things and doing some research recently I discovered some things that have led me here. But that's a whole other story and before we get to that you have a deal to keep. Out with it."

Arielle was filled with mixed emotions. On one hand, she felt excitement that someone might have some explanations to what led her here. On the other hand, she felt trepidation with the thought of losing a potential long-term friendship. *If*

I don't open up though I'll always question my decision and we'll have it between us. So where would that leave us anyway?

"You drive a hard bargain Maya. Okay, here goes. About six months ago I started having this reoccurring dream which turned into a vision."

"What kind of vision?" Maya felt her Fire symbol pulse to a slow steady beat and her hands grew hot. She became more uncomfortable and wished the man on the other side of her wasn't taking up so much space.

"It begins with me standing in front of the Great Pyramid, you know the famous one. Then a mysterious entrance reveals itself to me." She cleared her throat before continuing, "I follow a tunnel from the entrance to a secret room. The whole time things are kind of cloudy so I never get a clear picture of where the entrance to this room is." She stared off in the distance trying to recreate the image in her mind and it came clearly.

"Once inside, walls filled with colorful hieroglyphics surround me. Then this large stone with writing all around it begins to appear."

Interrupting her Maya asked impatiently, "Is there a crystal hanging from above?"

She kept the vision clear in her mind. "Yes."

"Let me guess. It hangs on golden rods?"

Arielle broke her concentration, turned with her whole upper body and locked eyes with this mysterious woman who felt like she could be her sister. The question hung in the air as they stared at each other for what seemed like eternity. "Yes." She shifted in her seat to settle back in. The array of bangles on her arm clanging together broke the silence.

"Do you recognize the writing on this stone? Is it Egyptian?"

"I'm not sure. I don't think I would know the difference."

"What about on top? Are there symbols on top by the corners?"

Still dazed by the turn of events she put her head back in her seat and rubbed the bridge of her nose then her right eyebrow hoping this would alleviate the tension headache she felt coming. "It's funny you ask that. It was only in the past few weeks that one appeared."

"Is it the one on your back?"

"Yes it is. How did you know that?"

"It only makes sense. I imagine that is what made you decide to take this trip?"

"Yes. I didn't know what or how I thought I would find some answers but it kept gnawing at me and I had to come…" Arielle's voice trailed away. "After the symbol began to appear I noticed shadows of three other people in the room and I felt that we were all there to do something. Something really important."

"We are."

"We?"

"Yes *we*." Maya pulled out her bag from under the seat in front of her. She reached in for the book. Flipping it open to the dog-eared page she found what she was looking for. Showing the page with the four symbols to Arielle she asked, "Which one are you?"

"Oh my God!" She leaned back again and both hands whipped up to cover her eyes. "This is too much! I can't believe what I'm seeing. It's…It's this one." Pointing to the image for the Water element.

"How? Where? Where did you get this?" cried Arielle. Tears filled her eyes as she realized there really was a purpose. It wasn't random and it has meaning. An odd sense began to fill her. A burden of responsibility as she came to the conclusion that it meant there was something important for her to do.

"This is me," said Maya pointing to Fire then proceeded to tell her story of how and what she found out about the symbol, Thoth, the Great Pyramid and their mission.

*   *   *   *

An hour later, Maya yawned and rose to stretch, exhaustion was setting in. While she waited for the man beside her to let her out so she could move around she noticed a man rising at the same time about ten rows back on the other side of the plane.

She watched in curiosity, his slim waist and broad shoulders capturing her attention. He turned and their eyes met. Her breath caught in her throat. Lingering there as a bolt of electricity passed between them. They took each other in and for a few seconds she felt lost in time. Did she know him? Had they met before? There was something very familiar about him.

His thick dark brown hair looked like he had just woken up and had run his fingers through it. A widow's peak added an intense sexiness to his rugged appearance along with a days growth of beard. Maya estimated he was probably in his late thirties or early forties. And those eyes, protected by thick dark eyebrows and eyelashes, felt like they were seeing the unseeable.

With his head slightly angled, he gently bit his lower lip, raised his eyebrows slightly and offered a thoughtful smile. She didn't know how but from that distance she was sure she could see his eyes sparkle. He nodded at her. Her heart quickened. Her breathing became shallow. She could feel her face redden. *What am I doing? I can't afford any distractions on this trip and I am certainly not ready to think about men yet!* She quickly averted her eyes breaking their heady gaze but she could still feel the heat of their contact.

Arielle looked up at Maya wondering why she hadn't moved. "Are you all right?" When Maya didn't respond she lifted herself up slightly to see what was captivating her friend. "Phew, wow! He's a dream! You've obviously caught his eye girl."

"Shhh…For Pete's sake." Embarrassed for being caught gawking at a man she tried to regain her composure. After sitting for so long she was stiff and hardly moving gracefully. "You're imagining things. Besides he's not my type," she whispered hoping Arielle wouldn't notice the hesitation in her voice. She was glad the man beside her had disappeared to the washroom, missing this conversation.

"Come on. Not your type? Give me a break."

"Look I just want to stay focused on the reason we're here." Putting her hands on her hips she leaned backwards to give herself a gentle stretch. "Entertaining a notion about some guy is just not in the cards right now." She hoped by saying the words out loud she would believe them but inside she felt like jelly.

"Maya…"

The sharp look she gave Arielle stopped her before she could say anything further. "No. Let's leave it at that…Please." Without saying anything further she walked in determination to the rest room. *Keep walking. Don't look.* But she couldn't resist. Out of the corner of her eye she glanced over to his seat and felt a sting of disappointment noticing that he'd moved out of sight already. *Just as well…*

* * * *

"This part refers to the Great Pyramid of Giza and the passage to the secret chamber," said Maya. They'd slept for a few hours and woke to a very boring airline breakfast. Huddled together, reading from one of the books Maya had brought with information about the Emerald Stone, they were careful not to spill their coffees.

"Look here, it says that there are few with the courage to dare passing through the portal of darkness. I wonder what that means?" questioned Maya.

"It sounds like the portal of darkness might be like going through the dark night of the soul. You know, facing your inner demons, just like you've experienced this year. What do you think?" Arielle asked.

"Mmm…Could be. It does make sense."

They continued reading together.

Maya pointed to another section in the book. "See here it talks about the crystal and revealing the great mysteries but then it talks about having the courage to dare entering the dark realms."

"The crystal I guess is the Herkimer Diamond you mentioned earlier, it follows your theory."

"I agree. It's this part about the dark realms that bothers me. It sounds like more than just the dark night of the soul. It reminds me of demons and ghouls and I don't like it one bit," Maya said with trepidation as she experienced chills throughout her body.

"I don't believe for one minute that you can't handle yourself. I can feel the Fire in you and I wouldn't want to be the one to come against you."

Maya chuckled.

"What's so funny?" asked Arielle.

"I haven't told you yet about my experiences with fire."

"Oh goody, you've been holding out on me," Arielle said sarcastically. "Okay give."

"Brian couldn't cope with everything that was happening and we had a few fights. One fight in particular really did it for him. I think it was probably the key turning point in our relationship. He was really making me angry and I felt my body burning up inside. It just kept getting hotter the angrier I got with him. Then this ball of fire flew out from the tips of my fingers and hit a garbage can beside him."

"Did anything happen?"

Clearing her throat Maya said, "Yeah. The can melted."

"Wow! What did Brian do then?"

"He looked at me like I had horns or something."

Arielle burst into a roar and laughed for a few seconds. "Would I have loved to see that!"

Giggling in response. "I guess it is pretty funny now that I look back but it certainly wasn't very funny at the time. It was pretty scary. This was even before the symbol showed up and I didn't know what was happening to me."

"Has anything else happened since then?"

"Well, I've been practicing with the energy."

"And?"

"I spent the last couple of months extremely frustrated. I couldn't seem to control it but then last week a friend of mine, Emma, helped me to let go of the pressure I was putting on myself. We were practicing in her backyard, trying to start a fire in her pit and I was finally able to do it."

"That's unbelievable! Have you tried since then?"

"A couple of times. I'm getting better at keeping focused but I don't know what would happen if something challenged and upset me. I still need to work on it...A lot."

Looking at Maya with wide eyes she asked, "So what do you think you are supposed to do with this gift?"

"I don't know that I'd call it a gift. But I think that Fire is the connection to the crystal. I think it's what activates it."

"What do you mean?"

"Even before I knew about this crystal in the pyramid I felt a strong connection to Herkimer Diamonds. I bought one when all this started and it's like I can feel it calling to me. It's hard to describe. It's like I am a part of it."

"Part of the crystal?"

Clearing her throat Maya continued, "I've been learning how to meditate and lately I've been holding it too." She leaned forward grabbing her denim bag. Loving denim, she couldn't resist when she saw it a couple of weeks ago. Well at least it was on sale, half off its regular price of two hundred and forty dollars. She'd never spent that much on a purse before but she was learning to give herself permission to splurge now and then.

With long thin straps it hung low by her hips with multi-colored beads that dangled from the bottom of the bag. The top folded over like a flap and it was big enough to carry her essentials including a notebook and a couple of books. She pulled out the Herkimer from a leather pouch. "This is it."

"Neat. Looks like it has baby crystals growing on it."

"Yes, apparently that's common among the larger ones. Anyway, one day I was in my favorite new age store where I bought it and I sat in a corner meditating. Helena, who works there and is quite a talented reader put some other crystals at the four corners around me for grounding and protection. While I sat in the center I noticed that my energy was getting lighter and lighter and everything around me was feeling very hazy. I pulled myself back because it scared me and I didn't know what to do next."

"What happened?"

"Helena kept people away and later told me that I was disappearing in front of her eyes."

"Get out! Seriously?"

"Yup. She said my whole body started fading away." Giving herself a shake as she remembered the experience.

"How did it feel?"

"Creepy but amazing and wonderful. It was like something was calling me to come and somehow I could feel a part of myself in there. I've never been able to recapture the feeling since."

"You're probably trying to hard. Maybe if you just relaxed…"

"That's just it. I can't relax. Every time I meditate I know that I want to experience it again."

"I'm sure it'll come to you again when you're ready. I just had a thought. Perhaps it *was* meant as a calling, like a message for you to recognize and decipher. Do you really think you are the one to activate the crystal?" asked Arielle in awe.

"I've had a few visions where I was deep in the woods with gigantic trees all around me and a really large Herkimer rose up magically from the ground. It speaks to me telepathically. Sometimes it just calls me closer but there was one time just a few days ago that was different. It told me that a long time ago a dark force tried to steal my powers and caused a devastating explosion."

"Oh my gosh! Did it tell you anything else?"

"It said that the explosion killed my physical body, shattering my spirit into pieces. But one very significant piece merged itself into the crystal and it has been sending its signal out for thousands of years in search of the rest of me. As I healed through the lifetimes I learned to draw back those shattered pieces until enough of myself has been restored and that's why now, I am able to hear the call. The crystal's final message to me was I am the key to the universe and protection will be provided to me as I find my way home."

They sat in silence.

Does she think I'm deranged? She must. Who wouldn't? "What are you thinking Arielle?" she asked tentatively.

"Um. I'm very emotional." Large tear droplets spilled onto her cheeks and ran down her face. "I could see this massive explosion erupting and I felt as though I was running. I think I was there when it happened. I think that the four of us, whoever we are, lived during that time as friends. I feel massive destruction and loss beyond comprehension." Leaning in to Maya, she reached for her hands, damp from wiping her own tears. "I can feel us. I can feel the beats of our hearts. The others are close. I can feel them. Can you?"

"Yes. Yes I sense that too." There was no denying any longer, as much as she might want to.

They held each other's hand tight. Maya thought about the dark force that once destroyed her, if it was true, and shuddered.

Chapter Twenty-two

Douglas sat in first class on EgyptAir flight number 984A filing his nails, drinking his coffee and smiling with confidence at the thought of Maya being on the same plane, behind the curtain in coach.

He caught sight of her briefly while they waited in the departure lounge. It was the first time he had seen her in this dimension since she was a baby. Waiting for this time, in Egypt, where all his plans would come to fruition, he had kept his distance all these years. Visiting her only in the ether and in her dreams. He had monitors track her activities and keep him posted, providing him with pictures every now and then as she grew up.

Nicholas has indeed done an excellent job. Despite his stubborn ways at first he has grown from a neophyte into a valuable acolyte. Yes, I think it will be time when we return to initiate him to the inner sanctum. I have big plans for him. It delighted Douglas to know that Nicholas will be so pleased and honored to continue his grooming, working even more closely together.

He felt rested after sleeping several hours, with the help of the sleeping pills Vivienne always kept in stock for long flights. They were only a couple of hours away now from landing and the thought exhilarated him. He glanced at Vivienne who was busy studying the brochure outlining the daily activities for the tour.

The others were on the plane as well, of that he was sure. Douglas had kept his participation in their awakening to a minimum, only getting involved at critical moments. He didn't even know their names, only working with coordinates.

He was looking forward to identifying them from the mass of people on this trip. It was part of the game he wanted to play, challenging himself and Vivienne by keeping their identities unknown.

Even though they were as important to the activation as Maya he had a personal motivation in taking such an active role in her awakening. She refused his advances once before, it wasn't going to happen again.

* * * *

Vivienne sat beside Douglas preoccupied with her own thoughts and plans for victory in their inevitable destiny. The shy demure persona she displayed on these public trips was a clever masquerade. No one knew how much he relied on her for her insights and guidance.

The toughest part of her job was keeping him grounded. His emotions often got the better of him, putting them in precarious situations leaving it up to her to come up with a plan to get them out of trouble. She thought about his irrational desire to buy the house in Salt Lake City, putting it in their name, and the pending SEC investigation. She knew at the time it was a mistake and now there was a direct link on paper to them.

Casting a brief glimpse in his direction she prayed for help and guidance to prevent the dire situation from interfering in her plans.

All of our efforts are coming to fruition and everything is at stake now. I'll need to watch him closely...He'll be at the peak of his dreams and his emotions will be volatile.

Chapter Twenty-three

It was chaotic and hot in Terminal two at the Cairo Airport even though the temperature outside was only sixty degrees. Maya scanned the crowd looking for Arielle after they somehow got separated from each other but she couldn't see her anywhere.

She followed the crowd trying to figure out where to go next but so far all she could see were signs in Arabic. Finally finding a billboard in English she realized she had to look for the proper airline to determine which security-screening checkpoint to go through. She kept scanning for Arielle feeling intimidated and alone in this foreign country.

There were so many people it was impossible to move very fast and when she reached the security area she was filled with dread. There were hundreds of people waiting to clear security with only two desks open. Maya was overwhelmed with the yelling and screaming going on in the lines. The security standing guard with weapons caused the jitters in her stomach to return with a vengeance.

"Maya!" shouted Arielle. "Maya I'm over here!"

Hearing her friend she turned to look behind her and saw Arielle waving her arms above her head. Maya waved back relieved. If she wasn't so hot, irritable and frightened she supposed it could have been a funny sight watching the skinny blonde woman, jumping up and down, her bangles bouncing on her arms making clacking noises.

Arielle worked desperately to move through the crowd to reunite with Maya, but by the time she was only five or six people behind it was Maya's turn to go through security. She could see Maya getting upset and wondered what was happening.

"I'm sorry I don't understand. What is the problem?" Maya was growing agitated. The guard wasn't letting her pass through. He was jabbering away in Arabic and waving her passport in the air.

"Maya, what's going on?" shouted Arielle from behind.

Maya was on the verge of crying. "I don't know. They won't give me my passport and visa back."

A security guard approached Maya. He raised his machine gun up and across his body. "Quiet! You must wait." He made eye contact with Arielle. "You, be quiet!"

"I don't understand, what's wrong?" Maya pleaded. Being so close to the gun made her life feel threatened.

"I said quiet! We are checking your records."

"My records?" He took another intimidating step closer. Maya decided to shut up. She glanced quickly in Arielle's direction and waited. Her heart was racing. She felt the energy in her spine start to build. *Oh God no! Stop!* She attempted to focus her breathing and thoughts but she had never tried to stop the Fire before and didn't know what to do.

The guard behind the desk spoke to her in Arabic and passed her passport back. "Go!" He nodded and waved for her to move.

Relief flooded through her body and she released a nervous sigh as she collected herself and walked away.

When she reached the dimly lit baggage claim area she joined the tired and frustrated crowd that was gathering around someone holding a sign that read Mystic Tours & Travel. Once there she was told that they had to wait for all their bags to be unloaded and lined up before they could claim them.

"Maya! There you are! I was so worried about you. Are you okay?" questioned Arielle plopping herself down in the seat beside Maya.

"I'm still pretty shaky."

"Why did they detain you?"

"I have no idea? They said they were checking my records."

"Maybe they were just trying to prove their superiority by intimidating a young defenseless woman. Creeps."

"Probably. There couldn't be any other reason."

"Talk about a nerve wracking experience to start off the trip."

"That's putting it mildly. My nerves are shot already." It was only four-thirty P.M. in Egypt and she wasn't sure how she was going to last through the evening on only a few hours sleep over the past two days.

* * * *

"Thank you for sharing your room with me," Arielle said to Maya as they got off the elevator and headed into the massive lobby of the hotel. "I don't know what I would have done if I had to stay with that crazy woman the whole time."

Maya was glad she paid the few extra dollars to have a room to herself on this trip and now it was coming in handy. "I couldn't leave you with her, she gave me the creeps. Dressed all in black, wearing that strange cowboy hat with a black fur tail. How weird is that?" exclaimed Maya.

"You know I stood beside her on the plane while I was waiting for a restroom and she kept talking about the end being near and everyone will thank her when she rescues them. I just wanted to get a way from her as fast as I could. I can't believe we were assigned to the same room!"

"Let's make sure to stay clear of her as much as we can. There's something very wrong with her."

The bus driver had explained that the El Gezirah Sheraton Hotel, sitting right on the bank of the Nile River, is a luxury hotel in the heart of Cairo. He said it was located on the tip of El Gezirah and it actually sits on an island. The round tower design provides all the rooms with panoramic views of Cairo's landmarks. Even though it was a traditional Sheraton hotel and didn't really have an Egyptian atmosphere Maya and Arielle thought it was magical to be right on the Nile River, to say the least.

Maya felt surprisingly energized and looked forward to the evening ahead. She thought fleetingly about home but it seemed eons away now that she was in this old and distant land. A culture going back thousands of years surrounded her and she felt its presence. The air was still and unseasonably warm for a December evening.

The Andalus restaurant was alive with excited chatter as people meandered through looking for places to seat themselves at just the *right* table.

Maya and Arielle selected a table joining three women and one man. They learned that Margaret and Elizabeth were sisters from Finger Lake, New York. Jason and Veronica were highschool sweethearts from New Jersey. All four had been huge followers of the tour's spiritual leader, Pamela Griffin.

"Maya isn't that the guy you were ogling on the plane?"

"Huh?" Maya was lost in thought thinking about the water fountain they saw earlier in the middle of the Nile River and how the man-made fountain seemed oddly out of place on this historic river. "Did you say something?" She noticed that Arielle was motioning for her to look in the direction of the two men walking towards them. *Damn!* For some reason the words *I will be right here waiting for you* from an old song popped into her head when she saw who one of them was.

"Do you mind if we join you?" Speaking to the group of people but staring into Maya's eyes, the tall dark stranger watched her blush.

As the others at the table motioned for them to join the table Maya looked around the terrace and noticed that there were very few seats left and no place to escape to. Feeling tongue-tied she just smiled with nervous apprehension as the man from the plane sat down beside her.

"Hi my name is Arielle Stewart and this is Maya Maxwell."

Maya shot a fierce look at Arielle like she had just been betrayed. She felt a host of emotions swirl around inside, joy, sadness, anger, pain. *Why is he stirring up so much turmoil in me?*

"Nice to meet you. I'm Alex Delaney."

Maya's heart raced and she didn't trust herself to speak so she just nodded politely. She thought he looked incredibly handsome wearing black jeans along with a black crewneck sweater and a gray blazer.

"And I'm Cade McAllister."

While the rest of the group introduced themselves Maya glanced at Alex tentatively. She felt the fire rising up her spine but she ignored it believing it was just lustful feelings. After all, it had been a few months since she felt the arms of a man around her. Longer than that really since it had been almost a year from the time when she and Brian were close and loving. *God, stop it! What are you doing? Get a grip on yourself Maya.*

To distract herself she turned her attention to Cade. He had light brown hair. *A little wild—looks like he likes to gel it up. Here's another one with a widow's peak. What's with that?* His facial features were long and slim. His smile was quite charming even though it was a little crooked. She figured him to be around six feet tall with a very slim build. He had an earthy quality, wearing faded jeans, a white shirt and cowboy boots. *I didn't know people still wore cowboy boots.* All in all she thought he was a nice looking guy.

Maya remained quiet while everyone at the table shared bits and pieces of themselves.

"Where are you from Alex?" asked Elizabeth.

"I'm from Boston."

"Oh that's such a lovely town. I went there once for a weekend getaway. Is that where you are from too Cade?"

"Oh no. Actually Alex and I just met at the airport. I'm from Sedona, Arizona."

"Ohhh…I hear Sedona is really beautiful. I've always wanted to go there," cooed Arielle.

The tone of Arielle's voice caught Maya's attention. Not that they've been friends long enough to know all the different inflections but she could swear she heard the sound of a woman interested in a man. She continued to keep an eye on Arielle while Cade described the alluring qualities of Sedona's red rock countryside. *Yup, definitely a woman smitten.* Actually he was looking pretty taken in too.

"Looks like they are hitting it off."

Maya was taken back as Alex who had seated himself on her left leaned closer and smiled while he spoke. "It does look that way," she said. She couldn't help but breathe him in, he smelled so good. *I wonder what cologne he's wearing? I wish he wouldn't lean so close.* He was making her feel very uncomfortable. *Look at those eyes, they're so dark and deep…*

"I won't bite, I promise," he smiled shyly.

"Excuse me?"

"You seem a bit jumpy. Did I do something to offend you?"

"No," a little too high pitched, she cleared her throat. "No not at all."

From the moment their eyes locked on the plane Alex was entranced with this woman who was now sitting beside him. He thought the feeling was mutual but now he was definitely getting a mixed signal. She almost seemed annoyed with him and he couldn't understand what happened to alter the connection.

She turned away from him to listen to the conversation taking place between Arielle and Cade. Anything to distract her attention away from Alex. But it wasn't working. She could feel him next to her. The heat of his body was electrical—he was just too close for comfort. It was too soon to think about another man, especially right now. She had too much to learn and do over the next few weeks and he didn't fit in the picture.

Alex noticed that her hair looked curlier than it did earlier. He found it incredibly sexy. It made her look untamable—fiery and independent. Sitting beside her was driving him crazy. Normally if he was rebuffed in this way he would walk away. But he found he couldn't bring himself to do that with Maya. There was something very compelling about her and it was stirring up feelings he couldn't ignore. Taking a chance he took the plunge once again to find out more about this woman who was completely capturing his attention.

"Where are you from Maya?"

Why oh why can't he see that I don't want to do this dance? Of course you do, you just won't admit it. How can I? Will I ever be able to trust any man to accept me again?

"I live in Harrisburg, Pennsylvania. It's kind of dull there, very historical. I've been thinking about picking up and starting over somewhere else. We'll see what happens after this trip. What about you? Do you like Boston?" *Why did I just tell him that?* Finding herself feeling very self-conscious she nervously pushed her hair behind her ears.

He watched her movements and couldn't help but think how sexy she was. "Yes, it's pretty nice. I like being near the water. Actually what I like is listening to the sound of the waves hitting the rocks. The force of the air moving the water gives me strength for some reason. It's hard to describe."

Finding herself intrigued she leaned a tiny bit towards him. "I think I can understand that. I've always wondered what it would be like to live near the ocean."

Her voice softened and everything around them seemed to drown out. *She has such a magical effect on me.* "Do you have family, children?" He prayed for the answer he wanted to hear.

"Just my grandmother but she's in a nursing home. She has Alzheimer's and hasn't recognized me in years. My parents died when I was a baby and I'm divorced, no children." She winced at the mention of children.

He noticed the odd look on her face when she said children and he wondered why but he wasn't about to prod any deeper in case it would upset her. "I'm sure this will sound cliché but the guy must have been a fool to let you get away." Reddening furiously for an unusually bold statement he tried to compose himself.

Maya couldn't help but feel warmed inside for his kindness. "Yes, that's one way to look at it but he would probably disagree. I had a miscarriage and didn't deal with it very well. We started going our separate ways and it just got worse as time went by. I guess by the time I starting coming around it was too late."

"I'm so sorry to hear about your loss." He paused in reflection. "I know what that's like. But I get the feeling there was a lot more to your breakup than that." He raised his hand before she could respond. "Don't worry I won't pressure you for details…Yet." He smiled tenderly and winked. He wanted to reach out and take her hand but he restrained himself.

She looked at Alex and couldn't think of a thing to say. Where did the world around them go? She couldn't see or hear anything other than him. He seemed to have a very quiet disposition, even shy. She had the impression that it was uncommon for him to be bold with women even though he was very easy on the eyes. Who was she kidding? He was very handsome in a rugged way. A cool breeze passed through her and she shivered.

Without thinking he took off his blazer and put it around her shoulders.

"Thank you," she said awkwardly. The feel of his hand sliding across her back sent tingles up her spine. "What about you Alex? Family?" Against her self-imposed exile she found herself hoping he'd say he was unattached.

"My mom and dad live nearby in Cambridge. I have a younger brother who lives in Boston too. We're pretty close. He has a great wife and twin boys." His voice got a little raspy as he continued. "My wife and daughter died in a car crash about five years ago."

"I'm sorry," was all Maya could say. Her hand reached out and touched his before she realized what she was doing. A jolt of electricity passed between them and she looked up to meet his gaze. Their eyes locked.

Arielle elbowed her in the side. "Look that must be Pamela Griffin."

Maya's internal world spinned momentarily as everything around her and Alex came back into focus and she quickly withdrew her hand.

* * * *

Pamela Griffin tested the microphone she was handed. "Good evening everyone and welcome to Egypt. I hope everyone had a good flight. Even though it looked questionable as to whether we would be allowed to come to this country at this time, here we are.

"My name is Pamela Griffin and together you and I will visit many pyramids and sites in this ancient land. As part of this trip I will be facilitating workshops and meditations which will provide you with opportunities to rediscover those parts of yourselves that were lost many lifetimes ago."

Maya and Arielle looked at each other excitedly and squeezed each other's hand. Maya forced the electrifying feelings she experienced with Alex aside. *I can't let my emotions cloud my judgment. I have to stay focused.*

Pamela continued, "You have all been drawn here for a reason. Every one of us here has lived at least one lifetime in ancient Egypt. And now we are all finding ourselves at a fork in our path. Do we turn right? Do we turn left? Or do we continue along the road we are on? We are all old souls. Let us keep our hearts open and await our answers. It may either whisper to us in the wind or it may take the rug right out from under our feet so be prepared for anything to happen.

"Notice that I use the term we, because I am in the same boat as you. Yes, I am looking for answers on the road to enlightenment as well so we're on this part of our journey together. My husband Bill is with me along with a couple of my closest friends, Susan and Donna. We are here to help you so please feel free to ask us questions on the tour.

"Stay safe, be well, and enjoy your journey. Tomorrow we begin." Pamela handed the microphone back to one of the hotel staff members and joined her traveling companions for dinner.

* * * *

Their meal consisted of tasty chicken shish kabobs served with traditional Egyptian accompaniments of greens and tomato salad, tahini sauce and pita bread.

"This pita bread is amazing and it's still warm." Arielle said to anyone willing to listen.

The smell of the food being distributed while Pamela spoke made everyone realize how hungry they were after their tiring travels.

Cade nodded in agreement obviously enjoying his meal. "The tomatoes are just bursting with flavor. They don't taste like this in the U.S."

The music playing in the background made it difficult for everyone at the table to talk to each other without shouting. So it became natural for Maya, Arielle, Cade and Alex to group together in conversations while the other four at the table did the same.

Arielle did not hide the fact she was admiring the spirited look in Cade's eyes. "So what do you do in Sedona?" she asked.

"I own an adventure tour company."

She noted to herself that it explained the deep tan that set off his brown hair and eyes to perfection. "That must be fun. Do you enjoy what you do?"

"Very much. I get to spend my days outdoors, being one with nature and everything around me. Even the dirt under my feet, the birds in the distance, the scurry of critters along the desert ground." Looking sheepish he said, "Sorry, guess I got carried away."

Arielle tenderly touched Cade's hand and smiled sweetly while offering him reassurance. "Don't be sorry. It's wonderful to feel so passionate about what you do."

"What types of tours do you provide?" asked Maya.

"Mostly hiking, jeep, and horseback riding. The canyons are a magnificent place to experience being outdoors. The majority of the tours are just day trips but sometimes I get a group who wants to take a three-day package. Those are the ones I enjoy the most. Sleeping under the stars with the earth beneath me...It's where I'm most at peace."

Arielle found herself experiencing a very unusual déjà vu moment. She felt a part of herself, her consciousness, begin to flow in a stream of water, meandering around stones and rocks along a patch of red earth. Bubbles formed as she hit the bumps of stones that forced her to either push over top or swoop around, depending on the height of the ground beneath her and the size of the rock. At times she made sputtering sounds when the stream was low and when she merged into an open area her voice grew to a hearty cascade. She felt at one with Earth. When the image faded she looked at Cade and he smiled. She wasn't sure what she just experienced but she was certain it had to do with him. She felt an incredible sense of freedom and yet connection to Earth and Water.

Cade watched Arielle in curiosity. It looked like she was in some sort of daze, her eyes staring off into the distance. He thought her bubbly personality was adorable. Her skin was beautiful and glowing. Her darkly lined eyes contrasted the sparkling light blue, really bringing out their color. He noticed that her eyelashes caught her long golden bangs when she blinked. She wore a tan suede jacket over a black top and he couldn't help but think she was incredibly sexy in a very earthy way. He thought that he could sit there and stare at her all night but he decided to break the silent pause before he made a fool of himself. "Alex what do you do in Boston?"

"Nothing that matches the passion you feel. Actually after listening to you I think I'm more depressed than before."

"Sorry man, didn't mean to bring you down."

"Don't apologize. What you said was very inspirational. It just confirmed that I need to find my passion. Right now I'm a Vice President in a computer game company. You know, I have it all; position, wealth. I'm healthy and fit. Yet I feel restless. I thought I was living my passion before my wife and daughter died five years ago. But something like that changes you in ways you just can't imagine."

"So what brought you here?" asked Arielle.

"I was surfing the net one day and I came across this tour. I booked it just like that. Without a second thought. I can't explain it other than to say I can't shake this feeling that I've been waiting for this moment my whole life."

Maya sat silently, listening to the conversation. Trying to avoid the overwhelming feelings of compassion she felt towards Alex.

When Maya didn't respond Arielle asked, "How did your wife and daughter die?"

Maya kicked her under the table and gave her a glaring look.

"Ouch! What did you do that for?" Arielle muttered under her breath.

"That's really personal. Maybe he doesn't want to talk about it." This was just getting too much for Maya. *I need to get away from him before I do something stupid.*

Alex rubbed his hand along his chin and frowned, her behavior kept confusing him. One minute she was warm and the next she was distant. "That's okay Maya. I don't mind. I feel really comfortable with you guys." He took a deep breath before continuing. "I was away on a business trip and my wife, Julia and our daughter Katie were on their way to pick me up at the airport when the driver of a dump truck lost control. He swerved into the side rail but not before Julia hit the back of the truck. Her car flipped over several times. It was a freak accident and it killed them instantly." Alex looked down and studied his hands to hide his wet eyes.

Maya's mind was racing. *That's the three of us who lost our families in bizarre circumstances. What are the odds? Why have these things happened to us?*

Arielle jumped up from the table and gave Alex a warm embrace. "Alex, I'm so sorry. I lost my parents and brother in a freak accident when I was a kid." She pulled away, looking into his eyes. "The only way to survive is to believe that there is method to God's madness and someday you'll love again."

"I know. That's why I'm here. To wake up from a long sleep."

Arielle watched the look of longing on his face as he gazed at Maya and vowed to promptly give her friend a good talking to later tonight. She couldn't understand why Maya kept her distance from Alex in such a revealing moment when they were obviously attracted to each other.

Chapter Twenty-four

Douglas and Vivienne had a crowd of people around them listening to their ideas and philosophies on life. Suddenly he could feel Maya close by. *But where was she?* He could almost reach out and touch her energy but as quickly as it had arrived, it disappeared.

He looked to Vivienne but she just shook her head indicating she hadn't seen her either.

Oh well, tomorrow's another day. It won't be long now.

*　　*　　*　　*

Dinner had ended but many people stood around mingling, not wanting their first night in Egypt to conclude.

Alex yawned and pushed back his chair to rise. "Well I think I'm ready to call it a night. Good night ladies. It's been a night I'll never forget. I'll see you in the morning." He bent lower to embrace Arielle and gave her a kiss on the cheek but when he turned to address Maya, she gave him a cool stare.

"Good night Alex," said Maya as she quickly extended her hand to shake his. Her face gave away none of the tumultuous emotions going on inside. She wasn't prepared for the feelings he stirred up. *This wasn't supposed to happen. I'm not here for romance.* She fought hard to ignore the electricity between them. Her heart went out to him because she knew only too well what it was like to live as he had over the past few years. But she couldn't trust herself to stay alert to her destiny if she gave in to those feelings. She was convinced the timing was all wrong.

"I'll walk out with you, I'm ready to hit the sack myself," said Cade excusing himself. "Thank you for letting us join you this evening. It was a pleasure. Good night Maya." He leaned in to kiss her cheek. "And you…I really enjoyed your company." His kiss lingered a little longer on Arielle's cheek. "Good night," he whispered while touching her shoulder.

His touch sent ripples of pleasure through her body. "Night Cade…See you in the morning," Arielle said hoarsely.

"What the hell was that?" demanded Arielle as soon as she collected herself and Cade and Alex were out of hearing distance.

"What are you talking about?" Maya responded distantly.

"That poor guy poured his soul out tonight and it's obvious that he's head over heels crazy about you. How can you be so cold towards him?"

"I wasn't cold." Maya brushed away a few crumbs from her slacks.

"No? Then what was that handshake about?"

"I was being polite. Not everyone can be as openly affectionate as you are Arielle."

"That's bull. You are attracted to him and you just won't admit it."

She had to hold back the tears so she could speak. "You are right, I am attracted to him. But I'm not ready to give my heart to anyone yet. It's too soon. So please just give me some space about this."

Arielle felt bad for coming down so hard on Maya. "Okay. I might not agree with you but I'll do as you ask—*for now.*"

"Come on let's get out of here and get some sleep."

As they were walking out Maya noticed a flock of people around a couple. "I wonder what's going on over there? It must be people wanting to talk with Pamela."

Arielle strained to see. When she finally got a glimpse she shook her head. "Nope. It's not Pamela. I don't know who it is. Can you see anything yet?"

"Yes. Oh now I see them." Maya was finally able to get a closer look. "They're kind of an odd looking couple."

"That's exactly what I thought. They don't look real," Arielle said excitedly. "They kind of remind me of the aliens in that old movie Cocoon."

"What do you mean?"

"Don't you remember how they were able to look human but when they were alone they took their faces off like masks."

"Arielle that's silly. But you know, they do look sort of plastic."

*   *   *   *

Cade walked alongside Alex through the expansive lobby area wondering how to broach the subject on his mind. "Alex, this may be over the top and you can tell me to mind my own business if you want."

"Go ahead Cade, what do you want to know?" He welcomed the question believing anything had to be better than brooding over Maya.

"I get the sense that it's more than grief that has broken you down."

Alex slowed his pace. "You are very astute. Yes it is more than that."

"Would you like to talk about it my friend?"

"It's guilt," he blurted out as though the words couldn't wait to roll off his tongue and it surprised him. He stood still and looked down at his feet.

"Ah guilt—the silent killer. Why do you feel guilt?"

"Because I told Julia not to bother to pick me up that day. I told her I could take a taxi home but she wouldn't listen. Her and Katie missed me and they wanted to greet me at the airport and catch up on the drive home."

"You've carried this around with you all these years?" Cade reached out and rested his hand on Alex's shoulder. "It's not your fault. You can't blame yourself for their death. You've got to let it go and forgive yourself."

"I keep telling myself that but obviously I haven't been able to do it yet. I'm not sure what it will take but I believe that this trip will help me."

"And so will Maya," Cade said boldly thinking of the way the two of them looked at each other all night.

Nodding, Alex looked away. "If she'll let me in…"

*   *   *   *

Frustrated by her inability to sleep Maya turned on her bedside lamp at midnight.

"Maya? What's wrong?" Arielle asked groggily.

"I'm sorry I didn't want to wake you. I couldn't sleep and I thought I'd read for a while."

"It's okay. Don't stay up too long we have to get up early." Arielle turned over and fell back into a deep sleep.

Maya remembered a new book she bought over the Internet that had arrived yesterday morning—was it yesterday morning? Who knew anymore? The mailman delivered the package just as she was walking out the door to leave for the airport. She had tossed the book into her suitcase and forgot all about it until this moment.

She quietly slipped out of bed to search her suitcase, which still sat on the luggage chair virtually untouched, except for the clothes she changed into for dinner.

Here it is! She broke open the cardboard box that contained the book and tossed it into the garbage can. Running her hand across the front cover of *Ancient Secrets* she wondered if she'd learn anything different.

Waiting for some water to heat up in the coffee maker she went over to the window, slid the drapes aside enough to gaze outside. It was so dark she could barely see the outline of the Nile River. When the water was ready she made herself a cup of tea, propped herself up in bed against the pillows and opened her new book.

She really didn't expect very much because what she had read so far had been pretty cryptic and repetitive, providing her with only limited insight on what had to be done.

Although one of the books, *The Key of Wisdom* spoke of following their heart and not letting fear consume them. She was reminded that it said love is the beginning and the end. *Guess I'm not doing so well in that department.* From what she could gather she would have to conquer her fears about loving again if she was to succeed in her mission and that's what frightened her. She didn't know if she could do it. It was easier to keep her feelings of pain and anguish buried than allow them to come to the surface and have to face them.

Maya, almost ready to give up on the new book, straightened her back and continued reading for a few more minutes.

"Arielle, wake up." She jumped out of bed and reached to shake her friend's shoulders. "Wake up."

"What! What time is it?"

"It's one thirty."

"God Maya, what do you want?"

"I need you to wake up. I found out something new about the Emerald Stone." She waited restlessly while Arielle rubbed her eyes and sat up.

"Can't it wait until morning?"

"If I wait to talk about it I won't get to sleep at all." Maya pleaded for her to be understanding. "Here let me make you a tea to help you wake up." Getting the tea she soothed her friend as she moaned and groaned in complaint.

"So what have you learned that couldn't wait until morning?"

"There have been people who have reportedly actually seen the Emerald Stone."

"What?" Arielle rubbed the sleep from her eyes and sat up straight in bed.

"I thought that would get your attention," Maya smiled deviously.

"Okay give." Arielle took the cup of tea offered.

"Apparently there have been a few people over the centuries associated with mystery schools who have seen and touched the Stone. It is an actual *crystal* emerald stone. I don't know why but I never thought that it was an actual crystal. I always assumed it was just a green colored stone. But it makes sense if Thoth was an Atlantean Priest and they supposedly used crystals all the time."

"Well that clears that part up. But I don't understand about other people being able to see it. I thought the prophecy states that only the Chosen Ones would be able to do this?"

"That's what I believed too and it confused me at first. But this book doesn't say when and who these people were. If you remember I told you that the chosen four would come together in various lifetimes in effort to reach their destiny. So theoretically those people who have seen the stone could have been us in different lifetimes."

"If that's true then we're screwed."

"Why do you say that?" Maya asked disappointed with Arielle's reaction.

"If we were so advanced and participated in mystery schools and didn't succeed in bringing mass enlightenment to the world then how, on God's Earth are we going to accomplish it this time? I mean no offense but neither one of us have any real training." Arielle sounded defeated.

The room went silent. Both women felt abandoned and heartbroken.

Arielle sat on the edge of her bed facing Maya and said, "Okay, let's think this through before giving up so quickly. Every message we have received is that Spirit wouldn't have guided us this far if we couldn't succeed. Right?"

"Yeah…"

"Well maybe we just need to force ourselves to believe in it and keep going."

"Mmmm…That whole theory that you're never asked to do something that you're not capable of doing? Now you're grasping at straws. I don't know Arielle. You brought up a good point, we don't know what the heck we're doing." Maya felt defeated.

"Maya, snap out of it. Come on. Think!"

Arielle too restless to sit paced the room trying to think of clues to help them. She started tapping her temples with her fingers in an unconscious attempt to bring some ideas to the surface. After several minutes her mouth moved slowly from side to side and her brows furrowed together.

"Are you getting something?" asked Maya.

"Well what if…"

"What if what?" asked Maya impatiently.

"Geez, don't get cranky."

"I'm sorry, this is just so frustrating. Go ahead."

"Well I was just thinking that if we have seen and touched the Stone before then maybe some of the energy would have rubbed off on us and over the centuries we have slowly passed that knowledge to others?"

"Go on," Maya said feeling an increase in energy.

"Maybe getting so close in previous lifetimes has been preparing us for taking the final leap. Maybe the *world* wasn't ready before now."

"Psychometry and osmosis! That's it! You're brilliant!" Maya shot up, pulled Arielle to her feet, hugged and kissed her cheek.

"I am?" Arielle said with delight.

"Yes! It makes sense. This book also says that the Stone contains an all-encompassing force. The sum of all knowledge. If that's true then whoever has touched the crystalline stone could receive its energy and a transfer of knowledge could hypothetically take place. It also states that those people who touched them went on to become healers. If we *are* them, then the knowledge and energy already exists within us through osmosis.

"Osmosis? What are you a physicist?"

"Ha ha funny girl."

"What does it mean?"

"It has to do with liquid or energy flowing between one membrane to another until both sides have the same strength."

"Oh. That's a little too left brain for me. I know I came up with the idea but even *if* we do have the knowledge within us, we still haven't reached a level of mastery that we did in the past. How will we be capable enough to see this through in such a short period of time?"

"You certainly know how to take the wind out of someone." Both women plopped back down on their beds.

Maya was still looking for answers on her third cup of tea. "Are you ready to give up and go home?"

Stumbling over her words Arielle replied, "No, I never said that, but…"

"No. Stop. Look, we obviously have some talent. Your visions brought you here didn't they?" Not waiting for a response Maya kept going. "Okay maybe we're not masters yet. And no we haven't joined any secret mystery schools to learn the how to's of life and alchemy but we've been entrusted with an assignment and we're going to see it through. We can't let our minds rule this one."

"Wow you said that like you believed it," answered Arielle.

Maya's shoulders slouched. "I'm as afraid as you are but I couldn't live with myself if I give up so soon. I don't know what's in store for us and there's probably a really good chance we'll fail miserably…"

Arielle joined Maya on her bed, putting her arm around Maya's shoulders. "Hey, forget what I said. We're in this together and we'll figure it out. We better get some sleep."

Maya nodded and they climbed into their beds.

Arielle was about to turn out the light but she stopped. "You know, I just thought of something that happened earlier at dinner. It was really bizarre but maybe it has something to do with all this."

"Tell me."

Arielle described her experience where she felt her consciousness existing as water flowing over the earth while she was talking with Cade. "I don't know why exactly but I felt certain this happened because I was connecting with him. It left me with an indescribable feeling of strength and serenity."

"Do you think he's one of us?" Maya was already deducing that if Cade was part of this then it was quite likely Alex was too. They all connected almost instantly and it made sense. The thought sent ripples of fear through her veins and her heart pounded.

"Yes I do. He's just so earthy. Did you hear the way he talks about being outdoors and his love for the countryside?"

"Uh-huh," seeing the perfect opportunity to express her observations Maya asked, "You're falling for him aren't you?"

"Pardon the cliché but yes, hook, line and sinker. I've never felt this way before," she sighed with content.

"Stars and bells?"

"The whole works. I know this is going to sound like I'm in high school but do you think he's interested in me?"

"Are you kidding? He looked like he wanted to pull you onto his lap and sing a song at dinner tonight."

"What about Alex?"

"What about him?" Tensing up because she really didn't want to think about Alex any more than she had to.

"Do you think he's the fourth?"

Maya sighed in resignation. "My guess is yes. When he told us his wife and daughter were killed in a freak accident I couldn't overlook the fact the three of us have all lost our families and in the most unexplainable ways."

"Oh my gosh! It didn't even cross my mind but you're right it's too strange to be a coincidence."

"What I don't understand is why would the universe conspire to rip our families apart in such traumatic ways. It's so…"

"Cruel," offered Arielle. She wondered about Cade and hoped that he hadn't suffered the same anguish that they had. She made a mental note to find out.

"Yes. It just doesn't seem right."

"How are we going to find out if and what they know about any of this?"

"I'm not sure yet but I suspect that opportunities will present themselves. We better get some sleep, wake up call is six thirty in the morning." Maya reached over and turned off the light.

"Good night Maya."

Chapter Twenty-five

Arielle stood looking out the window in their room on the twenty-seventh floor. Dressed in cotton khaki pants, a white shirt, and walking shoes, she was prepared for the tours first day of activities. Her long hair was loosely braided and the only jewelry she wore was large gold hoop earrings.

She supposed she was grateful they were missing the scorching heat of the summer, but she thought it might have been interesting to experience it.

It was seven fifteen in the morning and she was waiting for Maya to finish dressing. "Don't take this the wrong way but I have to say you have a great body. You must work out."

Maya was pleased that her efforts of exercising regularly in the past few months were starting to show. "Thanks. Yes I run and do weights. I'm going to miss working out while we're here. It doesn't look like our schedule allows for much time to ourselves," pausing to give Arielle a once over she said, "You have a great body too."

"Oh please. I'm too thin. My arms and legs are like sticks. You fill your clothes out in all the right places."

"If we find some time I can always put together a plan for you to put a little meat on your bones if you're interested," Maya said while running a brush through her hair.

"I'm basically kind of lazy but who knows maybe I can be convinced to give it a try."

Maya pulled on a pair of black cotton pants and a short-sleeved white shirt. Even though it was December the sun was still strong during the day here and it was not uncommon for temperatures to reach the high sixties.

Like most other countries around the world the weather patterns had changed over the past few years with global warming. Plant and wildlife were being negatively affected, many growing extinct, and causing all kinds of changes in the environment.

Maya joined Arielle at the window. There was a thick morning haze covering the city of Cairo preventing them from seeing too far into the distance. All that was in sight were a few buildings and the tops of some trees; even the Nile River was covered in a fog.

"Come on let's go, I'm ready," said Maya turning to grab the black wind jacket she tossed on the bed earlier.

The elevator door opened and standing inside was Alex. His eyes twinkled and he gave them a bashful grin. "Well fancy meeting you ladies here."

"Alex, what a treat," offered Arielle in compensation for Maya's modest nod of her head. "How are you today? Did you sleep well?"

"Like a log. I was wiped. What about you two?"

Winking at Maya trying to loosen her up she said, "We weren't quite so lucky. We ended up talking until the wee hours." The elevator stopped again a few floors down and Arielle squealed in delight when she saw Cade.

He shook his head and laughed when he saw who was in the elevator. "Well isn't this a coincidence. Good morning all." He moved in beside Arielle, which seemed to fill him up with an invigorated feeling. He noticed her freshly washed face sprinkled with freckles across the bridge of her nose. God he enjoyed the way her bangs hung straight and low over her sultry blue eyes. He didn't know how she could be so cute and sexy at the same time.

"Morning Cade," said Maya trying to ignore the increase in her heart rate as she stood next to Alex. She could feel the heat from his body and the rhythm of his breathing. It made her nervous.

"We all seem to be gravitating towards each other," said Alex raising his eyebrows and watching Maya, hoping for an encouraging sign but he was disappointed with her coolness again this morning.

"Yes, don't we though," responded Cade cheerfully.

When they reached the lobby they decided to go out onto the terrace to see the Nile River before going back to the Andalus restaurant for breakfast.

The air was a little cool but the sun was rising and the day promised to heat up quickly.

Maya breathed in the view and lingered for a while, feeling its magic.

Alex walked up beside her and noticed the dreamy look in her eyes. *It doesn't matter how she wears her hair she always looks charming to me.* It was swept up today with a few wisps framing her face. He contemplated her long neck and how he'd like to kiss it. "It's hard to believe we're here isn't it?"

"Yes it is," responded Maya softly. "Can't you just feel the lives the Nile has nurtured?"

Alex picked up on the softening of her mood since the coldness in the elevator and felt relieved. "Even though all we can see right now are buildings that line the river banks, it *is* fascinating to think of the thousands of years of history it has seen. Joy, tragedy, life, and death. The flow of everlasting life."

Maya angled her head to get a better view of Alex. "You practically took the words right of my mouth." She observed that he was wearing black again. *It makes him look very exotic and a deep thinker. Whoa…stop day dreaming girl and get a hold of yourself.*

It was time she started to find out about him and what he knows but at this rate she didn't know how she was going to do that and keep her heart tucked safely away. "This might sound crazy but I believe that I was destined to come here and experience this. To taste it, to listen to it and to feel it." *Geez, what am I getting myself into?*

"I know what you mean. I've read about the pyramids and have always been fascinated by them. I haven't done anything impulsive in a long time but I went and booked this trip just like that." Snapping his fingers to demonstrate.

"It makes life back home seem very small doesn't it?" commented Maya.

"I couldn't have said it better myself."

"What *is it* you're looking for Alex?"

He wanted to scoop her up into his arms when she looked up into his face but he remained steady. "I guess I'm trying to understand my purpose in this life."

"This life? Does that mean you believe in reincarnation?" She had to fight an urge to reach out and touch his hands that rested on the railing.

"Honestly?" He thought her slight nod was very endearing. He gazed into her eyes and felt her depth, knowing that she too had experienced her share of pain. "Yes. I've been secretly reading new age and spiritual type books for a couple of years now. My family and friends would think I'm nuts so I keep it to myself."

Maya thought of Brian and nodded in understanding. "I know what you mean."

"I've just always had a feeling there was something bigger than running my business that I need to do but…"

"Everyone please join us in the restaurant, we will be giving instructions for the tour in just a few minutes," shouted a man dressed in safari type clothing.

"I guess we better get moving," said Alex. He lightly touched the small of her back and felt a fiery heat shoot into his hand and up the length of his arm. It's effect left him disoriented for a few moments.

The interruption of their conversation disappointed Maya, she hoped she would learn something that would confirm her suspicions about him. She reminded herself to have patience while they regrouped with the other two.

Maya, Arielle, Cade and Alex hustled into the restaurant and discovered that a buffet breakfast was set up and most people were already seated and enjoying their meal.

"I see an empty table over in the corner, if we hurry and grab our food we might still be able to sit together," suggested Cade.

Just as they sat down their attention turned to the man tapping on the microphone while he began his introduction.

"Ladies and gentlemen may I have your attention please. Welcome to Egypt. My name is Azizi and I'll be one of your tour guides on this trip."

Two other gentlemen came forward as Azizi motioned for them to join him. "This is Fadil and this is Kaphiri, they are also tour guides. Because of the size of this group we will split it into three. Fadil will take the group in this area." He was pointing to the left side of the restaurant. "Kaphiri will take the group in this centre section," he said moving and pointing to the middle of the room. "And I will take this area." Pointing in Alex, Maya, Cade and Arielle's direction.

Holding up a red sign he continued, "My group will be known as the red bus, Fadil will be the blue bus, and Kaphiri will be the green bus. We will hold these signs up whenever we make stops and there will be one on the windows of the bus so you can recognize which one you belong to. Does everyone understand?"

He waited for people while they nodded in comprehension.

"Good. Please remember your color."

Maya, Arielle, Alex and Cade all looked at each with a smile, recognizing that they would all be traveling together on the same tour bus.

"Before we leave for the museum I'll give you a bit of background on the River Nile. There is no better way to trace the evolution of Egyptian history than to follow the Nile. It has been Egypt's lifeline for thousands of years. It fertilizes the land beside it by depositing silt after the floods, which are now controlled by the High Dam at Aswan. Pharaohs, nobles and mortals have all built monuments and tombs to immortalize themselves along the river.

"Since time began here Egyptians have associated the River Nile with life, fertility and development. They care about it and nurture it. After all, it has been their source of prosperity and was the main reason in building the great civilizations beside it. Egyptians believe very much in reincarnation and recognize that the River Nile has been witness to thousands of love stories, giving them hope and promise of happiness."

Maya observed Azizi. Noticing he was about five ten and looked like he was in very good shape. She also noticed he took great care with his appearance. He wore khaki pants, a matching vest with many pockets and a white shirt. His hair was perfectly trimmed, short and black His smile was attractive and engaging. She considered his impeccable speech and recognized that he was a well-educated individual.

"Many songs have been dedicated to the River Nile and in ancient times Egyptians made sacrifices adding to its legends. Flowing for six thousand six hundred and ninety kilometers, the River Nile is considered the longest river in the world. It passes through nine countries. Tanzania, Kenya, Zaire, Burundi, Rwanda, Ethiopia, Uganda, the Sudan and Egypt. The River Nile has areas of waterfalls and deep drops making the trek very dangerous in some places.

"Egyptians believe that if you have lived one life near the River Nile you will surely return.

"We will leave the hotel in twenty minutes for our first journey of the day so please look for your tour guide with the correct color sign. I hope you enjoy your day."

"Well that was entertaining. He's obviously well educated," said Alex.

Looking at Alex, Maya couldn't help but smile at the way he kept pulling thoughts right out of her head.

They ate their breakfast quickly, gulping down the strong aromatic coffee in haste so they wouldn't be late for the start of the day's tour.

Cade and Arielle, who were having their own private conversation, got up at the same time. Arielle laughed and said, "I guess we should get ready to leave. I need to make a trip to the ladies room first. Maya what about you?"

"Sure I'll join you."

"We'll wait for you ladies in the lobby by the front door. Might as well grab seats together on the bus," suggested Cade.

Maya and Arielle glanced sideways at each other and smiled. "Sounds good to me," added Arielle.

"Did you learn anything about Cade that provides us with any clues?"

"Um, well I…Not exactly. We were just kind of enjoying each other's company."

"Arielle, how are we going to find anything out if you just keep flirting with him?"

"Geez, what's got you up in knots?"

Alex, that's what.

* * * *

"Her energy has increased from yesterday. She is close by. Do you feel it Kanïka?"

"Yes Melïon. She is getting stronger already." Pausing to take her husband's hand in hers she added, "My love, please remember we need to be careful using our Atlantean names in public. We do not want to trigger memories from the past that might cause any of them to remember who we are." She knew she was risking admonishment later by criticizing him but it was vital they be on guard every minute. *Perhaps he will let it go this time.*

"Yes, yes you are right my love. It is imperative that our plans follow the proper sequence." He did not like to be reproached by Vivienne but she was right. *Damn, I must be more careful.*

"She is being carefully protected. It is extraordinary that we have not seen her yet. Do you think she has been trained in cloaking?"

"I hardly think she has received that kind of training." Irritated that he had not been able to locate her tellurian body he did not appreciate Vivienne's reference to his failure. "Not to worry, my love, she will soon seek me out. I guarantee it."

Vivienne recognized an opportunity to please him to make up for pointing out his oversight. "Yes, she will come to you and our destiny will be guaranteed." She slipped her hand in his. "Come my love, it is time to board the bus before the crowd arrives. Which tour guide did you make arrangements with?"

"I spoke with Azizi, he seemed the most cultured and enlightened. The others, well they were ordinary. Here it is, the bus with the red sign."

"What cover did you give him?"

"I told him I am an Ambassador of the Cultured Arts here to research their history first hand. That will explain our aristocratic appearance sufficiently. I also indicated that I am highly psychic and would like to confer with him at the different sites."

"Good. That will be very believable. It will also put you in the limelight making you appear approachable and kind."

Wherever they traveled they made sure to be at the head of the line to guarantee they had first choice and selected the most desirable seats. Douglas insisted they always got the best of everything. *It's just too bad we have to resort to traveling on this bus like common people. Oh well, on with the charade, it's for a good cause.*

They sat regally together, appearing to be lost in conversation with each other but they were actually watching everyone board with a keen eye.

A rather large man boarded the bus and stopped beside Douglas, blocking his view of anyone else boarding. "Excuse me, do you know if these seats are taken?" The man pointed to the seats behind Douglas and Vivienne.

Feeling Maya's energy very fleetingly, Douglas grew angry with the stranger. *Get out of my way you fat pig! I can't see! Damn it!* "Not that I'm aware of," disguising his irritation he answered good-heartedly to the man who stood hovering in his way. "Vivienne did you see her? She's on this bus! I couldn't see, that idiot was blocking my view."

"No I couldn't see anything either. Don't worry darling, if she's here it will be much easier to have contact with her." *He's wound up too tight. I'm going to have to make sure to keep a very close watch.* She touched his hand allowing for a transfer of calming awareness to descend over him.

"Yes, this is very fortunate indeed. Did I tell you how beautiful you look today, my love?"

"Not yet but thank you for noticing." *Good he's settling down but he will need my skills more than usual now that we're getting closer.*

"That sweater looks lovely on you and your matching blue hat is quite charming. Are they new?"

"Yes I found them in a darling boutique in Washington the last time we were there."

"Good for you. I like it when you buy new things—you deserve them." It always made him feel powerful to have a beautiful wife by his side. But he knew better than to believe the persona of the housewife she often portrayed in public.

He marveled at the way she handled most of the monetary decisions in their household and business transactions. She worked closely with the lawyers and accountants to keep their money flowing in from their investments. It was just too logical and left-brained for him to be concerned with. He needed to be free to concentrate on the missions that were assigned to him by the clandestine sector of the government in return for keeping his knowledge of the Boiling Lake concealed and arranging all the circumstances necessary to ensure his plan for the new world began triumphantly.

He smiled smugly knowing there was no further news of the SEC investigation and his mole was now in place.

Luck is on our side. Soon I will be able to free myself from that tedious obligation and have retribution.

* * * *

"What about here?" asked Maya as she led the way down the aisle on the red bus.

"Why don't you go down farther. I see four seats available. That way Cade and Alex can sit across from us on the aisle."

"Do you want the window or aisle?"

"I'll take the aisle so you can have the window Maya. I know how much you like it. Anyway that way I can stretch my legs out."

Cade followed Arielle's lead and took the aisle seat, happy to be able to sit close to her.

Maya was equally relieved that she did not have to sit next to Alex. He on the other hand didn't feel the same.

Once they were settled in, the ladies on the left side and the men on the right, Maya leaned close to Arielle and asked, "Did you see that odd looking couple we saw last night after dinner at the front of the bus?"

"Yeah. Maybe we'll get the chance to get the scoop on them."

"What couple are you talking about?" asked Cade overhearing their conversation.

"We saw this couple last night talking to a crowd of people after dinner. They're kind of strange looking."

"What do you mean strange looking?"

"Oh Arielle here said they reminded her of the aliens in the movie Cocoon." Maya made an exaggerated motion of taking her face off and giggled.

"Oh sure laugh at me now but don't come running to me when they want to whisk you off somewhere," replied Arielle jokingly.

Chapter Twenty-six

Maya was surprised to discover that the city of Cairo was much larger than she anticipated. Azizi said that the metropolitan area consisted of 15.2 million people. The city was a mixture of old and new structures but it retained its very Old World atmosphere.

It was not as strict with women's dress as Maya was led to believe. Many women wore long dresses or pants and even though their heads were covered in pretty scarves or capes, for the most part their faces were not covered.

They drove by street cafes where men gathered for their morning coffees or smoke from what Maya learned later were called water pipes.

Most of the buildings, whether store, office or home dwellings were constructed with dull grayish stones. Occasionally there were doors or entrances painted in bright shades to add splashes of color in the monotone city. Many of the apartment dwellings were left unfinished. The windows were glassless, protected only by cloth from the wind, which carried the desert sand in the air as it traveled. Some of the windows and doors had nothing at all to protect the people or furnishings from the occasional harsh weather conditions.

Men with donkeys and carts sold their wares in the streets, often blocking traffic. The stores were an open-air concept with products arranged on tables encouraging people to buy.

"We are now in Tahrir Square where the Egyptian Museum is located. It is going to be very busy so please make sure to stick together as a group and follow the red sign I will carry above my head," said Azizi into the microphone. "If you get lost please come back to the red bus. We will be departing at eleven thirty for lunch at the Nile Pharaoh floating restaurant. You must be back at the bus by eleven thirty."

"Busy is putting it mildly. Look at all those people," Alex exclaimed as they got off the bus.

The four of them stuck together not wanting to get separated and lost among the hundreds of people.

Azizi led the way with the red sign held above his head as promised. "Follow me! This way please! Follow the red sign!" he shouted repeatedly.

They made their way towards the main building. There were stone walkways around the lot with small versions of monoliths and other stone carvings engraved with hieroglyphs. Trees provided shade in some areas for any overheated tourists to stop and cool off.

The museum building was constructed of a vibrant pink colored stone, which was oddly different to most others. The entrance was white in contrast and extended outward from the rest of the exterior. It had a rounded archway surrounded by two columns and statues of a Goddess. Azizi described the building as being a neoclassical structure.

As they entered the museum Azizi escorted everyone to an area to the right of the entrance. "This museum houses nearly one hundred thousand exhibits with the most comprehensive collection of Pharaonic art in the world. The highlight of the collection here is considered to be the tomb artifacts of the Pharaoh Tutankhamen, otherwise known as King Tut. Tutankhamen's tomb was discovered in the Valley of the Kings in 1923."

Maya noticed the *odd* couple standing close to Azizi. They were both dressed in high quality but casual clothing. The woman was wearing black slacks with a blue sweater set and blue hat. Her jewelry consisted of a gold diamond bracelet, a gold necklace, diamond stud earrings and a huge diamond wedding ring. *She obviously likes gold and they are definitely upper class.*

The woman's hair looked like it was a chestnut color. Perhaps a blunt cut, as it hung straight across the back of her neck. Maya guessed her to be around thirty-five to forty and she appreciated the fact that this woman obviously worked out—she looked firm and toned.

The man seemed to be very caring and considerate, constantly watching out for her, holding her hand and guiding her to move by the elbow every time someone needed to pass. One of the first things she noticed was his gray-blue eyes that glittered with the light.

He was wearing black slacks with a clingy brown silk shirt and a black jacket. He wore some type of signet ring on his left ring finger. *That's odd it doesn't look like a wedding band.* Even though Maya estimated him to be in his early fifties his hair was dark brown with no signs of gray. She couldn't tell if he colored it or not but it looked pretty natural. Maya admired his well-muscled shoulders and chest, emphasized by his snug shirt and thought even though he was rather ordinary looking there was something pretty damn sexy about him. She couldn't think of very many men who took such good care of themselves and had pride in their appearance, especially at his age. Self-conscious of being caught staring she slipped back out of sight as he turned his head to look in her direction.

"Look across the group on the right of Azizi. That's the couple Maya and I were talking about," Arielle whispered to Cade. "Aren't they kind of strange looking?"

"I don't know…Yeah kind of…There *is* something unusual about them."

* * * *

It was turning out to be a frustrating excursion. There were so many people it was hard to hear Azizi over all the other tours taking place at the same time. Pushed up and down the narrow aisles, trying to take in names and dates, Maya was growing weary.

The ground and upper floors contained individual rooms in addition to the aisles. Every room was so jammed packed with people she found it stifling. When she got to an opening at the end of the aisle she had an opportunity to stand back for a few minutes to breathe. Looking into a glass case was a statue of Thoth with a plaque that read:

> Thoth, the God of Hermopolis, he was the God of writing and science. Man with ibis head surmounted by a lunar disk, baboon.

*Hmmm, no mention of the Emerald Stone…*She was deep in thought when a voice behind her said softly, "Do you have a special interest in Thoth?"

Startled, she hesitated for a moment when she was approached by the couple she watched earlier. "Oh, I didn't hear you come up behind me. No, not particularly. I'm getting restless being herded through all these exhibits on a rigid schedule."

"Yes it is somewhat wearisome. Well try to enjoy the rest of your day," he said and she watched them walked away.

She was left to ponder the magical softness of his voice.

"There you are!" exclaimed Arielle. "I thought I lost you. One minute you were beside me the next you were gone. Did I see the Cocoon people stop to talk with you?"

"Hmmm?"

"Maya! Are you all right."

"Yes, I'm fine. I just needed some air. It's so crowded I felt claustrophobic. I saw this open space and took advantage of it. Then I noticed that I happened to stop in front of this statue of Thoth."

Arielle wanted to get to the goods. "What did they say to you?"

"He asked me if I had a special interest in Thoth. That's all."

"What did you tell him?"

"I said no, I was just frustrated with the pace of the tour and stopped for a break."

Arielle pressed for more. "What do they seem like?"

"She didn't say anything but he seemed nice enough. Very gentlemanly and proper."

"I wonder why he asked you about Thoth?"

"I don't know it did seem kind of odd. He was probably just being polite." *It did feel weird though. Like I was in a haze.*

"Come on we better get back with the group. I think the tour is just about over."

"Thank goodness. There are too many people here to enjoy it."

* * * *

"She lied about her interest in Thoth. We'll have to take it slow and give her some space," Douglas said to Vivienne as they walked away. *But time is running out…*

She nodded in agreement but sensed that he was frustrated. "I think I saw her with another woman and two men. The universe is working quickly if it has already brought them all together."

"Yes, we'll have to stay close and monitor the situation." He felt a sting of jealousy. *I can't let him get to her before I have a chance to draw her into our circle.*

*   *   *   *

The Nile Pharaoh floating restaurant reminded Maya of a river showboat. It had two levels. The lower river level had the main dining area, which was completely surrounded by windows draped with white sheer curtains scooped to the sides. The upper level had both an indoor seating area and an outdoor deck with groupings of tables and chairs placed at every other window. The colors were rich with gold, red and turquoise. Scenes of Gods and Pharaohs were painted on the walls.

Attached to the dock spanning the length of the boat was the oddest thing Maya had seen so far on the trip. Metal planks, painted in turquoise with decks holding tiny houses richly decorated in the same design as the boat. Ducks were standing on the decks outside the houses, eating enthusiastically from bowls of food. She wanted to say something to Arielle but noticed she was in the middle of a conversation with Cade.

"Cade look at this statue, isn't it bizarre?" Arielle touched his arm gently to get his attention. "It looks like a miniature version of the Sphinx but its head is like an alien!" Arielle exclaimed excitedly.

"Very odd. It looks like it's lying on top of a tomb." The box was painted in gold with black trim and top. As they stopped briefly to look Cade brushed his hand against hers. "I wished I could read hieroglyphics, I wonder what this cartouche says?"

Maya watched the closeness that was developing between Arielle and Cade as they leaned against the railing with envy. She wished she could let go of whatever was holding her back from feeling what ached to be released but she couldn't.

"They look good together," said Alex.

His deep voice startled her and her stomach tightened. "Yes, they do."

"Cade is quite taken with her. This morning on the bus ride he told me she's been in a recurring vision he started having a few months back about Egypt. He said when he saw her at the hotel he knew that it was their destiny to meet." Alex was trying to gage Maya's reaction. He probably shouldn't have said anything, but he couldn't resist. The universe seemed to be bringing the four of them together and he wanted to confirm it was connected to the reason he was there.

"Really? That's interesting. Arielle was having a recurring vision which led her here too but she was not able to actually see any faces." Maya said and waved to Arielle. "Come on they're waiting for us to go in."

"Listen, do me a favor and don't say anything to Arielle about this yet. I don't know if Cade would appreciate my talking about it. I probably shouldn't have said anything."

Maya didn't like agreeing to his request but there was no time for discussion right now. "Okay." Besides, she was holding back about her own visions for the moment and as much as she would like to jump right in to the real reasons they were all there she wanted more confirmation first. She didn't know whether to thank Brian or curse him for causing her to be guarded.

"Wow! The inside looks just as vibrant and colorful as the outside," said Arielle lightheartedly.

"I'd say even more." Maya was still annoyed with Alex for asking her to keep their conversation to themselves but she also found the new information picked her spirits up, especially after the disappointing trip to the museum. *I have to find a way to encourage Arielle and Cade to share their visions to see if they are similar, but how and maybe just as importantly, when?*

Sitting at a table for four on the left side of the boat, Maya observed the odd couple as they chose to sit at a table for six nearby. He seated himself facing Maya and she looked quickly away when he made eye contact with her.

Lunch consisted of fig and lemon chicken or fried perch, both served with a wild rice pilaf. Arielle ordered the fish while the others decided on the chicken. They chatted with each other pleasantly throughout their meal, keeping the conversation light until Arielle decided it was time to find out some more about Cade.

"Cade, in our conversation last night I got the impression that you are quite happy back home in Sedona. What prompted you to take this trip?" asked Arielle.

Her question captured Maya's attention. *That a girl!*

"Spending as much time outdoors as I do you get to know Earth. You feel when she's at peace and when she's in turmoil. When the unhealthy energy builds up she needs to rid herself of the toxic energy. I believe the turmoil on our planet is building to devastating proportions and that's why we're seeing so many freakish natural disasters."

Maya remembered her conversation with Emma and saw the connection. "You mean things like the horrendous earthquakes, hurricanes and fires that have been growing in number?"

"Yes…But the hurricanes are growing even bigger and even more will turn into tsunamis. Unstoppable fires are destroying our forests. Earth is purging itself of the contamination we are dumping into it both physically and emotionally."

"Don't you think that's a rather oppressive view?" asked Alex.

"You may think it's oppressive Alex but it's realistic. I feel the beat of Earth's heart and she is suffering. She will demand drastic changes or the quality of our lives will be greatly affected."

Their conversation was interrupted for a few minutes while the waiter refilled their glasses of water.

"Let's get back to why you came to Egypt," said Arielle reminding Cade where he left off. His passion for his beliefs stirred her heart and she couldn't help but enjoy the quirky way his right eyebrow raised higher when he grew animated, it emphasized his slightly off center smile.

"A few months ago I started having visions about the pyramids." He stopped to evaluate their reactions and when he realized there wasn't any judgment he continued. "They kept increasing in frequency until I couldn't function properly. I started having trouble sleeping and I felt depressed. I stopped enjoying the simple things. Anyway I thought that maybe I better just come here and see if I could figure it out. So here I am."

"I'd almost have thought you prompted Arielle to ask that question," Alex whispered to Maya flirtatiously.

* * * *

I know who you are. I know where you are. Come to me, my love. I have the answers you seek. Only I can provide you with what you need. Reading her energy fields, studying her thought patterns, Douglas communicated these thoughts to Maya telepathically.

Maya, what a lovely name for a lovely creature of the eternal burning flame. Your Fire burns bright my love. Brighter than I imagined. You are special indeed and hold the gift of life and I can show you the way.

He had to contain the jealousy he felt observing the man beside her, it was obvious that he was smitten with her and he needed to divert her attention. *He can't offer you what I can, little one. He'll never be able to help you traverse the galaxy and escape from this mundane world whenever you choose.*

* * * *

"Who knows, maybe she read my mind," Maya replied slightly annoyed with the speculation that she betrayed her promise. Feeling a sense of discomfort, she couldn't identify exactly what was bothering her. She assumed it was Alex's comment. Distracted from her thoughts, she angled her head slightly to the right and found herself looking straight into the eyes of the man who had spoken to her at the museum.

She didn't look away. She felt him gaze into the depths of her soul. Feeling unexpectedly aroused she flushed, and still he held her gaze. She felt magnetized, as though she couldn't look away. Everything around her began to fade. Her friend's voices drifted into the distance. It felt as though he was speaking to her.

We have met before. I feel that in the way you look at me. But why now? Why was your voice like silk brushing against my skin? Who are you? And why does it feel like you have the answers I seek?

"Excuse me miss, are you finished your meal?" asked the soft-spoken waiter.

When Maya didn't respond Alex followed the direction of her eyes. He was overcome with jealousy with the way they were looking at each other. *What is she doing? He's married for God's sake!* Anger consumed him but he remained silent. Looking away in an effort to stay calm, his emotions escaped in his breath with such force it sent Maya's water glass crashing to the floor. *Damn it! I haven't lost control in a long time.*

The sound of her glass shattering on the floor knocked Maya out of her trance. "What happened? Oh gosh, I'm sorry, did I do that?" she asked the waiter. Disoriented, her world seemed to shake around her. She felt confused. She looked at the gentleman again but he was engaged in conversation with the people at his table. *Did I just imagine that or did it really happen?*

"Please do not worry, I'll clean that up. Are you finished with your meal?"

"Oh yes. Thank you." Glancing around nervously she noticed that people were staring at her. She watched the waiter take her dish away and clean up the broken glass. Her temporary madness caused her to feel awkward and embarrassed. *What came over me? Where did I go? It seemed as though he was inside my head yet when I looked he appeared to be in deep conversation with others. I must be losing my mind.*

Alex noticed that people were starting to leave the restaurant. "Looks like it's time to go," he said curtly. He reminded himself that he didn't own Maya. She could do whatever she wanted. But it didn't help to dispel his grudging feelings towards the strange man.

Chapter Twenty-seven

"Are you okay?" Maya asked Alex as they walked together behind Arielle and Cade. He had been silent since they left the floating boat restaurant and throughout the bus ride on their way to their next stop. Now they strolled together with the tour group as everyone walked in pairs along the walkway to the Mohamed Ali Mosque.

"I'm fine, why do you ask?" he replied distantly. He watched the easiness developing between Arielle and Cade and secretly wished that it could be that simple between him and Maya. Confusion ate away at him, wondering why she was making this so difficult.

"You seem angry."

Turning towards her he said, "Can I be honest with you?" *Oh God, what am I doing?*

His wife used to complain all the time that he didn't open up to her and talk about his feelings. His natural tendency was to keep things to himself to keep the peace. He'd learned to bury things so deeply that often times he wasn't even aware that something was bothering him. But it would come out in unpleasant ways and it was usually Julie who was the recipient of his cutting remarks.

As much as he idolized their marriage for the year following her death he finally came to realize it had its flaws and perhaps they weren't as happy as he wanted to believe when they were together. He was often distant and kept busy working. He believed he was that way to build a better life for them but now he was able to see he wasn't really living and work was a distraction from noticing.

During his time of self-exploration since her passing he made a commitment to himself that in his next relationship he would do his best to talk openly about his feelings, even if it meant causing a disagreement. He didn't want to hide behind excuses any more.

"Uh…sure," Maya said uneasily.

Hesitating he was filled with second thoughts and abandoned his commitment, for the time being. "Nothing. Never mind," he said. How could he tell her he thought she was the most beautiful woman he'd ever seen and he was filled with envy by the way she looked at that other man. It was more difficult to talk freely than he bargained for but he was afraid he would push her away and lose any chance he had in developing a relationship.

Everyone's pace slowed as they approached the Mohamed Ali Mosque. It was a huge structure with white domed ceilings of varying heights and lots of windows.

Azizi waited for his group to gather around him. "Everyone must take their shoes off and leave them to the side," he shouted for everyone to hear. "There are no chairs or benches but you may sit on the floor to pray."

Chanting could be heard through loud speakers across the city, "Allah Agbad," repeated over and over.

Azizi continued, "The call to prayer is issued across the city fives times each day. No matter where people are you will see them stop what they are doing, kneel down and pray to Allah. Please walk quietly as you enter and partake in prayer as you would like."

Inside a huge chandelier donated by King Mohamed Ali in the 1800's provided a luminescent glow to the immense prayer area.

One by one they took their shoes off and ventured off into the Mosque. Maya stumbled while trying to slip off her shoes and Alex reached out quickly to brace her lower back with his hand. "Don't worry, I've got you." He felt an intense heat shoot out where his hand touched her. It dazed him. His heart softened and his moodiness started to melt.

His touch on her Fire mark sent waves of emotion through her whole body. She could not deny the electricity as much as she wanted to. She looked into his eyes and whispered a weak, "Thank you." It was the best she could offer. *I feel like an idiot for melting under that strange man's gaze. Here I've been trying to keep Alex, who I feel something earth shattering for at a distance and then I go and turn into putty for a married man. I don't know what came over me.*

Cade walked quietly up behind Alex after removing his shoes and said quietly, "Nice save. I saw the way she looked at you. You're in."

"Shhh, not so loud. I don't know. Every time I think I'm making progress with Maya she shuts me out."

"She'll come around, just give her time."

"What are you guys whispering about?" asked Arielle.

"Nothing. Just guy stuff," responded Cade in a low voice. He looked at Alex and gave him a reassuring nod.

They wandered around the mosque together, finding a place to sit in a circle and silently offer their prayers to the universe.

Maya thought about how much her life had changed in such a short period of time and was filled with such a sense of awe. Even in just the last few days, she felt like she was transforming before her very own eyes as her confidence grew.

After several minutes white rays of energy began to spark out from each of their heart centers—they spiked and waned. The group of four were as yet unaware of this energy.

The rays of energy strengthened in intensity, rising upwards to meet at an apex. Then flowing down to envelop the four, forming a circular shield around them. While they meditated the shield strengthened and expanded.

Each one began to sense a force greater than themselves. They opened their eyes at the same time and witnessed the field of energy surrounding them. In the moment each one made eye contact they mysteriously received a message telepathically.

Azizi came around to gather everyone to leave. Having received training in the ancient mysteries he too saw the white shield guarding them. "It is time for us to leave now," he said not wanting to interrupt them but they had a schedule to keep. He felt relief along with fear, for he knew this meant the time had come for the final test for humanity.

Reluctantly they rose slowly, looked into each other's eyes in wonder and amazement then proceeded to follow Azizi who guided them to the outside courtyard where he allocated everyone ten minutes to ponder their experience.

"I felt like we were bound together throughout time and space," announced Arielle, her eyes still wide in astonishment.

"Eternity," responded Cade and each one nodded knowingly not wanting to break the spell with words.

"It was like we were just embraced and blessed by the universe," added Maya. *Well if that doesn't confirm who the other Chosen Ones are I don't know what will.*

"Did anyone receive a message?" asked Alex.

Maya spoke up, "Yes I did. The message was *Stay the Course.*"

"I heard the same words," said Cade and Arielle together and laughed at their synchronicity.

"If no one else is willing to say it, I will," Alex said confidently. "We obviously have a connection to each other and we need to find out what it is."

"I agree," said Maya, "but now is not that time. I think we need to talk about this privately."

Alex sighed. "Okay. Why don't we all plan to get together after dinner tonight."

* * * *

The remainder of the afternoon was spent shopping at one of the most oldest and historic markets in the world, the Khan El Khalili Bazaar.

They bonded together, laughing and sharing light stories of their pasts. Walking down bustling streets filled with shoppers and vendors selling various shapes of alabaster bowls and vases, statues of Gods, Goddesses, and Pharaohs, paintings made from papyrus, jewelry, and fine assortments of oils and perfumes. The assortment was too numerous to name.

Cade and Alex stopped to look at some handcrafted walking sticks while Maya and Arielle continued on.

Maya admired a box made of Mother of Pearl and decided to buy it for Emma. While they waited for the friendly merchant to wrap the gift they overheard the two sisters they met on their first night in Cairo, Margaret and Elizabeth talking.

"He's quite handsome don't you think?" asked Elizabeth, the younger of the two, dreamily.

"Yes, very elegant and debonair," replied Margaret.

The conversation intrigued Maya and Arielle. The humor of these two older women swooning over a guy made them wonder whom they were talking about. They stayed back out of sight, picking up statues pretending to be interested but continued to eavesdrop.

"He's led such an interesting life. So many fascinating stories."

"Who would ever believe that someone who worked for the government could be so spiritual? His wife seems really nice too. They're a bit odd looking but they sure are fascinating to talk to."

Maya and Arielle exchanged looks of recognition with each other.

"Hi Elizabeth, Margaret. How are you?" asked Maya, coming out from behind the wall adjacent to the neighboring vendor.

"Good," they chimed in unison.

Arielle followed Maya's lead, "We couldn't help but overhear you talking about that couple that seem to be getting everyone's attention."

"Oh you mean Douglas and Vivienne," Margaret said with pride at providing this well-known information that had obviously been lost on the group that had attached themselves to each other. "Yes we met them last night after dinner. They look a little uppity but they are actually a really nice couple."

"Did I hear you say that he worked for the government?" asked Arielle.

"Yes, he's apparently an Ambassador for the Cultural Arts. He's here on a goodwill mission trying to establish friendly relations with the people of Egypt by showing respect for their history."

Elizabeth continued, "They said they would be in the lounge after dinner this evening. You should introduce yourselves and talk with them. We're sure you'd enjoy it. Last night he was telling us about the Pharaoh Akhenaton. Douglas said he was the second Hermes who rediscovered something called the Emerald Tablet."

Maya glanced quickly at Arielle. "Did you say the Emerald Tablet?"

"Yes. Have you heard of it?" Elizabeth asked in surprise.

"I seem to recall reading something about it back home," replied Maya. "Do you remember what else he said about it?"

"It's hard to remember but he said that Akhenaton came up against some resistance by using the concepts of living in truth and acting from the cosmic principles in the Emerald Tablet. He tried to instill the belief of believing in One God and One Mind. But he was cast as a heretic and died mysteriously. His body along with his wife's, Nefertiti, were never found."

"Sounds like this Douglas guy knows Egyptian history pretty well," said Arielle opening her eyes wide and glancing in Maya's direction.

"They're both very knowledgeable people about anything spiritual. You should talk to them." Looking at Margaret, Elizabeth said, "We should get moving. It was nice talking with you. See you later."

"Yes, it was nice talking with you too," responded Maya as the women walked away.

As soon as they were out of ear-shot Arielle turned to Maya and exclaimed, "Holy cow, did you hear that? We have to meet them tonight. They might be able to help us."

"But we promised Alex and Cade we would meet with them," reminded Maya.

"Oh that's right. Well they'll have to wait or they can join us."

"Arielle I'm surprised at you."

"This is too important, Cade will have to wait.

Maya's thoughts raced. She felt trepidation at the thought of being near Douglas. *It's not like anything is going to happen. He's married and besides what about how I'm feeling towards Alex?*

They continued to wander through the market, enjoying the lively atmosphere and eventually met back up with the men in time to return to the hotel.

Back at the El Gezirah Hotel Maya and Arielle let Alex and Cade know that they would see them later that evening in the lounge. They told them they were exhausted and needed to have a nap before coming down for dinner, they didn't want to impose and ask them to wait. The guys reluctantly agreed to meet in the lounge later and then went their separate ways for the next few hours.

Chapter Twenty-eight

The Ciao Italia restaurant provided a very cozy atmosphere. At nine o'clock in the evening it was quiet with the exception of a few groups of people who had also probably opted for a nap before dinner.

After leaving the restaurant, Maya and Arielle went to the El Gondool Bar and found themselves standing right behind Douglas and Vivienne.

Maya smiled to herself. *How's that for the universe conspiring to move them along their path?*

Douglas and Vivienne turned when they heard the ladies come up behind them. "Hello. I hope the rest of your day was better than the last time we spoke," Douglas commented to Maya in a considerate voice.

"Yes thank you." She flushed in embarrassment remembering the incident at lunch and tried to put it out of her mind.

"My name is Douglas Mercer and this is my wife Vivienne."

"Hello nice to meet you," said Vivienne politely.

"Nice to meet you. I'm Maya Maxwell and this is Arielle Stewart." Maya was grateful that she was not feeling the same pull towards him as she did earlier that day.

"Why don't you join us for a drink. We'd enjoy your company," he suggested.

"Well we're supposed to meet some friends but I don't see them yet," Arielle responded.

"They will be welcome to join us when they arrive. What do you say?" asked Douglas.

"Thank you, we will," said Maya nervously and exchanged a quick look with Arielle. She hadn't shared her experience at lunch with her friend yet. After all, it might have been her imagination taking over.

The hostess guided them to a quiet area in the back with a couple of comfortable looking sofas facing each other. Arielle slipped in first, then Vivienne, followed by Maya and Douglas at the end.

They talked about their hometowns and their backgrounds. They discovered Douglas and Vivienne lived in Bel Air, a town near Baltimore, and they visited Washington, D.C. frequently because of his close association with the government as an Ambassador.

After the waitress brought their drink orders Douglas decided it was time to take the conversation a little deeper. "So are you here just to see the sights or do you plan to participate in the spiritual part of this journey?"

"Maya, Arielle! There you are!" Alex's eyes narrowed for an instant when he recognized who Maya was sitting beside. He felt disappointment squeeze his heart. "We've been looking for you guys."

"Hi Alex. This is Douglas and Vivienne Mercer," said Maya. "Douglas, Vivienne, this is Alex Delaney and Cade McAllister."

Douglas extended his hand to both Alex and Cade and said, "Nice to meet you. I hope you don't mind, we arrived at the same time and invited these two lovely ladies to join us for a drink. Please have a seat with us. We were just getting to know one another." He smiled smugly knowing he had the upper hand.

"Don't mind if we do," responded Cade lightheartedly.

Alex was further irritated by having to sit on the couch opposite Maya but Cade seemed to take it in stride.

The waitress returned to take requests from the newcomers and disappeared to place the order.

"So Maya, you were just about to tell us what brings you to Egypt," reminded Douglas.

"We're all pretty much here on a quest to find some answers to the meaning of our lives. Myself, Arielle, Cade, and Alex are at different yet similar points of questioning our existence and what to do next."

Alex's irritation grew while he listened to Maya speak on his behalf to this man, who he was beginning to consider his adversary.

"And for some reason you all felt compelled to come here," said Douglas finishing Maya's sentence.

"Yes you could say that." She glanced towards Alex with worry. Feeling some strong vibes emanating from him made her uncomfortable.

"Sounds like you are all experiencing the dark night of the soul and you're seeking a path of spiritual purification and transformation." Douglas placed a cloaking sphere of energy around them making them invisible to others. He did not want to be disturbed during this conversation. "In other words you seek enlightenment by attempting to discover your relationship with the cosmos."

Even though he was speaking to all of them Maya felt his conversation was more personally directed towards her. She could feel the heat from his thighs next to hers and she shifted, trying to put some distance between them. *Why oh why did his voice feel like music in her ear?* "Where have you learned so much about spirituality?"

Douglas smiled knowingly. "Let's just say, I've been around a long time, studied extensively and have experienced a great many things."

"Do you have any advice for us?" asked Arielle after the waitress returned with Cade and Alex's Egyptian brewed beer.

"Not knowing the events that took place to bring you here makes that somewhat of an open question. But I'll ask you this…Have you all noticed seeing any particular sequence of numbers on a regular basis?"

Since Maya had become familiar with this theory she took the lead wanting the others to benefit too. "I see the numbers 11:11 all the time and variations of the number nine."

"I've noticed 11:11 a lot," added Alex.

"Me too," said Arielle enthusiastically and Cade signaled his agreement.

Douglas nodded in understanding. "Yes 11:11 is the most popular number that is seen. This happens because human DNA has been encoded to awaken at a certain point in time and these numbers trigger this. When you see a repetition of numbers your DNA is being activated and you should pay attention to what is happening around you shortly before and after it happens."

Despite his jealousy Alex couldn't help but be intrigued. "Activated for what?"

"To remember that we are spiritual beings having a physical experience and we have the ability to unlock our memories to who we truly are and what our specific purposes are. Maya, I'll take you for example. Now that you have released yourself from enslavement from your recent relationship you are free to move into higher frequencies and you are now able to call forward your destiny more quickly."

"How did you know about my divorce?" Maya asked in awe.

He leaned in closer. "I know many things that would surprise you." Reclining back he continued with a self-satisfied smile. "Meaningful coincidences have brought you here, *now*. You too Alex, Arielle and Cade. Some of you have been guided by your dreams and visions. Believe in them, they are helping you to perfect your art."

Arielle, Cade, Alex and Maya looked at each other in surprise.

They looked to Vivienne who spoke up. "He's very gifted, you'd be wise to listen," she said demurely.

Maya wasn't sure what to think except that she was more convinced than ever that he could help them find what they were looking for. *Why does he seem to show particular interest in me? He's so distinguished and intellectual what could he possibly find interesting about me? Maybe it's my imagination taking over again.*

"It's not your imagination," Douglas whispered into her ear yet again.

The feel of his breath so close was unnerving. His voice was like velvet and raised the beat of her heart. She felt the pull again. The same one that drew her in during lunch. Her eyelids closed softly, like a long, slow blink.

"How do you know these things about us?" interjected Cade. "Are you psychic?"

"In a manner of speaking yes. I can read your minds. I have the ability to project myself into the minds of others and see what is there."

"Did you always have this gift or was it something you learned?" asked Arielle, leaning closer so she could hear better.

"I've always been fairly intuitive. But it wasn't until I was recruited into a test group to determine if there was any validity to psychic phenomena that my talents were really developed."

"What type of test group?" asked Alex.

"Ah, that's a conversation for another time. It's getting late." He lifted the sphere from their circle and announced, "And I think we should call it a night everyone. We have another early day scheduled and tomorrow will be a big day. Please join us for breakfast in the morning. Let's meet for seven-thirty, we can talk more then." Douglas and Vivienne rose to leave. "Good night," he said confident that he intrigued them sufficiently enough to begin weaving his web.

"Get some sleep," winked Vivienne.

* * * *

"Was that strange or what?" asked Cade as they sat back down together on the sofa.

"I think it's time we talked about why we are all here and find out what our connection is to each other," Alex said with authority.

"I agree," confirmed Maya. "Cade why don't you start by telling us more about your visions."

"Well as I mentioned earlier today I kept having the same vision over and over again about the pyramids. More specifically I kept seeing the Pyramid of Giza. Somehow I knew these visions were connected with this great unrest I have discovered in Mother Earth."

"Tell us about the visions," said Arielle curiously.

"I am guided by a force to the pyramid and a secret entranceway is revealed. As I enter I suddenly have a torch in my hand. The pathway is low and very narrow and this crazy wind gusts around me and nearly knocks me off my feet but the torch never goes out. Finally the winds die down and I can see an opening into a room that glows with a green light. As I walk into the room I see that the room is actually glowing from torches placed on the walls and the light is reflecting off this luminescent green stone. It has writings on it but they are in another language which I can't read."

"Is there a crystal hanging above the stone?" asked Arielle.

"Yes there is." Looking at her in amazement he hesitated briefly before continuing, "It's held in place by a gold staff. Symbols are carved on top of four corners of the stone. In the vision I move to stand in front of the corner that has a symbol I am familiar with."

Arielle, touching his arm asked with tenderness and understanding, "Do you have the same symbol on your lower back?"

"Yes," he said quietly and placed his hand over hers. "Arielle, in my visions I also see you standing at the opposite corner from me at the stone." Looking at Alex and Maya he continued, "And last night in my dreams I saw you two take the other two corners."

Arielle smiled knowingly. "I've had similar visions, and now that I think of it I remember the gusts of wind in the passageway too. I saw that there were four of us but they were like shadows—I could not see any faces."

"My vision fades out after we approach the Stone and even though I don't see anything my gut tells me that we're there to do something important. Something that will help the world."

"Does your symbol have three interconnecting circles?" asked Maya, having already predicted which element was associated with Cade.

"Yes it does. But how could you know that?"

"Because each one of us represents an element of nature. I am Fire, Arielle is Water, I guessed by the way you spoke about your life back home that you are

Earth. The three circles linked symbolizes Earth." Maya turned towards Alex. "So that makes you Air. You do have one on your back as well right?"

Clearing his throat before responding, "Yes."

Maya proceeded to recount her own visions, her gift with healing and Fire, her discovery of the prophecy of the Emerald Stone, her connection to the Herkimer and how it brought her to Egypt. She told them about how she became friends with Arielle, the recent book she bought and their latest theories on their past life experiences with the Emerald Stone.

Alex's feelings for Maya grew stronger while he listened to her story. He grew more convinced there was a special connection that existed between them. He also felt a great deal of admiration for the way she was dealing with the quest they found themselves on. "So what is the connection with the elements?" he asked.

He felt grateful knowing he wasn't the only one. They were in it together and there was a purpose. And hopefully the memories of his father persecuting him as a child for his strangeness could begin to fade away now.

"It seems to be an important point but I haven't figured that out yet. The references I've read so far don't explain the reasons," responded Maya trying to remain hopeful they would figure things out in time.

"Okay so lets think about each of the elements and what they might symbolize spiritually," said Arielle. "Maybe that will provide some clues."

"Fire burns bright, like an eternal flame," offered Cade. "Burning away the old, it sets you free from the limitations of your mind."

Arielle smiled, feeling excitement build. He was quick on his feet, she liked that. "Good, keep going."

"I know that water is linked to the feminine energies, the astral plane and emotions." Cade continued, "Nothing can survive without it. To me it says drink from the fountain of life and nurture our emotional natures." Arielle was his Water, they blended and molded together, knowing this filled him with all the nourishment he could ever need.

"Air flows through us and around us. It heightens our awareness of all our senses and helps us to discover our inner worth," Alex hesitated, glancing quickly into Maya's eyes. "Air feeds Fire, providing the oxygen it needs to flourish and grow stronger."

"Earth is our center. It's nurturing and provides the space for our roots to grow," said Arielle. "It makes me think of the tallest of trees, reaching ever upwards."

Maya watched the three of them getting carried away with the intensity of their emotions. She fought to stay centered believing someone had to. "What have we got when we put it all together…Fire burns away the old, lights the way and sets us free. Water offers life, filling us up after burning away the limitations. Air flows through us heightening our awareness. Earth teaches us to reach for the stars, and dream big." She could feel Alex's eyes on hers but she avoided meeting his gaze.

After a moment of quiet contemplation Alex recognized the inter-relationship. "This sounds like a process for awakening and reaching higher levels of awareness. Isn't that what the Emerald Stone symbolizes? Each one of us must be the representation of the different stages. Cade you talked so passionately about your connection to Earth. Do you ever have unexplained occurrences with Earth or anything that grows from it?"

"How do I say this without sounding crazy?" replied Cade.

"If anyone was listening to our conversation they'd say we're *all* crazy. Go ahead," said Maya.

"The first time I experienced it was not long after the symbol appeared on my body. I was a child and my sister was sad that a flower she planted died. After staring at it for a few minutes the leaves started to move. So when no one was around I used to sit and will it back to life until two days later my sister came running in the house so happy that her flower was magically alive again. I'm kind of known around the neighborhood for having a green thumb because everything I plant thrives."

"That's awesome!" exclaimed Alex. "Maya what about you?"

Maya told them about her dreams as a child where her mother taught her to use her healing gifts but she forgot all about it until lately. She also described her experience with Arielle on the airplane and then she talked about her experiments with Fire.

When Maya was finished Arielle shared her love of how living near the water soothes her as well as her passion for painting water scenes. She also shared her experience from the previous day where she found herself living within the consciousness of water.

"Alex, have you discovered what your gift with Air is?" asked Maya.

"Well remember at lunch today when your water glass fell to the floor?"

"Yes…" she appeared confused.

"I was upset and the wind from my breath knocked it off the table."

"I thought something was bothering you. Why were you so upset? Maya asked.

"I can't even remember now. It was probably something stupid."

Cade jumped in to save Alex, recognizing his friend's discomfort. "This is great but what do we do now?"

"Considering our experience today at the mosque I think we should continue to practice meditating together as a group. We can try it again tomorrow at Giza and see what happens," offered Arielle.

"Great idea. I think we should also spend time getting to know Douglas and Vivienne some more. Arielle and I heard Margaret and Elizabeth say that Douglas talked about Hermes and the Emerald Tablet with them," suggested Maya.

"Great," said Alex with a slight sarcasm in his voice.

"Is there something wrong Alex?" asked Maya catching the insincere tone in Alex's comment.

"Huh? Oh sorry, no nothing's wrong," he said trying to hide his displeasure at the thought of spending more time with Douglas.

* * * *

Later that night, Maya moaned. Turning her head from one side to the other in her sleep. Covers sprawled across her body. Her left arm freed itself from under the blanket and reached up. Laying the back of her hand on top of her eyes. Her breath was soft, deep and steady. She turned her head to the other side leaving her hand to rest gently on the pillow.

"I am here for you," the voice whispered caressingly.

Soft noises escaped her throat. Her legs shifted and her body moved.

"Yes, that's right. You feel me here."

Her moan turned deeper.

"Come with me my darling. Take my hand," the voice proposed.

Pushing the blanket further away, her body shifted to the other side.

"Feel my breath on your neck. I need you. Reach for my lips and meet me here in the ether."

Her head tilted upwards to reach for his kiss. Another moan escaped from her throat.

"You are so beautiful, my love. I'll be your everything, come to me darling."

She floated into the abyss allowing her body to reach higher.

"I am for you. I want you," beckoned the voice.

A drop of sweat trickled down her back.

"Come with me. Come with me NOW my love!"

In the split second before opening her eyes she saw the eyes of a dragon. Surprised by her body's reaction to this strange plea, and the vision of the eyes she waited for the beat of her heart to slow down. Checking to make sure she did not wake Arielle she relaxed back into her pillow.

That was so real. I could hear him talking to me. His body felt like he was right here. She remembered Douglas whispering to her that he knew many things about her and telling her his interest in her was not just in her imagination.

She was getting the uncomfortable feeling that Douglas was her dream visitor and he sent the dragon's eye as her clue to recognize him. She wasn't sure what to think about the way he was reaching out to her. But sometimes she felt as though she couldn't control herself around him.

Chapter Twenty-nine

Maya and Arielle met Alex and Cade in the hotel lobby at seven-thirty A.M. the next morning. Entering the Andalus restaurant Maya saw Douglas and Vivienne already seated at a round table. As they approached the table Douglas motioned for Maya to sit beside him. *This is embarrassing. How can I look at him after that dream? Maybe it wasn't even him.* Cade seated himself beside Maya leaving Alex no choice but to sit between Vivienne and Arielle.

"Did you sleep well Maya?" Douglas asked quietly.

Is he toying with me? "Yes thanks. Did you?" Maya asked politely while she placed a napkin across her lap.

"Like a rock. I feel refreshed and ready for the adventures of a new day in this ancient land."

A waiter came around to fill coffee cups and take everyone's breakfast order.

When the rounds were done Alex started the conversation, wanting to make a good impression on Maya. "Well today's the big day. I'm really looking forward to finally seeing the Sphinx and the Great Pyramid."

"Douglas, you must have some insights about the pyramids. What can you tell us about them?" Cade blurted out in anticipation.

"Let's see…Well the Great Pyramid is geographically located on the center of the planet and the air shafts in the King's Chamber were built to be in a direct line with the stars in Orion's belt at that time."

Cade interrupted, "That's pretty common knowledge. What is your theory on why they were built in that specific location?"

"Since you asked…The base of the Great Pyramid symbolically represents the consciousness on Earth at its densest point. The peak of the pyramid is the point at which it connects with the Heavens and expands outward in a reverse pyramid shape, similar looking to an hourglass. That mid-point is a portal that activates pure consciousness to anyone taking an initiation in the sarcophagus in the King's Chamber."

They sat in silence absorbing the information while Douglas continued. "It is a gateway connecting above and below. A labyrinth to awaken the human mind to the mysteries of higher vibrations."

"As Above, so Below," Arielle nodded.

Douglas gave her a warm smile. "Exactly."

"This reminds me of our discussion last night around 11:11 and the DNA being activated. Are they connected?" asked Cade.

"Absolutely. The DNA activation is happening at a higher level now than ever before. People are being called *en masse* to action during this time to accelerate Earth's evolution."

"Why now?" asked Alex leaning forward on his elbows and resting his chin on his hands.

"You may have heard the Mayan Calendar ends in December of this year, 2012. It coincides with the final shift of Earth's pole star axis. Nostradamus predicted that there would be much chaos and destruction during this transition. A great alchemist by the name of Paracelsus foretold the same thing and also said that only one third of our population will survive this shift. Earth is purging herself of the waste humankind has left behind in our quest for power and technology."

The waiter served their breakfast and refilled their coffee cups. Pausing before he left he added, "Your tour leaves for the Sphinx in twenty five minutes. Can I get you anything else?"

Douglas looked around at everyone then said, "I think that will be all. Thank you. Let's eat and enjoy our breakfast."

Arielle thought about Cade's predictions. "This all sounds very much like what you have been talking about," she said looking at the man who had captured her heart. She turned to Douglas, "Cade's very in tune with Earth and he thinks we're on the brink of major catastrophes unless we change our ways."

"He's a smart man," said Douglas. He glanced at Vivienne sorely tempted to talk about his plans for energy in the New World but she frowned at him, shaking her head slowly in warning. The temptation was so great but he knew she was right.

"We'll talk more tonight if you like after you have experienced seeing the Sphinx and pyramids. I'm sure it will produce more fascinating discussions."

Maya was silent. Thinking about what Douglas said she felt the need to say a silent prayer offering her thanks to the universe for protecting and guiding her on her journey.

Douglas leaned closer to Maya touching his shoulder to hers. "That was a beautiful prayer. If more people offered their gratitude to Spirit we would be in a better place. I'm touched."

She looked into his eyes and everything swirled. Feeling like she was looking into the center of the universe itself she couldn't speak.

"I hope you don't mind. I read your thoughts. You have a beautiful heart and soul Maya."

She blushed in embarrassment and looked at Vivienne. "I don't know what to say."

"There's no need to be embarrassed and don't worry about Vivienne. You should spend some time talking with her. I think you will find you have a lot in common. If you look closely enough you will see what I mean. She doesn't open up to people very often but I think she would welcome you as a friend. So if an opportunity comes up please don't feel self-conscious."

Nervously she pushed her hair behind her ears and played with the necklace she wore. His shoulder was pressed up against hers and she was getting uncomfortable. Looking at Alex she noticed he was playing with his food. *He looks angry again.*

Douglas observed Maya watching Alex and pulled his shoulder away from hers. "You will recognize soon, if you haven't already that we have known each other before. I have looked for you for thousands of years and now here you are," he said with intensity. "Did you enjoy your dream?"

She choked on her orange juice and tried to gather her wits about her. "It was you!"

"Yes. I apologize if I took liberties with you but I did not sense any resistance. I would not have done anything if you did not want me to…"

Alex noticed Maya's cheeks flushing. He was very aware their conversation looked rather intimate and wondered what Vivienne was thinking. She didn't appear to be ruffled or upset. In fact, she seemed relaxed and comfortable as the others carried on a conversation together about how friendly and generally spiritual the Egyptian people were. Alex, on the other hand, was struggling to maintain his equilibrium over his feelings for Maya and the way Douglas managed to monopolize her time.

Feeling ashamed Maya didn't know what to do or say. She looked in Alex's direction again then looked down at her hands and quietly said, "This is confusing. Please you have to respect my integrity. You're married..."

Leaving her comment in the air, he looked at his watch and announced to everyone, "Well it's time for us to go. I'll look forward to catching up tonight." It irritated him the way she glanced at Alex. The thought of her reuniting with him fueled his anger to darker depths. *I will not lose her again. I'll have to make sure this bond of theirs does not get stronger.*

* * * *

"I think Alex is upset. What is going on between you and Douglas?" demanded Arielle in a low voice once they were seated on the bus.

Maya was still reeling with thoughts of Douglas and his admission that he visited her in her dreams to seduce her. "Nothing is going on." *Is it really possible? Can he really do that?* She was so confused, a part of her felt violated and another part felt shame, wondering why didn't she stop him.

"Well it certainly looks like he's flirting with you. Are you attracted to him?"

"Oh Arielle, I don't know. Okay yes I think he's attractive don't you? I mean come on he's extremely intelligent and handsome but that's as far as it goes for me. Besides he's married and I wouldn't let anything happen."

Arielle scrutinized her friend closely. "I just don't want you to get hurt."

"You are so sweet to look out for me but don't worry. I can handle myself. My interest right now is in finding out how he can help us. I can't explain it—I just know that there's a reason we met him and he has some answers we'll need. Time is running out Arielle, we only have nineteen days left and we need to capitalize on any opportunity that presents itself to get closer to being able to ignite the Stone," she pleaded, desperately wanting her friend to understand. "He obviously has strong psychic abilities and we know he's aware of the Emerald Stone right?"

"Yes," Arielle relented. "And he knew that we have been having visions. Maybe he knows about us and the prophecy." She paused to consider these points. "Okay I'll work with you on this but please be careful."

"I will. In the meantime we need to make sure Cade and Alex and are on board with this."

"That's going to be interesting." Arielle turned to see Alex deep in conversation with Cade and felt pretty confident he was talking about Maya judging by the sullen expression on his face.

* * * *

"Hey are you okay buddy?" asked Cade.

"Yeah." *No I'm not okay. I'm losing her to Douglas before I even had a chance.*

"You got to fight for her. He's just a passing fancy. There's as much of a connection between you and Maya as there is between Arielle and me. I can tell. This is a crazy journey we're on but we got to stick together. The four of us."

"I don't have any choice. What I feel is too strong to walk away. I have to see it through even if it means losing her. You were sitting beside her. Do you know what they were talking about?"

"No. I only heard her last comment asking him to respect her integrity. So he must have made a move on her and she turned him down. That's a good sign."

Shaking his head in disgust, "I can't believe he has the balls to do that especially with his wife sitting on his other side. You know I was watching Vivienne and she didn't seem bothered by his behavior in the least. Was it obvious or am I over reacting?"

"No it was pretty obvious."

"Maya seems determined that he can help us. I'm not happy about it but she is the key to activating the Herkimer."

Cade nodded in agreement. "We'll just have to watch her back and see where this takes us."

Chapter Thirty

"The Sphinx was carved from the bedrock of the Giza plateau. As one of the great mysteries of the world with the body of a lion and head of a king or god, it has come to symbolize strength and wisdom." Speaking into the crackling bus microphone, Azizi wiped his brow and continued in a clear voice. "We will be approaching the site in just a few moments. You will have some time to take some pictures from the platform and walk around when you get off the bus before we meet at the base of the Sphinx."

The energy in the bus was high with nervous excitement in anticipation of visiting the Sphinx and the Great Pyramids of Giza.

"Most people who see the Sphinx for the first time are in awe of its existence. It has a very mystical presence, which I am sure you will see immediately. Egyptians feel a great sense of pride for the Sphinx, as it is a symbol of strength and intelligence to our culture.

"The great prophet, Edgar Cayce said that Egypt was the repository containing the records of the ancient civilization Atlantis. He said that this repository was kept in an underground library, which he referred to as the Hall of Records but this library has never been found."

"Did you hear that?" exclaimed Arielle quietly, she looked first at Maya then tapped Cade on the arm. "I wonder if that has anything to do with the Stone?"

They were now leaning forward in their seats and huddled together, guarding their own mysterious quest.

"Who knows? Could be…But what we're looking for is under the Great Pyramid," whispered Cade.

"That doesn't mean they're not connected," interjected Alex.

Azizi continued to speak about its history. "Because of the changing desert terrain the body of the Sphinx has been covered by sand several times over many thousands of years. Being buried in the soft sand for much of its existence has actually preserved the Sphinx from eroding completely. The sand was most recently cleared away in 1905. Some areas are more eroded than others but you may be able to see traces of original paint near one of the ears. It is believed that the Sphinx was originally very colorfully painted.

"Here we are. Please meet me at the base in about thirty minutes." Azizi jumped down the final step from the bus and stepped aside for everyone to depart and approach the deck overlooking the ancient structures.

Nothing could have prepared Maya for the time that she would see the Sphinx with her own eyes. The enormity of its size was incomprehensible. But more than that its impact on her was impossible to absorb. It struck her in her heart center with force causing her to feel dizzy.

"I've got you." Alex was right behind her to steady her. One hand pressed up against her back, the other holding her by the arm. His heart jumped into his throat with the feeling of her in his hands. *God she's the most beautiful creature I've ever seen.*

Maya's emotions were so raw and unprotected. She turned to Alex with tears welling up in her eyes. "I…I can't breathe…" In that moment the tether between them merged into one and fastened tightly. She moved closer to him and they stood together. Their eyes riveted on the Sphinx. She did not know why but she needed him more than she would have liked.

Alex sensed her need and without speaking he pulled her closer, wrapping his arm around her.

Thousands of years of ancient civilizations saturated the dry and musty air and Maya instinctively understood what Azizi spoke of. A light breeze stroked her cheeks while she absorbed the mystical vitality emanating from the great and mighty monument.

Looking down, the people milling about the Sphinx and pyramids looked to be tiny specks in comparison. Guards on camels could be seen in the distance, sprinkled throughout the area. Beyond the Sphinx and the pyramids, only dry desert could be seen for miles with a few trees scattered here and there.

The Sphinx's body looked battered and worn with the exception of some areas, which were under restoration. The King or God's head still appeared very defined with strong features. Its jaw line was square and the headdress accentuated the cheekbones. Its eyes were large and kind. The most prevalent damage, which has remained unrepaired, was its broken nose. Despite the damage it had endured, its spirit was real and strong.

Standing on the hilltop overlooking this monumental statue, she could not contain the overwhelming urge to cry from the deepest part of her soul at its sight. Moving was unmanageable but she felt comforted by the warmth of Alex's arms holding her steady.

Something is happening inside of me. A shift of time… "Alex…"

"It's okay you don't have to say anything." He tightened his hold, never wanting to let her go. He wanted this to be a memory never to be forgotten, holding it sacredly in his heart.

She looked up into the depths of his milk chocolate brown eyes and watched them grow darker. "We've been here before."

"Yes. We have." He felt more sure of that than anything he'd ever experienced. The world stood still and everything disappeared around him except Maya.

Feeling the sands of time bringing them back together in this moment she leaned closer and he brought his lips down to meet hers. Their souls blended and fused as one. She slid her hand over his chest and surges of unequaled passion rushed through her. Their hearts were beating wildly.

Her breath was warm and inviting. He couldn't get enough of her. Her hand felt like it was searing a mark on his chest for eternity. They kissed with intensity as though nothing else existed except this moment. All the while his eyes remained fixed on hers and he watched the flame of her soul capturing his heart.

She pulled away to catch her breath. Her feet felt unsteady beneath her. "Alex…" *What am I doing! Last night I allowed Douglas to come to me in my dreams. He said we've known each other before and he's been looking for me for thousands of years. Yet here I am with Alex and I feel as though I've betrayed him. Which one is the truth?*

He sensed her pulling away so he held her tighter. Panic filling him. "Maya, don't pull away. I believe there's meaning between us, a reason we're here. I believe in you and me."

Her hand became firm on his chest but now it held him apart from her. "Alex, I need time. Please there are things I need to work through and discover about myself before I can be with anyone."

Anxiety took over his reasoning abilities. "It's him isn't it?" he demanded.

She was taken back by the severity of his words. "If you mean Douglas, no it's not that. This is about me and my desire to find who I really am deep inside. I've always been afraid of being alone. I need to make sure that whatever I do, it's for the right reasons."

He wasn't completely convinced that Douglas didn't have anything to do with what she was doing yet he could hear a measure of honesty in her words. "I care too much for you to be upset with you. As long as you don't shut me out I'll wait for you Maya."

"Thank you. I don't want to lose the friendship we've been building and it's important for our group to stay strong." She couldn't shake the feeling that she was taking a chance on losing something deep and real. *Finding my true self and what I'm capable of doing is worth the risk. I have to believe in that.*

* * * *

Cade reached out to take Arielle's hand while they witnessed Maya and Alex's embrace. He drew her close to him, their hands clasped together and he held hers against his wildly beating heart. "Do you feel that?" his voice croaked with passion.

Arielle couldn't summon any words to escape from her lips so she just nodded instead.

"Our hearts are beating in unison Arielle. We belong together, don't we?" He tilted his head in the direction of Alex and Maya, "Just like those two belong together."

Again she could only nod in agreement.

He tenderly brushed aside a long strand of her golden blonde hair clinging to her eyelashes and with great longing studied her features, a little at a time. Taking in her sparkling blue eyes that equaled the clearest of skies and the adorable freckles that streaked unabashedly across her diminutive nose and glowing cheeks.

She held her breath in anticipation, while taking immense pleasure in the way he looked at her with absolute wonder.

He leaned down and their lips connected, tentatively at first then with desire and passion.

When they released their kiss, he embraced her with both arms wrapped tightly around her body. Slowly he opened his eyes and he took notice of Alex and Maya.

Arielle noticed Cade's body stiffen. "What's wrong?" She pulled her head back to look at him.

"Something's happened with them. They look upset."

Watching the parting of ways on the platform overlooking the Sphinx, Arielle said, "I'll take him, you go to her."

Arielle approached Alex gingerly. "Is everything all right?"

Alex shrugged his shoulders and put his hands in the front pockets of his jeans. "I'm not sure. The sight of the Sphinx was overwhelming and we both felt a past life connection here. It brought us so close but then she pulled away. She said she needs time to sort some things out. I asked her if it had anything to do with Douglas. Maybe I shouldn't have asked but it just blurted out of my mouth before I could stop it."

"What did she say?" Arielle tried to comfort him by rubbing his arm.

After he repeated the excuse Maya provided, Arielle knew she had to try to smooth the rift. "Alex. I know things looked questionable between Maya and Douglas this morning but she told me that she just wants to find out how he can help us. You have to admit he's gifted and we could use some help. Maya made a good point this morning. We only have nineteen days left, that's less than three weeks, and we don't have a lot to go on yet. Douglas is aware of the Emerald Stone but we're not certain how much more he knows. Even if somehow we manage to find the hidden entrance and chamber are you confident we'll know what to do?"

"No." He shifted his stance and his shoulders relaxed somewhat. He couldn't ignore the fact that there was so little time left. "Okay I'll go along with this. But if anything happens to Maya I'll never be able to forgive myself."

"Maya's been through a lot. You're probably not aware of this but she's grown up a very lonely person. She lost a baby that meant everything in the world to her just last January."

His head hung low. "Yes, she told me she had a miscarriage…" He felt like a heel for the way he spoke to Maya.

Arielle felt this poor man's pain and wanted to help him win Maya's heart. "She's had a lot of difficulty dealing with her loss and her husband turned his back on her when she started discovering her powers and having visions. She's dealing with all this the best she can and she's trying to find her way. I believe in her and if you want her you'll have to believe in her too."

The thought of her husband abandoning Maya filled him with contempt and he vowed to never hurt her.

* * * *

"Hey kiddo. Wanna talk?" asked Cade. He approached Maya on the ridge, where she stood looking introspectively out into the horizon.

"Oh Cade, I think I just made a mess of things with Alex."

He pulled her into his arms as she burst into tears. "Come on, tell me what happened." He tilted her chin up to look at him. Compassionately he brushed the tears aside with his thumb.

Maya proceeded to share what transpired between her and Alex. Cautiously she said, "The thing is…Something bizarre is happening with Douglas. He claims that he's been looking for me for thousands of years."

"Do you believe him?"

"Yes and no. I believe I recognize him but I'm just not sure about the romantic aspect. I have to be honest with you Cade, I do find him attractive and it scares me. There are times when I almost feel like I'm not in control of my feelings when I'm around him."

"What about Alex?"

"That's why this whole thing scares me because I feel something very different and deep for Alex. I feel like I'm being pulled in two completely different directions and it's driving me crazy. I can't let anything happen with Alex yet—it just wouldn't be fair to him. I have to figure out what this pull is towards Douglas and I am convinced he can help us." She looked at him with desperation in her eyes. "What do *you* think?"

"I agree that we need to explore what Douglas knows. When I came on this trip I knew that time was running out and I couldn't ignore my instincts any longer but I didn't realize just how little time was left. I think you should trust your instincts Maya."

"I will. I know there's at lot at risk but I need to take that chance."

"Well then we'll just have to work together and support you. Leave Alex up to me. Are you okay?"

Taking a deep breath she said, "I think so. Thanks for being there and thanks for supporting me."

"Anytime. Now, let's go catch up with Alex and Arielle. It looks like the tour group is gathering at the base of the Sphinx." He walked alongside Maya, feeling sorry for Alex and worried that troubled times lay ahead for both of them. He hoped that Maya knew what she was doing and that she wouldn't destroy Alex in the process.

* * * *

Seething with anger and jealousy Douglas stayed back in the distance with Vivienne while they watched Maya and Alex closely. *How dare he kiss her! She belongs to me! I found her and I brought her here to fulfill her destiny.* His eyes smoldered from blue to black under his aviator sunglasses. *If she is provoking me she will learn that nothing good will come of it...*

"She pushed him away, that's what's important," Vivienne said, recognizing it was necessary to soothe his boiling temper. She was trained to hear his thoughts as if they were her own. Their connection was strong after sixteen years of working side by side, as a team.

She met Douglas through a friend of the family who had been in the army with him. She was twenty-five and engaged to another man when they met but when Douglas arrived at her home one night in tears over the loss of a friend during a mission things changed. She began to see him secretly and broke off her engagement after a month without any explanation.

Up until the time she met Douglas she felt like she was living an empty existence. Going through the motions day after day she wondered what her purpose in life was. When he started talking about humanity's survival in the coming years and how he would lead them through the cataclysmic changes into a new world order she recognized her calling almost immediately.

Leaving behind her friends and family, they eloped and moved to New Jersey to start a new life together.

They had been joined at the hip over the years and despite his faults he was brilliant at convincing people to follow him. He taught her many things, including how to communicate with each other telepathically and to be a master of manifesting her own dreams. She took her mission very seriously, spending time every day to advance her skills.

Recognizing that running a business was not Douglas' element she took various courses to ensure that they created and maintained the necessary funds to finance his ideas and build their empire.

Douglas' gift of seducing both men and women into investing their money and becoming a part of his regime was legendary. Vivienne learned to turn a blind eye and sometimes even encouraged the many women he bedded along the way, knowing it was part of developing their allegiances and building their cause.

The sacrifices had been great. Douglas demanded complete loyalty from his followers and she was no exception. She learned the cycles of his command, manipulating by flattering one minute and threatening the next. Depending on his mood she could either be treated like a queen or beaten down emotionally but knowing that she would play a significant role in changing the course of history was her reward and kept her centered.

Sixteen years later she was committed and prepared to make sure Maya was successful, whatever risks to her own life she had to endure didn't matter.

"She's been affected by you I can sense it," Vivienne said reassuringly. "That's why she pushed him away. She's doubting herself. We'll need to move quickly when the time is right." She studied him thoughtfully.

"Let's stay close enough to keep an eye on them," he said in a cool and calculating voice.

The excavated area around the body of the Sphinx was approximately twelve to fifteen feet deep and thirty to forty feet wide at the base. People meandered around the Khafre temples located in front of the monument examining the faded inscriptions on the stones. Heading over to the statue they inspected the different areas that had been restored over time.

The groups from each of the buses; red, green and blue were gathered together below the face of the great statue listening to a lecture on its history given by the psychic Pamela Griffin.

"The statue is disintegrating because of the humidity, wind and smog in Cairo. There are fissures along the joint lines that are being filled in with cement. You'll see the neck is badly weathered probably because of the years where the Sphinx stood above the sand from only the neck up. Much of the work you see being done around it is for restoration purposes. But there are a couple of doors excavated below the base where it's believed that antiquity experts are searching for hidden chambers leading to the Great Pyramid holding the secrets of Atlantis."

Douglas observed Maya, Alex, Arielle and Cade exchanging glances. His eyes shifted towards Vivienne to determine if she noticed. *Of course she's watching. She never misses a beat. I've trained her well.*

"We need to make our presence more obvious while we're here and at the Great Pyramid. Especially now that they suspect the entrance might be here. We must get close enough to Maya so she feels and sees us wherever she turns," said Douglas quietly.

"I agree but we also need to gain the trust of the others. She relies on them and they are drawing closer together," replied Vivienne conspiratorially.

"I'll leave it to you to surround them with filters to block their ability to sense any discordance in this operation. You should also monitor their dreams and remove any insights about us before they're able to manifest. I'll continue to focus on Maya. I don't want any distractions," he said with authority.

Chapter Thirty-one

The bus ride from the Sphinx to the Pyramids of Giza was taken in silence. Everyone was lost in their own thoughts.

Now they stood in front of the Great Pyramid, once again mesmerized by the magnitude of another structure. Pictures could not possibly reflect the greatness it bestowed on those in its presence.

"When this Great Pyramid was built it was four hundred and eighty-one feet high," explained Azizi to all the groups gathered together. "Over the years approximately ten feet has been lost off the top. Until the nineteenth century it had been ranked the tallest structure in the world. Each side slopes at a fifty-one degree angle and they are carefully aligned with the four directions, North, South, East, and West. Unbelievably the error difference between the lengths of each side is less than point one percent. This is an extraordinary feat and is one of the reasons there is much controversy over its origin and purpose." Azizi looked regal and proud of his heritage in his dissertation.

It's amazing to think he has spent his whole life living here and studying his country's history. It's obvious he's passionate about what he does. I guess that's what happens when you live your life purpose. Maya felt a measure of pride herself and was starting to feel like she was really beginning to live her destiny. The brief past few months of studying spirituality, while it prepared her for this time of her life, paled in comparison to the magnitude to this rite of passage.

"Some speculate they were built to be astrological observatories or places of cult worship. Some even theorize that they were built by extraterrestrials but this concept is not generally accepted even though in many hieroglyphics there are strange looking beings which are unexplained and definitely not humanlike."

Many tourists milled around the outer limits of the pyramid while others climbed the outside of the stones investigating the various corridors and escape shafts. Azizi had said it is no longer allowed to climb all the way to the top due to the decay at the tip through sandstorms and by visitors removing stones as souvenirs.

"Tomorrow you will make the climb to the King's Chamber which is located in the centre of the pyramid. It's a long and steep climb and not for the faint of heart. Your initial visit here today is in preparation for your ceremony if you choose to participate."

Pamela, knowing the group was disappointed, added enthusiastically to Azizi's speech, "Trust me, you'll need the time to adjust to the high frequency of energy before the meditation and ritual tomorrow. It's going to be wonderful and life changing for many of you."

"Thank you Pamela. I hope everyone enjoys your visit here. You have one hour to walk about before we leave for lunch," Azizi finished.

Many people stood back taking in the magnificent site with the Pyramids of Khafre and Menkaure in the background before walking about.

"I wonder if the entrance to the hidden chamber is actually at the Sphinx and not here at the pyramid like we thought?" asked Cade once they were alone together.

"It's possible," said Alex. "I've seen diagrams of the Sphinx and the Pyramid. I think I remember seeing a tunnel running between them that lines up with the lower shaft in the pyramid. The shaft connects to the Queen's Chambers then up to the King's Chambers." The confidence in his voice masked his shakiness. He was still trying to pull himself out of the funky mood caused by his conversation with Maya.

"It makes sense with your visions Cade. Didn't you say that you walked through a passageway to get to the chamber with wind gusting around you?" questioned Maya excitedly. She decided to follow Alex's lead and focus on bringing the energy back up in the group.

"Yes, that's true." Cade recollected the vision with ease. "It does feel like I'm walking a long way in the vision. Does anyone know if we're scheduled to return to the Sphinx on this tour?"

"I think the itinerary showed that we would be back there tomorrow morning before coming here," offered Arielle.

"That's good but my guess is that our time will be limited. We're not going to be able to do everything we need to do on this tour. There's just not enough time to explore and spend time alone." Alex rubbed his chin thoughtfully. "We'll probably have to abandon the tour group at some point and do our own thing."

"I agree but not yet. We should participate in the ceremony in the King's Chamber. I think it's important. Maybe it'll provide some insight for us," Maya said confidently.

"I'm disappointed we're not going inside today," pouted Arielle. The affect of being here had not been as forceful on her as it was with Maya. *I have a lot of sadness but it's mixed with joyful feelings too. I wonder what Maya was experiencing? Something awful must have happened to her.*

"So am I," Maya added in frustration.

"I have an idea. Let's make good use of the hour we have and split up into two groups," Alex said with eagerness. "We can walk around the perimeter and see if we can pick up anything unusual with the help of our elemental senses."

"That's a heck of an idea!" exclaimed Cade. "Ladies why don't you go around that way," pointing to the west, "and Alex and I will go east. We can meet back here and compare notes."

"I just had another thought," Maya said showing more enthusiasm. "What if we hold hands in a circle first and take a few minutes to center ourselves?"

Alex and Cade exchanged looks obviously feeling uncomfortable with the idea. "Here?"

"Yes here!" said Arielle in emphatic agreement, winking at Maya. "The male species will not die suddenly because you guys meditated in public for a few minutes."

"Beside, it's Egypt. The land full of mystery. No one will pay any attention," added Maya with a smile.

"I don't know. Cade do you think we can suffer this disgrace?" joked Alex.

"For the cause of human evolution? I suppose we can endure this atrocity."

For the first time since they arrived at Giza the mood lightened and they laughed.

They joined hands together in a circle, alternating male and female for balance. Looking at each other with anticipation they wondered what to do next.

"Okay I'll start us off." Maya cleared her throat and shrugged her shoulders to loosen up. "May the Light of the Universe shine upon us, guiding and protecting us along our way." She prayed for a spark of inspiration to lend a helping hand.

"Let's take a few deep breaths and allow the energy to flow through us and between us," suggested Arielle.

Closing their eyes, they drew deep breaths and felt the Light begin to surge through them.

Words from a long forgotten time and place revealed themselves to each one. They felt transported in time and felt the beauty of the power they once experienced in another world. The aroma of burning Boswellia incense swirled around them, promoting the expansion of their consciousness.

They spoke in unison, "We stand before you as ONE."

Maya recognized her cue, "I AM Fire!"

"I AM Air!" announced Alex.

"I AM Earth!" declared Cade.

"I AM Water!" proclaimed Arielle.

Together they completed their plea, "Reveal to us the great cosmic power for all to see! Expand and blaze through us to awaken the Earth and set it free!"

The symbol of Fire on Maya's back pulsated, growing stronger with each passing second. A fire within her erupted like a match being lit, bursting to life.

The luminescent white ray of energy came forth from their heart centers with more force than the first time at the mosque. The rays collided with each other at the midpoint in the circle. They blended into one beam and shot up to the Heavens.

Their hearts began to beat in unison. The ground tremored ever so slightly under their feet. When they began to tire from holding the energy it pulled back down and slowly dissipated until it dissolved.

They released their hands and slowly returned to consciousness from the spell. A level of knowingness passed between them not experienced for many centuries.

If anyone had looked real closely at that moment, they would have seen a warm glow of gold Light encapsulating them.

"Did you guys remember saying those words before?" asked Arielle with a hoarse voice.

"Yes. They sounded ceremonial," said Alex, stretching upwards and filling his lungs with a new breath.

The three of them looked at Maya expectantly.

"They are words from a prayer we created thousands of years ago. Its meaning is pretty obvious. They prepare us to unite with the One Mind. Thoth guided us then and he is guiding us now through Hermes." The level of Spirit within Maya was so overwhelming she felt almost numb and barely aware of the words coming forth from her own mouth.

"Well then I guess the humiliation Cade and I endured on behalf of men everywhere was indeed worth it."

Once again Alex broke the enormity of their circumstances with much needed humor and they enjoyed the intimate moment together.

"Everyone ready to walk about the Pyramid and give this a try?" asked Arielle.

They nodded in agreement and headed off in separate directions with a renewed sense of purpose.

* * * *

The sun was strong but the soft breeze sent a chill through Arielle's body and she put her arm through Maya's, they walked side by side interlinked. "I'm glad to see you smile," Arielle said nudging her friend. "I talked with Alex. He told me what happened."

Maya slowed down and looked straight ahead trying to forget the scene with him. Her mood mellowed again at the mention of their conversation. "I don't know how patient he's going to be but it was a good sign to hear him joking. I can't blame him. I must seem unpredictable to him but…"

"I know, it's something you have to do. You know what I think?"

"I'm afraid to ask."

"I think it never hurts for a woman to be a little unpredictable," Arielle said trying to lighten her spirits again. "Why don't we forget about that for now. I didn't mean to bring you down." She tugged on Maya's arm to get her moving again. "Come on. Let's get right up close to the side of the pyramid."

I am blessed to have found friends like Arielle and Cade. She couldn't allow herself to think of Alex right now. She needed to concentrate on the task at hand.

The blocks of stone that make up the pyramid are the color of gold sand. They are huge, anywhere from two to five feet high and it looked like an arduous task for anyone attempting to climb them.

"You know, here we are walking beside this massive structure but I still can't comprehend the reality of it. I mean, look at this thing. Look at the size of these blocks!" Maya exclaimed. "How could they have been moved much less lifted up that high!"

Standing arm in arm they stood gazing upwards in silence.

"I know what you mean," said Arielle. "It's like walking in a dream. I'm just a girl from Coos Bay, Oregon. Things like this just don't happen."

Maya collected herself out of her dreamlike state. "But they do and we're proof of that. We're here and we have a job to do, so we better focus."

"Right-o. Let's go." Arielle released her arm from Maya's; recognizing it was time to get down to business. "Any idea what we're looking for?"

"Why don't we focus on each step and tune in to our breathing. Let's try to ignore all the people around us and imagine that we're the only ones here."

They walked slowly without speaking. Turning the west corner, then the south.

"You getting anything?" asked Arielle hopefully.

"Nothing. The energy here is extremely high. My body feels like it's buzzing but I haven't noticed anything else unusual. No spikes or changes in the energy. What about you?"

"Same."

Stopping to stretch and take a drink from her bottle of water, Maya noticed Douglas behind them in the distance, out of the corner of her eye. *That's odd, he's not with Vivienne. I never see them apart.*

"I wished I brought my Herkimer with me. I can't believe I never thought to bring it," Maya said, mentally kicking herself. She lifted her hair off the back of her neck hoping the slight breeze would help her to release some of the heat still contained in her body from the meditation.

Arielle, watching Maya's attempt to cool off, felt grateful for putting her long hair into braids. They suited her hippie style of dressing. She refused to give in to fashion trends preferring to be free from societal expectations. She liked to wear big floppy hats, lots of bangles that made noise when she walked, and long flowing skirts. Yes, they were her favorites. They made her feel eclectic and independent.

Her mind wandered to Cade. Absently she removed the cap from her water bottle. She smiled as she remembered their kiss earlier. She took a few sips of water then put the cap back on. "Let's keep moving," she said distracting herself from indulging in thoughts of him.

* * * *

"Alex, wait. I feel something!" Cade said as they approached the Northeast corner of the pyramid.

At the same moment Alex noticed a subtle difference in the air. "What is it?"

"There's a shift in Earth's energy here. It's more electric under my feet. What about you?"

"It's like I walked into a different energy field just as we approached this corner. The air feels finer."

"Come on, let's walk around the corner."

The feeling began to fade about fifteen feet or so away from the turn. At twenty feet it was gone completely.

"It lasts about the same distance on both sides," observed Alex.

They retraced their steps inspecting the area on the pyramid. Touching the stones searching for something, anything that would reveal the nature of the alteration in the energy.

"Nothing. They all look the same," Cade said in frustration.

Alex ran his hands through his hair waiting for some sort of revelation and he began to laugh as Cade leaned his back against the pyramid.

Cade stared at Alex. "What's so funny?"

"Sorry, I just had a vision of you falling backwards into the pyramid through a magical door."

"Well if I go I'll drag you with me." Cade tried to be serious but couldn't help laughing with Alex.

"That would be comical."

"Well I give up here. We should continue and see if anything else comes up," Cade said ending their banter.

They felt discouraged, as the remainder of their walk was uneventful.

Maya and Arielle were sitting on some stone benches near the entrance to the pyramid waiting for them. They waved to Alex and Cade to get their attention when they saw them approaching.

"Did you guys have any luck?" asked Arielle as the guys sat next to them.

After describing their experiences Alex asked them if they experienced anything unusual.

"We noticed a difference in the same spot," started Maya.

"But it was very subtle," added Arielle in disappointment.

Maya noticed Vivienne coming from the same direction that Cade and Alex had just returned from. *I've never seen them apart yet Douglas walked in the same direction as Arielle and I and it looks like Vivienne followed in the guys footsteps. Are they following us?*

Maya brought her attention to Alex, as he said, "Don't get discouraged. This is a good thing. All of us sensed something different in the same spot so we're in sync."

"He's right," offered Cade in support. "Tomorrow we'll search around the Sphinx and see what we come up with. If the entrance is there we'll find it somehow."

*   *   *   *

"This is fantastic. They're getting stronger," Douglas said to Vivienne. "I wasn't convinced in their abilities but they are coming along nicely."

Vivienne nodded in agreement.

"Maya and Arielle noticed a shift in energy at the Northeast corner. Did the guys notice it?"

"Yes they did. They went back and forth along the corners investigating the area. It doesn't line up with where we thought the chamber was though."

"No it doesn't. I have to admit I don't know the cause of it. It doesn't make sense."

"Did Maya see you following her?"

"Yes she did. I pretended to be studying the pyramid when she turned around but it had the desired affect. Did you stay out of sight?"

"Yes. I put a shield around me so even if I was standing right in front of them they wouldn't have seen me."

"Excellent." *Diãntha, my love, the sound of your name in my heart is a clean soothing caress. I long to speak it in your presence. I know that you will recognize it and prefer it to your tellurian name Maya. It's lovely yes but pales greatly in comparison to the quintessential expression of Diãntha.*

Vivienne, reading his thoughts recognized his pattern of coming to believe in his own fantasy character. *Good. It will make it easier for Maya to trust him if he believes his love for her is real.*

Chapter Thirty-two

The tour group had dined at the Sakkara Nest restaurant for lunch. It was an outdoor restaurant lush with grass, trees and bushes like an oasis in the desert. Tainted only by the peculiar meat that bore a striking resemblance to the rumored camel's knuckles, which they heard Egyptian restaurants used to disguise and sell to unsuspecting tourists. Maya and Arielle could not bring themselves to eat the questionable meat and enjoyed just the side salads instead.

When they were returned to the hotel the group of four gathered in a meeting room with the rest of the tour group for an afternoon workshop led by Pamela. The chairs were lined up in rows in a u-shape with Pamela at the head. The walls were painted white with paneled sections in a soft canary color. Potted fig trees and wall lamps placed around the room added an extra warmth. Chatter filled the room as everyone waited for Pamela to begin.

She was a fairly large woman. Tall, big-boned and buxom. Her hair was a shiny sleek black, kept in a shoulder length bob with bangs to frame her face. She exuded enthusiasm and warmth in her manner of speech and people seemed to gravitate towards her embracing presence. She dressed with a stylish comfort and her most noticeable adornments were the over-sized gemstone rings.

Speaking with a slight lisp she began her speech on a serious note. "I know that each and every one of you experienced a reawakening on some level today. Retracing your steps in history is part of your healing. Every time you feel the need to visit some place—follow your heart. It's your soul calling you back to a time when you were left with unresolved pain. Even if you have no memory of that time trust that healing is taking place.

"We're at a crucial time in history. Enough of us must awaken and remember our true heritage. That we are all one. Sparks from the One Mind and each one of us has the ability to set us free from the endless cycle of birth and rebirth by recognizing our immortal essences.

"In order to do this we must focus with a determined mind and heart to live our life purpose. Discover what your calling or passion is and live it, share it with the world.

"But that in itself is not enough to reclaim our authentic selves. We must remove all the garbage that holds us back. How? By digging deep and clearing away all the anguish buried deep within our psyches. This takes perseverance and hard work but it needs to be done.

"The reward for doing this is renewed energy which will lead us to transmute our innermost being into gold. You will rescue your heart and find your treasure bursting with infinite Love and Light. Only by living your absolute truth can we save humanity." Pamela paused to take a sip of water and to allow the meaning of her words sink in to her audience.

"Now I know what you are thinking. That I am blowing reality out of proportion. Or I'm causing undue panic to suit my own agenda. Well let me ask you this. Have you been paying attention to what's going on around you? It's real and it's growing worse at an accelerated pace. In case you hadn't heard Hurricane Roger just wiped out islands from Granada right up to Bahamas just in the last few days and it's heading towards Florida with full force." She watched the nervous looks pass between each other upon hearing this news.

"And a massive earthquake shook through South Africa this morning wiping out the largest area ever by an earthquake. These events are occurring at an alarmingly increasing rate. We've burdened this planet for too long and time is running out.

"Make no mistake, we are reaching a time of transition in the history of mankind. And it will take every one of us to lift the veils and free us from reliving Atlantis.

"Like the planet, everyone here is experiencing a point of transition. You are crying out to free yourself from the burdens of bondage. That's why you signed up as part of this spiritual tour to Egypt, to the Sphinx and the Great Pyramid of Giza. There's power in numbers and what each one of you will do during our meditations and ceremonies will be magnified by one hundred and fifty percent. And that will go out into the world making it easier for others to follow.

"Our ceremony tomorrow will help you eradicate the burdens you and your life experiences have placed upon you. Then you will be liberated to live more fully. Live with the intention that the rest of your life will be the best of your life.

"I see this transition as the Phoenix rising from the ashes and rebirthing into a new star. That's what each and every one of you are and what the planet will be too, the *Phoenix Star.*

"You will all go back as teachers and do what you have been called to do in this life. There's not one person in this room who does not have a mission and after this trip you will see what that mission is with clarity."

The room was soundless with the exception of a few people shifting in their seats.

"I don't want to frighten you. I want you to stand up and take your place in the universe. We'll do it together. What's that saying? *United we stand.* You've all had a long day and it's getting late. I'll take some questions now then we'll have a break until dinner. Yes you." Pointing to a women to her right in the second row. "What is your question?"

"You talked about clearing away past pain. How do I know what I should choose to work on?" the woman asked.

"You have to chip away layer by layer. I suggest that you make a list of events or relationships that need healing. Prioritize them and work on them one at a time," said Pamela. She pointed to another audience member.

"I've tried healing experiences from my past but I find that the emotions come back again the next time something triggers it. Is there a way to heal it so it never haunts me again?"

"That's an excellent question. I'll share with you a method I find works with almost one hundred percent certainty. It's a lot of hard work and you have to dig and dig, getting your fingers bruised but it is worth it. The first step is recognizing your anger. That's not always easy. Sometimes we bury it so deep we deny it's there. But it is. You cannot heal your past without discovering and releasing your anger. First write it down, then give it a voice. Scream, yell or swear. That's not enough though. You must also have a physical release from your body. Beat a pillow or a punching bag. My favorite is taking a small towel, rolling it up and beating a bed. You might feel silly at first but trust me once you start, it wants to release and its force will amaze you.

"The second step is to heal the sadness that will naturally occur during this process. Allow yourself to feel sad, write about it and talk about it with someone close.

"The third step is to become aware of any fears that come up. Focus on them, write them down and voice them.

"The fourth layer is longing. What didn't you get in your relationships but always wanted? What do you wish could have been?

"And finally you will need to find forgiveness. Lewis Smedes said '*When we forgive, we set a prisoner free and discover that the prisoner we set free is us*'. This is the last layer to work through to rescue your heart and it's the most challenging. Probably because our egos like to have the power that comes from feeling wronged because then we can blame others for our lives. Forgiveness is a gift to yourself. Any more questions?"

"How will I know if I've cleared out all the anger?" asked another woman in the audience.

"You'll know when you fall to your knees from exhaustion and start crying. You'll know when you think of the event or person and it no longer triggers the feelings inside." Pamela nodded to the next person.

"What if I don't do the anger part but I do everything else?"

"Then you haven't healed. Releasing the anger is the only way to complete the process," said Pamela with irritation. "Next?"

The questions continued while Maya debated with herself about asking Pamela if she had any knowledge of the hidden chamber. In the end she decided to wait and look for an opportunity to approach Pamela in privacy before she left the room.

As luck would have it the opportunity did presented itself and she motioned for Arielle, Alex and Cade to follow her. Just as Pamela was walking away from the head of the room she caught her. "Excuse me Pamela? I'm sorry to bother you but I wanted to ask you if you could help us with something."

Pamela looked a little tired and irritable. "What is it?"

"Well um…I uh…We were wondering if you know anything more about the hidden chamber you spoke of earlier today?"

She eyed them carefully and looked beyond them into the distance. "You're looking for the sacred Stone." She paused and turned around looking for Douglas and Vivienne. "Ask them," she said and pointed, "they can help you on your quest." With that statement she began to walk away leaving Maya and the others speechless.

*　*　*　*

"Here they come. I want you to extend the invitation to join us for dinner and talk warmly with Maya. It will help her and the rest of them to feel more at ease." Douglas and Vivienne waited in the lobby for the group to approach. Being the masters of disguise they managed to give the illusion of just arriving.

Vivienne nodded in understanding and smiled affectionately at the group as they approached. "Hello. Our timing is impeccable. It's wonderful to see you all."

"Hi Vivienne, Douglas," Maya smiled and looked tentatively towards Douglas, anxiously pushing her hair behind her ears.

How charming, she's nervous to be near me. Douglas extended his hand to Alex and Cade, "Gentlemen." He noticed a slight hesitation on Alex's part but Cade appeared comfortable. *Ah, he's worried about me. Good, he should be, he'll not have her this time.*

Douglas moved a little closer to Arielle and touched her arm very lightly. "You look lovely tonight Arielle. But then you always look lovely and tonight is no exception."

"Thank you," said Arielle noticing Cade move closer to her side. *Like he needs to remind me of his presence, I'm not the one Douglas is after.*

"It was an amazing day. Wasn't it?" Vivienne asked. She noticed their nods of agreement but didn't wait for a response. "I'd love to hear about how you felt visiting the Sphinx and Pyramid. Will you join us for dinner?"

Surprisingly Cade responded enthusiastically, "That sounds like a great idea."

Following Pamela's pronouncement Maya, Arielle, Alex and Cade had a group discussion and decided not to fight the guidance that was being offered to them. It was pretty clear there was a reason they met Douglas and Vivienne and they prepared themselves to follow through with finding out why.

The atmosphere in the restaurant was relaxed and casual. Even Douglas and Vivienne seemed less formal as they joked and laughed with ease.

Douglas sat back and glanced around the table while they enjoyed an assortment of fresh fruit and cookies for dessert. He toyed with his signet ring, twisting it around his finger. It irritated him to discover he was anxious. To distract himself from this nervous gesture he leaned forward, put his elbows up on the table and rested his chin on his interlaced hands.

Taking a quick scan, Maya on his left. *This is her place, by my side. She'll see that soon enough even if she's resisting it right now.* He scowled inside watching Alex beside her. *He won't give up. He'll see he's no match for me.*

His annoyance was short lived as he examined Arielle and Cade. Pleased to see there was no resistance at the forefront of their minds. *Pamela opened her mind long enough for me to plant the thought and it worked. I don't even think she'll remember directing them to me. Even if she does she won't know where the thought came from and assume it was her guides.*

Not moving his position he continued to smile and participate in the conversations while mentally placing an invisible shield of protection around the table. *I don't want anyone to join us or interrupt our conversations. It's time to move in.*

Feeling the sphere enclose them Vivienne took her cue from Douglas. "I had the impression seeing the Sphinx caused a lot of turmoil today. Why do you think that is?" she inquired.

Arielle looked briefly at Maya and decided to speak up first. "I believe a lot of emotions were stirred up from a past life experience here. Maya and Alex seemed to be affected more than Cade and I. Isn't that right Cade?"

"Yes I'd have to agree. Although they were intense, these two were definitely hit harder," said Cade thoughtfully.

"Were any of you able to identify any specific memories?" asked Douglas.

Maya shifted in her seat, feeling a great deal of discomfort.

"What is it Maya? I know it was painful but it can't hurt you any longer," offered Douglas tenderly.

Tears appeared in her eyes unexpectedly. "While I was looking out at the Sphinx from the plateau I closed my eyes for a minute to steady myself because the emotions coming to the surface were so intense." She avoided mentioning she was in Alex's arms at the time. "Suddenly I was overwhelmed by cloudlike bursts of red flames. It felt like they were coming towards me." The memory was still too painful. She had to pause before she could continue. "I had the sensation of being struck and I couldn't breathe."

Alex started to reach for her hand, when he saw her pull away he withdrew trying to respect her need for space. But inside it hurt him to know she was in so much pain and turning away from him. He wanted to ask her why she didn't tell him about it when suddenly, a vision emerged. Startling him with its unexpected force.

"What is it Alex?" asked Maya as she wiped away tears with her napkin.

"I just had this vision of seeing the sky fill with flames and smoke and it filled me with panic. I saw myself running towards it. Do you think our visions are connected?"

Douglas saw an opportunity and his brilliant mind quickly seized it. "You were all experiencing a memory from your lives during the fall of Atlantis." He watched Maya carefully as his words sunk in.

Her eyes reeled back in her head. Pain exploded in her body. *What's happening to me?* She saw a black hole emerge in her mind. It drew her in till there was nothing but darkness.

Alex jumped up to grab Maya as her body hit her chair with enough power to knock it backwards. "Maya! What the hell is happening?" he yelled and looked to Douglas for help.

Arielle and Cade leaped swiftly to Maya's side. Vivienne said with control, "Douglas do something!"

"Maya, listen to me," said Douglas with conviction. Alex held her steady in the chair while Douglas leaned close. "Maya." He placed his index finger on her temple, his forefinger on her cheekbone and his thumb along her jaw line. Concentrating on sending her a wave of healing energy along with his message. "You are alive and healthy. That pain is from a distant past. It can no longer hurt you and now it is time to heal from it. Reclaim your lost essence and come back to your body." He spoke in a soft trancelike monotone voice.

Alarmed by her stillness, everyone waited for some sign of life.

"Diãntha, hear my voice. Your Spirit survived and you are living another life now. Your name is Maya. Do you hear me? I am Melïon. I'm here to help you. Your name is Maya now." Douglas was getting worried. *She shouldn't be taking this long to return. Come on my love. Diãntha, you must return.* Growing weary of waiting he commanded, "Come back and fulfill your destiny."

They were in a world unto themselves, enclosed by the sphere. No one paid any attention to the unusual and disturbing scene taking place at their table. Not even a noise could be heard throughout the restaurant as they waited to see if Maya would regain consciousness. The veil around them gave the false impression they were in another dimension.

He tried again in a lower and more commanding voice, "Come back and fulfill your destiny!"

Maya's eyes began to flit from side to side under her lids. Twitch. Flicker. She gasped a breath of air, then another. Her eyes opened and she struggled to get her focus. "What…What happened?" she asked in a thin whisper.

Arielle grabbed a glass of water and put it to Maya's lips. "You were unconscious Maya. You weren't even breathing."

Douglas took her hands in his and looked into her eyes steadily. "Maya. You are safe. Do you understand?"

She nodded disoriented. "I think so."

"I don't want to strain you any more." Secretly he hoped she had the strength of conviction to want answers.

"No please. I need to understand."

Douglas looked to Vivienne and she nodded in agreement. *Good.*

"Maya you recognized the truth of my words and were pulled back in time to Atlantis. You relived something that happened to you. I wanted to guide you and put protection around you so you would not physically experience it again but you went in too fast. I've never seen it happen so quickly before."

"Tell us about what happened there," she said shakily, her face still ashen from the trauma. She braced herself to hear the story.

"You were one of the great leaders in Atlantis. We were all leaders at some level and we worked together closely. You were working in your temple trying desperately to find a way to encode your master crystal with the secret mysteries so that the knowledge would live forever on this planet for future races to discover."

She covered her face with her hands and leaned forward trying to ease the nauseousness that was building. "Yes, I have a vague memory of that," she whispered.

Arielle was kneeling by Maya's side. Her hand on her knee to offer support.

Alex's legs grew weak from worry. He sat down in anticipation of what would be revealed next.

Douglas continued, "There were people, forces against you and what you were trying to do. An attack was launched not only on you but others." He paused briefly to watch her carefully. "Your temple was blown up. I heard what they were going to do and I wanted to warn you." *Lies mixed in with truth are very difficult to detect. She'll never find what's hidden in my words.* "I saw you on your terrace from the ground. The first blast had already detonated and you were trying to escape. You turned for one last look and faced the explosion rising up. It hit you Maya, full impact."

"I was killed instantly," she sobbed from the depths of her soul. She was filled with misery. Not only for the loss of her life prematurely but for the loss of her work, those she loved and her people. She let Arielle take her into her arms to comfort her, aware that this must be the message she received from the Herkimer in her dream.

"Yes. Your death was immediate," said Douglas.

Alex tuning into the memory relived the anguish he felt at the sight of her tower crumbling. He could not get to her in time.

Cade, standing beside Alex, firmly positioned his hand on his grieving friend's shoulder.

"There's more," said Douglas gazing with moistened eyes at them, one at a time. "Maya's body was never found. No remains, all signs of her just disappeared."

"What do you mean disappeared?" questioned Cade.

"No trace. No clothing or jewelry. Even her crystal disappeared." He looked directly into Maya's eyes to continue, "Vivienne and I looked for you for many lifetimes. We thought you were lost forever."

Arielle recognized this event as being the one Maya spoke about. She looked into Maya's eyes and was on the verge of making a comment but something in Maya's eyes asked her to keep this between them.

Vivienne spoke next in a calm voice. "Until a few months ago." Standing beside her husband, she put her hand on his shoulder and they exchanged knowing looks. "Douglas was travelling in meditation and he received a familiar signal. It was faint but it was there. He recognized it as your resonance. We couldn't believe it at first but it grew stronger as the days went by. He was able to follow traces of your thought patterns and we knew you were coming here."

"Why do you think you were not able to detect her until now?" asked Arielle.

"I believe her spirit was shattered into hundreds if not thousands of filaments. It's common in a violent death for the soul to break away into a few fragments and over the course of a couple of lifetimes the person will be able to reclaim these lost parts as they evolve. That's why it is so important to travel to places you feel called towards. When you travel back in time your cellular memories have an opportunity to heal allowing you to become more complete. However, Maya's case was so severe. Her soul was ripped apart so completely it is utterly amazing she's here today." He looked to her with adoration in his eyes.

"It's more than amazing it's miraculous," added Vivienne showing an unusual amount of emotion as she held back her own tears.

Douglas continued, "You have come a long way. You've worked hard and against all odds you are nearly whole again. I know what you experienced today was painful but you are collecting the final filaments completing your cycle."

"What do you mean completing my cycle?" asked Maya.

"This is your last cycle in this dimension. Not just you, all of us. Now that you are remembering and awakening it will be time for us to move to a greater reality and our success will be guaranteed."

"Douglas I think we should move to the lounge where we can be more comfortable and you can answer some more questions," said Vivienne.

"Good idea. Maya are you all right to move?"

"Yes. I'm feeling better."

Alex and Arielle offered Maya their arms to support her as they left the restaurant.

Chapter Thirty-three

He called me Diãntha. It was like a soft caress. Melïon, how did we know each other? What was our relationship? And Alex, what about him? Maya thought about Alex as they headed to the lounge. Willing him to appear from her memories. Some letters began to form in her mind. She focused, oblivious to her surroundings as she walked, and continued to summon his name to her conscious mind. Nared. She looked at Alex and recognized him. *Yes Nared.*

Douglas and Vivienne walked ahead of the others, it's just the way things were, he was always in the lead.

Vivienne whispered to him, "I think you should let Alex sit beside her. Before you object, please listen." Observing his irritation she continued with her reasoning. "If you try to alienate him from Maya he will turn against you."

"Actually that's not a bad idea. I just had a brainstorm on how to solve this situation. Follow my lead." They seated themselves in the lounge. Douglas feeling very pleased with his solution orchestrated his environment to his liking.

Maya found herself in between Douglas and Alex. She noticed something shifted between the men and she no longer felt the animosity from Douglas towards Alex. *That's interesting. Thank goodness. I hope Alex relaxes. I'm tired of the tense energy between them and I certainly don't feel like dealing with it tonight.*

A waiter came to take their drink order before they had an opportunity to begin discussions.

Arielle, who was sitting on the opposite sofa with Cade and Vivienne leaned forward to ask Douglas a question. "Do you know all of our names?"

"Yes, as a matter of fact I do," responded Douglas.

Maya jumped in, "I think I remember Alex's name." She looked at Alex whose curiosity was obviously piqued and she smiled.

"Well? Are you going to share it with us?" asked Arielle excitedly.

Maya looked to Douglas for confirmation before saying it out loud. She knew by now he could pick it out of her head.

"Yes you are correct. Your memory is improving. I'm very proud of you. Generally I would not recommend releasing this information because I believe that everyone must wait for it to come from within. But this is a special scenario and since I've already revealed yours I can hardly contradict myself. Go ahead." He gave her an affirmative nod, impressed that she had the foresight to receive his approval first. Quickly he projected himself into her thoughts to examine her memories. Finding what he was looking for he plucked it out before she had any awareness that he was present.

Teasingly she prolonged revealing Alex's name. She looked at him, then Cade and Arielle like a cat that had just caught a mouse.

"Come on Maya, tell us," said Cade impatiently.

"Okay I was just playing with you." She felt lighthearted and like the weight of thousands of years was lifting from her soul. She spoke his name, rolling her tongue to get the proper pronunciation. "Nared." She watched a look of recognition wash over Alex with delight.

"Yes…" Alex uttered and sat back to reflect on his name as the waiter delivered their drinks.

Douglas, in a very good mood and feeling generous paid for everyone's drinks.

"Can I make a suggestion?" asked Vivienne looking to the group.

"Of course," said Cade curiously.

"It's still relatively quiet in here. I don't think they start the music up until ten. Why don't we let Cade and Arielle take a few minutes to meditate on their names. With everything that's happened maybe it'll trigger their memories as well."

"That's an excellent idea dear," said Douglas. "I'll guide them in. Would you like to give it a try?" he asked Cade and Arielle.

"Absolutely," said Arielle enthusiastically and looked to Cade who was nodding in agreement.

Douglas brought a chair over and placed it close to Cade and Arielle. "I want you to take a deep breath and exhale. I'm going to help you to relax by bringing your attention to various parts of your body and I want you to mentally tell yourself to relax that part. Now, focus your attention on your scalp. Feel the sensations in that area and mentally tell yourself to relax your scalp." Taking a few minutes to work his way down the body they were able to allow their minds to escape into the alpha level where information from the spiritual dimension can be detected.

His voice was deep and low, "Now take another deep breath and relax even further. I'm going to count down from ten to one and when I reach the number one you will be in an even deeper level of relaxation. Ten, nine, eight..." he continued down to one.

Alex and Maya watched with anticipation. He had been surprised when Douglas had motioned for him to sit beside Maya, and now he found it extremely difficult to feel her so close and not reach out to touch her.

"On the count of three I want you to imagine there is a theatre screen about twenty feet in front of you. You will imagine looking at this screen through the area of your third eye, an area just above your eyebrows. One, two, three. You are now looking at the screen.

"Let yourself imagine living in a place filled with a lush landscape. You are walking along a pathway surrounded by rich green bushes with large flowers in every color. The aroma from the flowers awakens the senses. The leaves are swaying from a gentle breeze. The sun is shining. The winding pathway leads you to a crystal temple. You enter this temple and go down a staircase. In the center of this room a guide awaits you. This guide is wearing a long purple robe with a gold sash. As you approach your guide you notice that he is holding a paper scroll."

Vivienne monitored their psyches to ensure a rogue memory didn't pop up to alter the desired sequence. Douglas mentally communicated the idea he spoke of earlier to her so she knew what to expect.

"As you approach your guide take notice of the paintings on the walls or any other objects in this room. Your guide greets you and hands the scroll to you. You open the scroll and see your Atlantean name printed in gold letters. Take your time. Study it. Feel the vibration of the letters."

He waited for a few minutes allowing them time to formulate the letters. Cade was successful first and Arielle followed shortly after.

"Now acknowledge your understanding to your guide and thank him for sharing it with you. It is an honor to receive this information and you must treat it with reverence." Douglas guided them back out of the temple and the gardens. "Imagine your screen has now gone blank. At the count of five you will open your eyes, remember the name given to you and feel in perfect health." He counted slowly and brought them out of their meditation.

They stretched their arms upwards at the same time and laughed together.

"That was amazing Douglas," exclaimed Arielle. She leaned closer to Douglas and gave him a hug. "Thank you."

"You are very welcome."

Cade struggled to fight the moisture in his eyes. "That was very powerful."

"I can see that Alex and Maya are anxious to hear what names were revealed." Douglas laughed, "You better share it or you will have a riot on your hands."

Arielle spoke first, "My name is La-Rouna," she liked the sound on her tongue.

"La-Rouna," repeated Cade enjoying the sound and feelings it stirred. He reached out to take Arielle's hand and gazed deeply into her eyes. "My name is Barakü."

"Congratulations. You both did very well," said Vivienne warmly. "You have all made huge progress today and I can imagine how powerful tomorrow's ceremony will be for you, especially now."

"Vivienne we have not learned your name yet. Will you tell us?" asked Alex.

"Of course. It is Kanïka."

"That's a beautiful name. Thank you for sharing it with us," said Maya.

Douglas moved the chair away and sat back on the other side of Maya.

She felt his leg lightly touching hers but forced herself to ignore it. "How did we all know each other?" she asked.

"You and Kanïka were sisters. Barakü and La-Rouna were deeply in love and she was one of your cousins. Kanïka and I were also lovers and we were also your close friends."

"And Alex, or I guess I should say Nared?"

Ah here is the moment I've been waiting for. "He was yours and Kanïka's brother." His smile widened knowing he just assured his victory.

It took a great effort for Maya to maintain her composure. "Oh I see." The shock of the news made such an impact she did not hear the warning in the back of her mind. *Is that why I've resisted becoming involved with Alex?*

Alex's mind reeled with the news. *Brother! I know we were close to each other but...Brother? Why did I think we were intimate with each other? Maybe that's why she's so confused about us and needs time. Oh God, what have I done?*

"You were very close and Nared was very protective of you. I warned him of the plot against you and he tried to get to you too but it was too late." *Fabulous, it's working. I'm brilliant!*

* * * *

Cade could clearly see that his companions were trying to comprehend this latest bit of information. *I knew the minute I met Arielle that she was my soul mate. I'm pretty sure Alex felt the same way about Maya. This must be very confusing for him. Christ I'm confused.*

He thought about the camaraderie that instantly developed between the four of them and recognized the connection with Douglas and Vivienne. *Yes, this is not the first time we've functioned as a group.*

Maya still trying to grasp the misunderstanding of her relationship with Alex became aware of a something that didn't fit with Douglas' explanation. "Excuse me Douglas, but I have to admit I'm confused about something."

"Yes what is it?" asked Douglas comfortable he had not missed anything in his revelations that would cause discomfort.

"If the explosion happened in Atlantis, which I believe is true then why was this memory triggered at the Sphinx? It's a different period in time.

"That is a very good question and I can understand why it confuses you. I believe it is because both locations are very much connected through the Gods and the Akashic records of all of our lives are stored beneath the area of the Sphinx. Its energy was communicating to you and you reunited with your destiny in both the past and the future realms."

Maya wasn't sure she understood the explanation completely but something kept her from pursuing it any further. Her instincts were telling her it would make more sense at a later time. "Oh I see, thank you."

"My pleasure," responded Douglas.

"Douglas, last night you said you were recruited into a group to test psychic phenomena. What kind of test group was it?" asked Cade.

"A number of years ago I was a captain in the army. My intuition got my team out of dangerous situations on several occasions and word about this got around. It made my superiors very uncomfortable because I proved them wrong on a couple of missions. So they found a way to get rid of me. One of the generals heard about Star Gate and got my name on the list as a test subject."

"What is Star Gate?" asked Arielle.

"It is a remote viewing program that has been conducted by the CIA and other sections of the government under a variety of names."

"How is this program used?" asked Alex.

"People gifted with psychic abilities are trained to gather intelligence information from a distance in the ether. Over twenty million dollars has been spent developing Star Gate and related programs and activities."

"Were you accepted?" asked Cade.

"Yes. I went through a series of tests and was subsequently transferred to Fort Meade for further training."

"How did you feel about this?" asked Maya.

"At the time I was ecstatic. It was exciting and the possibilities of finding terrorists was very alluring to me at that time."

"Can you tell us some of the things you did?" asked Arielle hopefully.

"On one occasion I was able to locate a couple of hostages held in Lebanon which led to their rescue. Another time I discovered the coordinates of a ship containing chemical weapons in a Libyan port and we were able to seize the shipment before it reached its destination."

Arielle was impressed. "That sounds very rewarding. You must feel good about the work you did. Are you still active?"

"Unfortunately yes, but I'm working on something which I hope will free me from the obligation."

Alex caught the note of bitterness in his voice. "Why do you say unfortunately?"

Douglas' eyes connected with Vivienne's in hopes of easing the moroseness, which sometimes consumed him. "Those are only examples of the good things I've been asked to do. Regrettably I've also been given assignments which I'm not proud of and keep me awake many nights." Douglas did not fight the emotions and tears that welled up. "I apologize for being so gloomy but sometimes I can't control the memories that consume me." He tilted his head back and rolled his shoulders to ease the tension.

In a contrastingly sharp tone he added, "But those are private experiences and only Vivienne knows about the things I've had to do. Even she should not know but we are so connected I couldn't hide them from her if I tried."

An awkward silence descended the group. They felt a wave of sympathy for him. Even Alex found himself feeling remorseful for judging Douglas so harshly. He couldn't imagine the kinds of things he's had to do.

Vivienne realized she needed to change the direction of this conversation and bring her husband back up to a better place. *He'll brood here for hours if I don't do something.* She cleared her throat to get everyone's attention. "There are also a lot of good things that have resulted from his work. In his spare time Douglas discovered a way to travel to other dimensions during his meditations. He's experienced communication with a Higher Intelligence, which has helped him to become a more spiritual person. It's the reason why he's working on a plan to get himself out of the program," she finished with love and pride in her voice.

Douglas was quiet. He appeared lost in thought.

Maya became aware that music had begun to play and people were moving to the dance floor. But none of that interested her. She wanted to help Vivienne rescue Douglas from his sadness. "Does the remote viewing let you see into people's pasts?"

Vivienne mouthed a silent thank you to Maya for being so perceptive. *Ah my sister, you are uniquely gifted and I hope you are able to awaken to your full power in time. So much is resting on your abilities.*

Douglas made the effort to pull himself out of his despondency. "Yes. Yes I can travel backwards and occasionally forwards in time. It's easier to pinpoint major events in someone's life." He began to speak as a leader once again with increasing energy. "You know those moments that alter the course of one's life. In your cases, each one of you experienced a major incident during your lives that made you feel alone and abandoned. The impact was great enough to make you wonder why you didn't fit in anywhere. Always searching to make friends but it rarely worked."

Alex nodded to himself awed by Douglas' skillfulness. "Do very many people have this happen to them?" he asked.

"Not really. Only the small percentage of people who have incarnated to live their last cycle in this dimension. These people have evolved enough throughout their lifetimes to become teachers and lead others on their way to enlightenment."

"And you believe that the four of us are on a journey to become teachers?" asked Cade.

"Yes. It is your destiny," said Douglas with conviction.

The sound of the music in the background increased making it very difficult for them to continue their conversation.

Vivienne took this as a sign that their lesson for this evening was ending. "I think we should retire for the evening. You have a lot of information to process and everyone needs to get some rest."

* * * *

"What are you thinking Maya?" asked Arielle as they were pulling the covers back on the beds that night. They had been back in their room for about half an hour.

Taking turns to wash their face, brush their teeth, the usual rituals to prepare for bed. Maya had been very quiet the whole time, barely speaking a word.

"I guess I'm just trying to absorb everything that happened." She plopped down on the bed and burst into tears.

Arielle quickly sat down beside her and rubbed her back. "Maya, oh my goodness. What's wrong?"

"I'm so confused. I thought for sure Alex and I were lovers. I figured Douglas was just a distraction and I would just handle it. I assumed that when we worked through this Alex and I would end up together."

"Just because Douglas says he was your brother doesn't mean the relationship has to be platonic in this life."

"But it wouldn't make sense." Maya paused before telling Arielle that Douglas told her that they've been together before.

"That's ridiculous. He said he and Vivienne were lovers and they were your friends."

"I know but…"

"But what?"

"I'm attracted to him and I'm afraid that now that I know about Alex I won't be able to resist Douglas."

"Well maybe you're not supposed to resist. You keep saying you need to pursue this thing to find out what he knows. Who knows, maybe it's part of your destiny."

"Arielle! That's crazy. How can you say that?" Her whole body was trembling. Her thoughts spiraling downward into an abyss.

"You're in a very tough spot but it's obvious that you are the key to our success." Taking her friend's hand in hers, she looked her in the eyes. "Maya, you're going to have to do what feels right to you."

"That's what I'm afraid of." Her stomach was knotted in anguish. *I hate to admit it but Arielle's right. I failed humanity before I can't fail them again.*

She got into bed and pulled the covers up to her chin. "Goodnight Arielle."

Arielle drew her friend close and embraced her reassuringly, "Goodnight Maya."

There's something that's not quite sitting right but there's only one way to find out. She was learning some very valuable things from the master and she visualized putting these thoughts behind a steel door and locking it tight.

When she finally drifted off to sleep she felt herself being pulled into another realm of existence. She decided not to resist and slipped away with him.

Chapter Thirty-four

Arielle poked her head in through the bathroom door and shouted to Maya who was showering, "I'm going to call Cade and Alex to let them know we're going to be late for breakfast." They had slept in after having forgotten to arrange for a wake up call before going to bed.

"Good idea. I'll just be a few minutes," Maya shouted back.

They both managed to be ready for the day in a record breaking half an hour for two women. Arielle had arranged to meet Alex and Cade in the lobby at eight o'clock and they would be really rushing to be ready for an eight thirty departure.

The elevator stopped on the sixth floor. When the door opened the strange woman who Arielle was originally scheduled to room with walked in. Maya and Arielle stole a quick glance at each other. Every time they saw her she was always dressed in black and wore the same black cowboy hat with the black fur tail hanging down the back.

The woman sneered at them as she walked in. "Bitch," she whispered to Arielle.

Arielle was stunned, "Excuse me? Did you say something?"

"What's the matter? You think you're too good to be in the same room as me? Miss uppity, that's what you are."

Maya pulled Arielle closer to her wanting to avoid a confrontation.

"You'll regret switching rooms, you'll see. I could have helped you. Everybody here thinks Pamela is so wise but soon everyone will see that I'm the enlightened one, not her. I'm the one who can lead everyone to a higher place. My day is coming. You'll see and you'll be sorry."

Oh God what's taking the elevator so long to get to the lobby? Come on. Maya held Arielle's hand tight.

The elevator finally stopped on the ground floor. Maya and Arielle darted out as quickly as they could.

"You can't run from me. I can always find you," she said snidely as she stomped out behind them.

Arielle spotted the boys straight ahead waiting for them. "Cade, Alex! Thank God!"

"What's wrong?" said Cade with concern in his eyes.

Arielle turned to look back but the woman had disappeared. She described the altercation to Cade and Alex and gave them the background on almost being stuck rooming with the woman.

"I've never met anyone so wacko before," said Maya. "The hair on my arms and back of my neck were standing straight up. It was so creepy."

"Let's make sure to stay away from her," said Alex. He was so torn with mixed emotions seeing Maya and hated the thought of not being there to protect her. "Which one is she?" he asked as they walked through the lobby and into the restaurant.

Arielle and Maya looked around but couldn't see the woman anywhere. "I don't see her. Believe me you'll know her when you see her," said Maya shaking her head in disbelief.

Vivienne caught Maya's attention and waved. Having been so late to appear, another group of people had joined Douglas and Vivienne for breakfast. They went over to say good morning before looking for another table.

"Well good morning. Looks like someone must have had a difficult time getting up this morning," Douglas smiled and winked at Maya.

She was glad to not have any recollection of her dreams last night. *There's been so much to absorb I need some time.*

Arielle laughed and said, "Yes, we forgot to schedule a wake up call."

"Looks like you could have slept in longer," he added. "Our trip to Giza has been postponed until tomorrow."

"What? Why?" asked Arielle, disheartened.

"There have been some protests taking place in Cairo this morning and the travel company doesn't want to take any chances. They recommend we stay in the hotel for the day."

"Oh that's so disappointing. I hope no one's been hurt," replied Cade.

"They didn't say. It's probably nothing serious and they're just taking precautions. Vivienne and I are just finishing up here. We're going to head back to our room. I got paged during the night and have some work to do."

"That's too bad," said Alex. "I guess in your line of work you're always on call."

"Something like that. Why don't you join us for dinner tonight?"

They agreed to meet in the Italian restaurant at seven o'clock.

"Well, we'll let you get to work," said Alex.

They found a table and decided to grab breakfast from the buffet even though they now had enough time to order something fresh.

"There's that woman. She's pacing." Arielle pointed to the far left of their table.

"Where? I don't see her," said Cade.

Arielle looked again but she was gone. "That's weird. I know I saw her."

"Forget about her. What should we do today?" asked Cade trying to distract her.

The restaurant had emptied out and only a few people continued to linger over breakfast.

"I was thinking we could look through my books to search for some clues," suggested Maya. "We can't afford to waste any time. Anybody have any other ideas?"

Alex yawned and stretched his arms over his head. He didn't get much sleep last night and his nerves were on edge after the previous night's revelations. "I agree with Maya, we need to stay focused." He looked at the date on his watch and felt his stomach tighten. December third, only eighteen more days. "Why don't we check out the lounge. We could grab a couple of those sofas and hang out there." He considered suggesting using his suite but things were awkward enough and changed his mind.

"Come on let's go. We'll follow you ladies up to your room to get the stuff," said Cade.

As they walked through the lobby Maya had an eerie feeling and the hair on the back of her neck went up again. She looked around and thought she saw the outline of the woman with the cowboy hat but it happened so quickly she couldn't be sure. *I must have gotten spooked and now I can't shake her.* It left her with a very uncomfortable feeling.

Alex sensed her discomfort. "Are you okay Maya?"

"Yeah. Just a little tired. I could have used a few extra hours sleep. I'm not used to keeping this kind of pace every day." She had a difficult time turning to others for help. During her years with Brian he would tell her she was too needy and asked too much from him. In the last year or so when she stopped turning to him she started to finally learn to rely on herself. It was a scary thought to share herself and trust her feelings again with someone.

* * * *

They found themselves face to face with the deranged woman coming out of the elevator twenty minutes later.

Arielle and Maya jumped nervously.

Alex and Cade instinctively moved themselves in front of the girls to protect them. "What do you want?" barked Alex.

The woman began to circle them. Her face contorted as she hissed, "You'll never find what you're looking for. You're fools to think my master will let you."

"I suggest you leave my friends and I alone," Cade responded defiantly.

"Or what? What will you do?" she laughed in a nearly hysterical voice. "You think you are strong enough to come up against the master? I'd love to see you try," she said as she disappeared around the corner leaving behind a spine-chilling cackle echoing in the hall.

"She's crazy! We should tell Azizi about her. Oh Maya, thank God you rescued me from rooming with her," exclaimed a shaking Arielle.

"Something's obviously not right with that woman. It's like she's possessed or something. Did you see the way her face twisted up?" added Maya.

"She seemed a bit off when I first met her but not this bizarre," said Arielle shuddering.

"What do you think she means by master?" asked Cade.

Maya's shoulders were rigid and she tried to relax but it was no use. She forced herself to breathe. "I don't know but I suggest we be very careful and keep a low profile on this trip. I can't put my finger on it but I've felt something creepy, like a sinister force following me a couple of times."

"We should stay close together whenever we can. At the very least I don't think you ladies should go anywhere alone," insisted Cade drawing Arielle close to his side.

"Yes father," teased Arielle.

"Laugh all you want but I'm serious," he said.

She gave in, "Okay, okay. Let's forget about this for now and stick with our plans for today."

Papers spread across the table in front of them they scoured through copies of various excerpts of books Maya brought to Egypt.

"This is interesting," said Cade. He was sitting back on the sofa with his legs stretched out in front of him. Wearing faded blue jeans, a white T-shirt and cowboy boots, his blue eyes sparkled with intrigue.

Alex closed one of the books, taking note of where he left off. Maya and Arielle stopped leafing through the papers and waited for him to continue.

"This talks about the Brothers of Darkness. It says they walk among us remaining hidden from man. They've been present from the beginning of time and in order to become a master we must triumph over these mysterious forces and the shadows of our own fears."

"That makes me think of what I said earlier about the ominous sensations I've been experiencing," said Maya.

Alex nodded and rubbed his tired eyes. "You know I just remembered reading once that the closer you get to achieving your dreams the more difficult the obstacles become. The book also said most people give up when it seems like it's hopeless but that's when success is around the next corner."

Arielle added thoughtfully, "Maybe that crazy woman is a test for us. Something to distract us from looking for the Emerald Stone. What else does it say Cade?"

"It says that we must travel through the pathway of Darkness to find the secrets but we must always stay in the Light and the Light is symbolic of the sun shining at the end of the road." He paused to read ahead then continued slowly, "This is a bit confusing. I think it's saying that when we are confronted by Darkness we have to figure out if it's something that's coming from inside us and if it is we are supposed to send waves of energy throughout our bodies until it's gone. Do you guys get this?"

"I'm not sure if it's talking about feelings of anger, sadness and things like that or an actual dark entity like that delusional woman," Arielle said confused.

"Maybe they're one and the same," suggested Maya. "Maybe all of our baggage that we carry actually manifests dark forces in the shape of evil people or creatures."

Alex thought Maya was on to something. "Could be. Pamela talked about facing our wounds and healing our hearts in order to find our treasures or as this says, the Light at the end of the road."

"Are you saying we attracted this woman to stalk us?" Arielle asked with skepticism.

"Not necessarily. This book also says that if we examine our hearts and if our inner wisdom tells us that it's not a force we created it will make us stronger. Then it says we should put a circle around us, raise our hands and call in the Light to free us," responded Cade.

"So how do we know if we are manifesting an evil presence or it's a real dark force trying to stop us?" asked Arielle.

"Maybe we need to do the exercises Pamela suggested. Examine the different parts in our lives and work at healing the problem areas," said Maya.

"That will take too long. You heard her, she said it could take months to work through all of them. We don't have that kind of time," Alex said in frustration. He couldn't believe what he was about to say but they might not have any choice. "Maybe Douglas can help us. He did say he is able go back in time. What if he can help us clear away the obstructions?"

"It's worth a try," Cade said optimistically.

Alex sat up and looked around the room with a look of concern. He wrinkled up his nose trying to decipher what he was sniffing. "Do you smell that?"

The others made an effort to smell what was bothering Alex when suddenly the noxious aroma filled the air around them.

"Oh God! What is that?" exclaimed Arielle coughing.

Cade recognized it immediately. "It's sulfur."

"Sulfur? What would cause that?" questioned Maya waving the air in front of her trying to diffuse the odor.

Guttural sounds coming from behind startled them. The crazy woman abruptly appeared out of nowhere. "You can't hide. I'll find you no matter where you go!" she snarled like a crazed animal. Circling them, she shouted obscenities. Her voice became more menacing with every breath.

"What should we do?" screeched Arielle. "She's crazy."

"Get the hell away from us!" yelled Alex to no avail. He tried to move but her response was more forceful.

"You don't know what to do. Do you? I bet that turns you on doesn't it big guy? I bet it turns you on so much you want to do me! Come on baby. You're such a pretty boy I'd love to do you too."

Alex was shocked into numbness. Neither he nor Cade could bring themselves to get violent with a woman. Even one as crazed as her.

She reached out to touch Alex. He jumped back repulsed, but not quick enough. His arm felt as though it had been burned. Suddenly he was doubled over with unbearable stomach pain. "We need to try to put that circle of protection around us NOW!" he shouted. "Maya think of an invocation to the Light!"

Fighting to stay calm Maya racked her brain for something to hit her. *Think Maya! Think!*

The woman kept circling them.

The stench became unbearable for Arielle. She couldn't breathe. She began coughing violently. Gasping for air. Drops of blood appeared from her nose. "Hurry Maya!" she yelled as she wiped the blood with the back of her hand.

"Get in a circle!" Maya ordered remembering some things Helena had taught her during her months visiting the Heartsong New Age Bookstore. Frantically looking around she grabbed a glass of water on the table. There was no time to look for salt. She poured it around them to act as a shield of protection. Hoping it would work. Raising her hands skyward she began her plea, "By the powers of us four, the Chosen Ones, we stand before you! Fire, Air, Earth, Water! We call to the Light to descend upon us and around us! Protect us from the Brothers of Darkness!"

The woman circled in closer. Snarling. Becoming more impatient.

"Do as I'm doing. Lift your arms and say it with me!" Maya ordered the others. "Cade grab Alex and help him up!"

"By the powers of us four, the Chosen Ones, we stand before you! Fire, Air, Earth, Water. We call to the Light to descend upon us and around us. Protect us from the Brothers of Darkness!" they repeated the prayer following Maya's lead.

Maya yelled, "Again! Say it again!"

Alex fought the pain with all his strength to stand straight reaching his arms upwards. Arielle had no choice but to ignore the blood dripping onto her clothes and the floor to do the same.

The wild woman leaped towards Alex. "I'm coming for you lover boy!" She was hit with an electrical charge. She squealed. It forced her to jump back. She began shouting words in a strange language.

The room around them appeared twisted and darkened. But a shield of Light kept them protected.

* * * *

It was becoming easier for Douglas to find Maya in the ether and even sense a change in her moods. He and Vivienne were working on their laptops catching up on their journal entries for the past few days in their suite.

Feeling a tension building inside caused him to think of Maya. "I think something is beginning to happen," he said to Vivienne.

She acknowledged his statement with a nod and waited for him to update her on their circumstances.

Douglas was a master of his art and was able to go into the alternate levels within seconds. Sitting straight up in his chair, he took a deep breath and counted down, three, two, one and he was there. Once he focused on Maya in his mind he was able to detect her almost immediately. He returned to his room a few minutes later. Seeing what he expected he stood up from his chair. "It's time to go down and take care of the situation." They had been prepared and waiting.

There was a lot of noise and a large crowd gathering in the lobby outside the lounge area. Having already witnessed the scene he knew exactly what to expect. Douglas and Vivienne stormed through the mob of people and they arrived in time to see the wild woman lunging towards Alex. Douglas was surprised to see Maya, Arielle, Alex and Cade had managed to form a circle of protection around them but their efforts didn't take anything away from his objective. As instructed the woman was not giving up her charge.

He strode closer to the scene with authority. "Amin!" he shouted.

The woman stopped in her tracks. She turned to look at Douglas with piercing eyes and venom coming from her breath.

"Is that the best you can do?" taunted Douglas.

"Douglas! Stay away!" shouted Maya frantically, almost in tears.

"Don't get distracted. Stay focussed on the protection around you," he commanded. He turned his attention back to the woman. "Come now, I thought when we met again you would be a more formidable host."

"Are you challenging me? You cannot stop Lucifer! He will always return and in the end you will lose!" Her eyes turned coal black. She charged towards him. When she was close enough she prepared to pounce on Douglas like a tiger.

Standing firm he took a deep breath and released his anger with a swipe of his arm through the air. Without touching her a force of energy hit her with enough power to throw her back several feet, knocking her against a wall. Her head hit a bronze statue and she crumpled unconscious to the floor.

Douglas walked calmly towards her and stood over her dazed body. For a moment he felt pity for this empty woman who was so easily corrupted but only for a moment.

Maya and the others stood motionless in astonishment. Holding their circle of protection around them they watched Douglas perform what looked like an exorcism.

Making the sign of the cross in front of himself he spoke with clarity, "In the name of the Father, Son, and Holy Spirit I release this entity from you." As she started to come back to consciousness he reached down and shockingly pierced his hand right into her chest. She screamed in desperation and fought him with all her strength but Douglas appeared to have the power of ten men within him and managed to hold her down with his other hand. Lifting a dark mass of energy from her chest he spoke a prayer in a commanding voice and everyone watched the Darkness disintegrate into the air.

Vivienne walked quickly towards Maya, Alex, Arielle and Cade. "You're safe now." They released the energy they had been holding allowing Vivienne to come through. She hugged Maya then Arielle, comforting them. "It's okay, he knows what he's doing."

"What happened?" asked Arielle still shaking in disbelief. The bleeding finally stopped and she wiped away the last bits of blood dripping from the corner of her mouth and nose. Cade came to her aid and held her tightly.

"That poor woman was taken over by a dark entity. But it's gone now."

"I've seen things like this happen in the movies. It's hard to believe it takes place in real life," said Alex recovering from the ordeal, the excruciating pain in his abdomen had subsided but he still walked with a limp favoring the residual discomfort. He headed towards Douglas out of curiosity and the others followed him.

The woman lay limply on the ground. Douglas kneeled beside her taking her hand to soothe her wretched soul.

Maya, Arielle, Alex, Cade and Vivienne watched on as Douglas moved his hand in rhythmic circles over her body.

"He's retrieving and healing her fragmented soul," Vivienne explained.

The woman coughed gently and Vivienne offered her some water.

"Take it easy. Don't try to move yet," Douglas said gently as she made an effort to sit up.

Giving up her attempt she laid back down on the floor. "What happened?" she asked weakly, looking pale and disoriented.

"You've just been through quite an episode. Unfortunately you'll remember it in a moment."

A look of remembrance and remorse instantly washed over her face as Douglas finished his sentence. "Oh my God! What have I done?" She looked towards Maya, Alex, Arielle and Cade in anguish and began to sob. "I…I'm sorry." The words were simple yet filled with deep shame. What more could she say. How could she ever mend the wounds she had inflicted?

Still trying to comprehend the entire episode the group felt at a loss for words. Maya looked to Douglas for direction. He nodded in understanding and motioned for her to come closer. She knelt down beside the woman with the others following close behind her.

The group of people she attacked now surrounded this odd woman, dressed all in black. Her signature cowboy hat had fallen off leaving her greasy hair disheveled.

Douglas gave her time to release her emotions through her tears and when she calmed down he spoke in a kind voice. "The most important thing for you to do is to accept that you were temporarily taken over by an evil presence and that what you did, didn't come from you."

"How can I ever forget what I did?" she asked in despair.

"You can't. The only thing you can do is to forgive yourself. I suggest when you go back home that you can get some counseling to help you through this. I've had some experience with this sort of thing and I know people who can help you. If you give me your email address before you leave I'll send you their contact information."

* * * *

They were sharing a couple bottles of wine together with dinner several hours later attempting to soothe their rattled nerves. Reports had to be filed with the police for the disturbance, which consumed the remainder of the afternoon. They discovered the woman's name was Norma and she was from San Francisco.

"I don't know what we would have done if you hadn't come down," said Maya gratefully. "Everyone in the room disappeared when she went crazy. Thank goodness you showed up before the police. God only knows what would have happened to her if they arrived first."

"You're like having a guardian angel around. How did you just happen to come by at the right time?" asked Arielle.

"Vivienne and I were working in our rooms when I had a feeling something was very wrong. I couldn't stop thinking about Maya so I checked in through remote viewing and saw that you were all in danger. We came down right away and the rest is history."

"Well thank God you did," said Cade.

"Why do you think she became so possessed?" asked Alex.

"Norma has a tormented soul and it made her an easy target for the dark side," commented Douglas. "I talked with her while you were all giving your statements. She's been living on the streets since she was barely a teenager and she's involved with a drug dealer who is very abusive. Norma has psychic abilities, which she doesn't know how to control. All of these things added up together leaves her open to questionable energies."

"Do you think she'll get help?" asked Cade.

"It's doubtful. There are too many obstacles preventing her. If she had a solid support system behind her that would make the difference but she doesn't. There is no family to speak of."

Alex sat back in his chair and stretched out his long legs under the table. Taking a sip of wine he studied Douglas. "Why did you call her Amin?"

"I recognized the energy imprint of Amin. I have come up against this Being before. He is a member of Lucifer's order," he said cautiously.

The wine was beginning to go to Alex's head and he questioned if what they saw actually took place but he knew it did though because it was still very fresh in his mind. He couldn't deny Douglas was able to do things he couldn't understand and was coming to accept that they needed him. "How were you able to throw her against the wall without touching her?"

Cade jumped in before Douglas answered, "And what about pulling that thing out from her chest? I still can't believe it happened and I saw it with my own eyes."

"There are many hazards in my line of work but with it comes opportunities to learn how to control the mind and things around us. We are capable of much more than we realize. All it takes is learning how to access parts of the brain humans don't use and harness the power."

"It sounds dangerous," said Arielle shivering with the memory of the terrifying escapade.

"You are correct. There's only a few us in the world who know how to do this." Leaning forward he placed his elbows on the table. Raising his arms up to meet his chin he interlaced his fingers touching the tips of his forefingers and thumbs together making a v-shape. Purposefully he moved the tips of his forefingers to rest against his lower lip.

Looking intently at the group he lowered his voice, "We call ourselves the Secret Keepers. We act as guardians of this knowledge and protect humanity from allowing it to pass into the wrong hands. Unfortunately sometimes it does and we are called into battle."

The impact of his words struck Maya. Realizing this man put his life on the line to protect people like them made her respect for him grow deeper.

"Do you know who these other Secret Keepers are?" asked Alex.

"Many of them, yes." Anticipating the next question he added, "We are strategically located around the globe. Working quietly, undercover so to speak. Some are in very high places and you would recognize their names if I told you but I am obligated not to reveal this kind of information."

"Have they all been trained in the remote viewing program?" asked Cade.

"In a manner of speaking. The government has tried to keep a very low profile around the program and its success. To the point of wanting it to appear as if it was a failure. But in reality its training has been incorporated into very elite groups of people carefully selected around the world."

Directing their attention to the signet ring he added, "We wear this. It's a symbol of being a leader of the coterie. Vivienne also has one but she does not wear it in public."

"Douglas..."

"Ah yes. That's Vivienne's way of telling me I've said too much. I can ramble on sometimes especially with people I like and trust."

Recognizing the need to change the direction of the conversation Maya asked, "Do you think she would have tried to kill us?"

He smiled at Maya appreciating her consideration. "I don't think that was the intention. At least, not yet. Amin, or Lucifer wanted to frighten you."

"Why?" Cade's voice held a hint of foreboding.

Pausing, Douglas looked at each one of them and settled his eyes on Maya. "I'm sure you know the answer to that. Maybe it's time we talked about the real reason you are all here." *Everything is falling into place better than I could have hoped. The universe is by my side and our destiny is near. Soon our time will come. And when darkness descends on this world everyone will turn to me as the leader who can save them from themselves.*

"That could take a while," Maya said nervously. *I guess it's time to dive in and see where this is going to take us.*

Looking to Vivienne his eyes narrowed ever so slightly. "We've got time."

Maya described the events from the past several months beginning with her meeting with Nicholas in Nassau then all the coincidences that led her here. With the exception of her connection to the Herkimer and its message. *I'm keeping that tidbit of information to myself for now.*

Arielle and Cade watched Maya waiting for her to finish the rest of her story but it didn't come. Arielle raised a questioning eyebrow. Maya responded using a barely noticeable motion with her eyes to indicate her desire for Arielle to leave it alone.

Arielle followed her lead and spoke next. Repeating her accounts already shared with the others.

Alex was lost in thought about Maya. *I wonder why she left out one of the most important pieces to the puzzle?* Deciding to trust she must have her reasons his mind wandered. *She doesn't give herself any credit. Douglas might have resolved the situation today but she's the one who came through in protecting us.* Catching himself looking at her with longing he averted his eyes.

Cade and Alex took turns telling their individual tales while Douglas and Vivienne listened with interest.

"Do you *know* of the Emerald Stone Douglas?" Maya finally asked even though she already knew the answer.

"Yes, you could say that. I detected its existence a few years ago through my travels and experienced a strong feeling of recognition. When I explored deeper into the mysteries I discovered my link to them and to the four of you. Vivienne and I have been in search for them and you ever since."

"What is your connection to them?" asked Alex.

"Thoth or Djhuty as he's otherwise known, entrusted me with the responsibility of making sure you accomplish your mission. We were his elite priests and we worked closely together. That is why you have been drawn towards me. It is time for us to fulfill what has been written."

"But what if we're not ready? We haven't learned to tap into our memories they way you have," Arielle said with doubt and fear in her voice.

"You are closer than you realize. It is not necessary for all of your memories to return. When the time is right it will happen because you *are* the Chosen Ones. I've watched the energy building between you in the last few days and it will continue to grow stronger in preparation for the final test."

"Do you know where the Stone is?" asked Cade.

"Yes I do."

Cade straightened up in his chair. "Is the entrance to the hidden chambers at the Pyramid or the Sphinx?"

"The entrance is located under the Sphinx and there is an underground tunnel leading to the Pyramid's lower chambers."

"Will you take us there?" asked Maya with growing anticipation.

"Of course." Douglas raised both his hands to contain their excitement, "Hold on. Not so fast. You still have work to do. Your energy is not strong enough or pure enough yet to face the challenge. Tomorrow's initiation in the King's Chamber is part of your preparation and I can teach you some techniques that will assist you in reaching the higher realms."

"We don't know how to thank you," said Maya soberly thinking of the days events and what was to come. *Maybe with Douglas' help there is a chance we'll be ready in time.*

He smiled at her knowingly. "There's no need to thank me. Just be successful."

Chapter Thirty-five

Alex stared at the ceiling lit by the light of the stars through his window. Morning was hours away and the night was beginning to seem endless. He tossed and turned and faced the ceiling once again.

So much had taken place in just three days. His life had been turned upside down not once but twice. First he met Maya and fell in love with her almost instantly. He knew she felt the same even though she resisted him and just when he thought she was his Douglas threw a curve ball in their direction.

Sister! How could she be my sister? How could I have been so wrong? How could I have fallen so deeply in love with her? I believed with everything I knew that she was that missing part of me. That part that completes me. It just doesn't make sense.

Meeting Maya changed his world. It brought him alive again. He'd been living an empty life since his wife's death. Sure he'd had a couple of relationships but they were shallow and short-lived. *But Maya…there was electricity the minute their eyes locked on the plane.* She was all he could think about. *The way she walked. The way she talked. How she smelled. And the taste of her when they kissed.* The kiss that melded them together and now haunts him every minute of the day.

There had barely been any time to think since Douglas told them of the true nature of their relationship. *I don't understand how I could have been so wrong.* His pain and anguish continued to build the more he thought of her.

I give up! I can't sleep. Getting frustrated he threw the covers off and got out of bed. Running his hands through his hair he stood partially naked, clad in just a pair of blue boxer shorts. Looking around the suite he picked up the converter, flicked on the television and sat in a chair. Flipping from one Egyptian station to another he gave up when he couldn't find any English speaking stations.

Realizing that sleep was not forthcoming he decided to get dressed and go down to the lounge for a drink.

Sitting at the far end of the bar having a cognac he looked up and watched Maya walk in. His stomach knotted up and the pain in his chest wouldn't allow him to breathe. *Oh God, what are the chances this would happen?*

He observed her as she sat down at the opposite end of the bar. She ordered herself a drink then looked around.

She could swear her heart stopped beating when she saw Alex. *I can't very well ignore him.* He was the last person she wanted to see but she picked up her purse anyway and slowly strolled over to join him. Smiling shyly she greeted him. "Hi Alex. Couldn't sleep?"

He shook his head. "Obviously you couldn't either," he said with an effort not knowing how he would carry on a conversation with her while his heart ached so much.

"After the past couple of days you'd think we'd be so exhausted we'd pass out. My brain won't stop though. I get really restless when I can't sleep so I thought I'd better get out of the room for a while before I woke up Arielle."

"I don't usually have any problems sleeping. It takes a lot to keep me awake at night but I guess tonight was one of those nights."

When the bartender brought her the martini she ordered she took a long slow sip appreciating the strong taste and giving her time to contemplate what she wanted to say. *Should I ignore the situation or come right out and talk about it? He's probably too proud to say anything…*

Stealing a glance in the mirror behind the bar she caught herself admiring his brooding appearance and found it stirring up the feelings she was so desperately trying to bury. The silence grew to an awkward length and yet she felt somehow at ease sitting next to him sharing his misery.

I wish she would say something. Anything to give me some idea where she stands. It's probably not eating her up at all. Maybe it's even a relief to her.

"Alex…I just want you to know this is just as confusing for me. I thought, well I felt something very deep developing between us."

"But?" he asked uneasily.

Taking another sip of her drink she hoped it would ease her anxiety. "But I think we need to let this go." The words were out of her mouth and she couldn't take them back. Not now.

His heart felt like it was being squeezed in a vice. He couldn't bring himself to look at her, instead he reached for his glass and concentrated on the cognac. Feeling its fire burning the back of his throat as he swallowed a sizeable gulp of his aromatic drink. "I don't know what you want me to say Maya. Fine? Okay? No problem? I can't do that. It hurts. I didn't think I could feel this much pain again." He couldn't continue.

"Alex, please. If you think this isn't painful for me too then you are sorely mistaken. But it doesn't mean we have to throw away our connection. In fact, we can't. We need to finish what has been started. It will just have to be different than what our imaginations were attempting to create."

He could hear the truth of her words and the sorrow behind them. It caused him further grief to know he was adding to her worries so he decided to stop wallowing in his own. "I just want you to be happy Maya. That means more to me than anything else. If this is what we have to do, then so be it. I admire you for your convictions." Going against everything he felt inside he extended his hand to hers, "Friends?"

What a remarkable guy. I lost hope a long time ago that there were men like him that really existed. She allowed her hand to reach out and touch his ignoring the rise of heat along her spine, "Friends."

"Good."

They reached for their drinks at the same time and tried to ignore the spark of energy that blazed between their hands.

Silence fell upon them for a brief moment before Alex spoke again. "Can I ask you something Maya?"

Dread filled her stomach. *Alex please let it go.* "Shoot."

"Why didn't you tell the whole story tonight?"

Relieved to change the topic but hesitant to tell him everything for his own protection she responded. "Ah yes. Let's just say I don't want to give away all our cards just yet. Can we leave it at that?"

His respect for her continued to grow. She's a very admirable woman. He didn't know what she was up to but he'd put his life on the line for her and for all he knew maybe that's exactly what he was doing. "No problem."

* * * *

It's two o'clock in the morning. Where is she? Douglas had been trying to locate Maya for the past two hours. She wasn't sleeping and he was growing impatient at not being able to detect her energy imprint.

Everything was set up so perfectly. She should have been waiting and willing to come away with me tonight.

Chapter Thirty-six

"One of the main purposes of the pyramid initiation rite was for the neophyte to experience molecular changes, which would allow his soul to pass through the inner worlds. The sarcophagus is in direct alignment with the down pouring of cosmic rays," said Pamela.

The tour group had gathered by the back paw on the northeast edge of the Sphinx. They sat sprinkled around Pamela paying attention to her speech preparing them for their initiation in the King's Chamber. Some sat leaned up against the great monument while others were on the dusty ground. The air was cool and dry and electric with nervous energy.

Maya, Arielle, Cade and Alex listened intently. Their collective mood was solemn, appreciating the seriousness of this ceremony as another step on their journey to enlightenment. Douglas and Vivienne remained close by.

"I recommend using extreme caution before entering the sarcophagus. This ceremony should not be taken lightly and you must look within yourself at a very deep level to make sure you are ready. The voltage of electricity has been described as a fiery light and can only be endured by those who are completely aligned and purified on the physical, emotional and spiritual realms."

Many people exchanged uncomfortable glances with each other upon hearing the warning.

Pamela continued, "When we reach the base of the pyramid I want you to imagine that you are shedding your body of all material elements. Leave behind the veils of duality and center yourself.

"The passageways are very low and narrow. They are meant to be a symbolic representation of your journey. Walking through the darkness to reach the light. The stairway leading up to the King's Chamber is very steep and difficult to climb. It has been referred to as the 'Ladder of the Soul'. You should use this time on your ascent to reflect upon your life journey, marking it as one of the most important steps you will take towards mastery and freedom in this life."

The air around them seemed to grow warmer by the minute as it was filled with both excitement and trepidation.

"For anyone who is unsure of continuing I will be available to speak with you before we begin the journey. We will leave for the Great Pyramid in half an hour but first I will lead you into a meditation to give you an opportunity to speak with your guides to confirm your readiness. I know it's somewhat uncomfortable here without chairs but do the best you can."

Following the meditation everyone had an opportunity to stretch and walk about for a few minutes prior to leaving the Sphinx.

Douglas caught Maya's attention and waved for her to join him. Turning to Arielle, Cade and Alex she motioned for them to follow.

"Come with us. I'll show you where the excavated doorway is to access the tunnel across to the pyramid," Douglas said quietly.

Following him around to the other side of the Sphinx Maya could hardly contain herself. "You mean you can get to it from one of the existing entrances?"

"Yes, but the so called experts don't know what to look for so it has not been discovered yet." They approached an excavated opening near the front paw of the Sphinx on the Southwest side. Douglas pointed down below to a very steep small opening with a rather rickety looking ladder braced up against the side. "This is it."

"It doesn't look very safe," said Cade wondering how on earth he was going to get down there and through the door.

Alex studied the entrance. "It's padlocked. We'd have to break in and we won't exactly be able to do that in the middle of the day."

Arielle was not impressed. The top of the ladder was a few feet away from the top of the opening. She didn't know how she was going to maneuver herself to reach the first rung. "Are you suggesting that we do this at night?" she asked fearfully.

Douglas, who was completely focused on their mission, ignored Arielle's remarks. He didn't have time for timid behavior when they were so close. "These sites clear out at dusk so we can return once everyone has left. We'll have some tools and supplies to purchase. I suggest tomorrow we get ourselves organized, make some plans and come back here the day after."

Maya stood looking down the dark hole contemplating Douglas' scheme. *I can't believe we're standing here actually discussing breaking into the Sphinx!*

* * * *

"Get in a line please! You will begin your climb from here!" shouted Azizi pointing to the first area of steps leading up the side of the pyramid.

"If you have any difficulties with physical exercise or have any breathing problems please stay to the back of the line! It's a strenuous climb and we need to keep the line moving. If you're going to slow things down please keep to the back!" Azizi paced back and forth as he spoke to make sure everyone heard him.

The entry into the Great Pyramid was roughly thirty to forty feet above the ground. They had to climb seven levels of blocks to reach the entrance of the first passageway where they slowly filed in one by one. It was framed with a white metal gate, which was also kept padlocked during off-hours. They had an advantage of low lights lining the walls to light their way, which the neophytes from the Egyptian era did not have. Torches would have been the rule of the day.

Douglas and Vivienne went ahead into the pyramid while everyone else gathered together to form a line. They were the first to enter the pyramid and begin the journey upwards. He believed in either being the first or last in any lineup and this was a protocol he strongly enforced among his pupils. Always watch your back and never leave yourself exposed was his philosophy.

Maya, Arielle, Alex and Cade found themselves somewhere in the middle. This slowed their progress quite a bit but they were content to have the extra time to reflect and concentrate every step along the way. They felt energized and connected to each other after having some time to perform their activation prayer prior to Azizi gathering them together to line up. Its intensity grew yet again and strengthened their union with the universe to even greater levels.

The initial passageway leading upwards was so low and narrow they had to crouch over, with room for only one person at a time. The shaft descends at an angle of about twenty-six degrees and is one hundred and twenty-nine feet long. Dark wooden beams attached to the sides of the channel allowed them to pull themselves forward as they climbed the wooden planks.

The shaft levels off temporarily with a connection to the passage leading to the Queen's Chamber. Azizi stood watch letting everyone know as they arrived that they would have the opportunity to visit the Queen's Chamber on the way back down.

Maya stopped briefly to drink from her water bottle. She blew some air up to her bangs in a vain attempt to dry some of the sweat accumulating on her forehead while taking a quick look down the aisle.

Estimating the height of the tunnel to be only three feet high all the way through. She turned to Arielle behind her and said, "I can't imagine how anyone could actually walk through there."

"I remember reading somewhere these passages were built this way to allow the initiate to show respect for their journey in bending over, like bowing to the Gods," responded Arielle, out of breath from the climb.

The final walkway leading to the King's Chamber known as the Grand Gallery opened wider to allow for an ascending and descending pathway but it did nothing to alleviate the escalating temperature of the pyramid making it feel like a sauna.

They were relieved to finally be able to stand tall again. Although they still were required to be very careful making the climb over the ramped area. This area lacked a solid floor beneath with some areas even being hollow. It necessitated them to use caution to ensure they did not lose their footing along the one hundred and fifty-seven-foot gallery. Thankfully the wooden handrails provided a safety net.

Maya took great care with every step while mulling over the events that had brought her on this adventure.

At last she entered the King's Chamber after climbing the unusually large final step. Her jeans felt incredibly hot on her body, her T-shirt and jacket clung to her damp back. Trying to let her eyes adjust to the darkness she moved farther into the grand room providing space for others to enter.

Above the main chamber were five smaller chambers supporting the weight of the stones above and spreading the load out away from the main area. The top chamber had a pointed roof made of limestone blocks.

Feeling a need to be alone she walked to the sarcophagus and stood beside it. Leaving Arielle, Cade and Alex to fend for themselves. Paying no heed to the other people who were also congregating by the stone box she placed her right hand on the ledge and observed how the coldness of the solid black granite was in contrast to the stifling heat of the room.

Blocking the noise from the increasing number of people in the room she went to her center giving thanks to the universe for watching over her. She also wanted to calm her unsteady nerves but it was cut surprisingly short by a voltage of electricity radiating through the stone into her hand and up the length of her arm.

Pamela distracted her by calling everyone together in the center of the room.

Looking more closely Maya could see the high walls were made of finished pink granite. She also noticed sand or salt deposits had gathered on them over the years.

As everyone gathered around Pamela she said, "We have enough time here to allow for anyone who feels the calling to enter the sarcophagus. When you get in lie down on your back and cross your arms over your chest like this." She demonstrated how to position the arms just like the mummified pharaohs.

"Concentrate on your seventh chakra and its principles of mastery, spirituality, transcendence, bliss and illumination. Afterwards we'll come together in a circle and complete the initiation with an offering and a prayer of thanks. Have faith and know that even those who decide not to enter the sarcophagus will experience exactly the right amount of illumination that is appropriate for you at this time. God be with you."

* * * *

Maya estimated there were only twenty or so people waiting to undergo the initiation. Her heart beat wildly, echoing loudly in her ears. Clasping her hands together in nervousness she noticed they were sweating. Her hair was sticking to the back of her neck from perspiration.

Fifth in line she glimpsed around to see where her friends were located. She noticed that Arielle, Cade and Alex were behind her and had also been separated with a few people between each one. *I wonder where Douglas and Vivienne are?* Studying the room she searched in vain. *That's strange. They're always in my line of sight.*

She watched as people came out one by one. They appeared shaken and disoriented. Sentinels stood guard by the narrow end assisting people to climb in and out of the deep box. Making sure they were steady enough to walk.

It was Maya's turn. She climbed in, lay down on her back and folded her arms as instructed. The floor was cold and radiated into her body providing some relief from the intense heat of the pyramid.

The room closed in around her and she closed her eyes. Drawing a breath deep in her belly, sparks of electric light shot around her instantly. Vivid colors exploded in through her third eye to the center of her mind.

Facing her own mortality in that moment of time she felt her Spirit elevate above her body. Rising upwards towards the apex of the King's Chamber. Looking down she witnessed herself in the sarcophagus lying still.

Drawing ever skyward towards the bright Light her consciousness spiraled between the electromagnetic grids. Her vibratory rate rose to meet each increasing frequency that ran parallel to her own.

Memories of previous lifetimes and everything she had learned flashed through her awareness as swift as the speed of Light. She felt her connection to the Goddess, Gods, and the One Mind repeated in various cycles of times. The sacred flame burned brightly within her, reaching out to the source of all Light; the Great Central Sun.

Having completed its journey, Maya's light body began its descent back to re-engage with her physical body.

Her legs felt unstable beneath her barely able to hold her weight while she tried to climb out of the sarcophagus. She stumbled and the sentinels took hold of her arms and elbows to assist her trembling body. Still not fully alert she smiled meekly. "Thank you," nodding to both of them.

Maya, still wavering, braced herself up against the east wall for support. Her body was still vibrating at a higher rate and she was having difficulty clearing her head and bringing herself back into focus.

She felt herself meld into the granite walls. Feeling the energy contained within them along with the lifetimes of people traversing this great room.

Following her own initiation Arielle wandered over to join Maya. "Are you all right? You look pale."

"I'm still shaky but I'll be fine." She was suddenly filled with an overwhelming love for Arielle. She reached out and took Arielle's hand in hers. "How about you?"

"Same." Arielle backed up against the wall beside Maya and they stood holding hands in silence. They didn't need words between them to understand that they had just experienced a life altering moment.

Pamela gently called everyone into a circle when the initiations in the sarcophagus were completed. Her assistant, Beth walked around handing out index cards and pencils to the group.

"Beth is handing out index cards. I want you to write down the word *release* on one side and *receive* on the other. Once you've done that take a few minutes to think about what issues or circumstances you are ready to release and write that on the release side. Then you will write down what you are now ready to call forward or accomplish on the receiving side."

Giving everyone enough time to complete this task she continued. "Now you are going to concentrate on the cards and what you have written down for the remainder of the day. Keep it steady in your minds. Tonight before going to bed recall your initiation today and burn the card over a sink offering a prayer of gratitude. Wash away the ashes and know that the universe has made it come to pass."

Beth came back around collecting the pencils while people guarded their cards putting them away carefully in their pockets or money pouches.

"Okay everyone let's come together in a circle for the prayer!" Pamela shouted and clapped her hands together softly.

"This is an ancient Gnostic prayer. The words are 'Blessed Be this Queen on High that is Sacred to all who come to Her. Amen.' We are going to repeat it nine times to complete the ceremony. Repeat after it after me."

Their voices grew louder with each repetition while the words echoed back to them off the walls.

Facing the four corners, a ray of Light bounced through the circle shooting out from the hearts of Maya, Arielle, Alex and Cade.

* * * *

Douglas and Vivienne watched the beacon of Light fire up through the apex of the pyramid. "They're energy has doubled," he whispered to Vivienne. They had performed their own ceremony in private and now stood outside the chamber to observe from afar.

They witnessed a wave of energy circulate in front of them. The Light held strong and unknown to the group, time stood still for three minutes. But Douglas knew. He recognized the patterns moving through the electromagnetic gridlines.

One hundred and fifty people stood motionless like mannequins with blank stares on their faces. But Douglas and Vivienne remained unaffected because of their elevated vibratory rate.

"They are totally unaware it happened," Vivienne whispered back to her husband.

"This should be interesting to watch the reactions when they come out of their trance." He felt both threatened and a sense of pride towards Maya at the same time. *She is remarkable. I have to give her that. Her powers are growing immensely. If she continues to develop at this rate…She will be a force to be reckoned with.*

Vivienne nodded in acknowledgement hearing his thoughts.

A sneeze broke the silence. Blank faces were replaced with brief looks of disorientation. The Light faded and believing the meditation had finished they released their hands.

Douglas and Vivienne could hear the people murmuring among themselves. Questioning each other if they felt anything unusual. Those wearing digital watches noticed the numbers were flashing in zeros.

A soft chaos filled the room.

I need to show her the papyrus tonight. It is time to bring her closer to me.

* * * *

The stairway looking down from the King's Chamber appeared daunting. *It's amazing to think we climbed up all that way.* Still trembling, Maya wasn't sure if her legs would carry her on the descent.

Quiet nervous chatter continued as people were still speculating about why their watches stopped and why it seemed as though they had lost awareness of their surroundings for a brief period of time.

Alex, still struggling to get his feelings for Maya under control followed in step behind her down the Grand Gallery. Like the others he was sure that she must have had an extraordinary experience and wanted to make sure she was stable on the way down. During his own initiation he had traveled through many lifetimes but never was he able to confirm or deny his relationship with Maya and it frustrated him even further.

Cade and Arielle, on the other hand, looked star struck together as the experience deepened their feelings for one another.

The journey to the Queen's Chamber was long and trying. Maya kept bumping her head along the low passageway and had to contain herself from laughing too loudly as she listened to Alex curse every time he did the same.

"Are you laughing at me?" exclaimed Alex as he straightened up in agony when they entered the chamber.

Grateful for the opportunity to release some emotion she couldn't help but burst out laughing. Her eyes opened wide as she tried unsuccessfully to contain herself. "I'm sorry but it was funny!"

"Well I'm glad I could provide some entertainment for you." Even though he responded with sarcasm in his voice inside he felt giddy with delight knowing he made her laugh. *I love her laugh. It's so hearty.*

Arielle and Cade came through next. "What's so funny?" Arielle asked.

Glancing towards Alex, Maya thought better of humiliating him any further. "Nothing," she said and the look she sent Arielle told her to leave it alone.

The Queen's Chamber was much smaller in comparison. It's walls and floors, unlike the smoothness of the King's Chamber, were rough and appeared unfinished.

Maya's nervous energy was subsiding and she was beginning to feel more grounded. Looking around the room she noticed there were very few people attempting the walk. Feeling more light hearted she decided to join Douglas and Vivienne who were at the opposite end. "I didn't see you in the King's Chamber. Didn't you go in?"

"Vivienne and I went ahead of everyone and performed our own ceremony, then we came here."

Cade, who had joined them, asked Douglas, "Do you know what happened to everyone up there?"

Douglas explained what they saw and why people's watches stopped. "Now that you are receiving the new frequencies your minds and bodies are being prepared to act as gatekeepers. You need to learn to take the energy in, magnify it and project it back into the planet. This will assist in the final activation of the Emerald Stone."

"We don't have any recollection of what happened up there much less how to do what you say," commented Alex doubtfully.

"Not to worry, Vivienne and I are experienced gatekeepers. We can teach you."

* * * *

Exiting the Queen's Chamber and reaching daylight once again Maya felt incredible. Full of love, light and joy.

Standing by the base of the pyramid, the sun shining brightly, Maya, Arielle, Alex and Cade hugged each other in pure delight. Feeling on top of the world and ready to face their destiny.

Chapter Thirty-seven

Maya couldn't sleep. She left a note for Arielle to let her know where she was going so she wouldn't worry when she woke. They had decided to grab an hour or two nap before dinner but Maya was restless and couldn't lie still.

She discovered Douglas sitting alone in the bar. There was only a handful of people present. Conversations were low and occasionally the sound of laughter echoed in the room.

Strolling towards him she thought he looked very handsome. He was sitting back in the chair with one leg crossed over the other and appeared lost in thought when she approached him. "Mind if I join you?"

"Please do. I was just wondering if I was ever going to have some time alone with you."

Sitting down beside him in a cozy blue suede chair she sighed trying to ignore his comment. The waiter appeared right away and she ordered a glass of red wine.

Douglas motioned for another scotch.

Relaxing back she studied him while they sat in silence for a moment. He was wearing a slim fitting black knit top drawing her attention to his muscular arms under the short sleeves. His skin looked smooth and soft. *Oh he smells good.*

He leaned forward and clasped his hands together. "You can't avoid me forever." His voice was soft and melodious.

She stared at his hands unable to respond. *His hands...they are shaped just like mine! How can that be?* She had always been a little self-conscious of her hands and feet, she thought they were somewhat masculine looking and they didn't quite match the rest of her more delicate frame.

Pulling his hands apart he looked at them. Noticing the outline and contours of his knuckles then comparing them to hers. "Yes they are Diãntha." He marveled at the serendipity and reached out to hold her hands in his. "It's the universe at work. Another sign to show you we belong together."

She jerked her hands away, uncomfortable with his public display of affection.

"Sweetheart, why do you fight it?"

"This is crazy! You're married," she stated flatly.

"Vivienne and I are partners in every sense of the word yes. But it is societal rules that impose this nonsense that you can only love one person. Vivienne knows how I feel about you. She has helped me to find you."

Maya was speechless and confused. A part of her wanted to get up and leave but she couldn't. Her heart was beating loudly in her ears.

"My darling Diãntha." He moved closer to the edge of his chair. Leaning forward so he could take her in. So she could hear the psychometry in his voice. "I have looked for you for thousands of years. When I discovered you had survived I thought my heart would explode with joy. The thought of finding you again one day has kept me going. I lived like a shell of a man until the first time I detected your frequency."

She dared not look at him. Keeping her eyes steady on her hands was her only way of coping with his words. Her breath was shallow listening to his caressing voice.

"At last we are together again, having crossed space and time in our relentless search for each other that has culminated in the wilderness of Earth. Look at me Diãntha." He said pausing to wait for her to respond. "Please…"

She didn't know if she could trust herself but something inside was calling. She looked up and into his eyes and saw the depths of the universe spiraling there. She felt herself falling. Testing out his name, "Mel'ion." There was a familiarity resonating within her. "I don't know what to say."

He took her hands in his again and gently stroked them. "Your beautiful voice captivates my heart. I love to hear you say my name my love." His tone of voice went deeper. "I only ask that you use it in private."

She started to apologize but he prevented her by speaking quickly. "There is no need to apologize. You are not familiar with the ways of the coterie but I will tutor you. I teach the teachers and that is what you are. That is what all four of you are. But you've known since you were a young child of eight that you were different. You didn't fit in with everyone else and you've had difficulty coping with your loneliness."

Her eyes growing wider filled with tears. "How do you know so much about me?"

"Whenever we speak our souls merge with scintillating Light that pales the tellurian spectrum by contrast. I know you because we belong together. Nothing can ever separate us spiritually, nor keep us physically apart for long because our life charts require our physical as well as spiritual freedom."

Trembling she listened intently. Feeling her resolve falter she wanted his words to be etched into her mind so she would never forget them. Her eyes still fixed on his, she moved her thumb to return his caress along his hand. Her heart ached to believe and to be loved so deeply.

Warmth flowed between their hands. Maya's left eye began to twitch uncontrollably then images flashed rapidly through her mind.

"What is it Maya? What are you seeing?"

"I'm not sure…It's whizzing by so fast I can't make it out."

"Breathe deeply. Yes that's it. Slow. Now tell me what you see."

"I see myself or rather Diãntha. She seemed to appear out of thin air in a temple." She waited to observe what happened next. "I'm stumbling and I think that you are running towards me. Catching me in your arms. We are on the ground and I'm feeling very weak. I can barely speak but I'm trying to tell you something. I think I said tell Kanïka she was right. What does this mean?" The image was very disturbing and confusing.

"The initiation today escalated your memories," Douglas wavered. This vision took him by surprise yet suited his purposes. "Maya, what you just saw is extremely painful for me. I have to be honest, I tried to hold that memory back from you. It wasn't completely true when I said I never saw you again after the explosion."

"What do you mean?" she asked timidly.

"If you recall I said that your body was never found. Somehow at the moment your body shattered you escaped into another reality and traveled through time into the future." His mood turned very despondent and he took a moment to collect himself before resuming.

Maya stroked his hands to soothe him and calm her own growing unease.

"The vision you just witnessed. It was you returning from the future. You came back to give us a message but I was never able to decipher the meaning. You died in my arms." Choking back tears he couldn't finish.

Maya remembered. She felt a pain rip through her heart and body. "My body disintegrated while you were holding me." A vision of Melïon throwing his head back and releasing a scream of despair filled her.

"Yes." The memory was as vivid as if it happened only moments before.

"I don't understand, how or why did I disintegrate?"

"Darling, your body could not adapt to the change in vibrational frequencies traveling back from the future. I lost you twice, my love…"

Maya squeezed his hands tighter. It was the best she could offer in such a public place. *All this time he didn't know where I was or if I even existed. How did he bear that grief through all those lifetimes?*

Douglas glanced up and saw Arielle stroll into the bar. In frustration he nonchalantly withdrew his hands from Maya's. He was spent but pleased with her receptivity and the progress he was making. *I hope it doesn't force her over the edge when I show her the papyrus later.*

*   *   *   *

Alex watched Maya's hair gently sway around her face when she reached for her wine. Needing to put some distance between himself and Maya he gestured for Cade to sit beside her. *I'm not sure if I made the right choice. Now I have a clear view of her next to Douglas.*

They decided to have dinner at Ciao Italia. It seemed fitting after their initiations to enjoy a relaxing meal and a couple of bottles of wine.

The air was filled with scents of wonderfully pungent Egyptian cheeses and garlic cooking in the distance.

Alex absently carried on a conversation with Vivienne. Telling her about his initiation. It would have meant so much more for him if only he had Maya to share it with. Instead he felt empty inside watching Douglas lean close enough to Maya to touch his shoulder with hers. Their heads were bent low, deep in discussion.

Vivienne could feel the ache growing heavy within Alex. "Thoughts are things Alex. Your negative thoughts are potentially destructive. They will slow you down and affect the outcome. The more you have them the worse it gets until you become blinded by them."

Her words of advice added to his confusion. "Doesn't it bother you?" he asked nodding in the direction of Douglas.

"We have an unusual marriage. Society as a whole would frown upon it but it works for us. In answer to your question, no it doesn't bother me. At least not in the way you think." Being careful not to give anything away to alter their destiny she added, "Keep your thoughts focused on what you want to happen because what you focus on expands. If you are constantly dwelling on what you don't want that is where the energy will go and that is what you will manifest. If it is meant to be Alex it will be."

He reflected on her words and wondered about their hidden meaning. Glancing secretly towards Maya his jaw dropped as he observed Douglas remove his signet ring and give it to Maya to wear. His heart sunk when she took it and put it on her index finger. He watched her stare into Douglas' eyes in acknowledgement of his meaning.

Vivienne caught sight of this action. *He is so immune to what the outside world perceives about him. He justifies everything in his mind and thinks everyone else will have the same conclusion.* A spark of irritation at this indiscretion tore through her for a brief instant.

Reverting her attention back to Alex she did what she felt was right to pacify him. "Everything that happens to me, even in my darkest hours I know are for me. I look at everything as part of a great plan. Everything happens for a reason and every moment of my life is a stitch in the tapestry. I look at each event as a challenge to my learning and everyday I am pleased that I am so above the illusion."

Douglas pulled his attention away from Maya and cleared his throat. "There are things we need to discuss to prepare you to meet your destiny," he said gravely to the group. Feeling at the peak of his brilliance with Maya next to him on one side, wearing his ring, and Vivienne on his other side.

"There are seven stages of enlightenment to pass through before you will be able to activate the Emerald Stone. Some of them you have all already achieved. Others you have not." Noticing the alarm he intentionally created he attempted to calm their unrest. "There's no need to worry. Tonight Vivienne and I will perform assessments on the progress that each of you has made. Then tomorrow I will take you through a series of meditations to reprogram your mind to prepare you for the final test."

"What do you mean by reprogram?" asked Arielle not sure she liked the reference.

"Yes I can see where that term would cause hesitation. I simply mean that I will guide you to remember events that occurred either in this life or others that have created blockages or negative influences within you. Once we have identified them you will recreate the circumstance in your mind with an alternate positive outcome. Thereby reprogramming your mind and releasing the issues so they will no longer have any impact on you. Does that meet with everyone's approval?"

Maya, Arielle, Cade and Alex consented.

"Can you explain the seven stages?" asked Cade.

"Yes, of course. It's common knowledge in alchemy, which is the study of personal transformation. In understandable terms it begins with the union between our thoughts and feelings. Through much of our lives these two live in conflict with each other. When this union is accomplished you have a state of perfect intuition where all ambiguity is made clear. Does that make sense?"

They nodded affirmatively and waited for him to continue.

"The first step is connected to the Fire element, the burning away of everything that is thick and cumbersome. This is done through the destruction of the ego and letting go of attachments in the material world. This can take place gradually over time or in some cases a traumatic event can trigger it."

Their waitress interrupted the discussion as their food was delivered. He waited for her to leave before continuing.

"The second step can be a painful one. Your world seems to turn into chaos where you are forced to reveal your wounds because your heart will no longer allow them to be buried. The element associate with this step is Water."

"The third step is the first coming together of the soul and spirit. Where you take what has been learned and use it to drive your transformation, finding your hidden self. Air is the element that drives this stage."

They drank wine and ate their dinner while they listened closely. Vivienne observed Douglas quietly. Regardless of some of his methods to achieve his goals she admired the way he taught spiritual truths with passion. He had a very unique ability to grasp their concepts with ease and in fact, he was a genius.

"Next comes fulfillment of our true spirits through the merging of the masculine and feminine sides of our personalities, representing the Earth element. Typically your intuition develops stronger in this stage.

"The fifth step typifies the way of the enlightened warrior who dedicate themselves to sharing their spiritual insights and knowledge of higher consciousness to others.

"The sixth step is referred to as the White Stage where the purified soul looks into the eye of God to work with the Heavenly bodies becoming one with the White Light.

"The final level is a permanent state of consciousness able to withstand any tests with courage. This is what you will achieve upon reaching your destiny in the hidden chamber."

*　*　*　*

After dinner they moved to the lounge where the atmosphere was lively. The sound of music and laughter filled the room relieving the nervous tension of the past days in anticipation for their initiations.

After a couple glasses of wine Maya relaxed and allowed herself to loosen up. She joked and laughed with the others to let off some steam.

Cade and Arielle decided to let loose on the dance floor.

Alex tried unsuccessfully not to notice every time Maya reached out to touch Douglas. Standing up frustrated he announced, "I think I'm going to call it a night. I'll see you in the morning."

"Let's meet at breakfast to discuss the supplies we'll need at the Sphinx and make our preparations for the journey." Douglas stood to shake his hand. "Good night Alex."

While he walked away Alex reminded himself to give Vivienne's suggestion a chance so he switched his attention to concentrating on what he wanted rather than what he didn't want. He had to do something constructive to lift his misery.

Every time his thoughts returned to Maya he forced himself to concentrate on finding the Emerald Stone in time and achieving their goal. Now that they knew Douglas was aware of its location they were sure to be successful. *But what about afterwards? What will it all mean without Maya?*

Sitting down between Maya and Vivienne, Douglas determined the time was now to make his move. "Maya, Vivienne and I purchased something important at the market that we'd like to show you. It will explain a great many things to you. If you're not in a hurry would you like to see it?"

Maya thought the request a little odd but she couldn't see the harm in it. "Sure. Okay."

"Wonderful. Vivienne this is the perfect opportunity to show her. Let's go shall we?"

"Just let me tell Arielle I'm leaving. I'll be right back."

When she returned the three of them left together. Maya and Vivienne on each side of Douglas. He felt like the most powerful man in the world and unstoppable with his triad complete.

Why does this feel so bizarre? Maya's heart began to beat faster and her hands started to sweat. *What did I get myself into?*

They entered the suite and Maya's trepidation grew. After today's initiation she thought fear was a thing of the past. Apparently she was wrong.

Vivienne brought a tube out from the closet and opened it up. She withdrew a large papyrus. Maya thought about the paper paintings she looked at with Arielle. She wanted to buy one but she couldn't seem to find one that particularly appealed to her so she didn't bother.

Douglas took the papyrus from Vivienne and ceremonially unraveled it. He couldn't be sure of how she would react but she was proving to be one of his star initiates. Awakening at the most incredible rate he had ever seen he was reasonably confident she wouldn't spin out. Laying it across the table he waited for Maya to approach.

She was unprepared for the affect the papyrus would have on her. She faltered and couldn't breathe. She heard him say it was the Triad of Menkaure. Then everything closed in around her. The image was of the pharaoh Menkaure in the middle with the goddess Hathor on his right and a slightly smaller woman in remarkable likeness of her on his left. Douglas spoke but she could no longer hear what he was saying.

She looked at him and then Vivienne. Feeling paralyzed from the implication of the papyrus. Her thoughts were reeling. She couldn't think clearly. *What does this mean? What is he trying to tell me? Is he expecting me to enter into a relationship with both of them? It can't be, it's ridiculous!*

Mumbling words she couldn't even hear herself say she excused herself from their room. She bolted down the hallway to the elevator.

* * * *

She darted into the lobby unsure of how she arrived there. Dazed and unaware of her surroundings she bumped right into Alex.

"Maya! What's wrong? What happened?" The look on her face panicked him. She was unable to speak so he directed her to a sofa in the lounge area. "Maya you're shaking! Talk to me!"

Trembling she took a few shallow breaths and told him what happened.

Just as she began to calm down Alex's pent up emotions exploded. "Maya, just what are you getting yourself into?" he demanded.

His reaction took her off guard. Her defenses went up quickly. He was sounding like Brian did when he had turned against her. "What's that supposed to mean?"

"You know what I mean. You're getting yourself involved with him and who knows what he was trying to tell you with that papyrus." He had trouble finishing. This behavior was so out of character for him. "I think you should break your ties with him." He regretted the words the minute they were out.

Her Fire began to spark erratically. "Oh you do, do you? You have no right to tell me what to do. I'm in control of my life and I can take care of myself." Infuriated, she stood up and stormed out before she did something she would be sorry for later.

"Maya please wait!"

Chapter Thirty-eight

Douglas rose early the next morning to perform a quick scan on Maya's energy patterns.

Vivienne had recommended that he refrain from visiting her during the night. Suggesting that she needed time to digest the ramifications of the papyrus and that it might cause more harm if she felt him digging around in her head. Reluctantly he agreed but he missed visiting her.

She was sleeping restlessly and appeared to still be in turmoil. He jumped out quickly not wanting to disturb her any further. *Her reaction was more unpredictable than I would have liked.* But he held firm to the belief she would return to him.

A gentle tapping on the door distracted his thoughts. He took long measured strides. "Yes, what is it?"

"I have an urgent fax for you Mr. Mercer."

Douglas opened the door and took the envelope that was handed to him from the bellhop, "Thank you. Wait here for a moment please," he said and returned with an American ten-dollar bill from his money clip on the dresser.

"Thank you Mr. Mercer, have a wonderful day."

"Thank *you.* I hope you have a great day as well." Douglas closed the door and ripped open the envelope. His jaw clenched and his shoulders stiffened while he read the contents of the fax. "Damn! Those bastards! How dare they mess with me!"

Alarmed Vivienne asked, "Douglas, what is it?"

"It's from John." He tossed the fax on the table. "The SEC has filed the complaint and is pursuing their investigation."

Vivienne picked up the fax to read it for herself. Sitting down she gently rubbed her eyes to alleviate the tension. "The investigation could still take a while, we may have time to finish what we started," she said reassuringly.

"I know but I don't like the idea of not being there. I haven't received any progress yet on who tipped them off." He wanted revenge, he wanted to find out who had turned on them and punish them. But most of all he wanted to speed up the execution of his plans to free himself from the program, this however, was not an option at the moment. The date has been prophesized and there was nothing he could do to alter it. *Can we hold on for sixteen more days?*

*   *   *   *

Arielle snuck quietly into her room at five o'clock in the morning. Part of her wanted to wake Maya up to tell her about the glorious night she spent with Cade but she resisted and chose to climb into bed to snatch a couple hours of sleep.

Smiling sweetly, thinking of Cade she fell blissfully asleep feeling happy and in love.

The sound of the water running woke her up. *I wonder why she didn't wake me up before getting in the shower?* She drifted back to sleep until she heard the hair dryer.

She noticed that Maya was banging things around and cursing under her breath. Pulling away the covers she sat up stretching and rubbing her eyes. "Are you okay? You seem agitated," she asked gingerly.

Maya slammed the brush down on the counter. "Who does he think he is telling me what to do?" she demanded as she stormed out of the bathroom.

"Who? Douglas?"

"Douglas? No…Alex! That's who!"

"What happened? The last I saw you were with Douglas and Vivienne."

Maya hesitated before telling Arielle the whole story. *What if she reacts the same way as Alex? We need to stay together and we need Douglas.* She decided to take her chances and recounted first about the vision she experienced of returning to Atlantis after her death from the explosion and then her disintegration in Douglas' arms. Pacing the room unable to keep still she then described what took place in Douglas' room and afterwards her run in with Alex.

Arielle, thinking it was better to let her get it out, watched and listened in silence throughout Maya's tirade.

When Maya ran out of steam she spoke, "I know you're angry with Alex but let's back up and talk about the papyrus. It might not be what you're thinking. Maybe because of the odd situation with Douglas you presumed it meant something more sexual between the three of you. Who am I to say it isn't, but you can't deny there is a strong connection there."

"What are you saying?"

"You are destined to work with him. You've said it yourself. Now the way I see it you can either run away and hide for the rest of your life or you can face your fears and meet your destiny head on." She sat straight and crossed her arms waiting for Maya to react. "Well?"

Annoyed with Arielle's directness she sat down on the bed feeling defeated. "What would you do?"

"What choice do you really have? You are a strong and gifted woman. Pull yourself together and do what your instincts tell you."

Rubbing her temples, Maya resigned herself to the inevitable. "Have you noticed, despite the different hair colors, there's an uncanny resemblance between Vivienne and I?"

"Yes I have. But you guys *are* sisters after all. Now about Alex…"

Maya groaned and wished she didn't have to think about him.

"I might as well keep going since I'm on a roll," Arielle's voice was firm and determined. "Alex is one of the most gentle, caring and sensitive men I've ever met and I'm willing to bet he reacted the way he did because he couldn't stand to see you in pain and he wanted to protect you. By the sounds of it your emotions were so heightened I think you over reacted and you probably felt like it was Brian all over again. He's not Brian and he'd never turn his back on you."

Arielle gauged Maya's reaction to her words. Finding her more passive she took it as a sign to continue. "We have to be in this together, especially now that we're getting closer. So you'd better find a way to patch things up with him. The sooner the better."

* * * *

Cade was the last to arrive for breakfast. He couldn't contain his enthusiasm over his discovery that morning. "Hey guys! You're not going to believe what I found on my camera!"

"What could be so exciting?" questioned Arielle.

Before he realized what he was doing he bent over and kissed Arielle on the lips then sat beside her.

Totally unprepared for his public display of affection she blushed and looked away smiling. *Well I guess that doesn't leave any room for wondering. Oh what the heck. Who cares! I'm happy happy happy…*She wanted to get up and do a little dance.

"There's been so much happening I haven't paid any attention to the pictures I've taken. But for some reason I decided to look this morning. Wait till you see these!"

The group, including Douglas and Vivienne took turns viewing the digital photos and they were amazed at what they saw.

The first image was of the Great Pyramid taken at a distance from the bus plateau. It was like looking at an x-ray with the White Light revealing the area outlining the King's Chamber with a beam of Light connecting it to the top of the pyramid through a non-physical shaft. In close proximity to the area of where the sarcophagus lay was an image of a man.

"That's pretty wild!" exclaimed Maya.

"Wait till you see the next one. It's even more incredible." Cade took the digital camera and moved the picture forward to the next one. "Here look!"

They stared in astonishment at a picture of the Sphinx. A magnificent golden ray shone down from the Heavens to the excavated doorway they were planning on breaking into and a White Light illuminated upwards from the entrance. Behind the Sphinx in the distance was the Great Pyramid, from a different angle than the first picture, with an equally mystical apparition. A ray of White Light was beaming down on the pyramid exposing a doorway of White Light.

"That's absolutely phenomenal," Alex added thoughtfully. "If we had any doubts about what we are doing that should just about do away with them."

They passed the camera back and forth between them studying the pictures in detail.

Douglas noticed Maya was remaining quiet and there seemed to be an added tension between her and Alex. They were avoiding any contact with each other. *Interesting…*

"I figure we'll need some flashlights or oil lamps, whatever we can get our hands on. A crow bar or bolt cutters. Maybe a shovel and picks just in case." Cade was rambling unable to contain his enthusiasm to begin their plans.

"I'll speak with the hotel owner to arrange for someone to help us purchase what we need." Douglas stopped them before they could object to involving an outsider. "A few green bills will get us everything we need including discretion." Rising to leave he gestured for Vivienne to join him. "We'll meet you in the lobby in about half an hour."

"Maya is something wrong? You look kind of pale," Cade asked with gentleness.

"Actually I'm not feeling very well. My stomach is upset and I feel really wiped out."

"Listen, why don't you get some rest today. We can take care of getting everything we need. Arielle can check in on you later to make sure you're okay. Right guys?" said Cade.

Arielle and Alex agreed simultaneously.

Alex was filled with remorse for his reaction last night. *I should have been there for her. Instead I made her more upset.* He didn't know how but he was determined to make it up to her.

"There. Now go take care of yourself. Order up some ginger ale if they have any. That'll help your stomach," offered Arielle.

"That sounds like a good idea. I could use some time to myself to sort some things out and do some writing. Thanks guys. I really appreciate it."

* * * *

Maya felt incredibly relieved to be alone. The room she shared with Arielle was peacefully quiet.

She sat in the chair motionless for several minutes appreciating the silence. Getting up she made herself a cup of mint tea and pulled her journal and a pen out of her bag.

She'd barely had any time to write her thoughts since she arrived in Egypt with the exception of brief entries outlining the events at the end of each day. Since Brian left she came to love her time alone with her thoughts. Writing and exploring.

She propped a few pillows up against the headboard on her bed and curled up under the light blanket she retrieved from the closet. Sipping her tea she fingered the cover on her journal. She bought it just before the trip. She splurged on a beautiful hardbound book with flowers on the cover. It felt smooth to the touch. Carefully she untied the pretty ribbon that held it closed and opened to the first blank page.

Before putting her pen to paper she thought about her reaction towards Alex last night. She focused on moving aside her emotions around the situation and tried to view it from a new perspective. *Where is my anger really coming from? What buttons did he push?*

Brian came immediately to her mind and the anger started to resurface.

She thought about Pamela's advice about releasing anger and realized that she was weighted down by hers. *I'm never going to heal and be ready to fulfill my destiny if I don't do the work.* Thoughts of December twenty-first, now only sixteen days away filled her with anxiety and she knew that she had to salvage her Spirit by exploring the core of her emotions.

And so she wrote, pouring out her feelings of anger, disgust, frustration and resentment towards the man she thought she once loved and who abandoned her but as she dug deeper she came to recognize her issues were really with God, the universal energy responsible for her creation.

It was a pain that followed her throughout her life. She was furious with the universe for abandoning her as a baby, leaving her with a bitter old grandmother, forcing her to sacrifice the joys of childhood. Then thoughts of losing her baby girl Chloe brought outrage and grief so deep she couldn't breathe. *All for what? To prepare her for her destiny? Why should I care about that now when I was made to suffer loneliness and fear my whole life?*

The anger continued to build and writing wasn't enough anymore. She thought about the next steps and went to the bathroom to grab one of the hand towels. Part of her felt really ridiculous but she needed to try it. She had to find a way to cleanse her mind and body of these toxic feelings permanently.

The minute she raised her arm in the air her rage exploded in the downward motion. Vehemently she began to strike the bed with the towel. Swearing and calling out every derogatory name in the book she knew, she let her wrath out. Working into a frenzy, the years of living with feelings of being forgotten, unwanted and worthless spewed to the surface begging to be released.

Finally exhausted she fell to the floor in tears. Waiting until they subsided she leaned back against the bed. Wondering if she was done she called her feelings to surface. Testing her emotions she lingered for a moment.

Anger was replaced by sadness for all the years she lost, living a shell of a life.

She thought about Brian again and remembered a time when she loved him and her heart ached for their inability to grow along the same path.

Shedding more tears of heartbreak over the loss of her baby, suddenly more anger emerged so she got up and started beating the bed over again. When one arm got tired she switched the towel to the other hand and continued. Her heart beat furiously. Panting and out of breath she fell to the floor for a second time.

Astounded by what was buried so deep inside her she was determined to get it all out. When her breathing returned to normal she tried one more time but only had a few strikes left in her. She collapsed on the floor, completely spent.

When her heartbeat slowed down she began to laugh thinking about how wild she must have looked whacking the life out of the bed. *What if Arielle were to come in now?* The thought made her laugh even more.

She rose and collapsed on the bed. She picked up her tea hoping it would soothe her raw throat from shouting but it was now cold. Putting her cup down she reached for her pen and journal.

Allowing her thoughts to float up she began to write again. She recognized through it all she just wanted to be loved and cherished. Her anger had finally dissolved and she wrote about forgiving everyone and everything she felt wronged by; the universe for taking away her family, her grandmother for creating a lonely childhood, Brian for abandoning her, and even herself for not loving herself enough to be able to really love others.

Feeling liberated and fatigued she laid aside her journal and pen. She snuggled up under the blankets and slept peacefully.

* * * *

Maya was sitting at the little table by the window overlooking the Nile River when Arielle came in. She had slept fitfully for several hours. When she woke every muscle in her back, chest and arms were aching from the pounding she gave the bed.

"Hi. How are you feeling?" asked Arielle tenderly as she strolled to the table and sat with Maya.

"I slept most of the day so I feel better now with the exception of some sore muscles."

"Sore muscles? From what?"

Maya laughed at the image she had earlier of Arielle walking in on her while she was beating the bed cursing with the foulest language. She described her experience with her friend feeling love flowing through her body.

The two of them sat and giggled together. "That's hysterical. Now I've got this image of you beating the crap out of your poor bed. Did you have anything to eat?"

"Just some soup and crackers about an hour ago. I slept right through lunch. I was just reflecting on the past few days and enjoying some down time. How did your day go?"

"Pretty good. Douglas came through, of course. The hotel owner provided one of his staff to help us get everything. It was quite entertaining. We got to see some of the back streets in Egypt. It's pretty awful to see how so many of these people live. It certainly gave me a new appreciation for the things we take for granted back home. Anyway, I'm glad we had someone to help us. Douglas also guided us through the clearing meditation he talked about last night. It was really cool and I feel lighter and freer now. I think we all did."

"That's wonderful. It's too bad I missed it but I guess I had to do my own thing."

"I think it's amazing what you did. I don't know how many people would be able to dig that deep on their own. It's a scary thing to face our shadows lying hidden inside. You look a little tired still but I can sense a difference. You should feel proud of what you accomplished."

"Thanks. You're so encouraging." Hesitating briefly she decided to ask, "How is Alex?"

"On the quiet side. But we were busy most of the day so I think it helped to take his mind off what happened. Have you figured out what you are going to do?"

"I know I need to apologize. I just don't know when. We're always in a group and I certainly don't want Douglas around when I talk to him."

"If you're serious, Alex is down in the bar having a drink with Cade. We could go down and I'll distract Cade." She smiled thinking of all the ways she could get his attention. "I'm sure that won't be too hard to do."

"I'm so happy for you guys," she said wistfully. "I'll be ready in a minute. I just need to change."

Fifteen minutes later they walked into the bar. Arielle squeezed Maya's hand and whispered, "Good luck." She sauntered up to Cade. "Hey good looking, how about buying me a drink?"

"Hi gorgeous," Cade said with a seductive smile.

Arielle grabbed his hand. "Come on, let's go sit by ourselves in a dark corner and fool around."

Cade's eyes grew wide with the invitation. He slapped his buddy Alex on the back. "Sorry man, this is a better offer."

Alex's smile disappeared when he glanced behind Cade and saw Maya standing there looking awkward.

"Do you mind if I sit with you?" she asked tentatively.

He raised his hand in gesture, "Help yourself."

They sat for a few minutes with an unpleasant silence while Maya waited for her drink.

She tapped her foot against the chair in anxiety and took a sip of her soda water to wet her throat. "I'm sorry I over reacted last night, it was uncalled for."

Relief flooded through him. He'd been agonizing over how to bring it up. "I'm sorry too. I behaved like a Neanderthal. Telling you what to do. I don't know what came over me."

"I do. You were just trying to protect me. It's sweet really. When I took the time to think about it this morning I realized my reaction had nothing to do with you. It was anger with Brian and other things that I directed at you. I had to do some soul searching and I spent a lot of time writing and working through my feelings. It was very liberating."

"That's good to hear. Do you think you got it out of your system?"

"Well if I didn't get it out today then I don't know what it would take." She threw her head back and laughed, "Ouch!" She reached up to rub her neck. Her stiffness and pain increased by the minute.

"What's wrong?"

"Would you like to hear about my day? I think you'll get a kick out of it."

"Sure. I could use some cheering up." He was grateful that things were smoothing over between them but the thought of her and Douglas together still left a hole in his heart.

He did indeed enjoy her story and visualized her Fire letting loose. It seemed almost comical. "I'm certainly glad you decided to take it out on the bed and not me." He feigned fear and chuckled.

"So what's the plan for tomorrow? What time are we heading out?" she asked, deciding it was time to change the subject and get back to business.

"We want to make sure to give ourselves plenty of time before people start opening the gates at the pyramid so we decided to meet in the lobby at three A.M."

Maya gulped her water, "Three o'clock!"

They laughed again together and their easy camaraderie filled them with both joy and sadness.

* * * *

"Egyptian civilization existed far longer than most people realize." Douglas spoke to the group who had reunited for dinner. "Studies of the pyramids and their erosion point to the possibility that the Sphinx was actually built by Atlanteans who fled before the final destruction."

Douglas was relieved to see Maya sitting next to him and enjoying herself. He did not have an opportunity to speak privately with her today but he could wait. She was looking a little pale but certainly not sickly white like earlier today or last night. He refilled Vivienne's glass with red wine then Maya's and reached across to give the bottle to Cade.

Back in the Italian restaurant, they were finishing up their dinner. Dim lights and soft music provided a pleasant ambiance for their evening.

"Have you been able to verify that through remote viewing?" asked Arielle.

"Yes I have. The pyramids in Egypt, and around the world were built using mathematics that can be found in nature and man-made constructs from the simplest to the most complex things. These mathematics are known as the Fibonacci numbers."

"I think I've heard of them," said Alex. "Isn't that the formula where each number is the sum of the two numbers before them?"

"Yes. You are correct Alex." Douglas was happy to see him engage in the conversation enthusiastically. "These numbers have been found in the laws of universal harmony suggesting that this knowledge predated ancient Egyptian civilization by thousands of years with the Atlanteans."

"So what does all this mean?" asked Maya.

Tipping his shoulder to touch hers briefly, he winked and smiled at her. "Taking it further I've also discovered a link between the Great Pyramid and other sacred sites around the world."

The conversation was proving interesting and Alex was getting curious. "What other sites?"

"Easter Island, Tula and Tiahuanaco in Mexico, Canterbury, Stonehenge, Rosslyn, which is the site of the Templar church in Scotland, and others. These sites are all located on meridian lines connected to Giza—the center of the planet. These meridian or lei-lines are power centers."

Enjoying a sip of her wine and putting down the glass Arielle asked, "What makes them power centers?"

"Wherever major lei-lines on Earth's grid intersect, an energy field is created. These areas are known as vortexes or Golden Cities and each one has a unique structure and energy that keeps them and the surrounding areas protected from Earth changes."

"Are there any Golden Cities in North America?" asked Alex.

"Most certainly. There are five areas in the U.S. that will be protected over the next ten to fifteen years. Arizona and New Mexico is one area, Illinois and Indiana another, Georgia and South Carolina, Montana and Idaho and finally Colorado, and Nebraska."

"Is each state a Golden City?" asked Maya.

"Actually no. Golden Cities cover a very large area. Prophecies from the Ascended Masters indicate that people who awaken to spiritual enlightenment will gather in these areas and work together to practice *simple living*. Paramahansa Yogananda called them *White Brotherhood Communities.* I believe this process will be escalated along with the strength of the vortexes with the activation of the Emerald Stone so Vivienne and I are planning to investigate these areas and relocate when we return."

Douglas tilted his head closer to Maya and spoke softly. "We'd like you to consider moving closer to us darling. I know that you've been having the urge to make a change."

Maya shifted in her seat unsure how she felt about his request.

"Before you say anything I want you to consider it carefully." Taking his coterie ring off he pulled her right hand into his. Gently he laid the ring in the palm of her hand and closed her fingers around it. "Will you wear this tonight while you sleep?"

She was very conscious of everyone having witnessed his gesture and knew they waited for her response. Spreading her hand open she fingered the ring feeling the sides and top. She closed her eyes for a few seconds and when she opened them she took the ring and placed it on her index finger, accepting her role.

"Remember, my darling, this is the last tellurian incarnation we shall endure. Meaning that we will resume our rightful place and purpose eternally together, which begins as foretold from the heart of our Golden City. Isn't that right Vivienne?"

"Yes dear," acknowledged Vivienne. "So many good things are coming from this experience. We are truly blessed to have you with us." She looked to the others in the group. "We are blessed to have found all of you."

Chapter Thirty-nine

They met in the deserted lobby as planned at three A.M., not fully functional yet and groggy with sleep. The hotel owner arranged for Hanif to be on duty at the concierge desk to make sure they set off safely. Hanif was a soft-spoken man who had cheerfully assisted the Americans with purchasing their supplies the day before, for a generous fee of course.

Looking rather conspicuous carrying all their tools, Hanif ushered them into the Manager's office, careful not to cause any more attention to them in case anyone came down to the lobby. "I've ordered two taxis. They should be here any minute. I will come back to get you when it arrives." *Ah these American fools. Do they really think they will find the treasures they seek? Don't they realize how many have tried before them?* He left shaking his head.

"I can't believe we're actually doing this," Arielle's tummy was filled with butterflies and her hands were shaking.

Cade, who was pacing the room impatiently nodded in agreement, "It's pretty wild isn't it? I mean up until now this has just been a crazy dream. But we're really doing this."

"If you had told me a year ago that I'd be traveling through Cairo in the dark of the night with picks and shovels I would have said you were out of your mind." Alex yawned and rubbed the sleep from his eyes in disbelief.

Centering himself Douglas saw an opportunity to ensure their steadfastness and loyalty to their mission. "We are all being tested you realize. A final test, since this is end cycle, to engage and synthesize our temporal transfer of energy to guarantee our success in the chamber. You are all source talents that will ignite the Stone's signal. There are only four of you who can do that, which tells you the veracity of what has been foretold." He spoke in a serious and monotone voice to emphasize the magnitude of his message.

The door opened and Hanif poked his head through. "Your taxis have arrived."

Once outside Douglas tucked five hundred dollars into Hanif's hand as they loaded their supplies into the trunks of the taxis. Hanif pulled the drivers aside and arranged for them to take the Americans to the Sphinx without question, insisting they remain silent about this episode.

Feeling torn between loyalties to her friends and Douglas, Maya debated over which vehicle to travel in before deciding on her friends. She sat in the back with Cade and Arielle while Alex sat in the front. *We must be a funny site at this hour. Traveling with shovels, picks and flashlights all dressed in similar outfits of jeans, T-shirts, jackets and running shoes. Except for Cade who wore his cowboy boots. Even with his disheveled hair and a day's growth of beard he's quite a catch.* She felt a little envious of the ease of the relationship between Arielle and Cade and its lack of complication.

She had given Douglas back his ring while they waited for the taxi. Wearing it through the night had a calming and strengthening effect on her and now while they drove in darkness through the streets of Egypt she rubbed her finger where it was worn. *Maybe it's a combination of the ring and the releasing I did.* In her mind it didn't matter. She felt confident and excited about this excursion.

Nervous tension consumed them but they remained silent during the ride.

They stood overlooking the Sphinx from the drop off platform taking stock of everything they brought. The men selected their tools to carry. Vivienne brought a knapsack filled with power bars, fruit rollups and bottles of water. Maya and Arielle led their journey, holding the flashlights to light the way along the dark pathways.

The air was cool but their pace kept their bodies warm. The only noise that could be heard was the sound of their feet hitting the sandy hard ground and an occasional rustling along the ground. Wondering if they were scorpions or snakes kept them moving quickly.

Out of breath from their hike at the drop off point, with provisions in tow, they finally reached the entrance they planned to break into.

"Okay who's going down there first?" asked Maya pointing the flashlight down the shaft.

"I'll go," said Alex first.

"I'll come down after you," Douglas responded next. "Cade when we reach the bottom you can pass these things down."

"Sure, no problem. Let me know when you get the gate opened and I'll send the women down."

Alex wondered about the state of the rickety looking ladder and if it would hold his weight. He turned around and placed his left foot on the first step to test how sturdy it was. Satisfied it would hold him he proceeded to climb down.

Douglas lay on the ground holding a flashlight, stretching he passed it to Alex. When Alex was secure Douglas followed him down below.

The gate was bolted into the walls on a crooked angle. They confirmed it was only locked with a padlock making it easy enough to break it free with just a crowbar. "We're just going in for a short ways to take a quick look around," shouted Douglas up to Cade.

The walls and ground were rough. The passageway was low and very narrow allowing room for only one person at a time. It was very musty with very little air moving creating a raspy and prickly feeling in the throat.

They stopped about twenty feet or so, comfortable it was safe for the others to follow they retreated to the entrance. "Cade?" called Alex.

Peering down the shaft he responded. "Yeah. I'm here. How's it look?"

"Pretty cramped but it appears safe enough," responded Alex.

"I'll start handing you the rest of the stuff." Cade sent down a shovel, the picks, more flashlights and the backpack of food and drink. "Okay ladies, your turn. Vivienne why don't you go next?"

"That's fine Cade." She turned around and Cade took her by the elbow to provide her with support as she balanced herself on the ladder.

Once they were all down they picked up the supplies and formed a line to proceed.

Shadows danced on the walls and ceiling of the passageway from the moving flashlights as they walked. Before long it opened into a wider path so they were able to walk in pairs with lots of space around them.

Maya walked beside Cade. "It must have taken years to excavate this passage. It's obviously been well traveled."

Douglas and Vivienne led the way in front, Cade and Maya in the middle and Alex and Arielle behind the others.

"It's pretty spooky down here," said Arielle nervously. She felt claustrophobic knowing they were in this underground tunnel. "Aghhh!" she screamed and jumped as a couple of mice scurried around her feet from behind. She grabbed Alex's arm to calm down "Sorry guys. I guess I'm a little jittery."

Cade briefly turned to check on Arielle, without loosing pace with Maya. He smiled. *She's such a girl. Sweet, soft and all feminine. I love that about her.* He wanted to stop and wipe the smudge of dirt from her chin. He was reminded about her tripping slightly coming down the ladder and losing her footing. *She must have brushed her face with her dirty hands.*

Maya thought about Cade and Arielle's vision of this trek and became aware of the absence of the forceful winds they both spoke about. "Hey you guys, can we stop for a minute?"

Douglas and Vivienne stopped and turned wondering what Maya was thinking.

"Have you noticed there aren't any of the winds both of you experienced in your visions?"

Arielle looked to Cade who came up beside her. She had a puzzled expression on her face. "You know I totally forgot about that, what about you Cade?"

He shook his head. "So did I. But you know, that's not the only thing that seems different. I didn't get the impression that the passages were this wide."

Arielle and Cade looked blankly at each other thinking with great effort for a possible explanation.

"Vivienne you are exceptional with deciphering dreams and visions. What are your thoughts?" asked Douglas.

She pondered their situation and considered what to share that would not distract them from seeing their journey through to its final destination. "Your visions could be a symbolic representation of the meaning of your journey. The winds were meaning the force of the universe guiding you to this moment in time. The narrow space could reflect the limiting beliefs you are preparing to liberate, expanding into the larger consciousness of the chamber with the Emerald Stone."

"That's an excellent interpretation my dear. Well then, now that we have that clarified that let's move on shall we?" Douglas said as more of a statement than question.

Lining up in pairs again they started moving forward. Cade thought about Vivienne's explanation, but wasn't convinced her theory was accurate.

* * * *

"Looks like there's a fork in the passage up ahead," said Douglas lifting his flashlight higher for others to see. He grabbed Vivienne's arm abruptly, "Stop now!"

Cade reached out to prevent Maya from plowing right into Douglas. "What's going on?" Maya questioned in alarm.

He stood firmly holding out his arms in a protective manner. "There's a pit right in the centre of this juncture."

Coming up behind them Alex wasn't sure he heard right. "A what?"

"Oh my gosh. A pit? It's a pit!" Pebbles tumbled over the side as Maya approached closer. She listening to the echoes as they hit the sides of the black hole. Her heartbeat quickened.

They gathered together to peer down into the emptiness. Holding their flashlights over the pit, Arielle gasped looking down. "There are snakes down there!"

"Oh my gosh. You're right! There's tons of them!" Maya narrowed her view to focus in. "There's tarantulas and scorpions too!"

"Look to the right. Up ahead. I think that's a passage up into the pyramid. That's not the direction of the chamber though. It's to the left," said Douglas distracting their attention from the creatures below.

"But it's a dead end!" exclaimed Arielle.

"Yes I'm aware of that. But the hidden chamber is beyond that barrier. There's a marker on the wall that will expose the entrance."

"There's no way to get over there," responded Arielle confused. None of this was in her vision or Cade's. *It doesn't make sense.*

Alex studied the area. "We are going to have to try to scale the ledge around the pit. It's the only way."

"Yes, you're right," replied Douglas in agreement.

"What about the tools?" asked Maya.

"We will have to leave them here," said Douglas.

Maya felt the terror overcome Arielle. "Arielle you can do this. Just stay calm and focused." Faced with this crisis Maya's own trepidations threatened to consume her but she was determined to remain in control of her fears.

"I'll go first. I've been trained to maneuver in unpredictable circumstances. Watch my steps and follow them closely," ordered Douglas.

He moved with painstaking cautiousness. Making sure his footing was solid before taking the next step. Looking for ridges in the walls to hold as he progressed. "Okay I'm over. Alex why don't you go next? You can help me grab the ladies as they come across."

"Will do." Alex vigilantly traced Douglas' steps.

Once across Alex and Douglas helped Vivienne then Maya with their last leap across.

"Okay, it's your turn Arielle. You can do it babe. I'll be right behind you," Cade reassured Arielle and squeezed her hand.

Somewhat more at ease seeing the others succeed she started out. When she made it to the first ledge she looked down. Everything around her started to spin. Her hand reached out to scale the wall feeling for something to steady her.

"Don't look down!" shouted Cade when he saw her falter. "Keep your eyes focused on the rocks around you!" The area around the first landing was too narrow for him to come in behind her so he waited anxiously while she stabilized herself.

"I don't know if I can do this!" she yelled looking fearfully back to Cade.

"Arielle, listen to me. Yes you can. You can't stay there you have to keep moving," responded Cade feeling helpless.

Douglas spoke with a commanding voice, "Arielle. You are doing fine. I'll guide you across. Just do what I tell you."

"Okay…Okay…" *I can do this. I can do this.* She forced herself to get her racing thoughts under control. Then she took a deep breath and did as Douglas instructed.

She waited for Cade to join her on the last ledge before taking her final leap to solid ground. Doubting her ability to make the wider gap she needed Cade near her to provide her with the courage she needed. She was frailer than Maya and Vivienne and cursed herself for not working out. *Oh* my *legs are aching! That's it, when we get back I'm joining a gym.*

"You're almost here. Don't worry we'll grab you," shouted Alex.

Feeling the comfort of Cade's body near her own she drew in a breath. She bent her knees slightly to give herself a lift as she made the leap. She lost her footing and screamed as she reached out for the ledge.

Alex and Douglas lunged forward to grab her as Vivienne and Maya screamed for them to catch her. Alex caught her by one arm but she dangled in the air. Her were legs frantically kicking about.

"Help!" she screamed. "Help!"

"I've got you!" shouted Alex. He tried to pull her up but she was moving around too much. "Arielle, swing your other arm over and grab onto me!"

She swung her body but she missed his arm. Feeling the ledge, she grabbed on as hard as she could.

Cade could not believe what he was seeing. His stomach flipped over. His heart jumped into his throat. There wasn't anything he could do but watch in horror.

Douglas seized her other arm and together he and Alex pulled her up. Her feet scraped the sides as she tried to use them to propel her up.

"Alex have you got her?" yelled Cade.

"It's okay Cade! She's safe!" They dragged her up onto solid surface and Alex took her into his arms, "It's okay you're safe now."

She stifled the sobs erupting within her, turning away from Alex she watched Cade leap across the divide almost effortlessly.

Flinging herself at Cade he wrapped his arms around her and held her tightly. Pulling her away he took her face in his hands. "You scared me half to death! Don't ever do that again!"

Relief flooded through her and she burst out laughing. "I'm sorry it wasn't my intention to fall." She peered down into the pit. Shivering at the thought of almost landing at the bottom with the snakes.

* * * *

"What are we looking for?" asked Alex. He stood holding one of the two flashlights Cade had tossed across the pit.

They stood in front of the dead end passageway. The walls in this juncture were about seven feet high, six feet wide and twenty feet long.

"We need to find a pictogram in the shape of a Star David. Or more accurately two triangles, one inverted over the other with a Fire symbol matching Maya's in the center." Douglas paused briefly to cough some dust out of his lungs. He accepted the bottle of water Vivienne passed to him and swallowed several small sips trying to clear his throat. "It should be two inches in diameter."

They scoured the back wall searching for the pictogram. Brushing away sand and salt deposits with their fingers but found nothing.

"Maybe it's concealed on the sides. Let's split up and try searching on the adjoining walls," suggested Alex.

I don't understand. It should be here. While the others went over the sides Douglas retrieved a penknife from his pocket and began to dig away patches of stone. Getting more perturbed by the minute he dug furiously. *I couldn't have been wrong. It's impossible. Where is it?*

"Douglas face it. It's not here. We've gone over these walls with a fine tooth comb for over an hour now." Vivienne tried to get his attention but he wouldn't listen. Giving up she leaned over the knapsack and withdrew some of the snacks and water she brought. She passed them out to the others.

Tired and disenchanted they sat wordless leaning up against the walls eating and drinking. Sand and dirt covered their clothes, arms and hands. Their hair was gritty from the dust they stirred up in the air. After several minutes they observed Douglas slump to the ground.

"Douglas, Vivienne's right. It's getting late. We should head back before anyone arrives and coming looking for us." Maya resorted to her old ways of playing it safe and it bothered her but she couldn't see any other alternative. She wanted to reach out and console him. She never thought she'd ever see him look so defeated.

Annoyed with himself for letting the others see him weak he stood up. "All right. We're wasting our time here. Let's make our way back. Maybe we will be able to repair the busted gate before we leave. Alex and I were pretty careful jimmying it free. When we get back to the hotel I will view the signal line to determine if there is another passageway."

"There was another shaft by the back paw on the east side. Perhaps there's another tunnel coming across," suggested Cade.

* * * *

They narrowly escaped from getting caught as dawn's light filled the sky. Seeing an armed guard riding a camel in the distance they knew they wouldn't get far with the tools so they left them tucked near the gate out of sight. Hoping they wouldn't be discovered.

"We'll have a better chance of not being seen if we split up and meet in the temple. We can hide there until everything is clear," ordered Douglas. "Vivienne will of course come with me. Maya you go with Alex. Cade watch out for Arielle."

Deciding on directions they went their separate ways. The guard crossed the back of the Sphinx just as Cade and Arielle made it through the temple archway.

Douglas observed the situation. The six of them were within hearing distance in the spaces they found to stay out of sight. "We're not going to get out of here without being seen. There's too much open space before we can get far enough to catch a ride."

"What do you suggest?" asked Alex.

"We should stay here until people start milling through."

"Good idea. That way we can blend in and go unnoticed with others," added Cade.

They had to wait for about ninety minutes before they could get up and walk around. During that time guards occasionally rode by and the site attendants started their shifts. They used their water to clean themselves up so they wouldn't stand out from the other tourists.

Chapter Forty

When the group arrived back at the hotel around nine A.M. they decided to get a few hours sleep and meet in the lounge around three in the afternoon.

Alex, Maya, Cade and Arielle watched the television in the hotel bar that afternoon feeling dispirited by the tragic news.

"This is the single most catastrophic natural disaster in the history of the United States since 2005," announced the newscaster on CNN. "Hurricane Roger, a Category Five storm, which hit the Florida Panhandle, Alabama, Mississippi, Texas, Louisiana, South and North Carolina only two days ago has left these states in devastation. The number of hurricanes affecting North America has increased by twenty-five percent this year due to the increasingly long hot summer. This storm is expected to cost six hundred and fifty billion dollars to rebuild the areas hit.

"More than one-and-a-half million people were evacuated from their homes but hundreds of thousands refused to leave. The death toll is anticipated to be in the thousands resulting from a combination of drowning, dehydration and disease due to contaminated waters. Thousands of people are left homeless including children separated from their families."

Scenes of rescue workers in boats appeared on the screen. Helicopters were saving people trapped on the rooftop of their homes. Rioters roamed freely taking whatever they could carry. Some areas were now under the National Guard's control.

"The impact of this storm will have an even greater impact over time with the Louisiana wetlands now completely submerged. These wetlands were the most productive waterways in America producing and transporting a third of the nation's oil and a quarter of its gas. It also had the second highest commercial fishing capabilities. It took several years to rebuild after the damage in 2005 and there's speculation now that these areas will no longer be operable for these industries."

They watched in silence. The newscaster continued to provide an update on yet another hurricane building force along the East Coast. "Hurricane Suzanne, another Category Five storm, is expected to hit Georgia, South Carolina, North Carolina and Virginia. People are being evacuated inland as many areas are preparing for total submersion."

The mood of the group sunk even lower. Their disappointing failure to find the hidden chamber left them feeling haunted and powerless.

"Our time is running out," said Cade with a heavy heart. "Mother Earth is acting with force and speed. It's going to continue to get worse until we find the Emerald Stone and complete the activation on the twenty-first."

"Douglas will come through for us and everything will be okay," offered Arielle hopefully.

"Let's hope so," added Alex gloomily.

Cade was the only one who dared to share what they were all thinking, "Are we giving away too much of our own power by relying on Douglas to save the day? There's no denying he was totally wrong about where the entrance to the hidden chamber was. What if he can't find it? What do we do then?"

"He's the only option we've got right now Cade. I say we give him another chance unless something miraculous happens to point us in the right direction," said Arielle.

"I have to agree with Arielle," added Alex.

Maya nodded in agreement but remained silent, brooding over the time slipping away.

* * * *

Douglas grew more disturbed by the hour. The harder he tried to find the energetic connection to the Emerald Stone the weaker the signal became.

"You're trying to force it. You haven't slept in over thirty-two hours. Why don't you get some rest for a while," Vivienne said trying to console him.

Ignoring her he prepared himself to make another attempt to go into the ether. "This doesn't make sense. I've never experienced a static object signal redeploy before."

Vivienne came up behind him and rubbed his shoulders to loosen the hard knots in them. "Sweetheart you really should get some rest. Everything will work itself out if you would just leave it alone and let the universe reveal its magic."

He sat back in the chair letting his shoulders fall. "You're probably right my love. That feels wonderful." Closing his eyes he allowed his body to relax. "Will you come lie down with me? I need to be with you."

"Of course." She knew better than to deny him in this dire state.

He felt at risk of being exposed and disoriented. Satisfying Vivienne was his way of mending his construct. It might be a superficial method, especially today, but it was effective none-the-less. She was his and knowing she was committed to him and their purpose set his mind at ease.

They were opposites in many ways. She was rational and unemotional. He was unpredictable and sensitive. She was aloof and he was passionate. She was the businesswoman and he was the artist. They worked well together, blending both sides of masculine and feminine.

Nightmares of days in combat and missions he wished he could forget normally plagued him and rarely let him sleep for more than a few hours at a time. But today was an exception. He slept soundly for five full hours.

All I need is a cup of coffee and I'll be fine. Groggily picking up his watch from the night table he was astounded to see it was after six o'clock. *Damn. I wanted to check on the coordinates again before meeting the others downstairs. Oh heck, they can wait.*

Watching Vivienne sleep serenely he felt thankful for her always-present steadfast calmness. She was able to see clearly when his judgment was clouded by his occasional fanatical moods. "Kanïka darling, wake up. It's getting late." He gently rubbed her shoulder.

Still spent from their vigorous lovemaking she mumbled, "What time is it?"

"It's after six. Could you please make some coffee while I shower?" Not waiting for a response he knew she did not require a second request.

A shower and two cups of coffee later Douglas went into the ether while Vivienne prepared for the evening. With the coordinates of the Stone in mind he went searching. As he expected or hoped, he discovered a second tunnel leading to the entrance of the hidden chamber. The second tunnel he detected ran parallel to the one they traveled and came up behind the dead end wall bypassing the pit.

Satisfied, relieved and revitalized he recorded his new findings in his daily log and prepared himself to meet the others.

*   *   *   *

When Douglas and Vivienne joined them for dinner later that evening he appeared enthusiastic and determined. He explained his experience to the group of locking on to the coordinates of an alternate tunnel and the sacred room beyond the obstruction they encountered.

Douglas' confidence reassured the others of his talents and so they made plans to return to the Sphinx with a renewed sense of determination.

Not wanting to get caught running out of time again they decided to give themselves a few extra hours and left the hotel at twelve-thirty.

Total darkness surrounded them in the early morning hours on the Sphinx plateau. The night sky, filled with a thick layer of clouds, left them without the light of the stars or moon to help them find their way.

Remembering the penlight he kept in his travel pouch, Cade fumbled to retrieve it. He clicked the button to turn it on but unfortunately it was strong enough to light the way for only a few feet in front of them. Deciding it was better than nothing they traveled along the highland and down the rocky area with caution.

Throughout their trek they hoped that the supplies they had stored in the shaft the previous evening had not been discovered and removed, or even worse, the gate rebolted.

Finally reaching their destination they waited in the shadows, watching the light down below move around while Alex would hopefully recover the tools.

They heard a thud and Alex swearing, "Damn!"

Maya tried to peer down the shaft but the light was too dim to see anything. "Are you all right Alex?"

"Yeah…I just banged my head. Nothing serious." He wiped away a few drops of blood from his brow leaving a streak across his temple. He was relieved to discover their supplies along with the addition of a few rodents scurrying about his feet.

"Is everything still there?" asked Douglas impatiently.

"Yes, everything's here and the gate is just like we left it."

"Good, we're on our way down. Shine the light up the shaft," ordered Douglas.

They found the second excavated passageway just as Douglas had seen. It was somewhat narrower than the first but only marginally. There were a couple of zig zags in the tunnel before it straightened out.

Douglas' determination was contagious and they walked with stronger conviction than the previous night. It helped knowing the terrain and what to expect this time.

Arielle felt grateful they didn't have to climb over the pit again. What could be more terrifying than hanging over a pit filled with snakes and tarantulas? Your life hanging suspended before you not knowing whether you will live or die. She survived and that's mattered.

Maya was in the center row again, this time beside Alex. Her stomach fluttered at the thought of coming face to face with the great Emerald Stone. *It's been a fantasy for months. I can't believe we're only moments away.* She waited for some sort of signal or vibration from the Herkimer tucked away in a front pocket of her jeans to indicate they were getting closer and tried not to feel disappointed when she received none.

"We haven't really talked about what we need to do once we're inside," said Arielle.

Douglas knew exactly what he had to do when the time was right. None of them would leave the chamber alive once they opened the doorway to the other dimensions with the possible exception of Maya. But that would depend on her actions over the next two weeks. It angered him that he had to rely on them. He and Vivienne had bided their time waiting for this opportunity to escape the magnetic fields, which have kept them captive living these tellurian lives for centuries. Soon he would be able to travel at will. Expanding his circle of power to other worlds.

"According to the prophecies, if we are spiritually ready to experience the transformation all that we'll need to do is place our hands on the symbols and the activation will begin," said Maya.

Alex speculated on the reasons why Maya was holding back. *She's the key and she knows it. It won't work without her lighting the Fire of her soul in the Herkimer.*

"What about the prayer?" asked Arielle.

"Absolutely. It really seems to strengthen and focus our energy," replied Maya.

"It was more than that," added Alex. "I believe it's an integral part of the ceremony we created in Atlantis."

Douglas was intrigued, "Would you like to share it with Vivienne and I?"

"Well when we began meditating together as a group each one of us received the same inspiration to recite a prayer or maybe it's more of an invocation," said Maya. "Shall we show them?"

"Sure, why not…" agreed Arielle.

They stood together in a circle and repeated the prayer. Without an intention for a specific purpose its affect was minimal and provided only marginal warmth of energy flowing between them.

"That's the general idea," said Maya shrugging her shoulders.

"I can see how that would highlight your work. You should all be proud of the progress you've made in such a short period of time." Douglas said with an enthusiasm that concealed the apprehension he felt lurking in the corners of his mind.

Continuing on their trek they arrived at a split with a wall ahead of them and two passages branching off in either direction.

Douglas was surprised to see the additional shafts but did not reveal his thoughts to the others. "It's the one on the right," he said decisively. Looking to each of them he said, "You know what to look for."

Time wore on and again they didn't find the marker they were instructed to look for. Disappointed they backtracked and searched the middle passage next.

Growing frustrated and distraught Douglas could not comprehend being so misled yet again but he maintained his composure. "There's one more passage. Let's hope we saved the best for last."

Reaching the end of the last passage they stood motionless staring into a partially hallowed out area.

"It looks like whoever worked down here gave up digging," said Arielle.

Cade moved in closer to inspect the area, keeping an open mind. "We can try crawling through to the back wall. It's only about fifteen feet away."

Douglas stood beside Cade. "It's only large enough for a couple of us to squeeze in at a time. Cade do you want to work with me?" asked Douglas.

"Sure, I'm in."

The space was constricting and difficult to maneuver but they dragged their bodies along slowly. They edged their way and finally reached the back wall.

Cade's neck and shoulder was getting stiff and sore trying to feel along the wall looking for the symbol. "I don't see anything."

"I'm going to get the picks. I'll be right back." Douglas turned around and crawled back. "Alex, hand me the picks will you? We're going to try digging for a while."

Maya had a sinking feeling it was a useless effort but she remained silent.

Clouds of dust and sand were accumulating in the narrow space. Cade and Douglas coughed frequently and it was becoming more difficult to breathe.

An hour later Cade stopped pounding on the wall. He looked discouragingly at the holes they made. *This is crazy.* "Douglas we're not getting anywhere. I think we should call it quits."

"No I will not abandon this. Alex! Come in and take Cade's place!"

Cade returned to the others and climbed out, still coughing and completely covered in dirt. "I told him it was useless but he won't give up," he said bending over and shaking his hair.

"Alex!" shouted Douglas.

"I'm on my way!" Alex looked at Maya and Vivienne and was struck with wonder by their similarities as they both stood with their hands on their hips. They had the same emerald green eyes. Even their body shapes were remarkably alike. "I better help him out," he said in resignation.

The two men continued to chip away at the wall taking turns for the next couple of hours.

Alex was about to give up when he felt the wall soften as the pick hit its mark. His heart quickened. He coughed in excitement, "Hey! I think I'm breaking through!" He continued digging using more force.

Douglas pulled himself up beside Alex. Together they picked away at the wall until an opening the size of a small brick caved through. Frantically they continued to dig until it was large enough to crawl through.

They squeezed through and stood up. There was so much dust they couldn't see anything. Coughing and wheezing they looked around. Anticipating a magical sight they were sorely disheartened by the dark empty space before them. They could hear the others shouting to them in the background.

"Tell us what you see!" hollered Maya.

"Should we come down now?" asked Vivienne.

Silence.

Vivienne grew impatient waiting for their response. "Douglas is the Emerald Stone there?"

* * * *

Infuriated and humiliated Douglas was at a loss for what to do. *Something must be interfering with my plan.* In all his training he could not comprehend anything that was capable of tampering his signal strength. At least not since being a novice when a wave or disturbance transferred it and crossed an adjacent signal causing confusion.

He was in a foul uncommunicative mood. Vivienne knew to give him space and warned the others to do the same.

The journey back to the hotel at six-thirty in the morning was made in silence.

Vivienne found a moment to pull Maya aside when they exited the taxi at the Sheraton Cairo. "We will be in touch when we've come up with an alternate plan. It may take a day or two. Tell the others to wait before making any decisions."

* * * *

They were devastated after another unsuccessful excursion and went their separate ways to sleep it off. When they met for dinner they were still at a loss for what to do. Douglas was their only hope to find the Emerald Stone and they didn't know where else to turn.

"Rather than fight this why don't we allow ourselves some time to regroup." Maya continued thoughtfully, "Personally I'd like to make it an early night and do some writing."

Cade and Arielle said they wanted to spend some time together so Alex offered to make sure Maya returned to her room safely.

The next morning Maya woke feeling cut off from Douglas. She knew he was busy looking for answers but she had grown accustomed to his visits in her dreams. He always seemed to know what to say and when to comfort her or make her feel wanted and beautiful. *He's a busy and important man. I guess this is something I would have to get used to if I want to be a part of his life. It's not like I have any other commitments to stop me from being with him and there's so much I could learn...*

She spent the afternoon with Arielle, Alex and Cade. Having totally abandoned the tour they went shopping in the Khan El Khalili Bazaar to keep themselves occupied and lift their disillusioned spirits.

Believing they had exhausted their ideas and resources they felt lost and their only option was to wait for Douglas to discover a solution.

They split up into couples while they walked the streets browsing the shops. Alex was being careful to keep his distance physically but still felt compelled to get to know Maya better. Being her brother he could still offer her a shoulder to lean on. "It must have been very difficult to lose your baby. I'm so sorry Maya. I know what it's like to lose your family," he said tentatively.

Her head dropped in remembrance. "I guess you do. I'm still not over it."

"I don't know that you ever get over it."

"Perhaps…" She glanced sideways at him, appreciating his efforts to develop their friendship. "I think I believed that having a baby would be the answer to my problems or everything I thought was lacking in my life." She paused to look at an Isis statue. "Back then I wasn't open to taking responsibility for myself or my actions and all I wanted to do was lash out and blame someone."

"I think that's normal. I know that's what I did for the longest time too. I must have been unbearable for my family to be around," said Alex.

She stopped and touched his arm. "I'm sorry for your loss Alex."

Her touch took him by surprise and he just wanted to hold her so they could comfort each other but he held back, unsure how she would react. "Thank you," he acknowledged.

"You mentioned your family. Are you close to them?"

"Yeah, I guess you could say that," he smiled thinking of them. "Except they think all this is just a phase I'm going through. I must have been preaching to them or something because they got sick of hearing about it so I tend to keep it to myself now."

"Maybe that will change…you know…afterwards."

"That would be nice."

They continued to get to know one another while they walked. Sharing stories of their childhood and the things they liked to do. Maya talked about her desire to learn to fly someday and she learned that Alex's passion was hand gliding, which allowed him to enjoy being free with the wind.

Arielle and Cade trailed behind at a distance.

"When did you discover your love for painting?" asked Cade.

"Oh it was a real gradual thing. I dabbled with it for years when I was in high school but the more I played the deeper under my skin it got until it became a consuming passion. My Aunt Grace started showing them to neighbors and soon people began to buy them." She smiled remembering her Aunt's support. "She helped me to open up my studio where we sold my paintings along with other local artists."

"Your Aunt sounds like a wonderful person," said Cade taking her hand in his.

"Oh yes she is. What about your family? I got the impression you're not very close."

"You could say that. We get along all right but we just don't see each other very often. My sister Jodi lives in California and my other sister Tess moved to

Texas to be with her husband. Mom and Dad traveled a lot when we were growing up and most summers they shipped us off to a camp so we never really spent a lot of time together."

"Oh that's too bad," said Arielle sympathetically.

"Actually it's worked out okay. When we do get together for special occasions we have a lot of fun. The rest of the time we just do our own thing."

"Have you ever been engaged?"

"Naw…I've had a couple of semi-serious relationships but I've been holding out for the real thing babe." He scooped her into his arms and kissed her right in the middle of the street.

He made her feel like a schoolgirl all over again but at thirty-two years of age, she knew what she wanted now.

The afternoon excursion helped to alleviate the crushing disappointment of not finding the hidden chamber, even if it was short-lived.

When they finally received a call from Vivienne the next day inviting the group to join her and Douglas for dinner it left them speculating what the new plan was going to entail.

* * * *

"I believe there is someone deliberately sending disruptive waves across the Emerald Stone coordinates causing a transference of the energy. Unfortunately there is nothing further I can do while we're here. I need access to my equipment and contacts." Douglas paused to let his words register with the group.

"We'd like to invite you to return home with us while we do some further research," added Vivienne.

They passed looks amongst themselves, unsure how to respond.

Maya felt a rising sense of panic fill her thoughts. *Time is running out…How can we afford to return to the States and be back in time?*

Douglas touched Maya's hand and acknowledged her concerns, "I know you're worried about the time but we still have twelve more days and we don't really have any other options. I need my equipment to find out what is interfering with our destiny. I understand it is an odd request. But while you stay with us I could help you develop your gifts to ensure your success when we return to Egypt."

"If money is a problem for any of you we'll pay for the additional expenses. And if there is anything else we can do to help just let us know," offered Vivienne.

Cade thought about his life at home. He didn't have any ties to bind him there. The Earth under his feet kept him company but he had that regardless of where he was and as long as he was near Arielle he was happy. "I'm in."

"Me too." Alex wasn't sure if it was more painful to be near Maya or away from her. But he wasn't about to let her travel unprotected until this was finished.

Maya and Arielle glanced towards each other and nodded in agreement. "All right we'll come too," said Arielle.

"Good. We will proceed with making all the travel arrangements and provide you with the details when everything is set."

"Douglas do you have any idea who might be interfering with us?" asked Arielle.

"Not yet but I will find out and fix the situation. This is my promise and I always keep my promises."

Chapter Forty-one

BEL AIR, MARYLAND
11 December 2012

Maya gazed out the window in awe of the spectacular view from the guestroom in Douglas and Vivienne's home. Rolling hills and evergreen trees filled the scene for miles. She imagined how beautiful it must be in the summertime with lush green grass and flowers in the gardens.

Having missed their connecting flight in France to J.F. Kennedy Airport, the group took a detour to London where they had a five-hour layover. They arrived in Douglas and Vivienne's home in Bel Air, Maryland, at two-thirty in the morning after a long and tiring two days. Paige, their housekeeper had their rooms prepared when they arrived.

A soft knock on the bedroom door distracted her attention. She glanced at the clock on the dresser and was surprised to discover she had slept so late. "Come in."

It was Douglas. He entered the room and mindfully closed the door behind him. She was surprised to see how casual he was dressed. He was looking relaxed and comfortable wearing a navy tracksuit with house slippers. "Are you settling in all right?"

"Yes thank you. This is truly beautiful." She looked around the guestroom with fresh eyes. It was painted a lovely soft rouge with white accents. A queen size gold wrought iron bed took center stage with layers of sheets and blankets and lots of pillows in shades of complimentary reds and whites. The cream carpet was lush and felt wonderful under her feet. The smell of fresh roses filled the room with a heavenly scent. "I feel like a princess."

He walked across the room and gently stroked her arm. Brushing a stray hair away from her cheek he gazed into her eyes. "You are *my* princess."

Her heart sped up and her breath grew faint feeling him stand so near.

"You must trust that we will survive this situation, and prosper as a reward for our diligence. Far more than our personal destiny is riding on fulfilling our fate at Giza, and so we shall." Moving his hand to her chin he held it there. "I will be there for you when you feel overwhelmed or disoriented. I am in love with you Diãntha."

She gazed into his eyes, spellbound, not knowing how to respond. "Douglas…Melïon…"

He took a step closer, "Shhh…" He tilted her chin and brought his lips down to meet hers. He kissed her, soft and gentle at first. Growing deeper and more insistent as the moments slipped by. When he pulled away he stroked her cheek and looked intently into her smoldering eyes. "You deserve to be kissed that way. By a real man."

He watched the confused look wash across her face. "Yes I know your every desire, my darling, and I know you have not been made love to, the way a woman should be in a very long time. You have been waiting for me whether you realize it or not and I will not abandon you. That is another promise and as I said before, I never break a promise."

Taking her hand in his he kissed her palm. "Come down for lunch when you are ready my darling, the others are waiting." Turning away he left the room closing the door behind him.

She leaned up against the door, smiling to herself, entranced by the magic of his words. His ability to always know what she was thinking and feeling amazed her. She felt herself falling into him, his thoughts, his heart and his soul. It was scary and exciting at the same time.

* * * *

Maya took her time strolling to the oak staircase. Studying the beautiful mandala hanging on a wall beside one of the six bedrooms on the top floor. The center circle of the mandala must have been two feet across with rich brown leather intertwined around it. Long fluffs of cotton hung down decorated with richly colored beads and feathers.

A cluster of three wrought iron candleholders with white candles hung on the wall beside what Maya guessed was the master bedroom at the end of the hallway. The sage green walls complimented the soft cream color carpet runner and oak stained floors.

The sun shone brightly through the large open windows overlooking the front yard. Their house was one of only six in the sprawling estate neighborhood sitting on one-acre lots.

Because it was so late when they arrived in the middle of the night and everyone went straight to bed she wanted to take her time taking in the atmosphere of Douglas and Vivienne's home.

There was a little landing overlooking the curve of the staircase. As Maya approached she noticed a beautiful ginger cat curled up on the ledge. Its piercing green eyes watched her move. "Hello kitty. You're such a pretty one."

The cat responded with a meow and got up to stretch lazily. It snuggled around Maya's legs and purred affectionately. She stooped to pet her for a few moments before descending the staircase and watched the cat follow her.

Upon reaching the spacious landing she noticed a formal dining room on her left. This room had full carpeting in a taupe shade with a lighter shade painted on the walls. The windows were decorated with A-shaped rich burgundy brocade drapes accentuated with taupe piping around the edges. A gigantic glass table sat in the center of the room with chairs covered in the same burgundy material. She noticed the centerpiece was another cluster of three white candles on bases of wrought iron.

Vivienne and I have similar tastes in decorating. It's rich, warm and inviting just the way I like it.

Turning to her right she peeked quickly through the windows of two French doors. She assumed it must be their office. With a cursory glance she was able to see a couple of desks with computers, a printer and bookshelves. There was a glass cabinet in one corner but not wanting to be caught being nosey she kept moving down the hallway where she heard the sound of laughing and chattering voices.

"There you are. We were wondering when you were going to come down," said Alex happily.

Cade, Arielle, Alex, Douglas and Vivienne sat gathered around a large rectangular oak table in the kitchen. Maya was struck with awe by the grand windows along the entire back wall. "Hi guys. You're all so chipper today?"

"I guess it's nice to be back in the U.S. again," laughed Cade.

"There's coffee on the counter if you'd like to help yourself," offered Vivienne.

"Thank you that sounds wonderful." The aroma of freshly brewed coffee filled her senses. Even with their disheartening failure to find the Emerald Stone she felt alive with the promise of a new day. She walked over to one of the windows with her cup and savored its flavor. Looking in awe at the glass enclosed massive indoor pool filled with sparkling sky-blue water and an attaching hot tub. Lounge chairs adorned the sides of the pool and a Plexiglas table with seating for six under a canopy. Further out she observed a guesthouse on their property and rows of orchard trees in the distance.

Arielle came up behind her. “Magnificent isn’t it?”

“It’s breathtaking. Vivienne you have a beautiful home.”

“Thank you, we certainly like it here.”

Paige came in from the pantry off the kitchen. She was a petite pretty woman with black hair, cropped short around her face. Her eyes were dark brown and her high cheekbones were highlighted with full red lips. She was dressed casually in blue jeans and a white shirt. “Would you like something to eat? I saved some French Toast and bacon for you.”

“That sounds delicious Paige.” She’d never known anyone before with a personal chef and thought it was interesting how they were all very comfortable with each other, more like family.

“Sit down and relax and I’ll get it for you. I understand you’ve all had a very tiring trip back.”

Grateful for the pampering Maya pulled out a chair and joined the others at the table.

They chatted with Douglas and Vivienne about their home. Learning that they had moved from Baltimore just a couple of years before. “It’s a quiet community which suits our needs. We like to maintain low profiles,” he said. “I’m somewhat of a hermit when I’m not traveling and having the pool, a gym downstairs and our office right here allows me to relax more.

“It sounds like a great setup,” said Arielle.

“It suits our purpose. Vivienne has wonderful taste and she’s made it a very cozy environment to live in.” He smiled at Vivienne with pride.

When Maya finished her meal Douglas escorted them to the sunroom that had been converted to a studio. The room was filled with paintings; some hung on the walls, some were stacked in rows and others on easels waiting to be finished. They wandered around the room perusing his work.

“These are spectacular!” exclaimed Arielle. “I’m a painter too but my work cannot compare to these,” she added wistfully.

“Have you been to Giza before?” asked Cade, studying an amazing likeness of the pyramids at sunrise with an orange glow setting off the golden sands and the occasional puffs of clouds.

“No, this was our first trip,” responded Douglas.

"This looks so real I feel like the pyramids are actually right in front of me. It's amazing how you were able to capture them so perfectly. You are very talented. Have you always painted?" asked Cade.

"Actually my first experience with a paint brush was only a couple of years ago."

The looks of astonishment on their faces gave him great pleasure.

Pulling them out from the stacks one at a time, Arielle studied his artwork closely. *His use of color and detail is remarkable.*

Douglas silently came up behind Maya and whispered into her ear, "Are you avoiding me, my darling?"

She jumped, startled by his sudden presence. "No, of course not. Why would I do that?" She tried to keep her voice light but in truth, she was having difficulty in figuring out how to behave with him around the others and especially with Vivienne. He'd said Vivienne was happy for them but it was too weird and she felt embarrassed by the whole thing.

"I don't know but I get the feeling something is bothering you."

She softened her demeanor, not wanting to worry him and put her thoughts securely aside. "I'm probably just tired from the trip but I'll be fine."

"We can remedy that right away. Paige is an amazing chef and very health conscious. She will take care of us. If you like to work out I'll show you the gym and you can exercise any time you choose."

Grateful that he did not question the reason she offered she thanked him for his graciousness.

Taking her tenderly by the elbow he said, "Come with me there is a painting I want you to see." He guided her towards an easel tucked away in a corner of the room. "I knew that you would one day be here."

She was unprepared for the impact as he lifted the sheet covering a painting of her temple in Atlantis. She tried to choke back the tears but she was unsuccessful. Droplets fell onto her cheeks. "Douglas it's so beautiful." She reached out wanting to touch her pyramidal shaped crystal on a white alabaster pedestal. "You've captured the shades of purple and turquoise so magnificently." The crystal's energy radiated outward reflecting its colorful light onto the luminescent walls.

"They are the quintessential colors that represent you and all your brilliance, my darling. This is one of my favorite pieces and I painted it when I discovered your existence in this dimension."

She brushed away her silent tears and stood marveling in her memories of her home. He had painted her standing on the beautiful white alabaster terrace overlooking her abundant fragrant garden. Her hair was a reddish chestnut color, the length of her waist and looked like it blew gently in a breeze. She wore a flowing long white gown wrapped around one shoulder revealing her soft creamy skin.

Standing in Douglas' studio thousands of years later, she could smell the sweetness of the flowers, feel the breeze waft across her cheeks and see the vibrant colors of her temple as if she was actually there.

Seeing the others nearby, she restrained the urge to glide into his arms and kiss him. Her heart ached to give herself to him, to surrender her heart and her entire being to this man who almost seemed to know her better than she knew herself.

* * * *

Douglas invited them to join him in his office. It was an inviting room like all the others they had seen so far, with the exception of some unusual artifacts.

Two very ancient looking swords hung above his desk. Their tips touching each other diagonally. The glass curio, Maya glimpsed earlier, was filled with various stone pyramids and daggers.

On the credenza beside his desk stood a large two-foot long statue of a silver dragon, the same one Maya had seen in her dreams and visions. It shouldn't have surprised her, she knew, yet it did. Tears welled up in her eyes as her heart overflowed with feelings of love and connection to her destiny. She looked to Douglas, he smiled and nodded and she believed in that moment that everything was going to be okay. Their destiny was assured.

Alex couldn't take his eyes off the swords. "These look like ancient originals where did you get them?"

Sitting down at his desk Douglas spoke softly, "You've seen a glimpse of my abilities to transfer my energy into various forms so perhaps you will believe me. Others have not and persecute me in their minds as a madman. I retrieved them by crossing through the dimensions and went back in time. One belonged to me, and the other one belonged to my opponent. We fought to both our deaths defending our causes."

"How fascinating." Alex, who was speechless, speculated about him. *Why would he, a man of so many talents, be so interested in helping us?*

"I've seen that insignia on the handle before, what is it?" asked Cade. He studied the red cross with flared ends on the circular white base.

"It is the sign of the Knights Templar," answered Douglas.

Cade and Alex exchanged glances. "From the Crusades?" asked Alex skeptically.

"That's correct. You know your history."

"Yeah. I did some research a while back about them and the Priory of Sion. It's pretty interesting stuff. I didn't really pursue it because I read some contradictory things about the Knights Templar that made me uncomfortable."

Arielle and Maya joined the fellows around Douglas' desk to listen.

"Unfortunately there are a number of authors out there getting rich spreading paranoia. They do so by saying that spiritual organizations like the Freemasons, the White Brotherhood and others are plotting to take over the world. They claim to have the answers to spirituality and spout claims of devil worship by these groups."

"Right. I see your point. They are using sensationalism to coerce people to see things their way," commented Cade.

"Exactly. This is all tied in to Hermes and the Emerald Stone, The Philosopher's Stone, The Holy Grail, the Arc of the Covenant. They all promise the same thing, enlightenment through Right action and Right living. As Above, so Below. Did you know that our founding fathers used methods to incorporate the Hermetic concepts into their vision of democracy? Benjamin Franklin believed in these philosophies. George Washington was a known Freemason. He openly supported the Hermes doctrines. The eye in the triangle of light is on our nation's seal printed on the back of all one-dollar bills."

"Seriously? I never noticed that!" exclaimed Arielle.

"These zealots trying to discredit the Hermetic beliefs call it the 'New World Order'. The scroll under the seal translated correctly actually reads 'New Order of the Ages' which is meant to mark the end of the Piscean Age and the start of the Age of Aquarius."

Maya gazed upon the insignia. "Douglas doesn't your ring have that cross on the sides?"

"Yes it does."

The red telephone on his desk began to ring capturing everyone's attention and curiosity.

"I apologize I meant to mention this to you earlier. You are welcome in here whenever the door is open but when this phone rings I must ask you to leave and close the door."

They felt like they were intruding on his space and swiftly acknowledged his request and headed towards the door.

The telephone continued to ring. It seemed to grow louder with each passing second.

"We can resume our discussion about Hermes later and I'll tell you about his seven principles. They will be very important to your training."

They quickly left the office, each one wondering about the significance of the red phone.

Chapter Forty-two

Over the next two days they felt a tension rising in the house. People coming and going, meeting privately in the office with Douglas and Vivienne, the doors closed much of the time. The sound of the red phone ringing could be heard at various odd hours.

Maya's room was above the office and she was sure she heard it ring around four in the morning.

Paige was used to this type of behavior. "He does very important work and when it gets like this I've learned to stay out of the way. Sometimes I barely see them for days, only long enough to make sure they have something to eat," she explained to them the next morning.

Maya, Alex, Arielle and Cade spent the remainder of the previous day taking it easy, waiting to see Douglas again. They felt awkward roaming around the house by themselves. So they went for a long walk around the neighborhood enjoying the cold fresh air. Admiring the beautiful homes and picturesque scenery filled with rolling hills and orchards in the distance.

"Is it all right if I use the gym?" Maya asked Paige. Her legs and back ached from not being able to run for the last two weeks. She longed to get on the treadmill and feel her legs moving and her lungs working hard again. Even though she knew she would be sore for the next several days it had to be done. The longer she waited the worse it would get and there was already enough atrophy to reverse.

"Of course. I'll show you where it is," said Paige.

Maya looked to Alex, Arielle and Cade. "Anyone else coming?"

Paige showed them the way downstairs and left them to carry on with her errands.

Maya was impressed with the setup. The room was about twenty by forty feet with mirrors along one wall. There was a treadmill, a cross trainer, a bike, a step climber and a full set of nautilus equipment along with barbell weights. Maya thought she was in heaven.

They decided to get changed and returned to spend the next couple of hours taking turns on the equipment.

Maya showed Arielle how to use the weight machines and gave her some tips to get her started on an exercise program. Then she disappeared into her own world on the treadmill and tried not to pay attention to Alex beside her on the cross trainer but she found herself stealing glimpses of him now and then. He obviously worked out on a regular basis. His body was long, lean and well defined. Dark stray hairs on his chest peaked out from the top of his sweat soaked tank top.

He admired her svelte shape and the way her ponytail bobbed around while she ran. She had long strides and he was impressed with the nine minute mile pace she kept.

"When did you start running?" Alex asked Maya when she hit the cool down button.

"Huh? Oh I joined the track team in high school," she panted and grabbed the hand towel hanging on the treadmill to wipe the sweat running down her forehead. "I did okay, won a few races but I wasn't in it to compete. I just loved the feeling of running…or maybe I loved the feeling of running away from things."

"You're not running away from things now…At least not from finding the Emerald Stone."

She glared at him not quite sure how to take his comment.

Realizing he better change topics he searched quickly for something to say, "I caught a glimpse of the painting of your temple in Atlantis the other day. It was beautiful. It felt like I had a memory about to reveal itself of being there but then nothing came."

"That's too bad, you must have been disappointed."

"Yeah I was, I had a really good feeling about it. Maybe you'll live somewhere as beautiful again someday," he said getting off the cross trainer. "Well I'm done."

"Me too. Let's check on Cade and Arielle."

Heading upstairs to shower and change they passed the office. Hearing a heated discussion they stole a glimpse through the glass doors as they walked by. A man who looked in his mid to late-forties sat in a chair by the fireplace. He was dressed formally in a black suit and a light blue tie. His hair was dark and coarse looking.

Vivienne sat opposite him looking calm while the argument between Douglas and the man grew louder.

"I wonder what's going on?" whispered Arielle as they headed up the stairs.

"Did you see how angry Douglas looked?" questioned Cade.

Alex responded in a low voice, "Something big is definitely happening. I can feel it in the air." He wondered if it had anything to do with the Emerald Stone.

Maya worried about Douglas. She knew his job was dangerous but she'd never seen him look so infuriated and it made her feel very uneasy. Even his outburst in the tunnel didn't compare to the ominous sound of his voice when they passed the office.

* * * *

Occasional quarrels repeated with the same man and one other for another day. The office was sound proofed so actual words could not be heard outside of the room but it could not disguise the fact something was terribly wrong.

Periodically Maya and the others observed Douglas and Vivienne as they left for meetings outside the home. He appeared extremely agitated and even Vivienne, who was normally the epitome of calm, looked distressed.

Maya, Arielle, Alex and Cade were watching television in the living room on the fifth night of their visit. That is, they were trying to watch but the quarrels were especially loud making it very difficult to concentrate on the disturbing news of another attempted bombing at the New York Stock Exchange earlier that morning.

"I wish they would tell us something," said Arielle. "This sitting around waiting is nerve wracking."

"I know what you mean. The days are slipping away and we don't have anything to show for our time," added Cade.

Alex who was sitting in a chair beside Maya nodded. "I'm feeling pretty useless. The chaos in the world keeps escalating and the twenty-first is only one week away. We haven't even started any of the training that Douglas spoke about."

"Or made any arrangements to go back to Egypt," said Cade despondently. A major earthquake along the California coast the day before was devastating and he could feel Mother Earth preparing for something even more catastrophic. He feared what would happen if they didn't get a break soon.

"Maybe we should consider making our own arrangements for Egypt," suggested Arielle.

Maya who shared their fears and concerns finally spoke up, "Let's just hang in for another day and see what happens. Douglas is the only lead we have. If even the slightest other clue had presented itself then I'd agree we need to take action but we've had nothing."

"Maya's right, let's wait it out until tomorrow and if nothing happens we'll start making alternate plans," said Alex.

Arielle, who was cuddled up beside Cade on one of the sofas, leaned forward and whispered, "Don't you think it's strange that Paige has been in a lot of the meetings? I thought she was the housekeeper…What's up with that?"

Maya had been wondering the same thought since yesterday.

"She's obviously more than a housekeeper…" Cade's voice trailed with the sound of the office door opening.

"I don't care. Do what whatever it takes!" Douglas' voice was deep and ominous. Then he escorted the stranger out of the house.

They looked at each other with apprehension then focused their attention back on the television, not wanting it to seem like they were eavesdropping when they realized he was coming down the hallway towards the living room.

"Good evening everyone," said Douglas grimly as he entered the room. "I apologize for leaving you to fend for yourselves for the last few days but I've had some things to take care of."

Paige followed in behind Vivienne. "Would you like me to start dinner?"

"Yes that would be lovely. Some salmon would be nice tonight. Why don't you use that lovely wine and herb sauce," said Vivienne behaving as though everything was normal. "Douglas would you like a nice glass of red wine?"

Sitting in his usual brown leather recliner he strained a smile and nodded. "Yes dear. Open a bottle why don't you and let's share a drink together."

There's no point in pretending to watch this thing. Maya picked up the television converter and clicked the off button.

"I imagine you are all wondering what has been going on for the last several days," said Douglas. He waited and watched their expectant faces, weighing his words carefully.

"As you know I had my suspicions about someone working against us. We have been in touch with our contacts and after doing some digging we discovered

I was correct." He took a sip of the wine Vivienne offered him and closed his eyes in resignation. "It turns out our opponent is one of our closest business partners."

"How horrible," said Maya sympathetically.

"Yes, I...We are in shock and disbelief that John could betray us in this way—we've worked together for years and we trusted him. We also discovered he's behind another plot to destroy us financially. But we're on to him now and I'm taking care of it."

"Douglas."

He ignored Vivienne's attempt to quiet him. "Soon I will be able to track the correct signal line in the ether and locate the Emerald Stone. We should be ready in a couple of days. Vivienne I'd like you to make plans for us to return to Egypt. In the meantime I'll teach all of you about the seven principles and I'll show you how to make your connection more refined so you will be ready to face your final test."

Maya observed him carefully. She looked to Vivienne whose lips were pursed together and her expression was tense while she puttered in the kitchen alongside Paige. *What are they planning?*

* * * *

"The teachings of Hermes have remained hidden for thousands of years and known only by a few people. They've been touted as being occult since the times of the Crusades and many have been tortured and killed for dabbling in these mysteries."

Later that evening Maya, Alex, Arielle and Cade sat in chairs gathered around Douglas in his office listening intently.

"The seven principles of Hermes form the keys of all knowledge. They are the rules of life. Learn them, meditate on them and prepare for a whole new way of living.

"The first principle teaches understanding that we are all creations of God even the universe. But each creation is relative to the individual mind and what you think you see. For example, Maya you see the chair I sit in as wood but Arielle could see it as metal. When you understand this principle you can learn to control your world around you because everything is a manifestation of your thoughts."

"Do you mean if we create something we can change it?" asked Alex somewhat confused.

"Yes that's correct. Your subconscious mind is molded by your conscious thoughts but it is actually your subconscious mind that communicates to the universe, drawing forward your experiences. For example, if you consciously believe that money doesn't grow on trees then you will not be able to attract wealth in your life because you are programming your subconscious mind with this belief. When you change your programming you change your reality."

"Fascinating," said Arielle.

Douglas continued, "The second principle is correspondence. This is easiest to understand when you apply it to smaller projects first because the results are the most immediate and visible. When you are able to correct something at its most basic level subsequent levels are affected, changing the outcome."

"I'm not sure I understand," said Maya.

Douglas paused for a few seconds. "Take for example a typical couple who have been together for some time. As many couples do, they fight about the same things repeatedly. One of them gets upset and accuses the other of doing something to hurt the other. But if that person changes his or her approach and learns to express their *feelings* about the situation instead of laying *blame* then it changes the whole dynamics of the argument and it flows into other areas of their relationship creating space for more love."

"I see," said Maya in awe of the wisdom he embodied. *He should be the one Thoth passed the teachings on to, not me.*

"The third principle is about vibration. Everything vibrates at certain levels. A change in vibration results in a change in manifestation. Health and illness have different vibrations. Healers know how to change the vibration of illness to match that of health. Maya that is what you do with your healing gift. You balance the energy so it vibrates at the same level. Everyone can actually learn to do this. Emotions like faith and fear are the same. They just vibrate at different levels. You can change one into the other through thought.

"The law of polarity is the fourth principle. Everything has a polar opposite. Love and hate, faith and fear. Again they are the same differing only by the level of positivity and negativity. Change the rate of vibration and you change the emotion. These are things you can train your mind to do. It's not out of the realm of possibility. In fact, I will teach you how to do this later."

"It sounds like it's about taking something negative that happens and looking for a positive outcome," said Cade.

"In a manner of speaking that's correct. It only varies by the degrees in which you can train your mind to think."

Douglas explained the principle of rhythm next. "Everything that happens in life is part of a cycle. Birth, growth, decline and death. If you were to chart your life you would discover a cycle. You can learn to capitalize on this by meditating and discovering when your cycles are.

"The sixth principle is cause and effect. For every action there is a reaction. A good example is what Maya experienced. When she and her husband separated the effect that resulted was freeing herself up to a whole new world of possibilities and here she is. Through right use of this principle you will learn to consciously participate in the outcomes.

"The seventh principle is an understanding that all things have a masculine and feminine aspect. The masculine aspect is outgoing and creates change. The feminine aspect is receptive and creative. I believe all of you understand that everyone needs to develop both in order to be balanced fully functional beings."

"It's easy to understand but not so easy to develop," said Alex.

"True enough. Many of these principles are relatively easy to see and others are not. I can teach you how to access that part of your brain that is rarely tapped into to manifest all that you desire."

"Karma must come into play here. Don't you need to be careful of what you create?" asked Arielle.

"You are all excellent students," said Douglas thoughtfully. "That is why you are also ready to be teachers, with a little help and that is why you are here, because I teach the teachers. Yes, Arielle, there are some basic golden laws that must be considered with everything you do. What you program for must not be selfish, it must aid two or more people and you must treat others with respect as you would expect to be treated in return."

Arielle yawned. "Oh gosh, I'm sorry. I guess I'm not used to working out."

Douglas noticed it was two in the morning. "I've kept you up late enough. If you let me I'll keep talking. I'm used to working until the wee hours of the morning but you are all in training now and need your rest. We have so little time left but soon we'll be on our way again and this time we will succeed."

Getting up to put the chairs back by the fireplace they turned to wait for Douglas. Vivienne had already gone upstairs an hour earlier.

"Go ahead I'll be a little while yet. I have another phone call to make, then lock up and set the alarms."

Retiring to bed, Maya was disappointed at not having any time alone with Douglas since the day they arrived. She hoped that tonight she could talk with him but he dismissed them all, including her and it made her importance to him feel diminished.

*   *   *   *

Maya was lying in bed writing in her journal when she heard a quiet knock on the door. She got up and opened the door a crack.

"May I come in?"

Still feeling jilted Maya said, "It's late I was just getting ready to go to sleep."

"Just for a few minutes. I promise."

She opened the door to let Douglas in. When she turned around he drew her into his arms and kissed her passionately. "I've missed you the last few days. It's been so difficult knowing you were right here and I couldn't come to you," he said in a throaty voice.

She pulled away and sat on the edge of the bed. He sat beside her, taking her hand and caressing it. Her desire for him was stirred up leaving her disoriented and unsure of herself or her place.

"You are perfection itself, my darling, and I adore you beyond the capacity that mere words can express." He kissed her lips tenderly, wanting to savor her presence and celebrate the orders he issued moments ago.

She felt dizzy with anticipation but somewhere deep inside she felt a niggle of hesitation. It grew and escaped to her conscious level. "Douglas wait," she said softly.

"What's wrong my love? You must know that I love you. Let us enjoy each other." He leaned in to kiss her again. He could feel her breath. "Trust me I will please you beyond anything you've ever experienced before."

She looked into his eyes and for a split second she saw something that sent chills up her spine. A blackness like falling into a bottomless void. She knew she quickly had to put her thoughts behind a veil before he sensed her feelings. She searched desperately for an excuse. "What about Vivienne?"

"She understands our bond and only wants us to be happy."

"What?" Confused, she got up quickly from the bed. "No! Douglas I'm…I can't…"

"Feel the psychometry of my kiss and with it comes a promise of my eternal love."

"Douglas…I need some time. This is all so new to me…"

"Time is something I can give you. Sleep well, my darling and I'll see you tomorrow." He kissed her lightly on the lips again and left. Walking towards his bedroom he cursed himself for his slip and Maya for turning him away. *She's not playing very nice and if she doesn't watch it I will not be inclined to let her live once she's opened the doorway.*

Chapter Forty-three

"Here are your tickets." Vivienne distributed everyone's airline tickets out to the group. "We leave in three days. I made reservations at the Sheraton Cairo. I thought it would be best to stay in the same hotel."

They were having a hearty breakfast of toast and cheese omelets with broccoli after their morning workouts by the pool.

It was only ten o'clock in the morning but the day was already showing promise of being a productive one.

"Thanks Vivienne, it's really nice of you guys to go to all this trouble for us," said Arielle.

"It's as important to us as it is to you and the rest of humanity," acknowledged Vivienne. "We should be there in plenty of time with a day to spare. You know the galactic rift is expected to take place at 11:11 in the morning but I did some research and discovered that is Greenwich Mean Time, which is two hours behind Cairo time. So that means we'll have to synchronize our watches for the activation to take place at 1:11 in the afternoon on the twenty-first."

"Oh my gosh, I didn't even think of time differences!" exclaimed Maya. "Thank goodness you checked it out…That would have been devastating to miss it because of such a stupid blunder."

Douglas entered and joined them at the table. "Oh I see you've all got your tickets, Vivienne tells me we're leaving on the eighteenth. That means we have a lot of work to do in the next couple of days. We'll get started once I've had something to eat. I hope you are all rested up and ready."

"It's nice to see you in such a good mood," said Arielle.

He smiled smugly. "Indeed. I feel great. I've taken care of our problem and was able to pinpoint the location of the Stone."

"That's fantastic!" exclaimed Arielle.

Alex could not contain his curiosity. "Where is it?"

"Be patient. You have other things to focus on now. When we get to Egypt I'll share everything with you."

Uncertain as to why Douglas was being vague left Alex with an uneasy feeling. He shifted in his chair and glanced at Maya. *She seems a little on edge this morning I wonder if something happened. I hope she doesn't get hurt…*

* * * *

Completing the last of their meditation training for the day, Douglas had excused himself to attend to some business while they went for a walk to get some fresh air and clear their heads before dinner.

"I feel like I've meditated more in the last two days than I have my whole life," said Maya.

They should have been exhausted mentally but instead they were exhilarated and energized with sparks of electricity flying all around them. Determination to succeed with the activation of the Emerald Stone remained at the core of their motivation and they practiced visualizing their success several times each day, knowing the impending galactic anomaly was scheduled to occur in only five more days.

"I know what you mean. Some of those exercises were pretty wild. I had trouble keeping up after a while," responded Arielle.

Cade rubbed his eyes. "My head hurts just thinking about all the details we had to focus on. I thought it was going to explode when he kept shifting the colors in the scenes."

"It was tough but I'm amazed with the results. I've never been very good at visualizing but I can't believe what we were able to accomplish. I feel like a different person." Alex had to give credit to Douglas. "He knows his stuff."

"I can't believe I was able to transport myself into your house Maya. That was so amazing," exclaimed Arielle impressed with her newfound remote viewing abilities.

Maya smiled. "You were so accurate describing what everything looked like, even down to the flowers and ivy hand-painted on my kitchen walls. I was stunned."

Cade rubbed Arielle's back when he noticed she was shivering from the cold. "There's no question Douglas is a genius and knows how to use parts of the brain most people never tap into."

The sun had set over an hour before so any warmth it might have provided was long gone. The sky was clear and the air was cold and invigorating while they strolled through the neighborhood.

"I never really understood about the beta, alpha and theta brain wave levels before. I didn't realize that you could use these cycles to program your mind for different results," said Maya thinking about the techniques Douglas taught them. He explained that by practicing the mental exercises he trained them to perform you are able to train your mind to maintain your center while you activate it to work on projects.

"I know what you mean," said Alex. "I've read all sorts of things on manifestation but nothing ever explained how to do it properly."

"I've used prayer to help me in the past," added Arielle. "Sometimes it worked but often it didn't. It makes sense to use your imagination and project it on a screen. It was interesting how he explained that's how the universe receives your requests."

"I liked it when he said that as long as your requests are in line with your life purpose and is not just a selfish desire the universe will support you and manifest the coincidences to make it happen," said Cade.

They walked in silence for a while. Looking back on the past two days of intensive training.

Douglas took them through demanding mental exercises. Teaching them to transport themselves into objects, animals and people in order to get a frame of reference for a subjective understanding of the different elements, both inanimate and animate.

He made them touch and feel these things internally and externally through the mind. They had to change the scenery around them to add more complexity. They had to learn to use their imaginations more than they've ever used them before.

He trained them how to use remote viewing to project themselves to a given location and provide a description. They also learned to detect health problems in people they didn't even know.

"It's amazing how all four of us had remarkable accuracy rates," said Maya.

"Did you hear him say we are the elite of any group he's taught?" asked Arielle.

Alex thought about this comment. "Even if he was just saying that to influence us you have to admit we were good."

Maya recognized an opportunity to do some of their own research and jumped on the idea. "Maybe we should practice the remote viewing techniques on the Emerald Stone and see if we can find it ourselves."

"Are you suggesting we go it alone?" asked Alex in surprise.

"Not at all. I just thought it would be a neat experiment to see if we came up with the same thing and see how accurate we are when we get to Egypt."

Alex glanced sideways at Maya while they walked and raised his eyebrow. *Is there something she's not telling us?*

* * * *

Maya's stomach was knotted up tight and she couldn't convince her body to relax. *Something is wrong.*

There was an uncomfortable, even foreboding, quality in the air when they returned from their walk and it grew stronger as the evening wore on.

Gathered in the living room watching a program on television about the pyramids, Maya couldn't help but feel as though they were biding their time waiting for something. She was tired and wanted to go to bed but Douglas looked as though he was fixed in his chair unwilling to let the evening end.

"Paige do you have any TUMS or Rolaids?" asked Maya. I have an upset stomach and it won't settle down."

Even Paige appeared very uptight. She stomped into the kitchen, grabbed a bottle of Rolaids and pushed it in front of Maya. "Here you go."

Maya didn't know how to react to her rudeness. "Thanks," was all she could utter.

Vivienne gave Douglas a sharp look. Looking more perturbed he immediately stood up from the recliner. "Paige may I see you in my office. Now."

With her head hung low Paige followed him out of the room and down the hall to his office.

Vivienne seeing an opportunity to escape, rose from her chair. "I have a lot of things to take care of tomorrow and need to get an early start so I think I'm going to say goodnight."

Arielle sat up alert on the edge of the sofa as soon as they were alone. "Do you guys get the feeling something is going on?"

"Yes, they seem awfully tense. Whatever it is it must have happened while we were out earlier," said Cade.

"I don't like it. I feel so anxious and uptight I can't breathe properly," added Maya. "It makes me want to get out of here. Douglas is behaving so strangely...It's like he's avoiding going to bed and doesn't want to be left alone." Maya rose from the sofa. "Does anyone want anything to drink? I need some more water."

She went into the kitchen, which overlooked the sunken living room with a wood railing, to fetch the refills of water for herself and the others. While she filled a small serving bowl with some temptingly fresh cashews a noise in the hallway caught her attention and she peaked around the corner to see if Douglas was returning.

When she saw him leaving the office she was about to ask him if he wanted anything but stopped when he reached out and took Paige's hand. He drew her close to him and whispered intimately close to her ear. Maya's heart felt constricted. She watched him touch Paige's chin with his forefinger and then kissed her tenderly on the lips.

She felt disoriented and stepped back against the pantry. *Did I just see what I thought I saw? Am I delusional?* She shook her head in confusion. *I don't understand...*

She didn't have time to gather her thoughts as Douglas and Paige rejoined the group. He looked calmer and Paige's mood was forcibly brighter.

Maya's thoughts were jumbled. Her body trembled with turmoil raging inside. She struggled to keep her emotions in check and hide her feelings when she brought refreshments to her friends.

Alex watched Maya sit down on the landing stairs into the living room instead of a chair or sofa. He felt anxiety emanating from her and wondered if something more was bothering her than just the tenseness that they had been experiencing all evening.

Maya observed Paige sit in the matching recliner beside Douglas, which was normally reserved for Vivienne. *What is going on?*

It was two o'clock in the morning and her thoughts were distracted when Maya heard a noise outside the front of the house. She turned to gaze at the entrance when suddenly the door burst open. A team of FBI agents came crashing through.

Two of them held mirrors extended on long poles checking the rooms as they rushed in looking for people armed with guns.

Assault rifles in hand. "Get down now! On the floor face down! Now!" they commanded.

Maya screamed. She leaped up and darted behind a chair across the room. She watched in shock and terror as Douglas jumped up to defend himself and the others in the room. His actions were futile. He was quickly knocked down with a knee in the groin by one of the agents and forced to the ground.

She could hear echoes of Arielle screaming in panic while an armed agent came stalking towards her and Cade.

"Get out from behind there and get down on the floor now! Face down! Hands behind your back! Do it now!" demanded one of the agents aiming his rifle at Maya.

As quickly as she could summon her courage, she came out from behind the chair. She threw herself to the floor and was immediately handcuffed.

It happened so fast that it was a blur. She lifted her head looking to her right and saw Alex, Cade, Arielle, and Paige lying near her on the floor. They were also handcuffed.

Douglas was on the landing. Still in pain from the attack. An agent was pushing him down flat on the floor with his knee and put the cuffs on him.

Another agent moved closer to Maya. He aimed the rifle between her eyes. "Keep your face down!"

Only moments before this circle of friends sat scattered around the living room watching television in this picturesque home on a sprawling estate lot in the outskirts of Baltimore. Now this group of six lay on the floor while three agents stood guard. Rifles aimed at their heads daring them to move.

More FBI agents scoured the house tearing through room-to-room. Busting down doors that stood in their way, looking for others.

This must be a dream...It can't be real. Maya tried to stay calm. But her body kept shaking involuntarily. The pressure on her shoulders from her arms pulled together was so great she was barely able to keep herself from crying. She tried moving her hands but it felt like her wrists were being squeezed. *Oh my God I've never been so terrified in my life. I don't understand what's happening! Oh God, please help!*

She moved her head slightly to the side. Enough to get a glimpse of Douglas. He must have sensed her move. He lifted his head and looked directly into her eyes. He mouthed the words, "Stay calm. You'll be okay."

How can he be so calm? Feeling panic consume her she consciously slowed her breathing down. She repeatedly told herself to relax. Finally she was able to still her shaking body. She focused on the voices she heard in the distance. At first they seemed distorted and slow. She forced herself to concentrate and the voices began to sound clear again.

"We found one more upstairs in the master bedroom, she must be his wife. We got her just as she was reaching for a gun," announced an agent pounding down the stairs. "We've got her secured and the upstairs is clear."

Douglas gasped. His heart squeezed. It felt like it would explode when he heard that Vivienne reached for the gun. "She could have gotten herself killed," he muttered under his breath. *She's okay, that's all that matters right now.*

Douglas did not expect this to happen so quickly. The phone call he received earlier that night to warn him about the charges that were being pressed against him set the grim tone for the evening. He shared this information with only Vivienne and Paige. *The others would have panicked and everything would have been lost. No it's better this way.*

Yet even advance warning did nothing to extinguish the feeling of anxiety and utter helplessness the situation created. He had to trust that everyone's training would keep the group solid and strong in the next hours or days to come.

* * * *

Only an hour had passed but it seemed like they had been lying on the floor for an eternity.

"Okay everything's clear. Take 'em in."

An agent grabbed Douglas roughly and pulled him up to his feet. Then he was taken out of the house.

Two of the agents poked Alex and Cade on the shoulders with their rifles. "You two next. Roll on your side and get up slowly."

Alex's shoulder gave out under his weight as he tried to turn onto his side and he fell backwards.

"Slow I said!"

Once the men were removed the agents turned to the women. "Ladies, you're next."

Maya's shoulder had been pulled so tight it felt like it was almost out of its socket. "I can't get up. My shoulder! It's..." The pain was so great. When she tried to get up she almost passed out.

One of the agents grabbed her and helped her to her feet. "I've got you. It's okay."

Tears dropped from the corners of her eyes. "Thank you," Maya said meekly. She walked blindly out of the house. Feeling numb from shock. "Where are you taking us?"

The agent softened his demeanor towards her. "To a State Police office in Baltimore. Careful, watch your head." He put his hand on the top of her head and guided her into an unmarked car.

Sitting beside Arielle on the trip they were too dazed and scared to speak.

* * * *

"Sign your name in the book," said one of the State Troopers who was overseeing their entry into the station. He turned Maya around and removed her handcuffs.

She rubbed and inspected her wrists surprised they weren't bleeding. She learned his name was Agent Bunker and he was patiently waiting for her to register her name.

He took her down a hallway passing several corridors and escorted her into a room. "Sit here. Agent Rawlins from the FBI will be right in to question you." Leaving her in the chair he walked over to another desk, sat down and began to write his report, looking over at her occasionally.

The time passed slowly adding to her intense emotions. She nervously shifted, unable to sit still while she waited for the next twenty or so minutes.

The room was quite large considering there were only four desks but it was dull and dingy looking. A few small windows placed up high didn't provide much light, not that you could tell at three-thirty in the morning. The gray scuffed walls and beat up old wooden desks and chairs added to the dreariness.

Finally a man strolled into the room and sat down behind the desk in front of Maya. "I'm Agent Rawlins. Which one are you?"

His hair was dark blonde and thinning on top, he had a very chiseled face with a square jaw line and an athletic looking body.

"My name is Maya Maxwell."

He flipped through some papers. "We don't have your name anywhere on record. How do you know Douglas and Vivienne?"

"I, my friends and I met them in Egypt. They invited us to visit them before we all went home."

"Who are your friends?"

She told him their names and how they met on their trip.

"So you're telling me you never met Douglas and Vivienne before going to Egypt?" he asked skeptically.

"That's correct."

"Uh-huh." He wrote some things down while she waited. "And you all just left your lives behind to come and visit them? That must be a hell of a friendship you all developed?"

"We got along well, yes." She wasn't about to offer any more information than absolutely necessary. At least not until she found out what this was all about.

"When did you arrive from Egypt?"

They must already have this information. "We got in early in the morning on the eleventh."

"And what have you been doing during your visit with them?"

"Nothing much. We've spent time relaxing and going for walks. Just visiting, that sort of thing."

"Can you give me more details please?" Agent Rawlins interrogated. "What did you do? What did you talk about?"

Maya was beginning to get irritated. *You're kidding me!* "Let's see, we'd get up and go for a workout in their gym for an hour or two. Then we'd shower and have lunch."

"All together?"

"Yes, well usually Arielle, Cade, Alex and I worked out together. Douglas and Vivienne preferred to exercise alone so they'd spend time in their office. Doing work I presume."

"What kind of work?"

"I don't know. They didn't talk about their work with us."

"So what did you talk about?"

"Mostly about spiritual stuff."

"What do you mean by that?"

Flabbergasted, Maya shifted in her chair annoyed. She had to remind herself he was just doing his job. "We talked mostly about the pyramids and our belief in a higher intelligence. Douglas taught my friends and I some meditation techniques. Things like that."

"Did you ever meet any of their business associates?"

"No. They had some meetings in their office but we were never introduced to anyone they met with."

"Uh-huh." He wrote down some more notes. "Did they ever talk about these people?"

"No." *What is he looking for?*

"You never heard them talking about their business partner John Damaskas?"

Feeling uneasy at the mention of John's name she was reminded of Douglas' ominous threat. She kept her face still. "No, sorry."

Agent Rawlins continued to question her. Asking her the same questions over and over. "Agent Bunker!" he shouted to the trooper working at the desk near the entrance to the room.

"Yes sir?"

"Keep your eye on Maya. I'll be back in a few minutes."

When Agent Rawlins finally returned he sat back in his chair. He tapped his pen on the desk. Then he scrutinized her carefully "That's all the questions I have for you. We're going to let you and your friends go but I want you to write down your full address and phone number in case we need to contact you again. You should be more careful who you associate with."

"Can I ask what this is all about?" asked Maya timidly. She hoped she appeared completely in the dark and vulnerable.

"We are charging Douglas and Vivienne with first-degree murder. Their partner, John was found dead yesterday and we have reason to believe they contracted to have him killed." His voice was flat yet firm and intimidating.

"Murder? That's not possible!" Her thoughts were spiraling but she made every effort to remain calm.

"Oh it's more than possible. We have evidence to prove they ordered it. If I were you I'd suggest you head home. We'll be in touch if we need you."

"Can I go back to the house to get my things?"

"I'm afraid not for a while. We're going through the house and it will be off limits for several hours. I'll give you a number you can call later to see if it's clear for you to get your stuff."

Agent Rawlins escorted Maya to the lobby area of the station.

She was so relieved to see Alex waiting. "Oh thank God you're here." She lunged into his arms. Traumatized from the experience. Needing to feel safe. "I didn't know where I was going to go."

Surprised by her movements he wrapped his arms around her and held her tight. "Are you all right?" he asked. Feeling her pressed so close against him unnerved his resolve. He felt a wave of love wash through him all over again. He couldn't imagine a worse torture than the chaos toying with his heart.

"Yes. Still shaking and scared but yeah I'm okay."

Cade and Arielle were released moments later and they called a taxi to take them to a hotel until they could return to the house to collect their things.

They sat in silence waiting for the taxi. Not wanting to take a chance on saying anything that might prolong their stay.

Chapter Forty-four

Maya woke up sweating and gasping for air. She felt disoriented in the strange room until she remembered they had gone to a hotel.

Her dream was terrifying and very real. So real in fact she believed it might have been a premonition.

They were in the hidden chamber with the Emerald Stone. When they activated the Stone the doorway opened to the other realms and Douglas turned on them with a gun. He shot and killed them all, then leaped through the portal before it closed.

Sitting up in bed she rubbed her face with her hands and cried. *Is the Universe speaking to me?* She felt confused, hurt and betrayed. *Did Douglas really have John killed? Was he planning on killing us when he got what he wanted?*

She knew the answers deep inside but she couldn't bring herself to acknowledge them. She wept until there weren't any more tears left to shed. She made a firm decision not to feel shame or beat herself up for her stupidity, instead she wanted to embrace what the experience was teaching her about herself. *He made me feel beautiful and wanted. Whether it was real or not doesn't matter, I've never felt so alive and I never want to live an empty purposeless life again.*

*　　*　　*　　*

"Do you think they did it?" asked Cade. It was eleven o'clock in the morning. Alex and Cade were in Arielle's hotel room after getting a few hours sleep.

"I don't know. We do know that Douglas received a phone call just before we went out for a walk. When we came back it was obvious something happened. They seemed pretty uptight even though Douglas was trying to act normal," said Alex. "And he said that our opponent was his business partner, named John," added Alex, not wanting to believe the charge was true but it wasn't looking good.

Cade jumped in, "He also said that he took care of the problem and he knew where the Stone is now. Do you think he was warned something was going down and just let us get caught in the middle?"

"It does seem rather suspicious but they could just be coincidences," said Arielle.

Maya looked at Arielle reproachfully. "There are no coincidences remember?" *Do I tell them about my dream?* She mulled this over weighing the pros and cons. *What good would it do right now? It will just upset them more and distract them from our mission. Finding the Stone has to remain our number one priority.* She decided to wait until they were able to find out more information and make some decisions about what to do next.

"I'm just trying to give them the benefit of the doubt," responded Arielle. "Do you think they really have evidence to prove it?"

Alex was surprised by Maya's change of tone. He assumed she would be defending Douglas. "We'll have to wait and see I guess," he said. "Why don't we go to the restaurant downstairs and grab something to eat while we wait." They had another hour or more before they would be allowed back in the house to retrieve their belongings.

The headlines on the front page of the Baltimore Sun caught their attention as they walked by the lobby shop.

Alleged U.S. Ambassador and wife charged with first-degree murder.

They stopped short and stared. "Oh my gosh!" exclaimed Arielle. "I can't believe it's on the front page of the paper."

Alex picked up a newspaper and paid for it at the cash. "Let's go sit down."

"Does it mention anything about us?" asked Maya nervously.

"I don't see anything," said Alex scanning the paper while they walked.

Alex continued to read when they were seated in the restaurant and ordered coffee, "Mercer, a former captain in the army and his wife were charged early this morning for the murder of their business partner, John Damaskas. Both are being held for three million dollars bail."

He skimmed through the article. "It says that a warrant was authorized to seize computers, journals, and all other personal items relevant to the case. Three guns were confiscated. It doesn't really go into any specifics but there's no mention of us, thank goodness."

They sat stunned and speechless for several minutes after ordering breakfast.

Alex spoke first, "We haven't really had an opportunity to talk about what happened. It was a pretty brutal experience."

"I think I'm still in shock," said Arielle. "You know like numb. I feel like I'm walking around on auto pilot right now."

"It was the most terrifying experience of my life," Maya admitted with intensity. "I'm scared and angry. Scared at the thought that everything we've worked for may be lost and angry with Douglas at the possibility that he knew what was going to happen and didn't warn us."

"Not to mention the possibility that they are guilty," added Cade soberly.

Arielle could feel her emotions welling up from deep inside. "You know what?" she asked forcefully but not waiting for a response she continued, "I can't talk about this right now. I feel violated and scared and probably a whole lot of other things but I'll loose it if we keep talking about it."

Cade came to her rescue. "Then we should all stay on auto pilot and deal with things as they happen as best we can. When this is over we can work on healing from it."

"Thank you," said Arielle holding back tears.

* * * *

An FBI agent was fixing the busted front door of the house and preparing to leave when they arrived.

The inside was in complete shambles. The computers and all their files had been taken from the office. Books and papers lay scattered across the floor. The sofa cushions in the living room were upturned. Dry food, packaged goods and vitamins had been tossed on the floor and the cupboard doors were left ajar.

Maya was filled with many conflicting feelings. Regardless of their guilt or innocence it was disturbing to see Douglas and Vivienne's home ransacked. She felt like she had been punched in the chest and couldn't breathe. She couldn't deny she had feelings for Douglas as much as tried to remain detached. And even though she hadn't spent much time with Vivienne she felt an affinity with the woman who was supposed to be her sister in Atlantis. *You can't fall apart now. Keep it together Maya, keep it together.*

With anxious hesitation they proceeded upstairs to their rooms and found their clothes and personal belongings as carelessly tossed about as everything else.

"Looks like nothing has been left unturned," Maya said sadly to herself. It gave her the creeps to think someone went through all her things.

"Hurry up! We have to leave!" shouted one of the agents at the base of the staircase.

Gathering their things as quickly as they could they scurried down the stairs and out the front door. Alex signaled to the taxi driver to keep waiting. "Will we be able to visit them in jail?" he asked the agent.

"Yeah. Probably not until tomorrow though. They're still being interrogated."

"Thanks." Alex lay a gentle hand on the center of Maya's back to guide her down the stairs. "Let's go."

His hand felt warm and comforting on her back. She felt an overwhelming urge to turn to him and cry. Instead she collected herself, straightened her back and walked towards the taxi.

"God we were so lucky they're letting us leave. We could have gotten into serious trouble here," said Arielle.

"It's pretty amazing to think that even the press didn't get our names or publish them," added Cade.

Maya stopped to look one last time at the house. "We're being protected and guided," she said in a matter of fact voice.

Alex reached out and opened the car door for Maya. *We might be protected but what are we going to do now? The Dark-Rift is now only five days away…*

* * * *

They received clearance from the State Police for one of them to visit Douglas and Vivienne in jail the next day.

Since Maya had the closest connection with them it was agreed she should be the one to visit.

Alex, Cade and Arielle stood beside a trembling Maya in the reception area.

"We'll be right here waiting," said Arielle reassuringly.

Alex took her hand. It felt cold and sweating. "Are you sure you want to do this?"

"Yes." Even though her confidence was wavering she remained resolute in her decision. "I need to do it."

Not sure what to do next she stood facing the one-way window waiting. She heard a voice telling her to place her driver's license in the slot in front of her. She did as told and nervously waited again. After several long minutes her driver's license was returned through the slot.

"Douglas will be brought out first. Go through that door and wait in the third cubicle," said the invisible voice behind the wall. Everything seemed surreal around her, she couldn't believe she was in a jailhouse, it was too tragic and bizarre to comprehend.

Pulling herself together she took a deep breath and wiggled her shoulders. *Okay here I go.*

She heard a click and the heavy steel door opened. Her legs felt like rubber as she walked through and she just about jumped out of her skin when it slammed shut behind her. Piercing her ears with its deafening noise.

Her heart raced. She felt like she was quivering from the inside out while she waited in a small cubicle in front of a glass partition.

Douglas was brought into the room on the opposite side. He felt humiliated and heartbroken in the orange overalls when he saw it was Maya who had come to visit.

She felt a multitude of confusing feelings for him. *He's helped us in so many ways and I've healed a lot of things since we met.* Recognizing her resolve was weakening she forced herself to remember her dream. *Don't forget this man could be a killer!*

He smiled weakly and together they picked up the phones on both sides of the glass.

"Are you all right Douglas?"

He cleared his throat and spoke with a low voice, "Yes. Don't worry about me. I've lived through worse experiences. How is everyone else?"

"We're in shock, of course, but we're dealing with it."

"Maya I'm innocent. They're just trumped up charges. They've got nothing on us. You believe me right?"

"Sure I do." His words rang falsely in her ears and she wasn't sure why but she automatically went along with the charade. "I know you wouldn't murder someone."

"That's my girl. I knew I could count on you. We'll be released and we'll all be together again soon. I promise. You should go and visit Vivienne now she could use your support. Please tell her I love her and remind her of our destiny together."

Relieved she didn't have to participate in this conversation any longer she watched him prepare to leave. "Is there anything I can do for you?" she asked.

"No…But thank you for asking. Our lawyer will take care of things for us. You just look after yourself and tell Alex, Cade and Arielle what I said." He rose to leave, kissed his fingertips and placed them on the glass.

To keep up appearances she did the same.

While she waited for Vivienne she reflected on what would appear to have been a lost opportunity to get some answers but her instincts told her it would have been a waste of time. Vivienne's always been relatively quiet. *I wonder what she really thinks of all this? Can I get her to open up?*

When Vivienne was brought in Maya thought she looked younger and child-like without her makeup. Her hair looked a little stringy but overall Maya thought she looked pretty good. Considering what happened. *She certainly looks better than Douglas does. It seemed like he wasn't quite all-together.*

"Hi Maya, it's so sweet of you to come and visit me."

"I wanted to make sure you were holding up okay. You look good. How are you?"

"I'm good actually. Just a little tired because it's so noisy in the cells. They're treating me pretty well."

Weighing her options she thought her best move was to be honest. "Vivienne can you tell me what's going on? Douglas wouldn't really say anything and we are at a loss as to what to do next."

Vivienne's voice was soft and quiet. "I thought this day would come and to be truthful I'm glad. Perhaps this will be exactly what he needs to help him realize the error of his ways."

Maya was flabbergasted by her straightforwardness. "Is he guilty of the charges?"

Aware that the phones would be monitored she answered carefully, "That question is irrelevant right now and our time is limited. I have other more important things to tell you." Putting her elbows up on the table she leaned closer to the glass.

Following Vivienne's lead Maya drew herself closer to the partition and listened carefully.

"His corruption goes back many lifetimes. In fact, I suspect you may recognize the reality of what I'm about to reveal to you."

"Of course, anything. Please tell me."

"His teachings are based on truth but he weaves it in with his own hidden agenda so that everything sounds believable and even honorable." She paused, gazed directly into Maya's eyes to ensure she had her complete attention. "I'll use the Atlantean names so you know what I am speaking about. Do you understand?"

She must be trying to protect herself and him in case anyone overhears. "Yes."

"Melïon was not rushing to warn Diãntha of her impending demise. He was the one who plotted against her and was responsible for the explosion of her temple." She watched Maya's reaction and realized that it did not come as a complete surprise.

Maya closed her eyes. Her shoulders slumped. *I wanted to believe in Douglas. I wanted to believe that he loved me.* Reluctantly she realized she didn't have any choice except to resign to accepting the truth. She opened her tear filled eyes and nodded for Vivienne to continue.

"His intention was to reach her on her deathbed so he could secure her secrets and in doing so he would make it look like he was attempting to rescue her."

"But when Diãntha disappeared he was defeated," said Maya sadly.

"Yes. Kanïka discovered his plot. She turned to Thoth in desperation and told him everything she knew. Her sister's death was devastating to her and the survival of the mysteries became as important to her as it was to Diãntha. Listen carefully, Thoth took measures to prevent further attacks and moved the Emerald Stone. He orchestrated the building of the pyramids and the Sphinx in later times as a distraction to those searching for them. Don't forget Hermes was also known as Merlin, the master Magician. They are the greatest monuments of misdirection ever created."

"Wait a minute. Now I'm confused. The legends indicate that the Stone has been found during various centuries."

"It has, but only by the Chosen Ones. However it was not the right time for mass awakening. Humanity has not been ready until now to accept the new frequencies. But time is running out as you well know."

The reminder of December twenty-first looming nearer grabbed hold. Her breath felt constricted. "So where did Thoth place them?" her voice croaked.

"The secret chamber's location is calculated through the use of a Fibonacci spiral, which touches the apex of all three pyramids and circles in on itself at a site between the Sphinx and the Nile. The exact location is a mirror image of the star Sirius."

"How will we know where to find it?"

"There is a doorway to the underground tunnel beneath an abandoned building. I own the building under a numbered company." Keeping an eye on the clock she provided Maya with the address of the building with general directions.

Maya memorized the information. "I don't know what to say. How can I thank you?"

"Just find the Stone and live your destiny. Do you remember Diãntha's words *Tell Kanïka she was right*?"

"Yes. Do you know what they mean?"

"This was the period of time you traveled to in the future. Right here. Right now. You came back to warn me this would happen and I was right about the new location of the Stone. You see Thoth did not tell me where he moved them. I took a mathematical guess and I turned out to be accurate."

Vivienne witnessed the guard signaling to let her know that her time was up.

Her sister's courage and self-sacrificing actions overwhelmed Maya. She had so many things she wanted to say yet she was speechless. *She did all this to save me and the Stone from death and destruction.*

The guard started walking towards Vivienne to take her back to her cell. "One last thing you have to know," she said hurriedly. "Nared was not Diãntha's brother. You know their true connection. They are two halves of the same star. Meant to be together through the sands of all time. The memories you have of Melïon are not real."

The guard put his hand on Vivienne's shoulder. In her last breath before being taken away she said, "Douglas planted them in your mind. You have to go back to Egypt quickly. Before he discovers..."

"Wait!" Maya yelled and the guard nodded his willingness to allow one more question. The news sent Maya's thoughts reeling but she felt something else nagging her. She tried desperately to keep her head clear. "What about my baby?" she asked with a sick feeling churning in her stomach.

"I'm so sorry Maya...He couldn't take the chance of the distraction to take you off course." She felt her sister's pain and one single tear dropped to her cheek as the guard took firm hold of Vivienne's arm and pulled her to her feet, escorting her away.

* * * *

Pain and anguish mixed with a measure of excitement. Lost yet found. Maya teetered on the edge of reality. Noise blurring around her, she ignored the pleas from her friends to tell them what happened as she walked out of the police station.

Alex called a taxi and they waited on a bench near the street. He was worried about her. The color had drained from her skin and her eyes appeared distant and glazed. "Maya don't keep us in the dark. Tell us what happened!"

She told them about her brief visit with Douglas and her conversation with Vivienne, with one exception. She held back the news about her relationship to Alex. *I'm keeping that piece to myself for now. Things are complicated enough.*

Alex wrestled with how to react to the news. "Maya I'm sorry things have turned out the way they did. I know it has to be really difficult to accept. At least now you know why you didn't reveal everything to him. You must have subconsciously known something wasn't right." He wanted to reach out to her and hold her but he held himself back. He wasn't sure how she would react and he didn't want to add to her anxiety.

"I have to deal with the reality of the situation. He didn't love me. He couldn't have as much as I wanted to believe he did. It just wasn't real. I don't think he's capable of loving anyone." She knew Alex was right, she was aware there were risks allowing Douglas into her heart but her need to discover the truth drove her forward. However, recognizing this didn't alleviate the pain of betrayal she felt permeating her being and she succumbed to the flood of tears now pouring forth from her heart. She was oblivious to the world around her as her whole body heaved and trembled.

She heard the gentle sound of Douglas' voice telling her he loved her and a scream exploded. Tearing through her yet no one heard a sound while it reverberated in only her mind.

Arielle, who was sitting next to her, put her arm around her shoulder and held her tight. "What do you want to do?" she asked when the tears finally slowed and her body softened.

"We're going to be on that flight to Egypt tomorrow and meet our destiny," she said with a newfound calm resolution. Or was it desperate determination mixed with anger?

"Thatta girl," responded Cade. "We're in this together no matter what."

"We've come this far," added Alex. He couldn't stand to see Maya have to deal with all this alone. "Let's finish what we started."

* * * *

Feeling very agitated, Maya tossed and turned that night in bed. Staring at the clock, she watched the minutes move at a snail's pace.

She placed her hands on her heart, concentrating on giving herself some healing energy. Another five minutes passed, then ten minutes. She thought about writing or reading but she was too lazy to make the effort.

She stared at the glittering stars through the open drapes, thinking about Douglas. *I did what I had to do and I can't waste my time regretting it or beating myself up. The universe has guided us and we've learned to harness our talents. Now it's up to us to finish what we started.*

Memories of Atlantis and Alex returned to her in bits and pieces vanquishing away the final remnants of confusion she felt about whether she had really fallen in love with Douglas.

It wasn't real. None of it was real. He distorted the truth to suit his own purpose but the Light is on our side and he's been stopped.

She closed her eyes hoping sleep would now take her away but she was disappointed.

One hundred, ninety-nine, ninety-eight, ninety-seven. She counted down to zero but nothing worked, she was still wide-awake.

Finally she rose. Grabbing her jeans and a sweatshirt she dressed then slipped quietly out of the room.

She walked partway down the hall and stopped. *What am I doing?* She turned and walked back to her room. Touching her hand on the door handle she hesitated. She took a deep breath and turned back around.

Reaching the second last door she stopped and tapped softly. She waited and tried again, a little louder this time.

Putting her ear to the door she heard some rustling. When it opened she put her hand on his chest and pushed him aside so she could walk in. He had thrown on the pair of faded blue jeans he wore during the day and was pulling down his sweatshirt over his stomach.

He rubbed his hands through his hair the way he always did when he was confused. "Maya what are you doing here? Is everything all right?"

When she heard the door close behind her she turned to face him. "Alex…" She wanted to hear how his Atlantean name sounded in her ears, "Nared…" *Yes the truth will set you free.*

Boldly she moved closer. She grabbed his sweatshirt, bunched it up in her hands and yanked him towards her. She kissed him with single-minded determination.

He drew back his head unsettled and bewildered. The heat rising in his body left him torn, "Maya…"

"You're not my brother. It was a hoax to keep us apart. I love you Alex."

"What?" his voice cracked.

"Douglas lied about us. We are two halves of one star, meant to be together through the sands of all time."

"We're not? We're soul mates?"

"Yes…" They gazed longingly into each other's eyes, seeing the truth of both their history and their future together. "Come here," her voice a hoarse whisper.

All of his withheld love and passion came rushing forward as he scooped her up into his arms. Their lips crushed together and everything around them faded away. They became lost in each other.

He was that other part of her, she was willing to admit it and embrace it now. Before arriving in Egypt she believed she was becoming a whole person but then she met him and recognized that he was her other half. Even when Douglas appeared, somewhere in the back of her mind she knew it was only a test.

Now she realized she was not complete at all without Alex to share their lives together.

Gently he laid her on the bed savoring every second in her presence.

She reached her hand out to touch his in offering. The electrical pulse between their palms lit the flame on her back and she knew without a doubt he was her one real love.

His lips crushed against hers and their lovemaking became a blind madness to explore each other in body and soul, blending together as one knowing they could never go back to living a life without the other.

When they lay together spent he held her close and she began to cry softly.

Alarmed he asked, "What is it Maya?"

"I'm so sorry I put you through what I did." She pushed herself up beside him so she could look into his eyes. "I had to do it. I had to get close to him and find out what he knew. It's difficult to explain even to myself."

"Oh my sweet Maya. I can feel your heart inside mine. I'm just so happy you came back to me. Nothing could keep us apart. Not even Douglas. I love you not in spite of what you did but because of it. I admire you. It took a lot of courage to put so much of yourself on the line for everyone."

Tears of relief flooded through her. "You are so incredible."

"No, we are incredible together."

She settled back down in the nook of his chest and they lay together peacefully. "It's so amazing to think of how the universe conspired to bring us together again." Feeling safe and secure in his arms she decided to tell him about her dream of Douglas killing them when the portal opens.

"There's nothing to fear now, we're safe. He's locked away and we're leaving to go back to Egypt today. Our destiny is only hours away now."

I hope so. But a nagging feeling invaded her consciousness leaving an uneasiness resting there.

Chapter Forty-five

BALTIMORE, MARYLAND
18 December 2012

Douglas experienced a rift in his energy field. He felt weakened and momentarily powerless. When he examined the source of his angst he discovered that both Vivienne and Maya had withdrawn themselves from him.

The connection had weakened following the arrests but now they were gone and his search for the others was in vain.

The overwhelming sense of abandonment sent him to the ether looking for Maya and the others but all the electrical wires surrounding the jail were wrecking havoc with the signal lines. *Where are they? What's going on?* These thoughts plagued him for hours upon hours.

He pleaded with the universe to reveal their whereabouts but his efforts were futile.

They must have gone back to Egypt. I hoped it wouldn't come down to this but I've got no choice. It's time to get out of here. Maya's going to pay for leaving me again. Vivienne's absence is unforgivable. I will make her suffer and plead for her life...

* * * *

Maya and Alex became inseparable. Their presence filled the room wherever they went. Together they were strong, a complete unit.

Over the past few months Maya had worked at peeling away the layers of duality that kept her in bondage to the illusion of feeling disconnected to life.

Always searching for something outside of herself she finally discovered what she searched for was within all along. She tapped into a powerful source of energy she didn't know existed. Now that she and Alex were united, her Fire burned even brighter.

Alex felt like she breathed life and purpose into his wings. He wanted to soar like an eagle in the wind with Maya by his side. Everything before her seemed pale in her light and he realized how little of life he had been living. He needed her, not to do anything for him but just to *be* with him. To share their thoughts, feelings and experiences together as equals.

It was seven-thirty the next evening and they were sitting side by side in the Baltimore airport holding hands, waiting for their section to be called for boarding. Their flight had been delayed by three hours because of heavy rains but an announcement a few moments ago notified the passengers the flight would be departing in half an hour.

They were relieved to know they would still have enough time to make their connecting flight at JFK to Cairo at eleven P.M.

"Turning you into her brother was an ingenious idea when you think about it," said Cade.

"It certainly kept us apart but it could never have lasted." Alex squeezed Maya's hand tighter and looked intently into her eyes. "Sooner or later we would have come together. It was inevitable. Right Maya?"

She nodded and lightly kissed his lips.

The next announcement permeated the airport lounge. "Rows thirty to forty-five please proceed to the gate for boarding!"

"That's us. Let's go," said Alex anxious to be on their way.

"We're at the back of the plane. Why don't we wait until everyone else goes through," complained Arielle. "I hate waiting in lines."

They waited until the last of the people went through the gate before getting up. Just as they were turning the corner on the bridge to step into the plane they heard a commotion back at the entrance. Curiously they stopped to look.

Douglas was being held back by two flight attendants. "We're sorry sir, the dock has been closed. You cannot board the plane."

He was out of breath from running. "Maya!"

"Oh my God it's Douglas." The words caught in Maya's throat and she was barely audible.

Alex grabbed her by the waist and arm. "Get on the plane now! They're not letting him board. Get in quickly!"

Rushing in, Arielle looked desperately to the flight attendants. "You can't let that man on the plane! He was arrested for murder!"

One of the attendants stepped out of the plane to inspect the situation. She witnessed the man break away from her co-workers. He began to run down the bridge towards them.

"Hold the plane!" shouted a desperate Douglas.

Recognizing the situation could be dangerous the attendant ushered the group in, "Please go to your seats. We'll close everything off and I'll tell the captain to pull out and radio security! Please go quickly!"

Two attendants pulled the door shut. They fastened the locking mechanism as fast as they could. They banged on the control door to signal the pilot to pull away from the dock and they breathed a sigh of relief knowing security had been called and were on their way to detain Douglas.

"What the hell is he doing here?" demanded Alex as they slid into their seats.

"He must have escaped. There's no way they were letting him out. All the papers indicated the evidence was solid and the Grand Jury was indicting him," said Cade.

Maya sank back in her seat. Anger and fear consuming her thoughts. "This is too important to him. He's not going to let obstacles get in his way. He's angry now and he knows we're on to him."

"Maya's right. He's not going to stop until he finds us," added Arielle.

"Let him try," responded Alex defiantly. "He's taught us well. As long as we stick together we can use our talents against him to protect us. We'll do what we have to do."

Maya nodded in agreement gaining confidence. "I've had enough of him and his games. Our energy has become strong and the universe has kept us protected. We'll know what to do if we have to face him." The words sounded good but they were hardly enough to convince herself they were true.

"We need to decide on a plan. We're going to have to work quickly when we get to Cairo," Alex said confidently. He was proud of Maya. She was the key and the force behind them. He believed in her. He had to. There could be no room for doubt because he knew it would be their worst enemy.

* * * *

They ran through the J.F. Kennedy airport at ten-forty P.M. Desperate to reach their connecting flight to Egypt. There had been a backup of planes on the tarmac in Baltimore because of the delays and they had to wait for twenty-five minutes before take-off.

The weather wasn't any better in New York. In fact it was worse. They circled for another half-hour before being allowed to land on the slippery strip.

Their plane jostled around in the air. Arielle had watched the lightening strikes in the distance, filled with terror. Memories of the devastating flight killing her family consumed her. The thought of getting on another plane to cross the Atlantic filled her with panic while they ran.

Finally they reached the departure gate. Out of breath from their sprint only to discover the flight to Cairo had also been put on delay status.

Trying to catch his breath Alex asked the flight attendant, "Any idea how long it will be delayed?"

The woman looked wide-eyed at the group who looked frazzled. "We don't know at this point sir. The storm is getting more severe and it could be several hours before we get clearance."

"Do you know if there are any other airlines running flights to Egypt?" Cade questioned.

"You don't understand. All flights have been either delayed or cancelled."

They looked at each other in frustration. "What should we do now?" asked Maya.

"We don't have much choice. We're going to have to wait it out," said Alex. "Let's go sit down."

They sat and watched people pace in aggravation, calling friends or family to let them know of the situation. Voices grew louder. Babies cried and the storm grew even worse as the hours went by.

Maya, who had fallen into an uncomfortable sleep with her head on Alex's shoulder, woke up with a stiff neck. Her movement stirred Alex and he stretched his arms over his head. He nudged Maya. "Look at those two," nodding towards Cade and Arielle who were sleeping.

Maya smiled. "God, what time is it?"

Alex checked his watch. "It's three forty-three."

She looked over to the flight status board and cried out, "Damn! The flight's been cancelled."

"What?" exclaimed Alex. He rose to look around the area that was emptying out. None of the boarding gates were opened and the rain continued to pour down.

He nudged Cade's shoulder. "Cade, wake up."

"Huh? What's wrong?"

"The flight's been cancelled. Come on we have to figure out what to do."

They scrambled to get their things together and find an open ticket counter.

"Can you please tell me when the next flight to Cairo is?" asked Alex, his body tense.

"Sir, there's been flooding all around the city, Boston, New Jersey, right up the coast…"

Alex grew more anxious. "I understand all that but when is the next flight to Cairo?" he persisted.

He had a frantic look. The woman at the counter was nervous to give him the news. "The runways are not expected to reopen until tomorrow," she said.

"Tomorrow?" Alex checked the date and time on his watch. "You mean like today, Wednesday the nineteenth?"

"No sir, I mean tomorrow. Thursday the twentieth."

"The twentieth!" he shouted. He turned to look at Maya. Panic filling him. He ran his hands through is hair in desperation.

"That's right. I suggest checking back later tonight or tomorrow morning," the woman said dismissing him.

Maya, who had been standing behind him shook her head in disbelief. "This can't be happening! It doesn't make sense…it's like the universe is conspiring against us now."

"What are we going to do?" shrieked Arielle. "This is crazy. What if we don't get to Cairo in time?" She paced around them. Feeling trapped and inconsolable. "What are we going to do?"

Cade sensed she was on the verge of becoming hysterical. "Calm down babe. We haven't lost yet. Everything's going to be okay. I promise."

"Please don't say that! I'm getting sick of that word. No one knows for sure what's going to happen…" She felt so helpless.

Cade put his arm around her shoulder. "We might as well get a couple of rooms in a hotel close by and keep checking for the first available flight."

"I agree," said Alex.

They weren't the only ones with the same idea. Most of the hotels right near the airport were booked solid and the closest hotel they could secure rooms was at the Crowne Plaza New York-La Guardia, twenty minutes away.

They grabbed a few hours of sleep and spent most of their time keeping a close watch on the weather network and checking the airport for clearance updates. Leaving their rooms for meals only, they took turns gathering in each other's rooms.

The hours ticked slowly by. Testing their nerves and commitment to succeed.

At six minutes after five on Thursday morning Alex called the airport again. Feeling distraught with worry that they would be cheated out of their destiny. He waited for the inevitable announcement that the airport was still closed. But to his surprise this time the recording was different. "Hallelujah!" he shouted. "Maya, the airport's finally open!"

She jumped up from the bed where she laid sprawled watching the television. "Yes!" She jumped up and down and grabbed Alex around the neck while he held onto the phone.

He kissed her in relief. "Go get Cade and Arielle and let them know."

When they returned Alex waived to them to quiet down their excited chatter while he finished his conversation on the phone. "Yes, thank you," he said and hung up.

They waited expectantly. "Well?" asked Cade.

"We're on the first flight to Cairo at four-thirty this afternoon," he said with mixed feelings.

"Four-thirty?" questioned Maya. "What time does it arrive in Cairo?" she asked hesitantly.

"Eight-thirty tomorrow morning, Cairo time."

"Oh my gosh, eight-thirty?" bellowed Arielle. "How are we going to make it in time? We don't know the area…we have to figure out how to get there…" she plopped down in the chair and cried.

"Shhh…We'll have over four hours to find it. We know it's in the Giza area so it's not far," said Cade trying to reassure Arielle that all was not lost.

Maya looked into Alex's eyes with trepidation. Her shoulders drooped. She slumped into the chair beside Arielle.

Alex acknowledged their foreboding feelings. "It's going to be tight."

* * * *

They arrived in Cairo at eight thirty-three in the morning of December twenty-first. Five days after the harrowing FBI bust. Operating on frayed nerves and adrenaline after several days of little sleep and many setbacks they maneuvered through the lineups and delays to gain entry into Egypt.

Not wanting to waste any more time they decided to leave their luggage behind. They rented a car and drove to the El Gezirah Hotel where they planned to request Hanif's help in locating the old building Vivienne owned.

They reached the hotel at nine fifty-five A.M. Relieved to discover Hanif was on duty. He was surprised to see the Americans back again and obliged them with their strange request for a map and directions to an abandoned area of old Cairo.

"I know you must think we're crazy but we need some more supplies. A couple of flashlights. A shovel and maybe a crowbar. Did you by any chance keep the things we brought back the last time?"

"Yes, as a matter of fact I did. I must have known you'd be back," said Hanif chuckling. "Would you like me to arrange for someone to go with you?" he asked, curious about what they were up to now.

"That won't be necessary. We'll manage on our own but thank you for the offer," said a haggard Alex.

Hanif disappeared into the office and returned with the supplies. "Well good luck on your journey. Peace be with you."

Cade extended his hand to Hanif. "We really appreciate your help." Looking at Arielle, Maya and Alex he tapped his watch. "We better get moving."

"What time is it?" asked Arielle when they walked back to the car.

"Ten forty-one," answered Alex tensely. When they reached the car Alex suggested that Cade sit up front with him to give directions.

Knowing their time was running out played on their courage and steadiness. A day and a half had been lost with the delays. They feared that Douglas had escaped again. Was he out there somehow? Gaining on them? What resources did he have at his disposal?

The stone roads were bumpy, jostling them about. Recognizing the landmarks according to the map was challenging.

Most of the buildings were unfinished and appeared empty but occasionally they would see a family occupying one of them.

"It's eleven-thirty…shouldn't we be there by now?" asked Maya uneasily and leaning over Alex's shoulder.

"We must be getting close," responded Alex.

"I don't know…Something's not right," said Cade. "I got a bad feeling we missed a turn."

Alex grunted. He pulled off to the side of deserted road and looked at the directions. "Here I think this is where we went wrong," he said and pointed to a roadway they missed.

"Yeah, I think you're right. Damn! I can't believe I didn't see that. God I'm sorry," Cade said kicking himself for his stupid mistake.

Alex turned around and headed back. They were silent contemplating all the things that were going wrong on their journey.

Maya glanced at the clock. "It's twelve-fourteen…We're running out of time guys!"

Cade was studying the map. "Hold on, I think we turn right here. If the directions are correct the building should be down the end of this road."

Alex turned as instructed. He drove slowly.

"Yes! Stop! I think this is it!" shouted Cade excitedly.

Getting out of the car they stretched out their sore muscles. A strong wind blew up a dusting of sand around them and almost knocked them off their feet.

"It doesn't look safe," said Arielle coughing while gazing skeptically at the old decrepit three-story building. It obviously had not been occupied in decades. Sand had eroded the frame and there were fissures all around it.

Alex walked around to the back of the car, opened the truck and started handing the flashlights out. "Maybe you ladies should stay here while Cade and I check it out."

"Not a chance!" responded Maya forcefully. "We stick together all the way."

"But…"

"No buts!" Maya stopped Alex in his tracks. She moved towards the structure with long strides pushing against the winds. Not giving the others any opportunity to procrastinate they followed in behind her.

There was no one else around this part of the area so at least they didn't feel conspicuous walking into the building.

It was colorless and filthy. Sand deposits were along areas of the floor. The sun was shining brightly through the windows revealing the cobwebs hanging in the corners and around doorways. At the sound of their footsteps a scorpion scurried across the room and Arielle stifled a scream.

"According to Vivienne's instructions there should be a room back there," Maya pointed in front of her to the left.

"So far so good," said Cade as they located the room.

Maya walked towards the back wall. She dusted away sand with her foot. "It should be right here."

Alex, Cade and Arielle helped her sweep away the thick coating of sand and dirt. Maya got down on her knees. She felt around and found the latch. "Got it!"

Alex moved up beside her. "Here let me help."

Together they pulled but the handle wouldn't budge.

"Cade give me a hand," grunted Alex. "It's stuck."

Their efforts were futile. It wouldn't move.

Arielle ran out to the car and returned with the crowbar. "Here try using this."

"You must have been reading my mind babe. Thanks." Cade took it and wedged it underneath one of the wooden planks. Forcing all of his weight down, a piece of the door snapped off. Breaking away a few more pieces Alex was able to yank the rest of the gate free.

A gust of wind sucked down some sand from the room around them. Putting their arms across their mouth and nose to protect themselves they kneeled to inspect the opening. Metal bars were welded into the side of the wall providing a stairway down.

Alex picked up a flashlight. "I'm going down."

"Not without us," barked Maya.

The passageway was much smaller than the ones between the Sphinx and the Great Pyramid. The wind howled around them. Blowing sand in every direction making it difficult to see clearly.

"Arielle does this look familiar to you?" asked Cade breathless and eager.

"Yes! Yes it does!" she shouted. "I'm sure this is the same one in my visions."

"I think I see an opening up ahead!" shouted Alex who was in the lead. He started to run. "Look it's glowing!"

Maya, Arielle and Cade ran behind him.

"It's green! It's glowing green!" Alex ran faster.

The others followed suit.

Breathless they were forced to an abrupt stop before entering the chamber by the pyramid priest who materialized in physical form from the ether. "Halt! Who goes there?" he demanded. The ageless man stood firm guarding the entrance. Dressed in a long white robe with a gold sash around his waist.

They looked at each other in shock. Excitement and exhilaration were running high.

Maya moved to the front of the group. "We are the Chosen Ones here to activate the Emerald Stone," she announced proudly.

The priest refused to budge. "Identify yourselves!"

It was twelve fifty-nine P.M. There was only twelve minutes until the galactic rift would occur. They grew impatient with the delay.

"I AM FIRE," declared Maya.

"I AM AIR," asserted Alex stepping forward beside Maya.

"I AM WATER," said Arielle moving beside Alex.

"And I AM EARTH," proclaimed Cade moving up on the other side of Maya.

The priest glared at them and scrutinized each element carefully.

The group snatched an alarmed glimpse with each other. The priest smiled. "What took you so long?" he laughed and stepped aside to let them enter.

His humor melted their heavyhearted tension and they laughed in return.

Together they walked into the chamber. The sight before them was spellbinding.

The room glowed an effervescent green radiance. The Stone structure looked remarkably like the one she saw in Atlantis. Now Maya understood why she couldn't shake the image as much as she tried.

When they turned to acknowledge the magnificence of this moment with the priest, he smiled and bid them fair well. Disappearing before their eyes.

Turning to face the Stone once again, Maya's heart filled with an indescribable joy. She cried freely. She turned to Alex and they looked intently into each other's eyes. Joy filling their hearts knowing they were about to meet their destiny.

Arielle and Cade moved around the room reaching out to touch the sacred Atlantean writings on the luminous Emerald Stone.

"Cade they're warm to the touch." Arielle's eyes reflected the green light when she looked at him.

He nodded holding back the tears he felt rising up from within. He drew Arielle towards him and kissed her with the passion of lifetimes of love.

Maya closed her eyes. She breathed deeply. Preparing for the completion of her healing. A journey she now knew had lasted thousands of years. She walked, mesmerized by the most glorious sight of the largest Herkimer Diamond she could ever imagine.

Her heart raced. The flame on her back ignited. Sending waves of brilliant Light upward through her spine. Standing in front of the crystal, every cell in her body came alive. Begging to be reunited with the lost fragments of her being.

Alex came up beside her and could feel her vibrating. "It's time. Cade, Arielle, let's take our places." He gave a single nod to Maya. "It's your time sweetheart. Light the Fire."

Maya stood to face the marking of the Fire element on the Emerald Stone in the center of the room.

"Place your hands on the mark of your element," said Maya already entranced. Her Atlantean heritage taking over. "Breathe and connect with the Heavens above and the Earth below."

The green glow in the room grew brighter. Reflecting off their pensive faces.

"We'll repeat the prayer together until the energy is locked on and releases to the universe," instructed Maya.

"May the Light of the universe shine upon us, protecting and guiding us along our way. We stand here before you as ONE."

"I AM FIRE."

"I AM AIR."

"I AM EARTH."

"I AM WATER."

"Reveal the great cosmic power for all to see. Expand and blaze through us to awaken the Earth and set it free."

Their voices grew louder and stronger as they repeated the prayer a second time. The Light in the room increased. The Fire in Maya's body grew more refined and mighty. She felt electric.

Their energy expanded and connected as one. A rainbow of soft muted colors blended and surrounded them in a protective sphere of Light.

But a noise down the passageway distracted them. The sound of someone running came closer.

"Don't stop," instructed Alex, listening as the footsteps loomed near.

They chanted the prayer again while Douglas burst into the room. "Maya!"

"Stay back!" she shouted. Electrical sparks cracked in the air around them.

"You need me! You'll never succeed without me! It won't work! There are things you need to know!" He started to move towards them.

"I said stay back! You are not welcome here!" She looked to Alex, Cade and Arielle. "Hold the energy. No matter what happens you must hold the energy!"

Douglas took another step forward.

"Stop! Now Douglas!" The Fire within her burned. She knew she would do whatever was necessary to protect her friends and their destiny.

He laughed menacingly, "Or what? What will you do sweet Maya? Do you really think you can stop me?" Moving his arm around his back he withdrew a gun. He aimed it directly at Maya. "You're a fool to think you can change what I set in motion."

Her voice was low but powerful, "Keep saying the prayer. You will be able to hold the energy without me. Trust me," she ordered with conviction to Alex and the others.

"Maya, don't go!" pleaded Arielle.

"I have to!"

The energy faltered for a split second then resumed as she withdrew her Spirit from the circle. She did not want to contaminate it with what might happen next.

"Come to your senses, my darling," he sneered. His eyes were as black as coal. He changed his tactics hoping to win her over. "Please don't make me hurt you, I love you Diãntha." When he realized his attempt to win her over was futile his finger lingered on the trigger. Caressing it. His common sense told him he needed her. But his irrational whims were gaining control.

His words goaded her and ignited her fury. She would not let him destroy the opportunity to raise Earth to a new level of existence. She had the power to stop him. She knew it now.

Sensing the danger Alex broke into a cold sweat. "Maya!" Fear gripped in his chest. But he remembered his promise not to move. He watched as Maya lifted her arm over her head and down in front. "Maya don't do it! Don't let what he did poison you! This is not the way!"

Douglas seized the moment. "You should listen to him Maya. Let me make it up to all of you. I can help you in the New World." He was pushing her and he knew it. But he was losing the internal battle with his own demons.

His finger cocked to pull the trigger. An explosion of fire erupted from Maya's hand. She hurled it towards Douglas.

"Maya no!" screamed Alex and Arielle watching in horror as the ball of flame whirled across the room.

Her aim was perfect. Narrowly missing him. Striking the gun from his hand. Smashing it against the wall. Douglas fell to the ground unconscious from the force and heat of the blast.

"Maya are you all right?" screamed Arielle. Relieved that she came to her senses in time.

"Yes, I'm fine." She turned back to the circle but faltered, weak and dizzy. She willed herself to keep moving. What had she almost done? She would have been no better than him and it would have probably cost them everything.

"Hurry! Before he tries to get up!" Alex wanted to stop and take her into his arms to make everything all right. But he knew there was no time.

"How much time is left?" she yelled.

Cade glanced quickly at his watch. He was filled with panic. "Hurry! There's only fifteen seconds left!"

Maya drew deep within herself. Gathering the last of her strength and ran to her place at the Stone.

"Hurry! He's getting up!" screeched Arielle.

"I AM FIRE!"

"I AM AIR!"

"I AM EARTH!"

"I AM WATER!"

"Reveal to us the great cosmic power for all to see!"

The Earth rumbled under their feet.

Douglas rose to his feet, staggering and then began to move.

"Expand and blaze through us to awaken the Earth and set it free!"

A thunderous clap struck the air around them. Blinding white rays broke free from their heart centers. They shot forward to the Herkimer Diamond.

The rays activated the crystal. Bringing it fully alive. Colors swirled within its clear center.

Maya focused. Communicating telepathically to her Spirit within the crystal. Receiving her psychometry it recognized her. A tube of White Light erupted up to the Heavens through a grand opening.

Now running, Douglas lunged himself at the circle. But he slammed up against the force field around them, knocking him to the ground once again.

Their focus was unwavering. The green light from the Emerald Stone grew to a brilliant new depth. Blending and fusing with the Light from the Herkimer Diamond. It bounced upwards through the shaft of White Light. An extraordinary angelic sound permeated throughout the chamber with exquisite brilliance and clarity.

They became one with the Light. Vibrating to the highest of frequencies. The angelic resonance infused their bodies. Opening their hearts and minds in ecstasy.

Their souls elevated from their bodies in glowing orbs. Rising up through the opening. Traversing out to the world and the universe. Looking down upon the planet from on high they watched as Earth's energy shield transformed and repaired itself.

The Light swirled around and through the mountains, the oceans, seas and the lands. Reaching the towns and cities from continent to continent.

Their spirits watched. Enraptured as Mother Earth gave birth to the Phoenix Star.

When the genesis was complete they descended back down through Earth's atmosphere. Their Spirits re-entered into their bodies. The ground tremored and shook under their feet. Uniting Heaven and Earth at last.

The rays of Light connecting them retracted and they stood staring at each other. Charged with the love of the universe, they were forever changed.

They looked around for Douglas. But he was nowhere to be found.

Something on the ground caught Maya's attention. She walked towards the object. She bent over and picked up the signet ring Douglas always wore. It was deformed from the fire but she could still make out the cross.

Alex joined her and placed his arm around her waist. "He's powerless over us now Maya. His kind will not be able to survive in the New World, eventually there won't be any place for them."

Epilogue

GLENWOOD SPRINGS, COLORADO
9 August 2013

People around the Earth talked for months about the two days that disappeared without remembrance. With the exception of four people who would never forget.

Eventually a world filled with chaos, negativity and strife began to experience microscopic shifts of reality in the veil of time as the planet continued to heal.

Those who were ready, aligned with the higher vibrational frequencies providing inspiration for others to follow.

Maya, Alex, Arielle and Cade became aware that they had been gifted with the ability to transmit their energy to people they came into contact with providing subtle alterations in emotional states to those who were open to receive.

When they returned to America their first stop was to visit Vivienne.

They learned she had secretly sent a letter to Douglas through an inmate telling him what she knew, including her plan to help Maya. She feared for their lives when she learned Douglas had escaped but placed her faith in the universe and waited for the outcome. The letter was her way of freeing herself from the depths of his hold, which had lasted for thousands of years, and she did not regret sending it.

By then the group realized they could not return to their old lives. Knowing the world would change daily for some time to come they wanted to stay close to each other and decided to move to Colorado, an area marked as one of the Golden Cities.

Touring the state they bought two houses within a ten-minute drive of each other in the picturesque mountain community of Glenwood Springs. With mountains, lakes, rivers and spectacular views wherever they went it met all their needs to continue to develop their elemental talents.

Within a month each one had packed up what they needed and had everything delivered to their new homes. Shortly afterwards Cade and Arielle were married in a quiet ceremony with Alex and Maya standing up for them.

Sometime later they learned Vivienne had pleaded guilty to lesser charges of conspiracy to commit murder. She was released but could not leave the state of Maryland for a period of two years. She had made peace with herself and dedicated her time working in a woman's shelter, helping battered and abused women to develop self-confidence and begin their lives anew.

Alex sold his company and invested the proceeds in various enterprises where his only obligation was to sit on the board of directors. This freed up his time to start up a new adventure company in partnership with Cade. They took people horseback riding, rafting and paragliding, Alex's favorite activity.

Arielle fixed up a quaint old building and turned it into an art studio where she painted and taught children how to tap into their talents and create works of art with the paintbrush.

Maya was becoming known around town as 'The Healer' after an autistic boy threw himself into her arms while she was grocery shopping and he was miraculously healed from her embrace. People began to seek her out for help and her abilities grew stronger each day.

On a beautiful sunny hot summer day in August they sat together on the front porch of the house Alex and Maya bought, enjoying the view of the mountains.

"Alex! I felt the baby move!" shouted Maya in excitement. She never tired of the feeling, even when the baby kept her up at night she didn't complain. To her it was a reminder of the possibilities life offered when you opened your eyes, healed your past and allowed Spirit to guide your actions. Rubbing her tummy she wondered if healing was something she and her child would do together in the years to come.

"Where? Let me feel!" He jumped from the wooden chair and let Maya take his hand and place it on her belly. Just the day before Dr. Jamieson gave her and the baby a clean bill of health in her eighth month of pregnancy.

Maya laughed heartily. "Well Mr. Delaney I think I'm ready to take you up on your offer." Suddenly she couldn't figure out why she had stalled for all these months.

"My offer?" He looked at her blankly for a moment then suddenly he realized what she meant. "You mean you're finally coming to your senses and willing to do the right thing by our baby?"

"Only if you ask me nicely again."

Alex rolled his eyes in a fake gesture of frustration. He kneeled on one knee. "Maya Maxwell, will you marry me?"

She couldn't resist teasing him. "Where's the ring? How can I marry you without a ring?"

The stunned expression on his face was priceless.

"Alex I'm kidding!" She cupped his face with her hands she smiled. "Darling, of course I'll marry you."

"Congratulations man." Cade shook Alex's hand. "What the heck," he said grabbing his friend and gave him a hug.

"Well it's about time," Arielle said giving Alex a wink and squeezed Maya's hand in delight.

They sat together on the porch, staring at the mountains in the horizon. Watching the occasional cloud float across the deep azure sky. Each lost in their own thoughts reflecting on the events of the past year. Hopeful that the next phase of their lives would be the best phase of their lives filled with promise, abundance and most of all love.

978-0-595-39883-6
0-595-39883-9

Printed in the United States
73921LV00003B/76

9 780595 398836